UNION 57

Bennett Joshua Davlin

CENTERED
AMERICA
PUBLISHING GROUP

OTHER WORKS BY BENNETT JOSHUA DAVLIN

MAJOR MOTION PICTURES BY THIS AUTHOR & FILMMAKER

THE MEDALLION
Sony Entertainment & Columbia TriStar Pictures

MEMORY
Warner Bros. & EBE

BOOKS

FICTION

MEMORY
Penguin Books U.S., Random House Australia etc. Blanvalet Germany, Sony Books Japan

THE MODERN ART OF DATING
Centered America Books & Various Foreign Publishers

DREAMSPACE:ESCAPE C19
Centered America Classic Books & Various Foreign Publishers

CINE-GRAPHIC NOVEL

DREAMSPACE: Escape C19
Available only at www.centeredamerica.com

POLITICAL ONLINE ESSAYS

SHORT TAKES
Available at no charge at *www.centeredamerica.com*

THE "ESSENTIAL" ESSAYS
Available at no charge at *www.centeredamerica.com*

POLITICAL FILM SHORTS

The Secret of November 10th, 1619
Available at no charge at *www.centeredamerica.com*

The Political platform of the Non Treasonous Democrat Party (NTD)
Available at no charge at *www.centeredamerica.com*

The Second Era of Good Feelings: MAGA & NTD
Available at no charge at *www.centeredamerica.com*

UNION 57

Bennett Joshua Davlin

CENTERED AMERICA PUBLISHING GROUP
Published by Centered America Books
A Publishing Division of Davlin Productions LLC
269 South Beverly Dr. Suite 537 Beverly Hills, CA 90212

UNION 57

This book is an original publication of Davlin Productions LLC

This is a work of fiction. Names, characters, places, and incidents either are the product of the author's imagination or are used fictitiously, and any resemblance to actual persons, living or dead, business establishments, events, or locales is entirely coincidental.

PRINTING HISTORY
Centered America Books trade paperback edition / August 1, 2024

An application to register this book for cataloguing has been submitted to the Library of Congress.

ISBN
979-8-9881466-9-8 (paperback)
979-8-9881466-7-4 (Hardcover)
978-1-7358736-2-6 (ebook)

PRINTED IN THE UNITED STATES OF AMERICA.

10   9   8   7   6   5   4   3

For my late friend and fellow artist,
Glen A. Larson.

911 Call Transcript date redacted

911 Dispatcher: 911–

Caller: My baby--he has my baby!

911 Dispatcher: I need your name, ma'am--

Caller: The dog-

911 Dispatcher: Just try and calm down. I need your name-

Caller: Mrs. Willard!

911 Dispatcher: Where do you live, Mrs. Willard?

Caller: 401 Pinwheel Drive. Help us!

911 Dispatcher: T-try and tell me in a calm manner what-

Caller: I came home——he had two pots on the stove. He boiled our dog!

911 Dispatcher: Who was boiling the dog?

Caller: He's naked——has a pistol——laughing——

911 Dispatcher: Who's with you now?

Caller: My son and I. We're in the bathroom! He's breaking down the door!

911 Dispatcher: The police are on their way. Who is he?

Caller: My husband–FBI Agent Willard——

Call Terminated–

CONTAMINATION

One

They said men went insane on *The Watch*.

They said they hacked up their babies, killed their children and slit their wives' throats. The mutilations, eviscerations, raping . . . all unique, all different. When these insane carnivals of the macabre ended, more often than not it was a rope off the central staircase. . . . a television in the bath-tub. . or a pistol . . . yes, they all had their government issued .38's.

Why?

Why did these dedicated agents of the Federal Bureau of Investigation with spotless records suddenly commit familial homicide . . . executing horrible acts. . . gruesome acts. . . acts beyond comprehension?

There were few hints among the blood stained carpets, swinging nooses, and faces frozen in terror. All of the murders were committed in the middle of the night when the family was asleep. Only a handful had ever been spared: a teenage girl, returning home just in time to find her dead father lying face down on the front lawn. They say she was functioning well now with the help of neuroleptic drugs. The stories read like Grimm's tales for Federal agents. . . whispers in the halls of the J. Edgar Hoover Building.

Slowly the investigators gathered the pieces. . . random and chaotic in and of themselves. . . a security consultant who'd left the bureau in Milwaukee--dead, a field supervisor in Shawnee, Oklahoma with three children---all dead. . . a retired agent in Lima, Ohio with an aging wife--both dead . . .

Soon the list was three pages long.

Upon closer examination the incident reports insulted logic and decency—"the bodies of the entire family and the dead dog were piled into--reports that Agent Connelly fired his .38 at close range, execution style while four members of his family pinned their heads down on—Pedowski raped his eleven year old daughter and eight year old son, the entire family forced to watch, and then went on to..."

Slowly the pieces began to fit and take shape, forming the gruesome puzzle: the one clue that drew these strangers together from all parts of the country. At one time or another, they had all served on *The Watch.*

Agent Richard Rizzuti first heard about The Watch through hastily scribbled graphite in a FBI Headquarters bathroom stall:

"What made Agent Polk,
kill his daughter, slit his throat?
Beware the Truth is like a cancer,
some questions we do not answer."

The next day it was wiped clean. Only after his recruitment into the top secret operation could he fathom such twisted poetry. For only then was the existence of the program verified and its purpose disclosed.

Because Agent Rizzuti was now on *The Watch.*

A hand crept lazily over the chair.

The skin was ghostly pale--long slender fingers wrapping around the crystal champagne flute resting on the side table. The flute vanished behind the chair only to be returned a moment later with a sip less of the bubbly Veuve Clicquot "Grand Dame." Then the hand was gone--there was nothing but the chair.

It was an ornate reading chair with weathered burgundy leather and brass trimmings quite in keeping with the antique surroundings of the study chocked full of Victorian curios. Yellowed lithographic maps lined the red lacquered walls. . . a gramophone, record spinning. . . a couch upholstered in acanthus. . . and a mahogany bookcase housing eclectic titles from Clauswitz's "On War" to "The World Atlas of Wine".

It looked like any Edwardian study except for the six surveillance cameras mounted overhead recording the figure sitting in the chair and the thick record spinning on the gramophone.

Agent Rizzuti couldn't hear the music.

He stared through the thick Plexiglas window looking into the Edwardian study. This was the first of three rooms called The Suite—where the creature lived. With the speakers off, Rizzuti couldn't hear the clink of crystal on wood as the champagne flute was returned to the side table, but he also didn't have to tolerate that annoying record the creature kept playing over and over and over.

All Agent Rizzuti could hear now were the chatter of voices, the buzz of computers, and back up tapes. He stared at his own reflection in the glass. . . a thin face with deeply set Italian features. I'm just a Brooklyn boy, he reflected on his humble roots as if to wonder how the hell he got here—babysitting in The Twilight Zone.

He turned away from the window, examining the cramped control room. It reminded him of a space shuttle mission control with rows of computers and personnel running back and forth. . . all guarding this prisoner.

"Camera 3's out," the technician stared up from his horn-rimmed glasses.

Rizzuti wiped sweat from his forehead. Strange, although he'd been doing this for 87 days, the thought of entering the suite always sent shivers down his spine. He glanced at the wall of TV surveillance monitors, all recording different angles of the study. Camera 3 was out—the screen static filled. It might be the relay. . . those always seemed to be breaking these days.

Rizzuti's eyes crept up to the top corner of the control room, noting the four surveillance cameras shining down on his crew. Just as they were guarding the lone prisoner in The Suite, he knew that in some remote location, others were studying him. Such the nature of this dangerous operation.

"Get into the sound closet," a female tech spoke into the microphone, addressing the creature in The Suite.

There was a pause. She was about to repeat herself when the creature slinked out of his burgundy chair, it's shadow cast through the observation window, falling upon the faces of the technicians in the control room. A moment later, it shut the heavy iron door as it entered the sound chamber.

The sound chamber was a coat closet just off the study. Now tailored with four inch sound padding, the room was commodious enough for a single person. The massive iron door shut, a green light above it flashed on. As protocol dictated, failure to isolate the creature would lead to contamination for anyone entering the inner rooms.

Not contamination in a visible sense, thought Rizzuti. After all, contaminated subjects showed no visible symptoms until they spontaneously carried out the perverse tasks outlined in well documented mission briefs. . . when decent FBI agents murdered their families and perpetrated acts so perverse that they were classified, never to be disclosed. What men had been able to gather the mental and emotional strength to bring this thing here?

"Who's going in, sir?" the technician interrupted his train of thought.

Rich headed to the door--his action answering the question. It would take him a few minutes to get his suit biohazard suit on.

The airlock door closed.

Agent Rizzuti's biohazard level 4 suit looked like a space suit complete with a copper plated visor. It took him a few minutes to properly freezer tape the exposed seams. Then he switched on his respirator backpack, cool air flooded the pressurized suit. Now all he could hear was his own rushed breathing.

"You OK?" a voice called over his headset, "I'm reading a high heart rate."

He silently cursed at himself, shunning away fear. As air washed through the scrubbers, he felt beads of sweat forming on his forehead. Then the outer airlock door opened.

And he entered The Suite.

He negotiated the burgundy chair.

The room was smaller than it seemed through the observation window. Turning around, he glanced back at the Plexiglas observation window which from this side looked like a giant mirror reflecting his space suited guise back at him. He could hear Fred Astaire crooning on that horrible gramophone.

"Camera 3's just over the bookcase," one of his technicians directed over his helmet intercom.

Dragging the leather chair to the wall, he used it to reach the surveillance camera. From a tool-kit strapped to his chest, he produced a Phillips head screwdriver and unfastened the outer casing. He instantly noticed it.

"Yep, relay's burned."

To his right he glanced at the green light over the sound chamber. The metal door was still closed shut. He reassured himself that he was safe. Thus he returned to the task at hand never noticing the quarter inch gap in the sound chamber door.

The magnetic seal was finally concluded to be the culprit, but no one was ever sure. Manufactured by a company in Concorde, Connecticut, the buildup of grime on the sensor signaled the door was sealed, but impaired the locking mechanism. Subsequent study would reveal that this mistake could happen only once in every fifteen thousand times. As a backup, the sensor alarm ran self-tests every 120 seconds and that was exactly how long it took.

The warning calls erupted.

Shocked, Rizzuti stumbled off the chair. Flashing red alarm lights exploded in the room. Sirens screeched that ear piercing warning of a level one contamination breach—the sound sending his mind reeling.

"We have a biohazard breach!" screamed the voice over his headset.

He fell hard, the screwdriver bouncing loose. Quickly, he retrieved it, hopping to his feet. Only then did he notice the gap in the sound chamber door. It was true. He had to get the hell out of there. His stomach and intestines tightened into knots and he dry heaved in his suit. Stumbling backwards, he toppled over the burgundy chair as he rushed to the outer airlock. The iron door closed before he could reach it.

"It's too late!" he heard another voice in his headset.

Red sirens shined down on the inch wide hole in his space suit. He glanced at the screwdriver in his hand, noticing the red blood on the tip—it had punctured his suit. He vomited into his helmet, droplets of puke partially blinding his faceplate.

"I-I'm fine. I swear, I'm fine," nothing had changed he told himself, nothing at all. He was the same person he was a moment before. They had to be wrong.

Havoc raged inside the control room.

Techs gathered around the massive window staring at their frightened coworker as Rizzuti banged on the airlock door. . . pleading, his body simultaneously recorded from nine different angles on the wall of TV monitors.

Through the rear door a woman in a lab coat barged into the room. She was beautiful, mid 30's, with dark hair falling on a cold, chiseled face, "What the hell's going on?"

"Dr. Brandt," one of the techs addressed her, "the creature wasn't properly sealed--Rizzuti ripped his suit--"

Dr. Brandt pushed the tech out her way, rushing up to a control panel, studying the situation on the wall of monitors, able to see the two inch gap in the sound door. She made a lightning quick decision, "He's been exposed,"

"I'm fine," Rizzuti pleaded over the intercom, "I'm not contaminated! GUYS, GET ME THE FUCK OUT OF HERE!"

Everyone in the room knew the protocol, thought the woman. But this was one of their comrades, she had to act fast before emotions might foolishly dictate otherwise. The threat at hand, the evil nature of the creature, was too much to risk anything on feeling. Rizzuti now had to be killed—hell, he was dead before she arrived. She was now looking at the shell of a man, a body without a spirit, a thing without a soul. All eyes were on her as she lifted the cap on the control panel revealing a bright, red switch.

She pressed it.

Agent Rizzuti saw gas pouring into The Suite.

A white fog, illuminated in blinking red sirens, filled the air. He saw was the sound chamber door closing. He stumbled through the haze, weaving along the mirrored wall reflecting the copper faceplate of his space suit back at him. He banged gloved hands against the mirrored wall, pleading to faces he could not see, "I swear I'm fine," fear overtook him, "GET ME THE FUCK OUT OF HERE!"

Fred Astaire's crooning voice almost carried a mocking indifference as the record played.

They were going to leave him here—leave him to die, pumping the room with saran nerve gas! With a gloved hand, he feebly tried to cover the hole in his sleeve, knowing all along that a single droplet could kill him.

"You're killing me!" he screamed in half disbelief.

His stomach churned in hurricanes of panic. He felt his skin crawling--fluid climbing up his throat. Froth erupted from his clenched jaw. His mind swam as he collapsed on the Persian carpet. He dropped the screwdriver, sending it rolling under the heavy brush fringe of the couch.

Rizzuti ripped through the fabric of the space suit, trying to cradle his boiling skin. Fred Astaire continued to croon. He collapsed as his mind swam and his eyesight left him. He was fine and they were murdering him! Fluid rose up his esophagus, asphyxiated him. What could be worth this--his own life? Then the world went dark and all he could hear was Fred Astaire's mocking him as he died, choking on his own mucous.

1998

part two

DEFENDER OF THE FAITH

Two

1:42 PM (EST)
Elizabeth, NJ

He could see the whole skyline from his vantage point.

The Statue Of Liberty rose majestically in the distance. He could see the sister towers of The World Trade Center and thought he caught a glimpse of The Empire State Building. Soon the snow-storm would eclipse this view. He had been standing on the small ledge for ten minutes. It was cold. Snow fell in thick clumps that landed on his military parka, wetting his black ski mask.

Smoking the unfiltered Camel cigarettes, he liked to watch the airliners take off from Newark Airport, making their wide, arching ascents overhead. Then he'd glance down at the towers of pipe and steel beneath him; the petrochemical refinery looked like a mini metropolis complete with blinking lights and billowing smoke. Yes, a metropolis, he thought to himself, and he was the leader-- the defender of the faith, standing above them all.

"On my mark," he spoke with a foreign accent into his head-set.

A moment later a 727 rushed overhead. He was up so high that it looked like he could touch the gray clouds. This ledge was a small overhang, a mere stopping point along the ladder which scaled the massive, cylindrical tower. It was technically called the " combination fractionator # 4 of the Hydrofluoric acid alkylation unit". . . at least that's what the map said. His tower was not the tallest in The Union 57 Petrochemical Refinery.

It was chosen by mere chance.

The wind picked up, sweeping past him. Even with the parka and ski mask, the temperature was dropping near zero degrees Fahrenheit as the storm neared. Rubbing his palms together, he tried to conserve body heat.

He went by many names. . . foreigner, convicted felon, religious zealot, but he could still enjoy a good view. He liked to call himself a biblical name. . . not the popular ones like Moses, Joshua, or David. . . all from the Jew Books—and he refused to read the words of kikes.

"We should go now," a voice cried over his headset.

He wasn't sure who it was. With the radio headsets it could have been any of his twenty men. Had he been able to see him, he would have shot him dead. . . they all knew that. . . fear kept discipline within his ranks. Only cloaked in the darkness of anonymity could they afford to be brave.

He was harsh. He was strict. The name they had chosen for him was Nehemiah. True, it came from the old testament—the kike's book. Yet somehow he felt deep down that Nehemiah was not really a Jew bastard.

"This is Nehemiah," he grunted over the howl of the wind, "no one moves until I sound the alarm."

The black ski mask had deep slits for his eyes and mouth. Slowly he sucked on his cigarette again and paused to examine the lit end. How strange he thought that this would all begin with one cigarette.

Then the words entered his head. He knew the verses well . . . Nehemiah the servant of God who spoke through the King who commanded the building of the walls of Jerusalem. Slowly, he lit the rag as he reflected on the verses:

> *So I came to Jerusalem and there was three days.*
> *Then I arose in the night, I and a few men with me; I told no*
> *one what my God had put in my heart to do at Jerusalem. . .*

He placed the burning rag in front of the gas sensor bolted to the tower's exterior. The alarm began to blare. . . a screeching noise. . .louder than any police car he had ever ridden in. It was so easy.

Nehemiah was no fool.

When things fell within his scope of interest he would study them obsessively, grasping every fact, every minute detail. But he was erratic. Sometimes he preached preparation, other times, he'd lose his head and improvise. But today was a good day. . . today he was feeling quite calm.

From the video and pamphlets he had to study before he could visit the refinery, he knew that with the alarm the employees would gather at different stations for roll call. This point was true for everyone except the security and engineering teams. In the safety of their hermetically sealed, concrete building, they were able to discern if the alarm was real or just a tripped sensor.

And that was where he was going first.

So I went up in the night by the valley, and viewed the wall: then I turned back and entered by the valley gate, and so returned.

Nehemiah linked up with his men at the front door of the security building.

They burst into the surveillance headquarters. Nehemiah and his men executed head shots, instantly killing the fat, out of shape guards. Time always slowed down for him during the killing. When he was young, he was always told how hard it was to kill a man. On the contrary, he reflected, killing a man seemed to bring him a sense of complacency.

Nehemiah was not a sociopath. He had the ability to empathize and understand pain. Shooting men was not like shooting paper targets. But they were not real men— not the faithful servants of God. Once a man fell by the wayside, he could be smited without guilt. These were the harsh politics of faith. By the time his head cleared, all ten guards were dead. He and his henchmen rushed into the next room. He felt an energy flowing through him, like pure electricity--

*And the officials did not know where I had gone or what I had
done; I had not yet told the Jews, the priests, the nobles, the officials,
or the others who did the work.*

Nehemiah paused at the open doorway to the break room.

Inside the large room a group of engineers and plant personnel listened as a fat man with red suspenders held roll call. . . as if this were just another drill.

"Sanchez?" the fat man with the red suspenders moaned.

"Here. . . sir, but wish I was fishing."

"Too cold Sanchez," joked the supervisor, "go back to Mexico for that."

"Hey man," Sanchez feigned injury, "I'm Puerto Rican!"

"GET DOWN ON THE GROUND" Nehemiah and his men charged in!

"W-what?" the supervisor dropped his roster pad on the floor.

Nehemiah fired a single shot into Sanchez's face. The engineer type screamed: a sharp, shrill sound, crumpling over, blood running down cupped hands. That was as good an introduction as Nehemiah could have hoped for.

"Everyone down!" he screamed, "follow me and everything will be fine!"

"Is this a joke?" the supervisor watched in a detached state of shock. Probably thought it was a cap gun. . . a birthday hoax. . . crazy things ran through people's heads when they encountered this stuff, thought Nehemiah.

"Down on the ground with your hands open!" his accomplice screamed.

He and his men must look terrifying with their black ski masks, thought Nehemiah. The group panicked, clamoring the floor. He started in the back corner. With each step, he stopped, firing a single shot into the back of their heads—his silencer making the gunshots sound tiny:

Pop.

Pop.

Pop.

They shook and twisted in strange spasms as the holes in the back of their heads opened up, pouring out brain matter and blood. As life left them, the bodies emptied their bowels and bladders, belching and farting—never showed that in the movies, thought Nehemiah. The ones at the end of the row understood, begging and pleading about their children and families-

Pop.

Pop.

Pop.

Strange things happened in that room as he walked along the rows. Some prayed. Most were silent, shaking, covering their heads. Today they had woken up just like any other day and here they were--shot one by one, execution style like animals at the slaughter.

An overweight, black secretary whispered to a man in the next row as if he were fated to survive, "Tell my husband," she shook, "that I loved h-"

Pop.

Pop.

Pop.

"I'm an FBI agent," one of the last men in a suit cried, "do you hear me-"

Pop.

Nehemiah smiled, "Have plenty of those already."

Bullet casings bounced off the table, rolling through streams of blood, excrement, and spilled coffee. He reloaded again, the sounds of weeping and moaning echoing in his ears. Turning, he could see one of his accomplices raping one of the young female employees, blood trailing down her thigh as she called out to the supervisor.

The supervisor wept. He looked like Santa Claus, thought Nehemiah, his pot belly stretching his red suspenders, "you're killing us."

"Ready grandpa?" Nehemiah sighed, "a quick death will be much better than what awaits the rest of them," Nehemiah grabbed the old man by his ear, pulling his head down to his waste, placing the pistol at the crown of the skull, "go meet your maker."

Pop.

Then I said to them, "You see the distress that we are in, how Jerusalem lies waste, and its gates are burned with fire. Come and let us build the wall of Jerusalem, that we may no longer be a reproach."

Nehemiah headed into the hall.

He checked for the folded piece of paper in his pants pocket. He would wait one hour and then make the call. All this labor made him thirsty. He stopped at the water fountain and noticed a black patent leather shoe with a small, flat heal. He remembered no woman in clothing that would merit such a fancy shoe?

Then he heard the sound. . . like someone stirring in a room behind him. He turned, locating the source. The electricity wavered and died, the emergency lights clicking on, casting localized shadows down the hall. He stared down at his watch. Everything was going as planned.

By now, mused Nehemiah, all the phone lines were dead too. They were an island in the middle of a torrid sea. A volcanic island watching and waiting to erupt. When it did, the dead in those break rooms would be the lucky ones. It was time to speak to his Master.

So they said, "Let us rise up and build' Then they set their hands to this good work.

He returned to the control room, confident in his powers and skills. Yet like many great plans there was a problem that even Nehemiah could not anticipate . . . the product of coincidence mixed with chance--the unknown variable. And at that moment, the unknown variable was hiding in the closet at the end of the hallway, watching every move he made.

Three

Candice Cooperman's teeth rattled.

Rattling like the wind up chatter teeth she used to have as a child-- so intense it made her shoulders shake. Crouched down in the supply closet, her knees burned--

paralyzed with fear. She shut her eyes, but all she could see was the scene replaying over and over like a broken record: Supervisor Givens, his bright red suspenders, tears in his eyes as the man in the ski mask dragged his head down, placing the pistol at the crown of his skull. Then she heard the noise. . . muted gunshots:

Pop.

He crumpled.

Pop--

In a matter of minutes an eternity had passed—an eternity ripping her out of her world, bringing her to this dark, little supply closet where every sound beyond the closed door was like an echo of death. No. . . no she had to gather herself. . . think. . . think clearly! She was fine when she didn't think about that horrible scene...she was really fine. Her teeth were rattling again. . . she was going to die. Calm down, retrace your steps—how did I get here?

"It's like reprimandin' a kid," Lou told her.

The rental car smelled new and sterile.

"Reprimanding a kid, huh? Do all kids embezzle product from their employer?" she smirked.

"Don't tell me you never picked your parents pockets for Friday night."

Lou had a cute, dangerous smile, she thought. If he hadn't introduced himself as an FBI agent, she might have thought he was a pool hustler except for his nice suit which invested in him an air of sophistication. He looked like Chaz Palminteri, but his last name was Greek?

"Sumthin' bothering ya?" he asked.

Their eyes connected for a moment. Did he know? Could he see the grief painted across her face? She turned away, lights reflected off the hood of the Ford rental as they entered the fluorescent reality of The Holland Tunnel.

"You go to these plants a lot?" he inquired.

"All the time," in the reflection, she spied him glancing at her. Suddenly a wave of emotion swept across her—feeling and sensations so fleeting and powerful they had no names. She thought she might cry in front of this stranger.

"Look," she decided to take the offensive, "I'd handle him," yell at Larry? She had problems reprimanding her cat.

He weaved between traffic, "Look, I don't like being here anymore than you do. But he took stolen goods across state lines and that brings in the FBI. Juss' think of me as the buzz of an air-conditioner, just here to watch," followed by a pregnant pause and then, "maybe we could even get lunch afterwards?"

"I'm married," she showed off her wedding ring only to wonder a second later why she lied.

Well there went lunch.

Still he looked at her in such a way that she smiled. . . a slightly sadistic smile—the smile of a woman who knows she's captured the heart of a suitor, boxing and collecting it like a novelty: a gesture very out of character for her.

"If you're this tough on me," sighed Lou, "juss feel sorry for poor old Lawrence, the embezzling foreman--"

"Larry," she corrected him again.

She heard foot-steps in the hall and tightened her fists so hard she felt her nails dig into skin. Think Candice. . . try to calm down. She refocused. . .

"Slow down. Slow down!"

Larry Bagnowsky, the embezzling foreman, waved his hands in the air. He was not a pretty man. . . tall and thin. . . anorexic thin, the bones of his elbows poking out of his arms. He was sweating, his thin, little Adam's' apple bulging up and down. Candice, Lou, and him seemed to fill his tiny wood paneled office.

She'd been screaming. All she had to do was imagine her husband, Jordan's face superimposed on top of Larry's and the fire flamed itself.

"How did you steal those valves!" she pounded his desk.

Then she felt a hand on her shoulder. Breaking out of her spell, she turned to Lou, standing behind her. He nodded as if to say job well done, taking the paperweight from her.

"Larry," he placed the glass object back on the desk, "if I may call you Larry?"

"Sure," the foreman trembled, sitting down.

The mood was tense.

"Employee of the year, huh?" he pointed to a plaque on the wall.

"Yeah," he finished chewing the antacid tablets "it was a long time ago."

"You get an award for it?"

"Check for a thousand dollars."

"What'd ya get with the dough?"

"Big Sony Trinitron for the wife—and a power saw."

"My old man used to have one of them Craftsmans."

"Mine's a Black & Decker."

Standing there watching Lou, suddenly, it all made sense to Candice. The FBI agent was a pro, using her as the bad cop while he played the role of trusting confidant. Look at them, she thought, like two old friends chatting it up.

"Larry," Lou opened his briefcase, grabbing one of the two cell phone batteries and plopping it into his phone, "I can call up the FBI office in New York City right now," he held up the cell phone, "it's on one a little speed dial and they'll be all kind of hell to pay. . . cops with big fluorescent FBI letters on the back of their wind-breakers and guns and handcuffs. We don't want that, right?"

"How'd you find out 'bout it?" he seemed to deflate like a balloon.

"Found a whole pile of Union 57 valves down by the docks an' they weren't taking no slow boat to China. So you were stealin' new valves and forging the invoices."

"Excuse me," Candice interjected.

Lou's harsh look silenced her. For the first time he flashed that steel underbelly. . . don't underestimate him, she thought, this guy was a pro, a cold FBI field agent whose advances, small talk, and flattery were just part of the job to size up the strangers he had to use

Jesus, she' d been bathing in her little spell of power while all the while she was the one being manipulated! The numbing pain in her left temple, the type she got when eating ice-cream too fast, flared up. She was a woman on the edge and didn't need this crap!

"I would have done the same thing, Larry," Lou turned back to the foreman, "it's tough for me, ya know, an underpaid FBI field agent. Got four kids' orthodontist bills and the wife wants the new Liz Taylor scent down at the mall. Every month she's got another perfume-"

"Your wife?"

"No. . . Liz."

"Yeh. . . right," he stared at the cellular phone, "it's a bitch."

"Tell me, how'd you get those valves to the docks with nobody seein' it?" the way he said it thought Candice, so nonchalantly, when it was the biggest puzzle to them all.

"Drainage pipes under the plant--we carted em from there to the dock.

"Ingenious. Now look, Larry," he neared the desk, "I'm gonna offer you a once in a lifetime deal."

A deal! Larry was the stinking bastard who called her "baby" and "hungry ass"--the slob who forced her to drive out to this stinking plant in New Jersey! If she hadn't been out in New Jersey, things with Jordan might've gone differently.

"Alright...sir," Larry collapsed in his chair, snatching up the offer as he scribbled out his confession.

"I-I'm gonna go to bathroom," she stormed out of the room, grabbing Lou's cell phone, trying to give her actions justification, "I want to check my messages."

The Agent cautiously watched her leave the room, making sure that he didn't lose his prey now that his claws had sunk into flesh.

"You have no messages," the electronic voice spoke over the cell phone.

Candice teared up, letting the phone drop to her side. Did she really expect Jordan to call? It would sure have been good today. No, he was gone—he wasn't calling ever again.

She stared into the mirror. Candice had a way of staring at herself that was unnatural, sort of raising her eyebrows a little too high. She thought she looked like a gawky ostrich with breasts and hips that were too small. Hell, she was twenty eight years old alone.

She never bothered to notice that she was a striking woman, blond hair. . . tall and lean with porcelain like skin. She never thought that her small breasts gave her a streamlined look with delicate, distinct features. The pain hit her.

She motioned to the stall—on top of everything she had a bladder infection! Shouldn't have drank all that coffee in the car. . . caffeine affected her so strongly. After urinating, she still felt like she needed to piss.

Then the alarm sounded. Another fucking drill, she sighed. She'd been out at plants for the past six months and through five drills already. It was so common place . . . she didn't even bother racing to her evacuation station like she did the first time. Her bladder would keep her right where she was. She pressed her legs against the stall door, tightening all the muscles below her waist. It was a trick her roommate had shown her in college for bladder stuff.

She thought about Felix her cat and how she had forgotten to leave food out for him this morning and-

Pop.

The burst of sound was loud enough to be heard over the blaring alarm—as if someone popped open a bottle of champagne. She discounted it as another random noise from the plant when she heard someone enter the bathroom.

"Anybody in there?" a voice screamed from outside the room.

She was about to answer when she realized the voice was not addressing her.

"No," the second man replied. . . a deep, guttural male voice echoing off the tile walls. He was in the bathroom, maybe kneeling on the floor. Was he staring underneath the stalls? Then the door slammed shut.   She was alone.

Stepping into the hall, she noted that the offices were empty--doors open. The sounds of the alarm muffled her foot-steps, but she could still hear that strange popping, so foreign to her, getting louder with each step. It was coming from the open break-room door at the end of the hall.

Pop.

Like an engine backfiring.

Pop.

Like jumping on bubble packing wrap.

"You're killing us! You said things would go smoothly! You're killing us! You're killing us!" the voice was so full of anger and dismay like a child whose parents break a promise to him.

Peering through the open doorway to the break room and kitchen, the thoughts of an emergency evacuation team disappeared. She noted the twisted image with shocked dismay. . . blood everywhere. Lou was laying on his back dead and a man with a ski mask pressed a gun to Supervisor Givens' head.

"Please," the supervisor pleaded, "plea-"

Pop.

He crumpled.

She saw a red thing, like loose tissue flying out of the old man's face: his body collapsing onto the floor. The room began to spin. The alarm, the weeping, the sound of her heart beat had suddenly built into a thunderous climax, burning her ears, sending her mind into a mad vortex. The hallway danced around her . She could no longer see the figure, but when she shut her eyes-

Pop.

He crumpled.

She rushed into the hall, dry-heaving. Then she fled to the only door that wasn't open—a janitorial closet. Once inside, she crouched down. Faint light crept through a grill in the lower portion of the door. Squatting down, she held her knees, staring through the vent. They were moving bodies out of the kitchen, dragging them by their, tracking long bloody trails with their victims' heads. She saw Givens and Lou.

Suddenly she remembered his phone--Lou's cellular, she was still clutching it! A terrorists—all black boots stood outside the door as she fiddled around for the power button. As she turn it on, the phone made a loud that almost made her pass out. The terrorists turned and her heart stopped. Then the electricity died and the terrorists spun around walking back down the hall.

In the half-light of the supply closet "FBI 2" glowed on the green screen. She pressed the "send" button so hard, she thought she cracked her nail. There was a long pause and she wasn't sure if it connected and then-

Four

2:48 PM (EST)
Alexandria, VA

The phone rang.

Tom Grant scratched his ass and tried to remember the night before. But days and nights faded into one long continuous blur. People used different words to describe Tom Grant. . . impulsive, uncontrollable, and of course: genius. Tom's mind was laser sharp. When he worked he only worked. And when he drank, well, he wasn't a good drunk, but he was learning.

Peering out the door, he examined his living room. . . walls covered with antique military lithographs. . . bookshelves lined with countless works on battle strategy from Peloponnesian tactics to Stalingrad. . . technical briefings on explosives and detonator devices. . . a stylized photograph of a U2 taking off at dawn. . . stuff only anarchists and mothballed pilots would use to decorate their home. Littered about his floor were empty beer-cans, an M16 Operator's manual, pizza boxes, a ballistic missile guide, Chinese take-out--anything that would deliver. Looked like the local IRA headquarters, he sighed.

He glanced down, examining his quickly forming gut, a patch of fat on an otherwise lean, wiry frame. He brought home a bottle of Jim Beam when he started this drunken marathon, determined to reach an enlightened state of inebriation. But without a goal, the mission degenerated into one lifeless blur punctuated by local trips to the liquor store for additional provisions.

How long had he been here? He counted the days on his fingers since he was rendered unemployed: a week. A week's worth of boozing and eating and falling asleep to the late show. Oprah was the only thing he actually scheduled. She was a newfound passion. He enjoyed watching her, listening to her soothing voice, the way she coaxed her guests.

Oprah brought him great peace.

Ring.

The phone broke his train of thought, but he refused to answer it. Hell, he hadn't taken a call in seven days and saw no reason why he should break tradition now. His machine clicked on.

"Remember us, your coworkers? We're at the office cleaning out our desks. Call us. It's game day!"

The line clicked dead, but the ringing continued. He realized it was his cell phone and did his best to ignore it. Despite how much he tried to ignore it, the question popped into his mind: now what? Drive out to Colorado and hike ? That's what he used to fantasize about doing if he were fired. Look at him now, holed up in his apartment, afraid to leave, squandering the last of his money on booze.

Because Tom Grant didn't want to be part of the real world. Fuck the real world with its nine to five men and women living out their ordinary lives, going to their ordinary jobs. All along, who protected their homes, their way of life? The so called real world was a fantasy of money, love, kids in the backyards with swing sets and college tuition: fixtures of a well-groomed illusion.

Far beyond the boundaries lay the real world of poverty and ancient ideologies tripping into modern times--ethnic cleansing and bloody *coup d'états'*. Truth in this closed society called The United States could be found in the men who spent their lives keeping such forces at bay: the sentinels at the gate.

Of course Tom Grant was not interested in the truest of sentinels, the marine grunts crawling around on foreign beaches, shooting up enemies. Tom came from a wealthy upbringing. . . the skin of his palms was smooth and soft.

A perfect candidate for CTJTF.

The Counter Terrorist Joint Task Force, CTJTF, appealed to Tom from the beginning. A think tank for the most horrible terrorist acts. The ten man, FBI sponsored group poured through books, news AP's, briefs, declassified dossiers, and old mission profiles in order to formulate the perfect terrorist act-- the one to top all others. . . poison in the water in Denver--nuclear bombs in Chicago.

Death was all fun and games at CTJTF. How many people could you kill? How quickly could you do it? How much money would you demand? On the other side, who would act as the Chief Facilitator? How would The Joint Chiefs and The White House be involved? What special operative force would you suggest to deploy: Navy SEALS, Psyops, Delta Force? But not anymore.

As of last week, it all got shut down.

The phone continued to ring.

Tom turned down the volume knowing that it was just his coworkers making sure he'd be there for Rabb's Hail Mary. Named after the leader of CTJTF and Tom's mentor, a man called The Rabbi, Rabb's Hail Mary was an anomaly of FBI intramural football. Three years ago one of Tom's team-mates accidentally caught the ball and was so terrified of the rushing onslaught that he not only ran off the playing field, but led his compatriots to the closest bar and proceeded to get thoroughly drunk.

"What?" he picked up the phone, "I can't hear-- it's all static," he realized the drapes were open--a maid in the apartment next door stared at his naked back-side. He couldn't tell if she was mortified or pleased, "call back on my-"

"They're killing us," the voice was stronger this time—a female.

"Who is this?" he covered his ass with a pizza box, shutting the blinds.

"I'm on Lou's phone. Lou's dead," she said it like he should know Lou.

"Is this a prank?"

"I have little time. All of them are dead. They're killing us."

The prankster was beginning to get on his nerves. Tom had that weird feeling, unsure of how he should react. He searched the confines of his brain for some clever response, but drew a blank, finally adding, "Tell the guys I'm going to the game."

"What guys! What game!" she almost screamed, "I'm in a closet in the Union 57 refinery in Elizabeth, New Jersey. Are you listening-"

"Shut up."

"What k-k-kind of hot-line is this?" the woman stammered, "you're the FBI! They're going to kill me! Don't you have anything to say to me?"

"Good luck."

He was about to end the call when she cried, "Lou Pauzpolis was here! Y-your number's on Lou's speed-dial--"

Lou. . . Lou Pauzpolis. Who the hell was he? Her voice was so desperate. He had to admit, she was a good actress. . . a damn good one, "Who's going to kill you?" he inquired.

"Gunmen."

"How many people are dead?"

"They killed all the hostages,' she stammered, " except one girl."

"Where were they killed?"

Her response was quick, "In the break-room."

"The break-room, huh?" he picked at an in-grown toe-nail-- need to clip that before the game, "where were you during all of this?"

"In the bathroom."

"Number one or number two?"

"Number one—what does that matter?"

" Do they know you're there?"

"They found my shoe, but--"

"You left your shoe? You're in the dog-house now!"

"I didn't mean to! You have to help me, please!" it was the sexy vulnerability in her voice that made him continue. He imagined her tall, "two men are searching room by room and mine's next!"

"Is there a door open to a room they already checked?"

"Yes, but I can't. "

"If what you're tellin' me is true, you'd have no time for can't do's."

He resolved to get dressed and then hang up the phone. But there was another question nagging him in the back of his head like an annoying fly he couldn't swat. How did he know Lou Pauzpolis? Over the phone, he could hear her rustling about, the crack of a door and then-

"I'm in the other room," she whispered, "hiding under Larry's desk."

"Is there a window?"

"Yeah, it's foggy. Could I get in an air-vent ?"

"Only in the movies. Air vents can't support much weight. "

Then it hit him. Lou was going to ref the intramural game, but he'd been dispatched out to New Jersey for something. Oh shit! "W-w-what's your name?" he stammered, his mouth growing dry.

"Candice. . . Candice Cooperman. They're coming back into the room."

"Quick," cried Tom, "get under the desk!"

The line clicked dead.

Was he just being stupid?

He sat there for a long moment, catching hints of his own reflection in the closed window. Then he pulled out The Yellow Pages. It took him a moment to find the number. What did he have? A caller an FBI agent/ football ref—but his number was on Lou's speed dial and-

"Union 57 Corporation," the operator answered, "how may I help you?"

"This is Special Agent Grant with the FBI," OK, so he told a little lie, he had been with the FBI--sort of, "I need to speak to someone about a possible breach in security at your Elizabeth, New Jersey location."

"Is this a joke?"

"I need to speak to someone in charge!" another pause. He thought she'd hung up, "Are you listening to me?" he barked again. He needed to speak to someone in security. He'd tell them what he knew, see if this thing were real before he involved anyone else in it.

"Yes s-s-sir, I am," the Operator stuttered, "I'm-- uh. . . I'm j-just gonna need a minute to figure out who I'm supposed to transfer you to."

Five

"**A**nd in front of *tout le monde*," followed by a snicker.

Benjamin Bronk turned away from her, examining the restaurant: a conflation of dim, golden lights, arch deco spires, and windows opening onto a wintry, slush filled 7th Avenue. The establishment was called *Petrossian*, an attempt to conjure up the ambiance of its Parisian predecessor complete with the maitre d' and his up-turned nose. When they arrived, the little man took great pains at finding an open table despite the fact that the restaurant was empty.

Benjamin's life held little time for daytime lunches. And the conventional restaurant dinner in which it was compulsory to listen to everyone's I have's and I do's, bored him. Benjamin often lost himself in the complex chasm of his own mind. Only a second before had he realized that the afternoon crowd had suddenly turned to gray haired men in Turnbull & Asser suits, playing raconteur to their buxom, twenty year old secretaries who listened intently, their champagne glasses never running low. The mating rituals that abound, Benjamin raised a lone eyebrow at the sight.

"Is that not the funniest, Benjamennnn?" she had that way of stressing the end of his name in that tight North Eastern drawl--as if chewing on marbles.

"Quite funny," the reporter, Erica Morales smiled, feigning a keen interest in everything she heard, but then again, thought Benjamin, it was her job to listen. He admired her features. . . early twenties, the skin around her eyes began to wrinkle into fine lines. She was cute in an ethnic way, Italian, possibly Hispanic. Suddenly the realization struck him. Did he, Benjamin Bronk, with his overflowing head of slightly graying hair and wrinkled face of forty years, seem like just another suitor with his prospective prey? So seedy!

Two waiters in starched linen jackets rushed the table, simultaneously presenting the fifty grams of Beluga caviar on tiny, silver dishes. A third server poured the remains of the *Cliquot Grand Dame* with the curious talent of letting the foam rise to the very top of the elongated flute without spilling over.

No, Benjamin turned to the third guest at the table, the one dropping little hints of French between her ha ha's and ho hums. With her along, no one mistook Benjamin Bronk for a suitor attempting to jump this young reporter."I guess Benjamin is not very talkative today," the third guest chatted on with the reporter, "or he didn't think it was funny ha ha ha," her laughter was refined, like water drops sneaking out of a tight faucet.

Yes. . .this was Mother.

Just look at her.

Born to entertain in festive Manhattan soirees-- seated around a regency table smothered in orchids and *Zuber* wallpaper. Mother knew how to pierce the chit chat, drawing the proverbial spot-light upon herself. Mother was the Queen. Mother remembered the Ritz Hotel. Mother's godmother was Marjorie Oelrichs.

She had a tight, puckered Irish face despite the fact that she only claimed the lowland, Episcopalian, Scottish side of her family; the group from which she inherited that proud, jutting chin. When she spoke, her lips were still, only the chin vibrated back and forth. With gray hair and a tight skinned face from acid burns and cosmetic surgeries, Mother looked no older than her sixty years and from a distance might even pass for fifty--in the right light of course.

Ageless or not, she was still the woman whose Park Avenue apartment was photographed in Vogue every time she decided to strip the thick layers of paint off the walls. She had all the accouterments of good taste: three groomed corgis--just like the queen--ever so English--and don't forget the sprawling mansion on Ocean drive complete with the Rolls Royce with wicker interior. Mother did not understand the words "unnecessary expense".

Take for instance the '54 Bentley housed and maintained in an uptown garage at the annualized cost of $60,000 with another $94,0000 for the Chinese chauffeur. And after Mrs. Van Horn was followed from Bergdorf's and savagely robbed--he admitted the story never quite made sense with Bergdorf's tight security--Mother now took only to take cabs. She taught the chauffeur how to tend the balcony bonsai garden.

Benjamin griped and complained and although he didn't inherit her view of possessions, he did understand it. Wealth for Mother was never about money, it was only about the good taste to have it.

Of course he managed to provide the money.

When Benjamin's father keeled over at the stock holder's meeting in August of 1971, Benjamin was only eighteen years old. It was strange how exacting his father was with financial figures and yet so loose with his own will. Locked out until 21, the family holdings were handed over to trustees appointed by the bank which was still owed millions in loans. It took 4 years of legal battles before he and his brother took control of the family holdings.

He sold off the food industry holdings, the gas station chain, and the international shipping firm. Was it the right move? Forbes Magazine nicknamed him "The Man Who Broke the Bronk". He framed the article over his desk.

What they didn't know or couldn't see was that Benjamin Bronk—tall and wiry in his boxy Anderson & Sheppard suits, black hair, and jutting Princeton jaw, was a perfect candidate for the task at hand. He had the insight to grasp the bigger picture. The other divisions were making money, but their continued success was dependent on the original source of the Bronk fortune:

The Union 57 Corporation.

Benjamin refocused, building Union 57 into the third largest refiner of crude oil in the world. It held interests in upstream drilling in Indonesia, the Middle East, Venezuela, and was a pioneer in deep water drilling in the Gulf of Mexico. Union 57's chemical branch manufactured everything from pesticides to-

"Benjammen," Mother's chin shook, bringing him back to the restaurant

He remained silent. Maybe she'd leave him alone--he could sip his champagne and think.

"Benjammen," Mother pressed, "are you listening?"

The journalist flashed a smile at him, a smile as fake as Mother's grin, but it was all part of the game. She was here at the request of this New York socialite to cover the charity ball and Kipps Bay something or other. He was here to shed a new angle on Mrs. Bronk, the socialite and mother.

"Both of you," Mother scooped some caviar on a cracker, "must try some of this Beluga. It's simply fabulous!"

When Mother wasn't looking, the journalist glanced down at the caviar, shooting a questionable look at Benjamin as if to say *fish eggs?* He smiled. Yes. . . she had to be Hispanic.

"I hear you have a wonderful apartment for entertaining? Why did you pick The Post House for the charity dinner?" the reporter continued.

"Well to be honest," Mother bit into her cracker with tiny bites, "since I was picked to throw this *soiree* for a hundred people, it's not going to be in my home. Who knows who some of those old hoyas will invite--personal trainers and florist friends poking their noses around my apartment. Is that a Chagall or not a Chagall? We're out of salted peanuts in the foyer. And the corgis go mad when there's a crowd, barking at the servers, pissing all over the front hall. Can't have that," she smiled, "of course you're not going to print that."

Benjamin watched the scent of scandal melt the glaze from her eyes. He gave mother a kick ever so lightly. She ignored it and in breathless exclamation pressed on as if divulging some great secret, "Most of the guests are so cheap. Half of them never even bid on the silent auction: that's the real money raiser. Do you know that you have to make room for at least ten extra slobs who just show up without even paying for a seat? Ha! What are you going to do? Have a knock down in the middle of the place? Ha ha ha. Anyway, the Post House cut me a deal on the liquor," she took another sip of champagne, "the liquor thing was a joke . . . you're supposed to laugh now, dear."

"Hahah."

"All joking aside I do have a magnificent story about The Post House that you can print," she peered off into space as if she could actually see the prefabricated lie, "when I was young, which was not long ago, my husband and I ate there and. . ."

The reporter rocked in her seat. She must've thought she was going to an afternoon drink with the Rockefellers and ended up with the Addams Family, sighed Benjamin, drifting back into his own thoughts. . . the world faded away.

"Just look at him," Mother pointed to her own son lost in thought, "looks like he's about to break into tongues ha ha ha. . . that was a joke too, darling. You're supposed to laugh."

"Hahah."

But Benjamin didn't hear them.

Often times he didn't hear any small talk or chit chat that went on in the world; indifference wasn't really the correct term, but more of an extreme detachment. Benjamin had no time for pleasantries. He did everything intensely. . . working seventeen or eighteen hour days when necessary. He sometimes drank too much Tequila, Don Julio or Patron, and ended up sleeping with too many of his female assistants in the Drake Hotel. Free time though was rare and so these vices never really had to be confronted.

When it came to his children, however, he was a devoted father. People marveled how this cold, character, who cared so little for his own wife, could be so caring for his children. He would leave work early to share a meal with Anastasia, his five year old daughter, and Benjamin Jr. and then return to work. As for personal time, he usually stayed in his separate bedroom reading historical biographies--he had 007's whole collection on videocassette and never tired of them. Often times he might stay up till four in the morning dictating memos, then shower, and catch twenty minutes of sleep during the car-ride from Sutton Place to The Union 57 Financial Center where-

"Benjamenn, wake up!" Mother's chin jutted.

"That's a very funny story, think my readers will really enjoy that, " the reporter smiled. Perhaps it was the fact that she was getting along so well with Mother that she became so bold, "tell me, Mr. Bronk, are there any points you would like to add to the comments on Nightline last night?"

"Nightline?" Mother tried to hide a gasp.

My, thought Benjamin, what an aggressive little girl this Ms. Morales was.

"Tell me, " Mother regained her composure, "what did you and Mr. Koppel have to say to each other?"

"Secretary of State Giardino and I exchanged some choice words on EPA rulings. The fact that the cost of refurbishing the oil refineries of America will be greater than what it cost to build them all. Yet the administration refuses to tax foreign oil refined under no EPA restrictions."

She flashed a stoic, icy look. They seemed like two bull-dogs about to fight. The tension was white hot.

"I'm going to go to the bathroom," the reporter excused herself.

"Little bitch," Mother smiled, watching Erica until she turn the corner, "is this an attempt to run for public office or you trying to public suicide?"

He stiffened, "I just got a little tired of all the—hell," he threw up his hands.

"Just like your father. Spoke your mind? What a sense of filial responsibility you've garnered for the general public with your prime time--"

"It wasn't prime time-

"For nation-wide television. Your brother probably has calls into me right now from London! You know he has that gastric problem when he gets upset. Next time you decide to go preaching-just go get a good fuck, she sighed.

"What?" he almost hopped out his seat. Once you started Mother there was no stopping her.

Puckering her lips, she looked as if she were discussing the weather, "I mean, it's much cheaper than an outburst on public TV. Simply use some discretion. Your father, may he rest in Hell, had a secret exit from his office so that he could skip out for flaunts without-"

"I don't want to talk about Dad."

With a raised brow, Eleanor stared back into the past, "He always had the most beautiful mistresses. Adultery's quite acceptable as long as it's done tastefully."

"I don't need to hear this."

"Oh, quit blushing. I'll tell you this, Benjammen, your father and I didn't have the fights that you and Amanda have. She's left you again."

"News gets around fast."

"No, darling, mothers just know. Your tie doesn't match. A dark pinstriped suit and a summer plaid tie in December? You, the most impersonal of people wearing your problems on your chest. And now you've taken to the prime time."

"I told you, it wasn't prime time-"

"Where did she say she was going this time?"

"The house in Lyford Cay," he shrank under the words.

"Lying little bitch," she sipped her champagne, "Beatrice's daughter saw her lunching at Gotham with a swarthy gentleman in a black turtleneck and a pony tail. What a scandal, eh!"

His stomach churned, but he tried to hide it. The kids were stuffed away in a friend's apartment with a friend's nanny, while she toasted over *Lynch-Bages* with *l'amour de jour*. Why was it that he only wanted her when she was chasing other men? Was it that he only loved what he couldn't have or was it that these adulteress tirades were simply staged to attract his attention?

"I'm sure she'll be slithering about the city on her back for the next few days, jumping from one bed to another," continued Mother, "and the children?"

"Haven't seen the kids since she left yesterday."

"Benjammen! Goats have kids! Bronks have children. Just get that little Nazi of yours, Mueller-"

"He's my chief of security!"

"Well he looks like a little Nazi. I could imagine him chucking Amanda into the East river. Should never have married into such an old family. In my older age I think you should mix up the genes every third generation or so, marry a Catholic--hell even a Jew as long as they don't invite their relatives to Christmas dinner and all. . . ha ha ha," she chatted on with a giggle, "hope your children have the good sense to marry an ethnic type. We need new blood to combat your wife's incessant habit of falling on any stiff prick around."

Jesus, now she was a geneticist! "You've become quite vulgar in your older age. Is this a sign of senility?"

"Look at Trimble Lawrence's grand-children. Can't tell me they aren't in-bred with those sloping faces and gaggling-"

"You're being crass."

"Well I can be, damn it--oh, welcome back," the jaw pointed upward. The reporter returned to the table, vacillating on whether she would sit down and continue, "so good to see you again, darling. Was about to send out the search party, thought you'd drowned."

The journalist averted Mother's gaze. Her body language was defensive, arms crossed, "Tell me, Ms. Morales," continued Mother, "shall we continue talking about the Kipps Bay Club and the Charity dinner or would you rather dig into more of my son's political views?"

Without a pause: "Kipps Bay Club's quite sufficient."

"I know the owner of your fine paper," Mother flashed her signature, tight lipped smile and actually moved her lips this time, "write a word of our private conversation, I censor the text and my son's Nazi henchman will toss you in the East River. . . ha ha ha."

The waiter tapped him on the shoulder, "Call for you at the payphone."

"Benjamin Bronk," he stated crisply into the phone.

It was Mueller. The man's gruff accent resounded across the phone line from the security headquarters in the Union 57 building, "We have a sort of problem. . . kiddo," he was one of Benjamin's closest acquaintances-- the only one who called him "kiddo, "an FBI agent called, claiming a hostage take-over in the Elizabeth plant. Security checked the phone lines, they were cut."

"How'd he claim to know?"

"Claimed a female caller had contacted him," answered Mueller, "she's at the refinery and witnessed the employees gettin' killed by gunmen."

"Send out a company security crew to investigate," continued Benjamin, "wouldn't worry about it. Sounds like a bad prank. Have New York run a remote security check—"

" When I said all phone lines were cut, I meant the security lines too."

There was a CPR poster mounted next to the phone and for a moment Benjamin thought he'd need it. His whole body tightened. In case of an emergency when an explosion might sever regular phone lines, the security lines from the sensor equipment were buried in underground lines encased in tubing--telemetry would always be available to the New York headquarters. The security line could only be breached inside the main engineering complex.

"What we gonna do?" asked Mueller in a calm voice.

Bronk's thoughts raced. Could it be? Could it actually be happening? All men had their deepest, darkest fears that they buried in the pits of their mind. Benjamin was precariously close to his own. He shook it away .

"Who knows about this?"

"The operator who took the call in the Baltimore office and my assistant."

"Detain them all—at any cost."

There was a slight pause followed by, "Understood."

"Mueller, I need you to get Amanda and the far away--put em on a jet to Zurich. Do you have any family around?"

"Well, got a brother in Patterson."

"Tell him to take a long trip," added Bronk, "now I'm going to need a chopper on the top of the Union 57 building in fifteen minutes. The chopper will drop me off at the Falcon in Teterboro--get the jet prepped."

He would give them the flight plan only when they were ready to take off. He didn't want anyone to know where they were flying to in such a rush--even Mueller. It might turn the wrong heads.

"I don't understand," asked Mueller, "why fly to a refinery across the river?"

"I'm not going to the refinery."

He said goodbye to his mother, telling her to contact Mueller as soon as she paid the bill. He failed to say good-by to the journalist. She didn't exist. Nor did the gray haired raconteurs and their buxom secretaries. Benjamin Bronk was no longer in the *Petrossian Restaurant*. . . nor in New York City. He was in a well-crafted nightmare, a terrifying déjà vu. Fifteen years ago he foresaw the a vision of terror, something they said could never happen.

It was snowing when he stepped onto the cold street. He still had his overcoat slung over his arm. Snowflakes melted against his burning, dry cheeks. His pulse beat so strong that the veins in his neck throbbed. Could Mueller find his children in time! He would need the men on the plane to work out the details. This thing was going to explode in the next few hours.

He only hoped that he could get to Washington in time!

Six

4:30 PM (EST)
Washington D.C.

"White House," the operator answered sharply.

The White House telephone line, 202-456-1414, received an average of 48,000 calls a year, each one answered skillfully by a highly trained staff of operators. The White House Switchboard had the power to interrupt general phone conversations, tracking down VIP call recipients anywhere in the world. The Chief Executive, his Press Secretary, and even staffers might give speeches, press announcements, and briefings, but the switchboard was the everyday voice of the President of The United States.

"White House, Washington D.C." she coldly repeated herself.

"I would like to speak to the first position operator," the caller requested in a foreign accent.

"First position operator?" she hesitated, repeating his words.

Another role of the operator was to screen callers. With seven years of service this one had heard it all: old ladies complaining about their electric bills, weirdoes giving political advice, pranksters talking about the weather. She searched her gut instinct, this one felt real. She transferred the call.

"Yes?" the first station operator was equally as dry as her predecessor.

She did not take basic calls, but worked on private, Presidential communications, answering The Executive and Chief on a myriad of questions ranging from emergency calls to movie rentals. They said that Kennedy used to call his first station girl in the middle of the night, looking for can openers and sandwiches.

"I require a fax line for a NODIS," the caller struggled in a chopped accent.

NODIS stood for a "no distribution correspondence". These official correspondences often originated from embassies, the military, or a number of internal security services. This request was not out of the ordinary and from his African or Middle Eastern accent, she assumed that the call was authentic.

She disclosed the confidential fax number. A minute later, the correspondence was digitally faxed into the White House main-frame computer routed via the e-mail system to the next rung up the ladder of authority.

In order to filter through the thousand messages a day that the White House received, a system was developed over the years to disseminate and filter information for the President. Without such protocol, the Chief Executive would be overwhelmed with mountains of material and requests too numerous to be handled by any one, single person. Thus, each President came into the White House dedicated to cutting White House staff only to ultimately add more filters to simply digest the ever-growing outside world.

The fax flowed to the office of the executive secretary. This particular staff member, a female in her mid-thirties, read the correspondence as it flashed on her computer screen. She quickly decided to advance it to the next station: the White House Situation Room, ear-marking it "CRITIC alert". The message was electronically routed away.

A millisecond later, it flashed onto the massive DIDS screen of the lesser of the two White House Situation Rooms. Commonly called "The Sit Room--the brain center for sensitive data. Information flowed from all channels of government: CIA, NSC, State, but only in the Sit Room with the help of three VAX computers, and an assortment of DIDS equipment projecting information in a thousand forms, did the smaller tributaries combine into a complete river of knowledge.

The Sit Room was manned by a White House national security assistant. All day long the assistant read blurbs passing over the screens like stock exchange ticker tape, deciding if any blurbs were of "Presidential Importance." If so, this assistant would pass the information onto his superiors. Only messages from US ambassadors abroad could circumvent the Sit Room, going directly to the Secretary of State's desk.

In this case, the assistant was a man in his mid-thirties who had been working since six that morning, doing some double time so that he could leave the next day for a long needed vacation in Dutch St. Maarten. Alone in the room, he began to nod off when the CRITIC alarm beeped, announcing a parcel of information which his subordinate had decided was worthy of special attention.

The words of the letter reflected off the screen and onto his face as he read this correspondence and took note of the names at the lower right corner: the bureaucratic hands it had passed through on its way to him.

He dialed his superior's office, "Sir, I think I have something you should take a look at, sir," damn, why had he said sir twice? Made him sound stupid, "it's a letter," he was careful not to use sir this time, "I'd like to e-mail it up."

"Terminal's off. I'm stepping out for a conference with the President-"

"This will only take a minute."

Secretary of State Giardino moaned, "Be down in a minute."

The assistant hung up the phone.

He scanned the monitor, reading the fax for the sixth time. The document was somewhat crude with incorrect grammar and misspellings as if a foreigner had written it, which went along with what the operator said.

Technically he was not supposed to decide if the message was valid. His function was to pass on information to his superiors and aid them in their decisions. But, he did have his own gut feeling . . and that feeling said that he should call the travel agent because he wasn't going to Dutch St. Maarten tomorrow. Hell, he probably wasn't going anywhere for awhile. He read the note again, noting the misspellings and poor grammar:

THIS IS CRIMSON FIST.

WE HAVE TAKEN CONTROL OF THE UNION 57 COMPLEX IN ELIZABETH NEW JERSEY. WITHIN FIVE HOURS THE FOLLOWING PERSON WILL BE FREED AND FLOWN TO AN AIR-SIGHT IN TRIPOLI LIBYA. THE ITALIAN GOVERNEMENT WILL RELEASE ALI YNES, AHMED KARBIAM, ATOUA ALIT TOURNEDA. THE ISRAELI GOVERNEMENT WILL RELEASE ABU SAIDWAR, AHMED KHANDLAM. THE UNITED STATES GOVERNEMENT WILL RELEASE HIS HOLLINESS, THE AYATOLLEH OF SUPREME ENLIGHTENMENT.

UNITED STATES WILL PREPARE $34,000,000 FOR AN EXCHANGE IN NEW YORK CITY. WILL PLACE A SECOND CALL IN THREE AND A HALF HOUR (8:00 EST) AND GIVE MORE DETAILS.

ALL FLIGHTS TO AND FROM NEWARK AIRPORT, YOU WILL CANCEL. NO ONE, NON-GOVERNEMENT OR GOVERNEMENT WILL TRESPASS WITHIN A 2,000 YARDS RADIUS OF THE PLANT. WE HAVE 148 HOSTAGES. WE WILL KILL 3 HOSTAGES EVERY HOUR UNTIL OUR DEMANDS ARE MET. FALURE TO FOLLOW ALL OUR DEMANDS WILL LEAD TO THE MASS EXECUTION OF ALL 148 HOSTAGES.

ALLAH BE PRAISED.

LONG LIVE THE CRIMSON FIST!

Seven

4:43 PM (EST)
Elizabeth, NJ

He was in the room!

Huddled under Larry's oversized, wooden desk, Candice Cooperman pressed her knees against her face. She wanted to curl into a ball, to climb inside herself and disappear. Sweat trickled down her forehead, running into her eyes. She was afraid to move--afraid to breath. Every footstep in the room unleashed a lightning bolt which shot up her spine. She focused on his combat boots stained brown with dried blood-- she knew he was the one that murdered the Supervisor.

He was going to find her--murder her just like he murdered the rest of them! No, Tom wouldn't want her thinking that way. . . calm down. Try to think. She shut her eyes-- remembered coming home a month ago. . . Felix rushing out from under the chair, greeting her with a purr. The note rested on the floor—that thought was definitely not going to calm her down.

More footsteps!

How many were in the room? Peeking through the crack of the baseboard and the desktop she made out three white guys—one had red hair. Surely they spotted her feet and butt poking out of the small gap at the base of Larry's desk! Something was set atop the desk—it nearly gave her a heart attack.

The terrorist stuck his arm under the desk, rolling up the sleeve of his jacket, exposing his pale skin as he thumbed the device--a metal box with a button atop it, the whole thing freezer taped around his wrist, "Leave me, I must consort with The Master," she heard the voice, gruff with a thick German accent.

She didn't know how long she sat there, listening to the sound of her own pulse as he typed? He shifted his feet and nearly gave her a heart attack. Then he stopped. Had she been discovered?

Standing, he exited the room. She waited a long moment, considering what to do before she shot out of the desk. She saw the sleek, laptop computer and followed the cord leading from it to wall mounted phone jack. The screen was filled with a conversation between this terrorist and some superior:

I am your Defender of The Faith. We have neutralized the plant—all are dead.

All are not dead. I am told one is still alive. You must-

The battery saver turned the screen black. She had no time to—but the question haunted her: what had the person on the other line meant by "I am told one is still alive?"

She heard someone in the hall!

Candice grabbed her overcoat, pushing open the small window. The sun was setting--a gray crown of light running across the horizon. The sting of the snow on her bare, right foot greeted her to the icy landscape. Wind whipped through her hair the sudden slap of cold air reviving her like a cold shower. Her heart beat so fast she thought it might explode. Then she saw it.

Under the entranceway awning of the building laid the pile of bodies. . . everyone from the break room--rotting corpses, arms and legs pointing up, stiff in the icy wind. Beyond them she could see terrorists clearing out the parking lot, creating some kind of pattern out of oil drums. What kind of terrorist action was this? They killed the hostages, used meditation chambers, and made funny patterns in the parking lot.

She felt distanced and detached for the first time. Maybe it was the pile of bodies or the fact that she had evaded certain death three times. The flood of emotions ceased. Instead, she felt like an invisible observer walking through this madness, observing outrageous acts, unable to participate in them.

She was invulnerable to these predators. Look at all the tribulations she had endured and still she lived! She was aware of the snow falling against her face, waking her gently from her dream like state. She came to a metal ladder bolted to the side of the building. Voices in the snow seemed to surround her.

She climbed upward, thinking that she could climb out of this mad world, climb back to reality, climb back to the life that seemed so far away now. The snow seemed to swallow her up. . . she felt like she was climbing a ladder straight into an endless snowstorm. Then she reached the roof.

She collapsed on the cold surface.

The snow on top of the building had melted, creating small puddles of water. Most of the roof was coated in a black tar, she could make out hazy shapes in the falling snow. . . a sign in bright orange letters reading STAIRWELL DOOR WILL LOCK AUTOMATICALLY.

Watching the mist rise up from her mouth, she tried to gather her thoughts. She wouldn't survive out here long--lying flat on her back, she glanced up at the gray sky growing ever darker, snowflakes falling into her eyes and freezing her lips.

She wanted to speak to Tom, to hear his voice. She speed dialed him.

"Candice?" she heard Tom through the phone, "is that you?"

Suddenly she didn't feel so invisible. Her moment of clarity was lost. She clutched the phone near her face. She was lying underneath an air-conditioner compressor. Then she heard it. Despite the fact stairwell door had closed--

Someone else was on the roof.

Eight

"Candice?" Tom Grant asked.

The phone call was like a wild roller coaster. He wanted it, expected it, but the moment he was hooked in, he just wanted it to stop. . . the lurking chance that he'd make the wrong move. . . so little time to think!

"I'm on the roof," she answered.

"The roof?" he was puzzled. What the hell was she doing on the roof? She was trapped under the desk in an office when-

"Tom, there's someone here. What do I do?"

He was clothed in his tattered hockey shirt and sweat pants. having vacillated between staying in the apartment or heading to FBI headquarters.

"He hasn't seen me yet," Candice whispered.

The nagging question resided in his mind. Was this a cover, a ruse by terrorists—or hell, even the intramural football team he was about to play, "Are you hiding behind something?"

Her response was barely audible, "I'm under an air-conditioner compressor—I think that's what it is."

"Candice?" he tried to sound reassuring as the television spun around him. He suddenly realized that in his nervous spasm, he was turning around and around in circles, "there have been a lot worse scenarios than this-"

"Like what?" she was near tears.

"Well. . . " yeh, Tom Grant, what situation was like this? Think of something to say. Think! "well. . . EgyptAir Flight MS64 in 1985."

She made no response. He could imagine the footsteps all around her as she hid under the AC unit, "There was an airplane that was hijacked by Arabs and Germans," he continued, "and a guy named Patrick Scott Baker was taken by terrorists to the stairway outside the parked plane and shot in the head."

"Uh," he could hear her grunt in fear.

Maybe this wasn't the best story. Still, he pressed on, "The bullet only grazed him and he fell off the gangway and under the plane. He walked away with a little scar-- had nerves of steel to pretend that he was dead. That's what you've got to have right now, big brass balls."

After a long silence he heard her faint reply, "I don't have balls, Tom," she paused again, "I hear him walking back to the stairwell door. . . there, the door shut. He's left!" he could hear her sigh, energy pouring out of her.

"How can you be sure?"

"I saw him return through the door. There are things I need to say. They're all white guys," she pressed on, disclosing facts about a meditation chamber, a man with a detonator, geometrical patterns in the parking lot—he wondered if the hypothermia was getting to her.

"I'm feeling really light headed, Tom-"

The phone beeped three times. A sick, queasy feeling formed in his gut.

"What's that?" she asked.

Honesty was the best tact no matter how much it hurt, "It's the warning signal on your phone. Your battery's low."

"Oh no," she sounded more disoriented. Maybe he hadn't noticed it before? How long had she been exposed on the roof?

"We need to end the call," he added, "to conserve power."

"I can't," she was near tears now, vacillating between light headed delusions and nerve shattering fear, "I c-c-can't Tom."

"Be brave."

"I'm afraid of the dark. You don't know anything about me," she sounded like a pouting girl--a beautiful, pouting girl, "I'm memorizing your phone number off this damn thing. It's the only thing I have now. . . your number."

He had so little time! No. . . calm her down. If he didn't calm her down with conversation, she'd do something drastic, "You were great getting out of there."

"Do you think so?"

"You were marvelous. You're like a Navy Seal."

"It's s-s-so cold here, Tom," he was losing her.

"Wrap yourself in a tight ball," he instinctively huddled into a fetal position on the bed. Shutting his eyes, he pictured a gravel filled roof, the air-conditioning unit overhead, "I want you to think of a warm place. The best place you've ever been. Can you do that for me?"

"Fiji."

"Fiji?" somehow he didn't peg her as the world traveler.

"I remember a sunset in Fiji. Was snorkeling off this island and I broke through the water--the sun was setting--a blue that went on forever," she sighed, "thank God I have you, Tom, an FBI agent."

Honesty was the best thing, he thought reassuringly, "I'm not the FBI. I'm just an unemployed analyst. What do ya' think of that?"

"Help me picture you," she continued, "what celebrity do you look like?"

"Celebrity?" he grinned, "Bond, James Bond."

A pause, "There were a few Bonds. Which one?"

"Connery of course. Bet you look like Ms. Moneypenny, strong--reliable."

"Ugh, she never gets her man."

Beep. Beep. Beep and then. . . silence.

"T-T-T-tom," she stammered, "tthere's someone else up here."

The line clicked dead.

Tom stood alone shaking. Only then did he hear the banging against the door. He turned just in time to see the door rip off its hinges. Then lights blazed down on him and smoke erupted so that he couldn't see the intruders that stormed in and-

Nine

"Status, Alpha One?" Team Leader's voice crackled across his headset.

Alpha One turned around on his roof-top perch. The hunter green Land Rover appeared black in the sulfuric street-lights of Queensway Avenue. Parked between Whiteley's shopping mall and the Bayswater tube station, he tried unsuccessfully to make out Team Leader seated behind the automobile's tinted windows. London traffic poured down the street heading to Hyde Park.

"I'm on the roof," Alpha One answered in his mild Scottish accent.

London was experiencing one of those typical winter evenings. Overhead, clouds reflected the city's lights, tinting the evening mist with a touch of ethereal orange. He could hear traces of music in the apartment building below him. Ironically, he had climbed to the roof-tops by scaling the wall of "The Spy Shop" on the corner of the block. Dashing across jagged tiles and chimneys, he negotiated tight tucks and leaps like an agile cat.

Technically Alpha One was a member of The Counter Revolutionary Warfare Unit of B Squadron: 22 SAS. His unit consisted of four soldiers: all headed by his team leader sitting in the Land Rover. Although he couldn't spot them, Alpha Two was stationed on the roof-top directly across the street, armed and ready with his marksman's .22 caliber rifle and infrared scope. Alpha Three simultaneously worked his way along the roof-tops from the other side of the city block. Alpha Four was on top of Whiteley's Mall with a set of high magnification, surveillance goggles, coordinating all of his team-mates.

"Alpha One here," he continued as he darted up a slate roof, "about to cross the threshold to the target."

Alpha One sported only the bare essentials that his job required: his night-vision head-set, surgical gloves, a black nylon jumpsuit, Teflon bullet-proof vest, and an alpine climbing harness attached to his waist. His skinny, angular face and balding forehead were covered in flat, black, grease paint. He carried no rifle, a side armed

Glock .40 with silencer serving as his only weapon and a tool kit for special purposes.

"Alpha One, descending," wasting no time, he unfurled the cord of climbing rope, securing it to the chimney of the building. Deftly, he locked the rope and carabiner into his webbed climbing harness. Winding the rope through the rappeler's belay, he walked face-forward off the rooftop.

Rappelling Australian style or "face first" as the yanks termed it, was an interesting experience to say the least. The world seemed upside down to Alpha One as he walked face first down the building. A car driving on the street below him looked like it was actually riding along an asphalt covered wall. The window along the building's façade looked like well-proportioned holes in a brick covered floor. Quite disorienting.

In Edinburgh during his childhood, before he was Alpha One, he used to scale buildings like this on High Street, relieving stylish flats of their high tech video-recorders and jewelry. Once he even stole Sean Connery's VCR from the house the actor kept but rarely frequented on The Royal Mile; that one he kept as a souvenir. It was when he tried for the larger stuff like televisions and cappuccino machines that he got caught and was forced into the military. Now he sort of did the same thing for Queen and country. Then again this apartment wasn't just anybody's London flat.

And he certainly wasn't here to steal a VCR.

"Alpha One," Alpha Two situated across the street with binoculars continued, "the room is clear. I'll buy pints when it's over. Think there's a skank bar nearby with Burnes Night on," he mimicked a bad rendition of a Scottish accent, "yee can wear yee' skirt and all!"

"Expect that from an English wanka'," Alpha One jibed. He paused for a moment. Hanging upside down over the window--he glanced inside the room. You could never beat the man on the ground in this type of situation. So he personally scanned the room before entering. Skillfully, he turned his body around, resting the points of his boots on the window ledge. A taxicab rolled three stories beneath him, casting hints of light between his legs.

"Going in," he unhooked himself from the climbing ropes, strapping the infrared goggles onto his head. Leaving the dangling rope behind him, he tripped the lock on the window and entered the flat.

Warm air coated his face.

He swung his Glock around using his body to aim the weapon. Standing in the small study, he noted piles of books with Arab titles and soiled plates, "Room secured," he whispered into his headset.

Alpha Two surveying from the opposite building said, "I see the target from the side window. Wanka is about to enter your room. Get ready!"

Alpha One tensely bit his lower lip, holding the taser gun at head level, just an inch from the closed doorway. The door opened. Alpha One caught a glimpse of the back of the target's head. The soldier shielded his night goggles while he discharged the taser gun at the base of the target's neck. The blast of electricity was enough to take down a bison. The next moment, he could see the target shaking, tongue waggling, eyes closed, neck arched. Alpha One grabbed him as he collapsed, carefully lowering the unconscious body to the floor.

From the medical kit , he produced the 600cc syringe of digoxin. Through his night goggles, he flicked the syringe twice with the tip of his finger, depressing the plunger until a thin stream of fluid was ejected from the needle. For the first time he noted that the target was wearing a t-shirt and boxer shorts. Pulling the shorts of the man's left leg up, he searched for the femoral vein, just medial to the femoral artery. He injected the syringe.

'Aiighh," the target began to jerk in quick contortions. Spit frothed at his mouth. The Arab opened his eye, but he was still in a state of shock—then his heart stopped.

The dossier stated that the target's name was Said Gewarn: the self-appointed leader of the Crimson Fist. His renegade group had its hands in the Lockerbie bombing over Alpha One's own homeland, killing all four hundred on board. A participant in the Rome airport massacre, Said was fingered as the man who shot the twelve year old, American girl point blank through the head. But the goal of the mission was to interrogate Said without him knowing it.

M15 still needed these terrorists. They tracked Said when he entered Heathrow Airport under his forged Pakistani papers. He'd been overconfident, a characteristic that often proved useful in his daring murders for the jihad. Now he had gone too far, thought Alpha One, and had pissed somebody off.

Thanks to the dijoxin, Said's heart had stopped beating. Alpha One felt for a pulse—it was light and feeble. He set the target's hand over his heart.

The Agent raced to the window, reattaching his harness to the climbing rope. He heard someone rustling around in the bedroom. Quickly he shut the window and scaled back up the roof. In his wake he heard the shrill shriek of a woman's voice.

Scaling down the side of The Spy Shop, Alpha One changed clothes before darting over to the parked Land Rover. Minutes later, two paramedics rushed Said into an ambulance. They told his wife to meet them at St. John's Hospital and sped away, administering a dose of digibinde, an antidote to the dijoxin and IV fluids and a lactic ringer. Yet, instead of heading along the park to St. John's, however, they raced through the park, pulling into an abandoned South Kensington garage in the shadows of Brompton Hall.

"Abu?" Team Leader sighed.

Team Leader was a fat, stocky officer from the midlands. A chain-smoker, he lit his fresh Marlboro Red with the old butt . Said awoke--ghostly white, he tried to regain his senses, his head flopping to one side as he mumbled in Arabic. The building smelled of gasoline. A few dusty cars surrounded them while a lone light bulb swung overhead, casting ever changing shadows against the far wall.

"This will calm you down," Team Leader injected the syringe of thiopental into Said. He waited the prescribed three minutes for the "truth serum" to work, "Abu, you're with the Crimson Fist?"

"Crimson jihad is me," Said had a distant glazed look. . . thiopental always made subjects look glassy eyed. . . half drunk, Team Leader mused.

Smoke curled from Team Leader's cigarette, spinning designs around Said's face. Team Leader glanced at his wristwatch, he had nine minutes left before they had to transport the subject to the hospital, "Said,' Team Leader continued, "I want you to tell me everything you know about the Union 57 Oil Refinery in Elizabeth, New Jersey."

Said began to speak.

Ten

Tom Grant was blindfolded.

He was stuffed into a car. It was moving and he figured he was no more than a block away from his apartment when the blindfold was ripped away and he saw the faces of his captor. Fear turned swiftly to anger as he studied the spacious stretch limousine and noted the muscular black man in his mid 50's with salt and pepper hair.

"Rabb," he sighed, "I should have guessed."

"Blindfold's kinda kinky, huh? Scared the hell out of you. Serves you right, not taking my calls all week."

Tom's former boss didn't bother to turn on a light in the vehicle. They were bathed in a darkness -- he smelled whisky in the air, heard the clinking of ice. The streets cast temporary illumination through the car, multicolored lights dancing across Rab's face, illuminating the dark eyes—eyes like an owl, mused Tom. Around the man, he always felt like an inexperienced, kid, but then that's how you were supposed to feel in the presence of a genius.

The Rabbi was a living legend in the intelligence world: *summa cum laude* from Georgetown University, an aide de camp to General Westmoreland in Vietnam, never married, maybe he never knew how to return home. . . lost in the government channels, he'd spent his life pioneering counter terrorist activities. His real name was Nebuchadnezzar something or other--no one could pronounce it. The colorful ethnic heritage lent him the nickname: the Rabbi.

"Shit Rabies, this bastard don't even know who I am," the gaunt man leaned forward in the darkness—looking like an old Cowboy from some John Ford film. Tom hadn't even noticed him. Tall and fit, he was also in his 50's with leathery skin and a graying mustache which framed sharp cheekbones.

"Why are you calling him Rabies?" inquired Tom.

The cowboy smirked, a crease of a smile peeking out from under his mustache, "In Nam, we played intramural football against each other. He played so nasty I named him Rabies—lot more fittin' than Rab," Tom caught hints of a Texas accent, "shit, didn't even know there was such a thing as a black Jew."

The Rabbi was a unique man. The child of Jewish, Ethiopian refugees who emigrated to America. Searching for a region similar in climate to their homeland, they settled in the outback of Texas where Rabb was born. They were both outsiders, thought Tom. It was Rabb who took the chance three years ago, offering him the position at CTJTF when no one else would touch him.

Rab handed a flask over to the man with the mustache, "Tom, never listen to a man named after overpriced booze."

The mustache curled around the man's long stern nose as he feigned insult. These two were indeed old buddies, thought Tom, "How many people can thank a fine cognac for their own conception."

Tom made the connection, "Of course, Major General R.M. Crandal."

"Well. . . keep goin'," prompted Crandal.

"You were the principle investigator in the Desert One debacle. In '81 you were Chief of SOCOM under Reagan. Your critique of the faulted storming of Grenada helped your subsequent appointment to head of The Ranger Regiment at Fort Bragg."

"That's the thing about special forces," sighed Crandal, "they can only publish your fuck up's. Very disheartening. But Grenada brings back fond memories. Reagan always knew how to do it right. Storm the beaches-get a tan-"

"Except that most of the special forces op.'s fed incorrect intelligence to each other," rebutted Tom, flaunting his knowledge, "one allied strike team fired on another thinking they were the enemy-"

"Yes," Crandal leaned forward, "but one must never lose sight of the point. We still got a good tan. And ya' talk 'bout me like I'm dead—like I'm written up in some encyclopedia," he should be, mused Grant, "this is all your doin' Rabb," the Brigadier General passed him the flask.

"At least they talk about you," grabbing a crystal glass from the limo's bar, Tom's mentor poured him a shot of bourbon, neat.

"You gotta' point there," Crandal winked, "tell me my young Turk, you know an awful lot about me as if you're kinda envious. Why the hell'd you want to be an analyst."

It was meant as a mere joke, but the question stung. Rabb shot a fleeting glance towards him. Tom drew back to thoughts of his past, thoughts he had pushed away for much of his life—the reason he was never allowed into The FBI. He felt flustered and directed the attention on the events at hand, "She gave me few details," he held his cell phone for all to see, "but I think she'll call back."

"Who?" asked the General.

"Candice," he responded in a matter of fact tone. Only then did he realize that the two men had no clue what he was talking about.

Crandal turned to Rabb, "Candice? I just know that we have an Arab terrorist situation in New Jersey. What do y'all know about The Crimson Fist?

The Crimson Fist, thought Tom, how were they connected to any of this. Candice had said nothing about terrorists, "Those are Arab terrorists. My eyewitness never said anything about Arabs."

"Well I got a hostage rescue team in route to New Jersey and some boys down in Baltimore checking up on a hunch from British SAS," interjected the General in a gruff tone, "we're all supposed to be further briefed on the   plane.

"The plane?" asked Tom.

Rabb pointed at Tom, "As usual, the answer's right under your nose."

Tom examined the crystal tumbler. Passing streetlights illuminated the etched imprint of the executive seal of The President of the United States.

6:55 PM (EST)
In Route Between New York and Washington DC

"What do you mean they're not taking my calls!" Benjamin Bronk thundered into the speakerphone. He rested his weight against the leather chair of the Falcon 20 jet. The interior of the craft was paneled in rich, mahogany wood, trimmed in gray piping.

"We faxed The White House the data and the briefs just like you said," added Mueller from the speaker, "they said it was a military operation and basically don't let the door hit us in the ass on the way out. I'm still goin' ahead, checkin' the surveillance tapes from the plant and all, but this tact ain't workin."

Benjamin's mind reeled. A faint burning in his stomach refused to stop. He loosened his collar and noted his panicked face in a mirror just over the couch. What could he do? No one was listening--too much was at stake!

"I called some buddies of mine—old friends from the FBI," added Mueller, "think you'd do better by turning that plane around."

"What?" asked the billionaire.

"I hear some the guys in charge are headed to New York—LaGuardia Airport. It's second hand info, but probably your best chance."

Benjamin took a breath, "Keep looking for my kids, Mueller."

"You got it boss."

Benjamin turned around. He needed a drink, but he'd wait and pour one after he spoke to the pilots. They'd just cleared rough weather over New York City— a storm system approached, swallowing up the whole northeastern seaboard. Now they were going to have to go right back into it again. He had to reach them—to tell him his secret before it was too late!

Eleven

Abu Singhalfa hopped off the bus.

The Iranian immigrant pulled back the sleeve of his parka to see his wristwatch: fourteen minutes late. The female manager, only in America would he have a woman boss, had given him a warning. Little bitch! Darting across the parking lot to the convenience store, he passed a customer gassing up a Honda.

Bright fluorescent lights made his white uniform glow. Glancing around the aisles of refrigerators and food, Abu couldn't see the manager. He poked his head over the counter, maybe she was loading up the time trigger safe? No.

She must be in the bathroom.

With a small sleight of hand that he had perfected, he snatched a pack of cigarettes from the shelf directly below the security camera. They were Marlboro Reds--just like Lee Van Cleef from the shoot em' up movies. Motioning out the door, he examined the lot. The man in the Honda had left. A woman gassed up her station-wagon. The full-service area was empty. Through the haze of fluorescent lights he couldn't make out the stars overhead. Since he worked the late shift for the 24 hour station, he enjoyed walking near the street in the slow hours of the early morning, smoking his Marlboro Reds, examining the night sky.

He lit up his first cigarette of the night and decided to tidy up the garage, get things in order so that by the time his manager got out of the bathroom, he could claim that he'd been there awhile. He inhaled on the cigarette and wondered what it would be like to be Lee Van Cleef—his favorite TV hero. Glancing up at the fluorescent Union 57 Gasoline sign, he unlocked the garage door. The door slid back over his head and the screaming began.

Shadows rushed around him.

A light flashed in his face! He glimpsed pistols. . . they were yelling at him. Turning around, he rushed back across the parking lot. The woman at the station wagon pulled her hair out of her head with one hand, pointing a gun at him with the other. What the hell was going on? She dropped her hair, a wig on the ground, and chased him. He broke for the street to lose them.

"GET DOWN ON THE GROUND!" she screamed.

More lights! A vehicle came charging across the street, crashing through a wooden sign he made to advertise discounted oil changes. Turning around, Abu could see more lights spinning and rushing around him-- more voices screaming!

"No steal!" he cried.

Lights encircled him. Men with black faces stood before him, screaming. In the confusion, Abu couldn't understand what was being said, "No steal. . .no steal," he whispered again.

"GET ON THE GROUND RIGHT NOW!" the man in black cried.

"No steal," Abu repeated almost to himself. He dropped the cigarette.

It was the cigarettes. They had seen him stealing the Marlboro Reds. He knew Americans didn't tolerate that kind of thing, but this use of force was--well--they didn't even do this in Iran!

"GET YOUR ASS ON THE GROUND RIGHT NOW!" another voice cried.

And all for cigarettes-

"I WILL SHOOT YOU! DO YOU UNDERSTAND THAT!"

"No steal," he prepared to reach into his coat pocket, to produce the cigarettes. He would show them-- he only took a pack--certainly not worth—

"I--" his teeth rattled, "I-I-I g-give them b-b-back."

"HE'S REACHING! HE'S FUCKING REACHING!"

Bright orange flashes exploded.

Abu never heard the sounds of the pistol. Suddenly the ground was pulled out from under him. His chest hurt. He felt heavy and nauseated, coughing something wet onto his face. They were circling now. He could no longer hear what they said, lights buzzing like fireflies in his head.

Hands touched him through his uniform. His body felt stiff and numb--like it wasn't his anymore. . . he was so tired. The images and sounds died away--all he could see was the bright Union 57 sign spinning around and around in the dark, night sky until it became like a fluorescent ball, round and bright and much larger than the moon, itself.

Twelve

Secretary of State Vincent Giardino was a pig.

But everyone called him "The Razorback." Of course, no one called him the nickname to his face. On television, however, Tom conceded that the political figure resembled a wild, tusked swine with razor sharp hair along its spine.

Barely five feet high, the terse, little Italian had escaped from some dank, longshoreman's hell-hole in the Bronx for the University of Arkansas on a football scholarship. It was in Little Rock that the gruff New Yorker acquired his nickname and first met the Tennessee born, Marshal Tucker Cormon.

"And I knew we were going places!" Giardino liked to say.

When Marshal Cormon ran for Congress in the great state of Tennessee, the clever little Razorback was at his side, biting opponents, bluffing the competition, snorting and screaming. The two were invincible. When Cormon defended the record industry against censorship, Anne Leibowitz photographed the mega-hip duo for Rolling Stone Magazine. Cormon wore a white, starched suit with a halo affixed to the breast pocket; the Razorback chose the pitchfork and horns.

Four years later, Cormon was the youngest Democrat Governor of his state; the Razorback was his cabinet chief. Then during their Presidential race, when the Memphis call girl scandal broke on the eve of the New Hampshire Primary, the old Razorback proved himself in a decisive Larry King show when he extricated his superior from certain political destruction by ranting and raving about the conservative witch-hunt trying to destroy them both. Brash, affected, and mean spirited he could get the job done.

With reelection less than ten months away, President Cormon's poles were rock bottom and Giardino had been slapped with a sexual harassment lawsuit by a summer intern. When Tom, Rabb, and General Crandal sat in the confines of the Gulfstream IV which rose high into the sky, bouncing through clouds, more than just a terrorist crisis was chipping away at the administration.

Rabb and Tom sat at the far end of a conference table. Giardino sat on the other side, flanked by a tall, nervous man with a bulging Adam's Apple. The lavatory door behind the Razorback opened and out stepped a third with curly hair, a pock marked face, and narrow slit-like eyes. Tom noted that Rabb turned away from the man, averting his tense gaze.

"The man to my left," Giardino pointing the bulging Adam's Apple "is Arthur Toblongee, White House Liaison for Central Intelligence Agency."

Arty nodded his head like a wounded dog, "Please to meet both of you."

"I'm familiar with your writings, Mr. Toblongee," Rabb spoke in the jocular tone of one colleague addressing another, "recall your recent dissertation on Sino American Counterintelligence-"

Arty's eyes sparked and the Adam's Apple pounded upward, "You must be the. . . " he refrained from using the nickname.

Rabb completed the sentence, "The Rabbi."

"Well," Arty shot up out of his seat, "it's an honor to make your acquaintance. I followed your career back to the cult infiltration in the 70's."

Cults, thought Tom? He had never heard of Rabb dealing with cults?

"Counter terrorism now," Rab smiled, "too much religion in any man's life isn't good."

Giardino rolled his tongue over a molar, "We don't have time for small talk. Six hours ago The Union 57 Refinery in Elizabeth New Jersey was taken over by an Islamic group called The Crimson Fist. In a ransom note they've specified a money exchange tonight in New York City which is where we're headed."

"Doesn't sound like The Crimson Fist's style," added Rabb.

Giardino did not appreciate the interruption, "And why would your opinion differ from our experts?"

The black man deferred to Tom. Grant shifted in his seat, wondering why the hell he was here as his lips moved, "The Crimson fist were the alleged backers of The World Trade Center bombing. They're more than your average Muslim extremists--they believe that in hands on attacks—in seeing the frightened eyes of their victims, they are somehow strengthening their claim for Jihad. They believe they are the only true defenders of the faith."

Arabs, wondered Tom? Candice had spoken of blond haired white men. . .a far cry from middle-easterners. She did say that the gunmen had spoken a foreign language. Somehow this whole thing didn't make sense to him-

"I'll share something we at NSC have known for awhile," added Giardino--

He spoke of NSC as if it were its own country. As Tom knew, CIA, FBI, Defense, could all work against one another based on the current, political forces at work. Because of the ulterior motives of these bureaucratic groups, Dwight D. Eisenhower formed an intelligence gathering network in 1948 dedicated to the soul interests of the Executive and Chief. This organization evolved into The National Security Council which orchestrated its own covert operations, independent of Congress during certain administrations-an issue that got President Reagan into some trouble with the NSC's "Arms for Hostages".

"The Crimson Fist's self-appointed leader, Said Gewarn," continued the Secretary of State, "has been in England for the past twelve months. M15 tracked them to an apartment in central London. Through interrogation, we thought we had The Union 57 link in the US. Agent Osbourne," he nodded to the pock marked man who stood in the corner, "had FBI pursue this link to no avail.

"You didn't him?" the Rabbi was gruff with the man. It was the first time, realized Tom, that Rabb acknowledged his presence.

"The subject fled," responded Osbourne--his voice tense and high pitched, "and was shot."

"The link wasn't there," added Giardino, "he was Said's cousin—pumped gas at a Union 57 station."

General Crandal tried unsuccessfully to hide a chuckle, "Right on Dick! Hoped you at least gassed up."

Tom couldn't restrain himself any longer, "Sir. All the employees are dead the terrorists are clearly not Arab," he felt Rabb kicking him under the table, but pressed on, "the information is confirmed by an eyewitness."

"Yes!" Osbourne smirked, "tell me Mr. Grant, why the hell would terrorists murder their own hostages? The worst they can do is blow up some oil tanks, light some black smoke into the sky. So why, pray tell, should we believe that they'd murder the hostages!"

"How can you claim to have prescience into their thoughts," Rabb drew the force of the storm back on himself, "you don't even know who they are or how they took over that plant!"

"We don't know as of yet," Osbourne strained force on the final word and then grinned, "or maybe we should let Grant call up Mrs. Cooperman. She seems to know everything else! " he chuckled incredulously, "most curious how a woman claiming she is a--well what do we call her--a lucky visitor, should witness every key sequence going on there and contact an agent of yours— don't you agree?"

"What're you insinuating?" Tom shook with anger--sweat trickled down his chest, "my number was on Agent Pauzpolis's speed dial!"

"Oh yes, Union 57 told us that too. What was the connection—this Lou person was reffing an intramural football game for you?" Osbourne had the annoying habit of smiling at his own self-proclaimed ingenuity, "hardly merits being put on speed-dial, eh?"

"Great!" Tom threw up his hands, "you going to bate me into confessing that I'm a Muslim fanatic too?"

"No," interrupted Rabb, breaking the tension between the two men, "because the Secretary of State obviously requires a task of both us. You didn't invite us here to discuss this operation with you and your advisors."

"You're quick, Mr. Rabbi. I like that," the Razorback tossed a second piece of paper down the table. It fluttered in midair, then slid along the polished wood, stopping between them, "That was received less than an hour ago."

Tom read it:

ELIZABETH NJ, 10:45 PM. WILL SEND THE DROP POINT 5 MINUTES BEFORE. TWO BRIEF-CASES WITH 3.4 MILLION DOLLARS IN CASH. SEND NEBACHDUNEEZER THE RABBI AND ONE OTHER COURIER. ONE BREEF CASE PER MAN--FALURE TO FOLLOW INSTRUCTIONS, 87 HOSTAGES DIE

"Notice anything special about the note?" inquired The Secretary.

"Spelling's pretty bad," Rabb glanced up at the Razorback, " so Mr. Grant and I are decoys--we transport the packages while you attack the plant?"

"Yep." smiled Giardino.

"We won't have 3.4 million dollars. . .will we?"

"That money's hard to come by these days. And with what? Six hours' notice. But I find it more than a troubling coincidence you were requested as the go-between and your associate of many years, Mr. Grant, is the only one who was contacted by this person inside the plant."

"And if we disagree?" asked Rabb.

"We'll arrest Mr. Grant," jabbed Osbourne, "for disclosing information to Union 57 and jeopardizing the lives of all of those hostages."

"Leave him out of this, Dick!" lashed Rabb.

"Nebuchadnezzar," he spun around, "I've had enough of your shit!"

"Gentleman. . . gentleman, " the Razorback silenced them like Nero at the gladiatorial games, "we're a team here. Now we just received the drop point only 10 minutes ago—so let us prepare."

The airplane began to dip forward, initiating its descent into New York City. Tom felt a chill run up his spine. Now he was human fodder for a senseless diversion. There were no Arabs—he was sure of it! To felt nauseous when he realized that up to now, he had only hurt Candice Cooperman's chance of survival. He get to the bottom of this—to find out who these terrorists were—why they were using a fake Arab cover. Only then could he begin to help here.

Thirteen

10:38 PM (EST)
Elizabeth, NJ

He'd left her.

The apartment was ransacked. Clothes strewn about. . . the windows open. Icy air billowed into the room, lifting the curtains high towards the ceiling.

Huddled in the center of the room, papers spun around her in a maelstrom of autumn wind. Shivering, she examined the note through tear stained eyes, reading it over and over until the letters blurred into strange hieroglyphics. But the real reasons weren't in the words of that note.

He left her because she wouldn't eat veal and fish, because she hated golf and Bermuda and his flossing in bed and those damn boring Doctor parties with idle small talk. Clutching the note in clenched fists, she squeezed so hard she could feel the fibers of the paper tearing into flesh. He left her because he didn't want to have children. Because he didn't want to have her children-

"Aiiighhhh!" someone screamed from the darkness.

"Uh!" Candice Cooperman awoke.

A single light burned sulfuric yellow above her. Gripping the cellular phone so tightly that the buttons pressed into her soft palm, her eyes adjusted to the dim light of the room. It was just a dream, she gingerly reassured herself. Then she remembered the situation she was in. The last thing she remembered was being trapped on the roof, paralyzed with fear, shutting her eyes as the terrorist approached-- the bitter expectation of a bullet in her head.

She heard a noise!

The surface beneath her was a metal grating and beneath that she could see the empty stairwell crisscrossing below. Above her head stood a door painted in blazing fluorescent letters: "ROOFTOP EXIT, CANNOT REENTER".

She leaned on her side. The elbows of her business suit were worn thin. . . as if she had been dragged from the roof into this stairwell? Curling her freezing toes in the half darkness, she realized she was missing both shoes.

Candice was still cold, but not as cold as she had been on the roof. Heat rose from the lower deck of the stairwell, warming her aching body.

Questions. . . many questions. How had she gotten here? Were they keeping her prisoner? Were they going to interrogate her or just add her corpse to the pile of bodies stacked outside the front entranceway?

Tom!

She had to contact Tom! Pressing the power button of the phone, the green screen lit up only to die the moment she hit FBI#2. She remembered the phone, her only life-line to the outside world, was dead.

A momentary wave of exhaustion rushed over her. It was as if she had passed from one world into another. Here in the dark confines of this stairwell there were no gun men, no gunfire, no roaring winter wind— she was safe here. Then she saw the two eyes peering at her from the darkness-

All the air was sucked out of her lungs.

She tried to speak, but couldn't summons the strength. The cellular phone fell to the floor. Instinctively she pushed herself along the grating, scraping the back of her legs, pressing against the cold, cement wall behind her. She thought she might pass out again.

The eyes didn't flicker, blink, or move. Like a cartoon, she could barely make out the two white ovals staring at her-- the mist of the stranger's breath rising into the dark stairwell.

"L-l-l-leave me alone," her hands shook, "just go away."

The eyes turned away. Stepping out of the darkness of the corner, the stranger avoided her gaze. She caught sight of him for a moment. . . a head of frizzy, red hair streaming by and the flash of his face-fat , red cheeks-- a pair of black glasses taped on the end to hold them up. He didn't look like a gunman, more like a shy child. He dashed down the stairs, a blur of a plaid shirt and scruffy jeans—a head ambling comically about as he moved. She studied him from the landing. He was wearing a gray, plaid shirt and blue jeans.

"Wait," she found herself speaking in astonishment, "y-y-you can't leave."

He stopped on the lower landing. Was he angry? Going to fetch his gun? Was this stranger following her commands? What the hell was going on?.

"A-a-a-are you the one who dragged me off the roof?" she asked.

He stood silent.

"What's your name?"

"Gummy."

At least he was speaking. . .it was almost as if he were in shock. That must be it, she thought, he had to be another survivor like herself, a victim who'd lost his mind in the face of what he'd seen this afternoon, fleeing to stairwell.

"My-m-my my mother used to make this Gummy ," he burst into a spasm of energy and words, "like the hard toffee, but they looked like gummy bears and ya could lick a gummy bear's ass and it stuck to your tongue."

"What?" she beckoned, "come back up the stairs."

The way he looked at her, the sudden twitches and gestures, he was more of a wild, untamed child than a man. She realized that the right side of his face was paralyzed, hanging in an odd way like dead flesh. His eyes were red and irritated, chafed marks flowing down his cheeks which hinted of past tears.

He noticed her studying his eyes and pointed to her own tear filled ones, "See, yours do too," he grinned. It was the first time he'd addressed her.

The shock of the day, the shock of everything brought tears to her eyes. She was at a loss for words. Who was this person? If he were a victim, what was a crazed looking man like him doing in the Union 57 oil refinery?

The stranger bit the lower part of his lip, rolling it around between his teeth, slurring his speech as he continued, "My babies need to play. Babies. . . like Gummy 'cept their bums don't crack when you lick 'em. What's your name?" he suddenly changed subjects.

"Candice," she stammered.

"Candice," he paused for a moment, "that's a pretty name. Like Gummy Bear, Gummy Bear," he smiled. That must be his name.

"Why are you here?"

"I came to play with my babies," he stated in a matter of fact tone, sticking his finger in his ear, "you're an angel, huh? Back in Orange, Momma brought me to Griffith's Pharmacy to pick up the card—Werther's, Juicy. I kept the card. Uh-huh, Gummy Bear don't forget 'bout you."

From his pocket, he produced a dog-eared greeting card—an angel rendition of a blond women with towering white wings and a halo rising over the embossed text of a birth announcement for Tara Cheryl Runyon, born in Orange, Texas on March 5--she couldn't quite make out the year.

"Who is Tara?"

He giggled and she wasn't sure if he were answering her or not, "Gummy was so good. Pa liked to drink all day--Old Granddad Whiskey--b-b-breakfast of champions--and he didn't want ta' be disturbed otherwise you know how he'd beat Tara up. Momma said he killed her 'cause that night she wouldn't quit cryin' 'cept you and me's know the real truth," he winked, leaning forward whispering, "you took Tara to heaven," then he screwed his face up, "where are your wings?"

He thought she was the angel from the card. What, was he retarded? "Who brought you here?" she asked.

"Nehemiah, so I could play with my babies. They love Gummy Bear--OlefinsNapthas," he broke into a long train of words without pause or punctuation, "LongResid'sParaffin'sAlkaylate'sAluminumChloride. No Gummy for them, makestheirteethrot," he finished with another toothless smile.

Then a thought began to dawn on her, "You see these things, Gummy?"

He pointed above his head, "I see Paraffin. Paraffin likes angels."

"Describe paraffin to me."

"The little carbon and his four hydrogen bullies. He can never escape em. The big meanie hydrogens, surrounding him, tossing their bonds at his head. I feel sorry. Paraffins like me," he opened his palms, "Olefins cute like a caterpillar with carbons, four of em for a spine and his double bonded booty. Paraffin doesn't like him. He says Olefins usually crude," he whispered, "the hydrogens always hanging off his backside like he can't find toilet paper. That's why he likes to face me carbon first. I got a picture of him, wanna see?"

She nodded. He reached in his pocket, producing a dog-eared page from a chemistry book. In the illustration was the chemical diagram of Olefins just as Gummy Bear described: a series of four carbon molecules with a double bonds on the end followed by a series of hydrogen molecules.

Gummy Bear was actually visualizing chemicals floating around him, thought Candice, describing their chemical construction as if they were as real to him as she was. For Gummy, the dark stairwell was filled with imaginary chemical cartoon friends, Angels, all the foundations of his own private imaginary world, she thought. They surrounded him, entertained him in his private reality.

"Do you see the other chemicals?" she asked.

"No."

"Why?"

"They're not here now."

"Why are you here, Gummy Bear?" she pressed the point.

And with a child's frankness, he answered her. In a single instance, the world stopped for Candice Cooperman. It was as if the energy drained out of her body. She felt sick to her stomach as if she might vomit. Suddenly she understood the sinister secret and was unable to do anything about it. Her cellphone battery was dead and she couldn't reach Tom!

11:00 PM (EST)
New York, NY

Tom took a deep breath. . . and coughed.

He was overwhelmed by the wall of cigar smoke and idle chatter. In comparison to the rest of his day, this moment seemed surreal. Standing at the long curving zinc table in the cigar bar, his knees felt wobbly. He felt his heart race. He noticed three or four women, blondes in tight leather jackets with face lifts. . . possibly mid-fifties on the other side of the bar. A little man with a shaven head, garbed in a black suit smiled back at him. Any one of them could be a terrorist.

"You OK?" asked Rabb-- his back to the wall the tall black man had an excellent view of the bar.

"I'm alive," answered Tom--eyes scanning the room.

A bartender approached the two nervous men, "Made up your mind yet--drink or cigar?"

"No," answered Rabb. The Bartender left. Rabb's eyes never left the crowd of faces around them.

Then he saw it. Tom addressed the tiny microphone attached to his collar, speaking to General Crandal in the control van and the handful of Delta Force troops in the bar, "I see him."

11:14 PM (EST)
New York, NY

"What!" cried Crandal, "boys, talk to me!"

Remy hated the cramped bunkers of the minivan. Through the tiny television camera implanted in the edge of one of his soldier's glasses, the General could see Rabb and Grant standing at the bar, eyes drawn off camera.

"What does he see?" cried Crandal, "turn your head and let me see damn it!" he barked at the soldier with the video camera attached to the rim of his glasses. For moment, Remy could see the top of someone's head bobbing through the crowd, working his way towards the two men.

"No one fires unless he threatens!" cried the General. He glanced at his wristwatch. His strike force was already positioned in the freezing cold tunnels under the Union 57 refinery—the attack was almost ready to begin! He turned to the other officer inside the minivan, the one in charge of contacting Colonel Sharpe at the Elizabeth New Jersey headquarters, "tell them to prepare for the attack on my mark."

"Yes sir."

"Now somebody talk to me!" he barked at the agent with the camera attached to his eyeglasses, "turn the fuck around so I can see this character!   He   could hear Rabb whispering through his head set, "He's coming closer-

"I   think   he's   reaching,"   another   soldier interrupted, "yes--he's definitely reaching for something in his pocket. It's a gun! I SEE A GUN!"

11:15 PM (EST)
New York, NY

Tom saw the pistol.

The figure was six feet away--a woman blocked his view. Clumsily he reached for his weapon and felt Rabb's firm hand push him away.

11:16 PM (EST)
New York, NY

Remy could see the figure on his monitor, tall and thick-chested. He also saw Rabb drawing his own gun, rushing forward--

"Take your shot!" cried Crandal.

"No!" Rabb froze, shouting over the sounds of the bar.

"Whad'ya mean, no!" Crandal whined.

11:16 PM (EST)
New York, NY/ Macanudo Club

Tom glanced up.

"Do not take the shot!" Rabb cried over the noise of the bar, "do not take that shot! STAND DOWN!"

He saw the stranger swing the gun underneath a woman's cigarette, lighting it. It was a fucking lighter! Tom shook feeling spent and empty. He noted the nameless soldiers turning around, returning into the sea of people to their initial positions. Only then did he feel the gun poking at his lower back.

Rabb? No. Rabb was standing in front of him. The soldiers across the way were returning to position, their heads turned.

"Take six steps back into the bathroom along with your partner," the voice grunted into his ear.

"Uh--" drop to the floor. That's what Rabb had told him, but Tom froze. Why the fuck weren't they watching him! He tugged at Rabb's shoulder. His mentor instantly understood what was going on. Calm and controlled, Rabb followed him as he walked backwards, the weapon poking into his back.

The voice was like a slow, soft whisper in his ear, "Walk right into the bathroom. Make one move and you're dead."

Fourteen

I am alone.

The flash of a single moment--the sounds of the bar, the chatter, laughter of nervous friends, the mauve and ivory toned lights, the clink of liquor bottles vanished away from Tom Grant. All he could think about was Candice. The white tiled room glowed from the harsh fluorescent lights overhead. The Rabbi stood in front of him, arms in the air.

"Don't turn around," the voice behind barked, "take the weapons out of your pockets," the gunman's lips were barely an inch from Tom's ear—a hint of mint on his breath and traces of scented soap on his wrists. His palms were sweaty--arms stretched tight around Tom's neck, the cold muzzle of the gun pressed to his temple.

"You collect em both and give them to me."

Tom and Rabb pulled their guns out of their pocket. With a bent wrist, the Rabbi collected Tom's weapon, lifting them both by the stock as he set them on the tiled floor. The pistols made a clinking noise as they slid back to the gunman.

"And don't think I didn't see the Federal agents at the bar," continued the terrorist as he knelt down, collecting one gun, pushing the other into the corner, "the bulges from their shoulder holsters were pure giveaways."

"Your suitcases with the money's in the bar," replied Rabb.

"What?" there was confusion in the terrorist's voice. Rabb didn't react, keeping a cold poker face.

Then Tom was thrown forward, slamming into Rabb--the movement like a final jostling, awakening him from his dreamy shock. He glanced back at the face. The terrorist was older than he guessed--early forties, he wore an expensive dress shirt, sleeves rolled up, with a plaid tie, draped lightly around an open collar. His bluish gray eyes burned with intensity--the jutting, aristocratic chin poking as he aimed Rabb's pistol at them both.

The Rabbi sighed in a gingerly voice, "I'm truly sorry to meet you under such difficult circumstances, Mr. Bronk."

Bronk?

How did Tom know that name? Bronk--the President of Union 57--the one which the security team had to inform before calling him back. That was the Union 57 operator's parting words to him earlier that day before the imposed silence. What was the chief executive of Union 57 doing with a gun in his hand?

"You recognize me?" the executive was shocked.

"Not at first," Rabb turned, facing him for the first time, "but logic dictated such. You would be the only one who knew about the crisis. The only one who cared enough to try and stop something like this. The question is why?"

"Very good," Bronk allowed the pistol fall to his side, " Mr.?"

"Rabb."

Tom sensed a perverse camaraderie between the two men, but couldn't fathom why. In this moment of confusion, anger welled within him. This guy was the sonofabitch that had a gun at his back only a moment before!

"Did you ever have a pistol?" inquired Rabb, his brow raised in curiosity.

"Not until you and the boy gave these to me," his jutting chin vibrated, "used the flat of my knuckles --saw it in a James Bond film once. . . I think."

Jesus Christ, thought Tom--knuckles!

"Inventive," complimented Rabb, "you're a very resourceful man. You must hold your work dearer than your life, willing to do all of this to save a measly refinery in your vast empire."

"No," he replied, "the Elizabeth facility was slated for shut down by the end of next year," beads of sweat trickled down his brow.

Anger welled. Tom rushed Bronk-- an impulsive act, his legs leaping forward, arms stretched out in front of him.

"No Tom!" cried Rabb.

Without a word, Bronk swung the pistol at his head. All the energy left him. Grant stood silent, deflated, staring down the barrel of the weapon. Bronk bit his lip, a tense, shaking finger wrapped tightly around the trigger.

"Stand down, Bozo," threatened the executive, "that was stupid," continued the billionaire, "you two aren't the leaders. But I have contacts in the government. You were with the General. And you ignored my warnings."

"Do go on," added Rabb with a distant look as if this man did not have a gun at Tom's head, as if they weren't in the throes of a violent encounter.

"The Agent who made the call to us. The one who had spoken to the female eye witness is telling the truth," he's talking about me, thought Tom, "the terrorists did kill all the hostages. But that's not the worst part of it-"

The fluorescent lights overhead died—then the bright flash of an explosion! The smell of gunpowder! The window over the toilets exploded, scattering glass across the room as the lights died and-

---

11:23 PM (EST)
Elizabeth, NJ / 20 ft. Under the Union 57 refinery in the drainage pipes

Major Peter Schubert was wet.

Standing in knee-high, freezing water for over an hour, he wished he hadn't discarded his diver's dry suit at the docks. Now he was clad in waste high, polyester, wading boots with an all-black ensemble: hip holster with a Heckler and Koch 9mm grip cock pistol, a heavy polar fleece sweater shirt, Teflon bullet proof vest, black ski cap, and black matte face paint spread over his face.

"Major, we're ready," a voice whispered in the darkness.

On his head, Major Schubert sported a starlight scope which required a meager amount of outside light for night vision. The goggles cast a green haze across their visual images so that as the Major studied the seven other members of his strike force, they appeared to be covered in a phosphorescent fungi much like the type he had seen while spelunking in Waitomo, New Zealand.

"All the charges in place?" he asked in a whispered voice.

"Complete."

His group in knee high water in the drainage pipe eight feet in diameter, staring up the ladder at a manhole cover leading to the surface of the Union 57 plant.

Major Schubert, Peter to his friends, could barely feel his icy feet. Still he stood perfectly still. Any movement might alert the targets to their presence. It had been much easier when he darted about the drainage tunnels, sawing through iron grill guards, setting the C4 explosives underneath the designated points of the refinery.

Following orders, they had set explosives under the crude heavy distillates, the coking unit, and underneath each of the three main compounds where hostages were being held. The C4, a soft, malleable, putty, explosive, were wired with 2 inch long detonators hooked to multi-cell batteries.

The detonators were linked via a remote signal to Schubert's modified wristwatch. The chronometer looked like a pilot's watch with an inner face that acted as a detonator. By adjusting the second hand to midnight he could detonate the explosives. By setting the watch between one and six he could selectively detonate various explosives—a real pyrotechnic show to arm them with the element of surprise.

"Any word on Polcheck?" whispered Thompkins.

"No," Schubert gritted his chattering teeth and cleared his thoughts of Polcheck. There was no time for such thoughts.

Positioned in a mess hall in Camp Mackall inside Fort Bragg hung a banner declaring the credo of the Army Ranger: SURVIVAL: **S**ize up the situation, **U**ndue haste makes waste, **R**emember where you are, **V**anquish fear and panic, **I**mprovise, **V**alue living, **A**ct like natives, **L**earn basic skills. This was the guiding credo for the Army Rangers otherwise known as The Green Berets or as this elite, special unit was called: The Delta Force.

To reach Delta Force status, these men travailed an arduous agenda of preparation. The Army Rangers had one of the shortest training courses in the special forces, only fifty eight days, but it was living hell. In that time, they were beaten, insulted, abused, overworked, and pressured to the limits of human tolerance. Each man was proficient in parachuting, bridge building, sabotage, trapping, helicopter rescue, and hand to hand combat. Later stages of training for the even more exclusive Delta Force, referred to as Phase II, included proving an IQ of 110, the ability to march 30 miles in 12 hours with a fifty pound backpack, running forty yards in twenty four seconds, and special advanced anti-terrorist training at the Mott Lake Compound. The course culminated in a tortuous air drop into The Uwharrie National Forest where each man had traveled forty kilometers over ungodly terrain while hunted by dogs and a blood-thirsty team from the 82nd Airborne division.

From this advanced agenda of training, Delta Force was refined into the preeminent hostage rescue team. Their Delta Force branch had been deployed in the Achille Lauro incident as well as numerous other hostage crisis. Delta Force was created to deal with last minute contingencies, rushed operations, the stressful, last minute surprises-- in other words, when your ass was on the line, you wanted them storming in to save it.

Major Peter Schubert's Team was a C-2 classification: the second ranking in the hierarchy of team rating--he never knew of a team that received C-1 ranking. Therefore, his group was preeminent in the world. The seven man A team, as it was termed by Delta Force, was cross trained in duties and consisted of a senior noncommissioned officer--himself, a master sergeant, an assistant, a light weapons expect, an engineer for sabotage, a medical expert, and a radio operator, using UHF, VHF and Morse code at eighteen words a minute.

Polcheck had been the communications officer.

Attempting to stay warm and perfectly still at the same time in the drainage pipe, it was hard not to think of his fallen team-mate. The mission never planned for them to have to spend an extended amount of time underground, wading in the freezing cold water. Schubert craved action, not this quiet waiting.

And he couldn't stop thinking of Polcheck.

It was the landing that did it. Under the time constraints they opted for the Gemini "Sub skimmer": a rubber dinghies propelled by a silent, outboard motor. Setting off from The Goethals Toll Bridge between Richmond Island and New Jersey, they reached Newark Bay in fifteen minutes. On their way in, they passed the series of US Navy SEAL attack ships moored at Kill Van

Kull: a support team of fifty soldiers waiting for Schubert's team to launch the attack. He was not only to attempt hostage rescue, but create distractions, blowing up the pier. This would allow the backup teams to make the hazardous landing without the gunmen standing atop the metal docks, holding the high ground. If not, the backup team would take serious casualties in such a compromised amphibious landing.

Once their Sub skimmer reached the set location, his team put on diving gear, deflated the rubber craft, allowing it to sink to the bottom of the bay for future retrieval. The team used dry diver's suits constructed for cold water applications with a LAR 4 SCUBA system, a special closed circuit breathing apparatus recycling the used air, scrubbing it of the carbon monoxide and tell-tale trail of CO2 bubbles which floated to the surface.

Everything went as planned. They treaded through the water at the far northern perimeter point where the olefin plant was located, carefully meandering through the darkness, setting explosives along the massive pylons of the pier. In order to reach the deeper inland position where the majority of hostages were thought to be detained, they wound their way under the pier, entering a drainage tunnel in the southern sector.

Then the surf kicked in. It was difficult enough to cut a path under the docks to the drainage tube and saw the metal grating protecting the mouth of the drainage line --all without attracting the attention of patrol guards overhead.

Treading water twenty feet below the elevated pier, Schubert broke the surface in order to set his bearings. The surf was choppy--he had to fight not to fly into the pylons of the pier. After ten seconds, he triangulated his position from the maps he had memorized during the plane flight briefing. Overhead he could see the guard, smoking a cigarette, walking perimeter along the grated pier floor.

Then a series of waves came crashing into the dock area. Schubert spun around, trying to drop below the surface, but was thrown into the steel pylon. . . cutting a gash across his forehead, disorienting him for a moment. Cringing, he watched as his men were sent scattering like flowers on a raging river, falling out of fixed formation, slamming into the pier supports.

He thought they would surely be spotted at that point, but the guard never looked down. They quickly snapped the grating at the pipeline cover and entered. It wasn't until they were well into the drainage pipe that they realized Polcheck was missing. They were already fifteen minutes behind schedule--Schubert chose to continue.

That didn't mean that he didn't care about his fallen comrade. The vision burned within him. . . a gunman finding the wounded or injured Polcheck, calling a full alert. In the interrogation, with enough torture, Polcheck would divulge everything. . . no one could hold out under torture. By then, rationalized the Major, they would have already overtaken the plant. Major Peter Schubert was a Delta Force soldier and tried never second guessed himself. Bright, alert, arrogant, he understood that they were here because they were the best. Only they could free the 148 innocent lives possibly at stake.

"Listen up," he whispered, "nobody makes a move until the Cowboy blows the whistle," the Cowboy was their nickname for General RM Crandal. No one disobeyed the Cowboy. The chain of command was set in stone: Schubert took his orders from his field leader. The field leader took his orders from Colonel Sharpe. Colonel Sharpe took his orders from General R.M. Crandall. And

General Crandall? Shit, he took his orders straight from the God almighty.

The Major glanced down at his chronometer. They were late--very late. But luck was with them. The call for the attack hadn't yet come. Now he was in position and ready to kill.

"Ready with the optical," whispered Thompkins.

Thompkins threaded the thin maneuverable wire through the grids of the manhole cover. The long, black snake of a device fed back to a tiny LCD computer screen which was handed to Schubert. The other men shut their eyes, the light would disorient their adjusted night vision. A flicker of light and Schubert could see the grounds of the refinery above them.

"How's it look, sir?" asked Rice.

Schubert ran the fiber optic on a 360 degree scan. . . all the same," This is too easy," he smiled, white teeth contrasting with the black face paint, "dumb bastards cut the electricity to the plant. There're no lights out there!"

11:24 PM (EST)
New York City, NY

"UP AGAINST THE WALL!" a voice cried in the darkness.

Tom saw flashlight beams scattering along tiles. Wood and paint chips were everywhere. Three of the plane clothed soldiers, brandishing guns knocked the pistol out of Benjamin's hand, slamming the billionaire against the wall, sweat and blood flying across the room. They spun him around, three flashlights beaming into Bronk's eyes.

Rabb rushed close to Benjamin, "A terrorist would never want to take an oil refinery. And why would they kill the hostages?"

"Get these handcuffs off me and I'll tell you!" his blue eyes beamed.

"Unlock the cuffs," ordered Rabb.

"But sir--" the soldier persisted.

"Take them off!" thundered Rabb.

His mentor was an intellect that hungered for entertainment, thought Tom in a moment of clarity. His mentor was overwhelmed not because of the 148 hostages or even being held at gun point, but because he was stumped--there was finally a puzzle which he could not solve and it was driving him crazy.

"What the fuck's goin' on!" cried Crandal.

Rabb turned around, greeting his old friend. Crandal stood, arms akimbo, in the doorway of the bathroom, the door laying on its side now. Behind him the crowd from the bar stared down the hallway at the scene.

"Why in fuck's name is this suspect uncuffed!" ranted Crandal. Tom could

"Shut up," screamed the Rabbi, "and listen for once—you old dog."

"I'm Benjamin Bronk," the executive introduced himself in a cold, business-like manner, "the CEO of Union 57-"

"There must be an echo in here, cause I hear ya talkin!" screamed the General, "and I know you don't want me to put a bullet in your head!"

"Let him speak, Remy, we don't have much time!" barked Rabb, "this is my fucking ass on the line! We have a strike team in a holding pattern that could cost them their lives. Now let the man speak!"

"A strike team!" Bronk's face turned ghostly white.

"Fine Rabies, one minute," cried the General, glancing down at his wristwatch, "be quick, Mr. Bronk" barked Remy, "I've troops to in the that are growing cold and impatient!"

The executive stared into space gathering his thoughts and then, "well first of all, I bet a million dollars that they've turned off the electricity to that plant. With that they've created the greatest threat ever to face U.S. national security. You don't realize it because--"

Fifteen

11:30 PM (EST)
New York City, NY

"You don't know how a refinery works," Benjamin Bronk continued.

"Ugh, Chemistry 101," moaned Remy.

"I'm not going to be technical--not enough time. A refinery is really simple," Bronk straightened his plaid tie, "take a cake for instance," this example grossly out of place to Tom, "you take the flower, the sugar, the butter--"

"Get to the point, Julia Child!" barked Crandal.

"Give him his five minutes of perfunctory bullshit," blasted Rabb,

"You're pushin' my buttons, Rabies!"

"For a cake, Mr. Rabb," Bronk refocused his attention on the black man, "the individual ingredients are in and of themselves useless. But you can mix them together to make a cake. In order to facilitate the growth of the cake you use a catalyst, something that facilitates a reaction. In the cake, we use yeast and heat. The two elements together create a reaction with the ingredients, causing the cake to rise in the oven. It's a reaction that must be carefully observed. Jump around in the kitchen and you cause the cake to collapse. The catalytic reaction is almost always unstable."

The bathroom was suddenly transformed into a lecture hall. Despite the fact that he didn't like him, Tom had to admit that the executive had a natural way of controlling of a room: commanding the attention of his own captors.

"I buy my oil from different areas," Bronk ignored the comment, "we use catalysts to isolate and change useless parts of the oil. As an example, part of the sludge becomes petroleum jelly. The catalysts are a range of volatile chemicals pressure sensitive, temperature sensitive, often hydrophobic—meaning they react harshly with water. We expend a great deal of care keeping the catalysts in their suitable environments."

"So you use highly explosive stuff to get to the good shit?" added Remy.

"Yes," Bronk added, "have any of you heard of The Bhopal Disaster?"

"In India?" Rabb answered.

"December 2nd, 1984," Bronk sighed, "a small half acre large plant owned by a subsidiary of the Union Carbide Crop.--no relation to Union 57--was producing agricultural fertilizers. Workmen washed out pipelines in an area storing a catalysts called MIC-Methyl Isocyanate. Remember the Tylenol cyanide scare? MIC is a cyanide family member-lethal to humans. Nobody really knows exactly what happened that day. Water probably made it into the pipes through a valve accidentally left open and then into the tanks storing the MIC.

The MIC spontaneously reacted, combining with the water, triggering a runaway reaction producing dimethyl urea, releasing CO2 and heat! The MIC polymerized and—no need to be so detailed," he corrected himself, "it created a toxic cloud of vaporous cyanide. Shortly after midnight, people living in the squatter village in Jayaprakash Nagar woke up feeling asphyxiated. Soon there were thousands of people on the street, running about, lost in a strange, hazy fog, gasping for breath, an awful stinging sensation in their eyes. Within sixty seconds, people started to collapse and gag. The wind was blowing hard all over Bhopal that night. No matter where the survivors ran, they were enveloped in this cloud extending over 40 kilometers.

Symptoms of exposure were numerous: respiratory alkalosis, chest pain, bronchoalveolar lavage, but the most common cause of death was total paralysis of the brain's respiratory center--a complete shutdown of breathing controls. People were conscious and awake, unable to remember how to breath, laying their suffocating like fish out of water."

"Wait a minute," interrupted Crandal, "you sayin' this fertilizer plant killed all those people?"

"Don't you ever reads the newspaper?" cracked Rabb.

"Figures show that the half acre plant," continued Bronk, "ended up killing anywhere from conservative estimates of 5,000 to 20,000 people with at least 200,000 injured."

"Are you trying to draw a relationship between Bhopal and Union 57?" Crandal jumped to his point again, "I may be a poor Texas boy, but I can tell ya' we ain't in India."

"Texas, huh?" Bronk's eyes lit up, " heard of the Texas City explosion?"

"Sure, who hasn't? In '47, a freighter carrying something nasty-"

"1400 tons of ammonium nitrate exploded after a fire broke out on board and destroyed the entire ship. The secondary explosions from the ship were so strong, they rattled windows as far as 150 miles. Leaping flames set off the Monsanto Chemical factory producing a combustible ingredient of synthetic rubber called styrene. The fire crews weren't able to deal with the new chemical compound. That chemical fire blazed out of control-- setting off another freighter."

"A lot of people died," Remy sighed. The topic struck home.

"576 people died--2,000 injured," elaborated Bronk.

"I got no more time for guessin' games. Union 57's an oil refinery," replied Crandall, "not a freighter-"

"Didn't you look out the window as you landed in New York?"

"Oh no," Rabb crumpled as if struck with a hammer. He supported his weight against the tiled wall, "there are other plants."

"Not just other plants," Bronk added, "forty five miles of fertilizer plants, oil refineries, chemical plants, tank farms, multiprocessors, storage stations, loading piers, moored super freighters filled with their chemicals cargoes. New Jersey has the highest concentration of hazardous industries using high risk technologies than any state in the country. New Jersey has over 150 plants using synthetic organic manufacturing.

My plant will explode setting off another refinery ten yards and a fence-line away. That plant will blow, destroying a fertilizer plant, an olefin plant, and a tank farm with jet fuel. That will set off. . . exponential growth setting off a toxicological apocalypse of biblical proportions!"

Chills ran down Tom's spine.

"Whoa--whoa," interrupted Crandal, "how big an apocalypse?"

"A chain reaction whose explosive force would level everything between Sayerville to Yonkers, Irvington to Brooklyn. And that's just the beginning! As a historical reference point, the half-acre plant in Bhopal created a poison cloud which was 40 kilometers wide, wounding 200,000. One freighter in Texas City leveled the entire town. Now imagine blowing up every plant between New York and Philadelphia--fifty square miles of plants churning out poison clouds!"

Rabb whispered," we're meant to be the hostages."

Like a mad man, the executive blew fog onto one of the bathroom mirrors. Taking his finger he traced out a diagram of the northeastern seaboard from Maine to Washington DC, "It all depends on the wind directions, you see. Shine a light over here so you can look at what I'm going to-"

"Wind Direction?" Tom paused, "of course--just like Bhopal?"

"Yes!" Bronk drew a large circle in the center of the map, "blowing up that plant would take each plant out one after another in a runaway chain reaction, not only creating a devastating series of explosions, but beyond that, creating and combining chemicals in a runaway reaction. The fire would create a hot pocket--change weather patterns, giving birth to firestorms like the Dresden air bombings, spewing poison clouds all over the eastern seaboard.

Imagine substances being stored at their stabilized temperatures suddenly being infringed upon, exploding, combining in a chemical vortex! A storm of death. New chemicals would be produced, combining with other radical chemicals just as the ammonium nitrate in Texas City created Styrene! Many of the new substances and old ones would be hydrophobic--if it rains, if the air pressure or temperature is different inside the holding tank than in our atmosphere, there might be more explosions! We're talking chemical fires, noxious and deadly substances lethal upon human contact.

Many chemicals would be affected by temperature and become more volatile, churning the cloud into one raging catalyst, producing a chameleon of deadly substances, lethal poisons, horrific toxins. By the time you organize the right device to stop it, the chemical cloud has changed!

In areas too far away from the blast to be incinerated, sleeping families would smell the sweet scent of Phosgene, like freshly cut hay, just before they suffocate in their sleep or their breathing centers shut off as it did in Bhopal, or their cerebral cortex would dissolve, their lungs burn out, their skin fall off, their eyes bleed, the list is endless!"

Silence.

"What's your projected casualty count?" inquired Crandal.

"Just guestimations," Bronk continued as if reading off statistics, "Bhopal was two and a half acres large, we're talking about forty squared miles of plant structure. I'd say we're looking at a lethal cloud with an eighty mile diameter in the highest population concentrations in the country. Then you have the subsequent fires, unburied bodies, rampant disease, subsequent plagues between 20 and 27 million dead."

More silence.

"Holy shit," shuddered Crandal, "holy shit."

"We sent all the technical information to The White House this afternoon," raged Bronk, "and no one read it! You can't attack. We need time to figure out how to stop them."

"Wait a minute," cried Crandal , beads of sweat forming on his wrinkled brow, "don't you have safety devices in these plants, fail safes?"

"Yes. Automated halon systems and automatic fail-safes everywhere and all these security devices could be circumvented by simply-"

"Candice said they disconnected the electric power lines," interrupted Tom. Bronk nodded his head affirmatively.

"How do you think they infiltrate the plant?" asked the General.

"We have security cameras placed in every plant entrance, the tapes are automatically fed to our downtown headquarters. I told the White House I'd be more than happy to share those with them."

"Have you reviewed them yourself?"

"I have a team doing that now."

Rabb calmly raised a brow, turned to his old friend, "Remy, you might want to call off your attack team?"

"Shit!" screamed Crandal to a soldier, "get Schubert on the horn!"

Sixteen

Major Schubert broke through the manhole cover.

He felt the cold wind whip across his face. His men fanned out in spread formation. Thompkins crouched along the side wall of the engineering building. Rice followed him as they raced towards the front corner of the structure. Schubert spied two terrorists stranding guard around a burning barrel. Snow fell in quiet sheets, muffling the sounds of their conversation.

"Point One," Thompkins reported over the Major's headset, "the rear is clear."

"Going in," Schubert sprinted forward, Rice at his side.

The guards wore hooded parkas. . . their first big mistake. They never saw the two special forces operatives race towards them. The Major jerked back on the first man's neck, his knife slicing through the cartilage of the man's windpipe. In a quick motion he broke the man's neck and turned to see Rice killing the other one. Warm blood poured out of the bodies, melting the fresh snow.

"Get ready on those explosives," grunted Schubert as they continued to the front of the building.

Rice rushed alongside the closed door, his MP-5 machine gun drawn. Schubert looked to his right and caught site of something piled under the awning. . . bodies? Were those actually bodies? Had they already killed hostages! No time for thoughts. He drew his MP-5 opening the front door. He could see the empty hallway streaked brown with dried blood. The Major reached for his chronometer, pulling out the adjusting knob in order to blow the-

"Stand down!" General Crandal screamed so loud in his head-set that he winced. Rice also flinched, voice berating him too, "stand down!"

11:55 PM (EST)
Washington D.C.

Secretary of State Vincent Giardino stood in the shadows.

Across the expanse of the marble portico, Giardino studied the figure silhouetted in trundle spotlights, positioning himself on an Astro-turf pad, setting the golf ball on the rubber tee and taking a practice swing—the club sounding like a rapier cutting through air.

The short, stocky, Italian heard the bad news a few minutes ago and scurried to the rear porch of The White House before he could be summonsed. He was not used to such a crisis. Secretary of State Vincent Giardino was the member of a profession based on public opinion. In this art, the weight and powers of statistics were more real than people. He could rattle off figures like a sportscasters and R.B.I.'s-- because his sole function was to please the majority of his 248,000,0000 constituents--and they were a tough crowd to please: 116,000,000 of them registered voters, 29,000,000 over sixty, 56,000,000 living in non-metropolitan areas, 57,000,000 in cities—thirty one percent of them registered Republicans, thirty nine percent Democrats, and thirty percent unaffiliated.

Within this conglomeration of millions of opinions on every topic from health care to The First Lady's hair style, a small vessel was thrown into the boiling, melting pot called The White House. Vincent did not think in terms of only the President being thrown in-- his view as an insider invested in him the larger picture of cabinet staffs working together, disseminating mountains of information that no President could do alone.

Within this proving ground, the Chief Executive's office was expected to set the direction for such pressing issues as "the pursuit of liberty" and "the general welfare of it people"— ambiguous concepts authored two centuries before by men who ruled a country of less than 25,000,000 people and a fifth the size of the current nation. The founding fathers never had to deal with abortion, civil rights, nuclear defense, sex scandals, toxic waste. No, mused the Razorback, they lived in a world of plantations and little slave girls serving mint juleps—and they had the same faults of their modern day counterparts. Only the tinge of history created statesmen, mused the Razorback. Hell, every President, before he became a distinguished blurb in some history book, fumed and screamed when things didn't go his way. Harding beat his wife. Eisenhower drank. Nixon ranted and raved at portraits of Kennedy.

President Cormon hit golf balls.

Leaning over in proper stance, the President of The United States gripped his titanium shafted driver. Rocking his hips, he swung with graceful ease-- sending the ball spiraling across the grassy expanse and into the trees as he cried, "Fore!" warning someone of the oncoming ball.

Clang! The ball contacted with something metal. Vince heard a rustling-- leaves shook a hundred and fifty yards away and he knew what was happening.

How far they had slipped.

Giardino first met Marshal Cormon long before he was President when they shared a room at The University of Arkansas. The Razorback remembered being seduced by Marshall's charisma--almost couldn't help wanting to be around the man, mused the Razorback---women were especially vulnerable to this trait. It was a fruitful friendship from the start. Marshal gave Giardino what his small, brutish, frame and demeanor lacked: a smooth finish. Giardino gave Cormon the protection of an entire football team.

Cormon was not rich, but came from modest beginnings and was utterly convinced he would achieve everything he wanted in life. During Vince's junior year, Cormon decided to run for student-body President of U.A. Over a pitcher of beer, Marshall recruited his best friend as campaign manager:

"It'll be great," he smiled, "hang posters, talk big —you're great at that."

"What do I get out of it?" Vince asked.

"The Student Body Leader appoints many positions--and later when I'm President of the United States, you could be my Vice President—"

"I like Secretary of State--hah! That'll be a good laugh."

It was strange how prophecies fulfilled themselves and the friendships of yesterday were perverted with time. Vincent Giardino did not regret his decision to enter politics. He was the son of a measly longshoreman and now look at him-- the Italian Stallion-- the Power Broker! Never would he have imagined facing such a crisis. Jesus, he thought, if he could only go back in time and—

Clang!

Cormon had hit another ball—sending it flying far beyond the spot lights. This time the sound of golf ball against soft flesh, a rustling in the trees--a voice cry out, "Fuck!"

"Are there snipers in those trees?" asked the President offhandedly.

Cormon knew, mused the Razorback, that the Marine snipers hid amongst the branches, armed with high tech weaponry, camouflaged with jumpsuits pasted with leaves. Cormon knew he was striking them in their bullet proof vests and their protective helmets just as he knew that beyond these guards were roving Marine patrols, a twelve foot high electrified fence, guard shacks and more guards, and a network of Missile defenses protecting the White House from death from above as well as hundreds of other secret service agents and advance teams, choppers, and Air Force One, to guard him every moment he was away from The White House.

When he became angry, Cormon suffocated from this protection--it stymied his love life, made him feel claustrophobic. He resented Giardino who could go home at any time, escaping the dog and pony show of power. That was why Cormon commonly asked him to spend his weeknights in The White House. The President wanted a partner in his prison cell. Sometimes Giardino would go a whole week without seeing the Chief Executive. Then on a whim, Cormon might invite him up for a drink or a cigar on the balcony and they would sit, slowly sipping Port, laughing and reflecting on issues of the day or stories from their numerous campaigns.

Still, thought Giardino, it was like talking to yourself, like conversing with a ventriloquist doll, unable to see the ventriloquist at all. Other nights, Cormon might stare into space, a prisoner of that facade of smiles and cool cobalt eyes. More often than not, Marshal had a young intern with him--the flavor of the month--blondes, brunettes, red heads--actresses and semi-call girls, Cormon screwed indiscriminately. It was well understood that his marriage was a sham and he openly entertained as long as the guests stayed in the Presidential quarters and left discretely by limo at sun up. The First Lady considered anything else a slight against her and you did not slight the First Lady.

Cormon was impetuous, spoiled, and a horrible womanizer. But the moment the stage lights were set , the

TelePrompTer in place, Marshall Cormon redeemed himself--, the camera loved him. On a television screen, his dreamy stare was Presidential regalia--his soft voice, genteel confidence. He was spectacular, engaging--he was the President of the United States.

Giardino on the other hand had gone through a failed marriage, lived alone, and had very little to go home to. Morality never played itself in his own self-analysis. Giardino perceived of the world as a place to take what you wanted. It was not power that he focused on, but the fact that if a man was willing to fight, he could have whatever things he desired.

"We have a problem," the Razorback spoke, "you've read Bronk's brief?"

"One of my aides reviewed it," replied the President, setting another ball on the tee—anger seething out, " you committed to a premature plan of action!"

Vince wanted to scream that Cormon could walk downstairs and run his own damned operation! Marshall would have made the same mistakes if not more. What the fuck did he know except how to smile at the cameras. Cormon sighed, gripping his driver, "Vince, this was all you. You had Osbourne as a loyal foot-soldier, you were supposed to act. I trusted you to do this—to make up for the favor."

The favor—the ultimate leverage. Unknown to the general public, a Senate Judiciary Committee was all over Vince for cash withdrawals from a reelection fund years ago—money he used to pay off a call girl ready to spill the shit on Cormon. And now Vince was looking at jail time and public vilification! The whole thing was over Cormon's refusal of a tax refund bill. Cormon now promised he'd support it—save Vince—if the Razorback took over the crisis.

"Vince, you're The Secretary of State of The United States of America," Cormon exploded, "I'm not even thinking about the polls in November. Tonight Vince, we face a crisis that may go down in the history books and I will not go down in history as The President who was THE BUTCHEROR OF MILLIONS."

Marshall stopped, collecting his breath as he set another golf ball. A cold gust of wind swept across the portico. Giardino smelled pine in the air, heard the ruffling of leaves, "I want you to continue under E.O. 12333."

Giardino was taken aback. Executive Order-- E.O.--12333 was a broad charter set by President Reagan in 1983, allowing for enlarged freedoms for the intelligence community in times of crisis--allowed for warrantless searches and seizures, theft, wiretaps , the ability to force people outside the intelligence community to serve as spies--even against their own will. By formally enacting the executive order, Cormon granted himself an air of legitimacy to whatever actions might be taken-- something to serve him well in Senate investigative committees or Congressional witch-hunts depending on the outcome.

"Are you sure?" Giardino paused.

"Vince, do you know what happened on November 9th, 1965?"

I'm sure you're gonna tell me, the Razorback thought to himself.

"The electric power from the Niagara Falls power station was severed. 80,000 square miles of the northeastern seaboard was powerless. Almost a million people trapped in subways. Thousands of hospitals shut down, flights unable to land. The looting and confusion was enough to scare the hell out of everyone. And that was a fucking power outage! Do you have any idea what even the knowledge of this threat would do to New York City, to Philadelphia, to the Northeastern seaboard, let alone having it happen?

I'd have the fucking National Guard firing on civilian looters. How would that look on the cover of Time? If Rodney King decision pissed the blacks off so much, what do you think they'll have to say about Big Business peeling the skin off their fucking kids' faces? And don't think the dumb bastards won't see it that way! They love a good riot--gives em a chance to restock the shelves. Hell, Americans love a riot. They riot after sport team victories. They'll kill before this one even happens--pillage midtown Manhattan, riot up Westchester--set New Jersey on fire—destroy Philadelphia. Even if we win—if word gets out about this thing we'll never stop the anarchy."

"Understood," with more than a note of subservience.

"Tell me, Vince, have you named this operation of yours?"

"Delta Forced named it 'Snakebite'--was supposed to be a quick attack."

"Trojan Horse would be a more suitable. Hell, we built all those cities around the damn industrial plants and now the beasts have awakened."

Vince stepped away from the Chief Executive. The Razorback knew he wasn't in control--just another piece of insulation to shield Cormon. Jesus Christ, he shuddered--now Crandal was their only savior. What the hell was going on? If what Bronk said was true--God, Vince couldn't even imagine the repercussions!

In an uncharacteristic move, the Razorback was reminded of the only big book he had ever read: *War and Peace*. On the Presidential campaign trail, he forced himself to read the tome as if to make up for all the classics he never completed. He started it during the New Hampshire primary and finished it on Super Tuesday. Even when it was over, he really never understood the book--just a bunch of rich Russians worrying about soirees until they finally had to haul their asses out and fight Napoleon at Borodino—then they sort of lost that.

Suddenly, though, Vince was struck with a certain passage about Napoleon, the most powerful man on Earth in his time. Tolstoy said that the decisions the French Emperor made were made freely--from his choices in battle to his taste in wine--dictated by no script nor story--just his whims and desires. Yet Tolstoy postulated that later historians would write that each of Napoleon's decisions were the product of predestination and inevitable fate. The Razorback recited the particular passage to himself. . . the only one he ever bothered to memorize. It sounded good at the time, but he now understood it so much better:

> *The King's heart is in the hands of the Lord.*
> *A king is history's slave.*

This moment was history, reflected the Razorback. He was absolutely sure of it and totally terrified. He had never been so scared in his entire life. He could never have imagined the horror--he thought he might throw up right there on the marble porch. As he stumbled away from his superior, the most powerful man on Earth in his own time, Vince watched the President's shadow stretch across the marble portico. The shadow was distorted, the golf club seemed as if it were growing out of the back of his head. Then just before the Razorback walked through the door, he heard the President slap another ball forward. Again, the distinct sound of the golf ball striking metal. And the Leader of the free world's voice calling out a moment too late:

"Fore!"

11:58 PM (EST)
Elizabeth, NJ

He was disoriented.

Blood kept running into his eyes, caking around his face, making his skin feel sticky and hard. He felt tired. . . so sleepy he could barely stay awake. He noted an awful, tingling sensation across the top of his head. He moved his right hand-- fingers creeping along the bloody gap in his skull, a strange liquid oozing from his open wound. He pulled away, wanting to vomit--his head was split open!

He was a Delta Force soldier and attempted to focus despite the fear, the pandemonium of confused thoughts. . . yes, he had trouble focusing on any single thing, falling in and out of a trance-like dream state. For a moment he thought he was back home, sitting at the dinner table, calling to his fiancée who stood in the kitchen, cooking his favorite dish: Chicken Poblano. . . then he remembered he was laying on the rocks.

The others. . . yes, there had been others with him, but he didn't know where they were now-- probably reached a safe point before they realized that he'd been swept up by the surf, crashing into the shoreline. He remembered hitting the rocks--the sound of a coconut against stone--that's what he thought.

"Do you want beans with your chicken?" his fiancée asked.

The surf broke. His toes felt numb and tingly. Again he broke out of the sleepy fog. There were lights on him, he could only see blurred images. He reached for his pistol, this time successfully drawing it out of the holster, attempting to hold it to his head and pull the trigger. But his coordination was so poor, he couldn't hold the gun, let alone pull the trigger. Something slapped the weapon out of his hand. He heard voices around him.

"Come here often?" someone laughed.

He heard the sinister voice in his ear, whispering, "Well well," he felt hands grabbing at his dog tags, "Sergeant Polcheck—I'm sure we have a lot to talk about."

part three
THE TROJAN HORSE

Seventeen

12:23 AM (EST)
76 Degrees Longitude, 43 Degrees Latitude
297 miles above the Earth

The retro rocket fired.

Rotating on its axis, the satellite pitched forward, a cosmos of stars glistening off its metal skin. Below the orbiting body, bolts of lightning quaked through clouds like steam in a smoldering pot. The winter storm swept down from central Canada, covering the Midwest, jutting its arms across the northeastern seaboard, spreading fingers far into the Atlantic.

After seven hours, the LACROSSE surveillance satellite initiated test procedures. Constructed by Martin Marietta Corporation at the request of the CIA for a cost of over one billion dollars, the satellite, one of a dozen manufactured, was deployed into orbit by the space shuttle six months earlier.

The concept of aerial reconnaissance was not new, dating back to The French Revolutionary War when a group of men called *aerostiers* climbed into their hot air balloons in order to watch pitched battles raging beneath them, sending information via tow lines to troops below. By World War I airplanes took up the task evolving into World War II's B-17 Flying Fortress which flew even higher, snapping automatic cameras over Axis territories. Now more than two hundred years after that first balloonist took flight with the hopes of seeing what others wished him not to see, the concept of aerial reconnaissance had reached into the very heavens themselves.

Over the past seven hours, the satellite fired its rockets at designated coordinates in order to reach geosynchronous orbit, its orbital speed matching the rotational speed of the Earth below. It now hovered over a single point. Powered by a tiny, nuclear reactor, LACROSSE had an image resolution of less than five feet from its target. If you were looking up at the heavens as it passed overhead, it could count the gray hairs on your head. By comparing the relative heat of different areas far below, LACROSSE could see through walls, utilizing frequencies of light invisible to the naked eye.

It began to scan the surface 297 miles below. Patched through an analog decryption system, the information was beamed to LACROSSE's control center at Sunnyvale, California. Sunnyvale decoded the signal, rebuilding the images, shifting contrasts, suppressing glint, restoring shapes to objects--creating one amalgamated picture: a complete image of all of the living organisms within the Union 57 Facility in Elizabeth, New Jersey.

Eighteen

Screaming.

Candice awoke in a cold sweat. The shrieking rang out again. She jumped, dropping the cell-phone so hard she jarred the battery loose. Scanning the cramped stairwell, she was alone. Gummy Bear was gone—maybe even to warn Nehemiah of her presence? She tried to control her fear when she heard the screaming again, stunning her--this time she placed it behind a small workman's hatch in the stairwell wall.

Opening the hatch, she peered out over a strange crawlway which ran forever. This area was over the suspended roof of the building-- steel support girders running into the darkness. . . hanging fluorescent lights and mounting, all supported above flimsy ceiling tiles.

"AAIIGHHHHHH!" the ear piercing scream rang out.

She looked back at the stairwell and saw the jarred cell phone battery on the floor. The battery! She remembered Lou's briefcase—he had a second battery, she had seen it when he opened his case while threatening Larry the embezzling foreman. If she could get to it, she could call Tom. Quickly, she took off her stockings, stuffing them and the battery just inside the workman's hatch.

The steel girder was cold as her bare feet crept along its boarders like some circus tight rope walker. Indeed, she was walking over a pit of crocodiles—just think of it as a game. Mentally, she worked her way back to Lou's office, negotiating wires and pipes as she walked along the girder.

"AAIGHHHHHH!" the scream almost toppled her over. She lunged out, grabbing at a curving pipe to support her balance. She was right over the screaming man—could hear his rapid breathing and grunts. She crouched down, taking a deep breath, collecting herself before she continued. But the scene beckoned to her. She couldn't help but peak through the crack in the fluorescent light fixture and ceiling tile.

Looking down, she became nauseous. It was the break-room, its floor stained with blood, the whole room stinking of feces and urine--the scent permeating even the tight crawl space overhead. Tiles five feet away were pushed away as if someone had been checking the crawl space.

She peered through the gap at the man, face covered in blood that caked along his cheeks, covering his right eye. His head was cracked wide open-she could see his skullcap parted into two sections just above where his hairline should have been. Clothed in a black jumpsuit, his pants were pulled down and tiny wires were attached to his shaved genitals. He was shaking, trying to move, but thick ropes tied along his head, mid-section, and feet, held him steady.

"Please," he pleaded, "d-don't shock me anymore."

On the next table laid a young woman--yes, Candice recognized her--the only living woman she had witnessed from the break-room carnage earlier that day! The woman's right eye was swollen shut. She was naked, a series of bruises formed on the fringe of her pubic hair. With long hair covering her face, Candice wasn't sure if she was dead or alive.

"Y-y-y-you've got t-t-t-to stop," stammered the bloody man.

"Can't do that," the one with the crusty boots, the one they called Nehemiah, loomed over him. She recognized his voice and could see thinning blond hair over a pale scalp. He rubbed the top of his head and she again noted the box with the button taped to his forearm, "now who are you?"

"Honest," the bloodied man whimpered, "I'm a security guard. I swear!"

"A security guard who wears night-sights?" Nehemiah scoffed. Candice caught a better look at the killer's face. He had a square chin with harsh, jutting cheekbones. Was he German, she wondered? "a security guard with an automatic rifle and dog tags," he screamed, "at least try and lie to me!"

"Please, for the love of God!" the bloodied man pleaded.

"What do you know of God? Now tell me what you were doing on the rocks?"

"He won't tell you anything—we've been doing this for hours," another man walked into Candice's range of vision, tall and skinny with jet black hair.

"Shock him again," Nehemiah persisted.

She heard a mechanical buzz and--

"AIIGGGHHH! AIGHHHHH!" the bloodied man lurched. His head and feet shook, penis stood erect and then fell flaccid. A thin stream of smoke rose from his testicles. The smell of bacon filled the room. Candice turned away, fighting hard not to pass out from the sight.

"We could shock him more," added the fellow outside of her line of sight.

"Bah," Nehemiah shook his head, "in Lubyanka Prison, Stalin used to have men's balls shocked for days at a time. This isn't the proper motivation--he's been trained to withstand torture. Get me the vial Gummy Bear prepared for us."

"The vial," the one in the ball cap seemed troubled, "I-I-I think we should wait. We should-"

"Get it!" barked Nehemiah.
The bloodied captive's eyes were drawn to the glass vial the other terrorist held. Nehemiah put on a set of thick gloves as he grabbed the vial, "Refineries are a lovely thing," continued Nehemiah, "lots of toys. This devil is used in a chemical reaction to produce jet fuel. It's called hydrofluoric acid."

"Jesus Christ," muttered the officer, "please don't burn me!" he whimpered like a child.

"Ssshhhhh," sighed Nehemiah, "we tried an easier approach. Now there's only one thing I want to hear from you."

"G-God, d-d-d-don't burn me man. Please don't burn me," he pleaded.

"Open your eye."

The bloodied man refused, squinting hard. Nehemiah gestured to his cohort. The terrorist with the cap forced open the man's eyes.

The prisoner grunted, trying to fight off his captors, jerking his head violently from side to side, "Polcheck's my name! Sergeant Randy Polcheck!"

"I told you I only want to hear one thing from you now," continued Nehemiah, snapping on a fresh pair of latex gloves while his cohort continued to pry Polcheck's eyelid open.

"W-w-what's that? Tell me!" the soldier pleaded.

"I want to hear you scream," sighed Nehemiah.

Candice felt ill. She held back tears. If she started crying they'd surely hear her!

"No no no no no no," continued the bloodied prisoner, "p-p-p-please. For the love of God! For the love of God!"

"This is all for God," sighed Nehemiah, aiming the vile over the man's eye.

"I'll tell you anything you want!"
Nehemiah poured the contents of the vial into the man's eye. Polcheck was silent--shaking with fear-- shocked by the apparent lack of pain.

"It's not going to burn your eye," continued Nehemiah in his German accent, "that's good," he ran a hand along the man's bloodied cheek, "let it pour into your tear ducts. Hydrofluoric acid doesn't burn skin or soft tissue like your eyes. But it's a tricky little creature— seeps right through your skin, searching for its sustenance: calcium."

"Ah!" the soldier winced in a slight flash of pain. His torso jerked upward as if someone stabbed him.

"There, it's discovered the bones of your cheeks."

"No!" he shook in bursts of pain.

"It's gnawing at your bones now," continued Nehemiah, "little pains at first--sharp and stinging as it draws the calcium from the surface. But its appetite is only wetted. This's just the appetizer!"

"Ahhh! It hurts!" cried the bloodied man, wincing in pain. His body stretched stiff, his toes curled in pain.

Candice thought she might fall off her pylon. She clung to the pipes overhead, trying to hold back tears. This was insane! Insane!

"Yes," continued Nehemiah, "it's hunger drives it deeper into the bone, sucking out the marrow rich in calcium, eating and eating and eating and-"

"AIIIGHHHHHHHH! AIIGHHHHH!" the soldier screamed, 'AAIIIGHHHH!" he spit blood so high that it cleared the crack in the tiled roof, splattering beads of saliva and blood onto the Candice's cold, steel pylon.

"I can make this all go away," continued Nehemiah, "the pain is dying down now as it searches for the far larger bones in your face and then it will progress to your neck and back. The pain has temporarily subsided before it reaches your spine. How many were with you?"

"Delta Force! AIIGHHHHH! Eight men. Eight men in the-aghhhh--eight men in the drainage pipes. Uh--uh--uh-- in drainage pipes!"

"Explosives?"

"Wired the plant for--uh--uh--uh—oh no--"

"For what?"

"Maximum confusion! To divert you so that we could--hostages! Rescue the hostages! Stop it please! Stop it please! It burning again!"

Blood erupted from out of his right eye, pouring down his cheek.

"What is the name of the leader of this strike force?" pressed Nehemiah.

"Major Schubert. Schubert! Schubert! AIIGHHH! Make it stop! PLEASE MAKE IT STOP! IT BURNS SO MUCH! IT'S EATING INTO MY SPINE! ITS EATING INTO MY SPINE! THE ANTIDOTE! MAKE IT STOP! AIIGHHHHH! OH GOD-- AAAIIGHHHHH!"

Casually, Nehemiah drew his pistol from his holster, "This is the antidote."

"Ahahah," Polcheck shook.

"Beg me to give you the antidote," Nehemiah flashed a sadistic grin, "beg."

"G-g-give me the-the antidote. For the love of God—AIIIGHHH! KILL ME!"

Holding the pistol to Polcheck's face, Nehemiah pulled the trigger. The bullet casing bounced around the room. Candice watched a thin stream of blood flood the table, splashing onto the floor--the same stream she had seen earlier in the day when Supervisor Givens was killed.

"I didn't expect Delta Force so quickly. We'll lose too many men trying to hunt them down," Nehemiah spoke to his associate, "The Master was right. Someone is still alive here—reporting back," the terrorist glanced down at the empty vial, "Let's give our Major Schubert a little surprise. Flush the pipeline with this stuff—when they come out running."

Now she had no choice. She had to get that battery--to save those men. She had to reach Tom before it was too late!

Nineteen

It was Benjamin's idea.

General Crandal needed a headquarters, somewhere to work in silence. Benjamin offered the top three floors of The World Trade Center, his former headquarters. An empty shell of offices and conference rooms, the halls were filled with tall brawny men hauling endless cases of equipment.

"Remy," asked the Rabbi as they entered the corridor littered with ripped and empty boxes, "wasn't this supposed to be a quiet little place to think?"

Like a consummate Luddite, reflected Tom, Rabb was opposed to super computers and technological devices. He believed that in the end, only the human mind could solve the questions the world offered and thus required only a quiet place to think.

"C'mon Rabies," the General rubbed his hands together, "gotta have my toys. Or we'd have to think for ourselves. You think for yourself lately?" he barked at a soldier standing in a side doorway.

The officer was flustered, "Well. . . uh. . . uh--"

The General walked past him, "See Rabies," Remy threw up his arms, "with the Ruskies gone, we've gone to shit. Oooyah!"

Twisting and turning through the maze, the General lit a cigarette, addressing Benjamin, "Bronk, quit a place you've created--more complicated than the Pentagon!"

They entered a massive room still under construction. . . exposed ducts and electrical wires hanging from the ceiling. Tom's attention was drawn beyond the scaffolding to the glass windows overlooking the Manhattan skyline. He noted the twinkling lights of New York below him, giving way the brownstones of the Village, rising again with the far off spires of midtown Manhattan. On the other side, he noted the commanding view of the Statue of Liberty framed against the twinkling lights of the New Jersey coast-line. Somewhere amongst those twinkling lights, thought Tom, stood The Union 57 Refinery and Candice.

They passed through the massive room. At the doorway, Tom noticed two soldier lugging an ice chest and a silver Champaign bucket, accouterments of Remy's eccentricities, he assumed. Heels clicking against the stripped, concrete floor, they entered an equally large second chamber.

"Me casa et su casa," Remy turned to them with arms open wide.

They arrived at the brain center.

The windows and walls of the room were eclipsed by a technocrat's dream of computers, monitors, and gadgetry, lining all four walls. In the center of the room stood a stoic faced, black soldier.

"Sir," the soldier turned to them.

Although he wore no official insignia of rank on his black jumpsuit, Tom recognized the face from his CTJTF days: Colonel Nathan Taylor Sharpe. Sharpe was one of the top ranking officers in Delta Force, slated to replace the General upon his retirement.

With a cold face, Colonel Sharpe addressed the group, "Two floors below us and three above are owned by Union 57. We've secured all floors with roving patrols. The men call it Fort Crandal. Outside Union 57, we've set gas alarms around the Union 57 perimeter and wired them to out computers. Satellite info should be in from Sunnyvale in a minute or two."

The group had an oddly tense moment as they waited for the telemetry:

"Well Remy," Rabb rolled his eyes "you've certain outdone yourself."

"If Congress gave me another four million you wouldn't believe what I'd have," he blew smoke into the air, watching it curl and crawl towards the ceiling.

Rabb rolled his eyes, "And I suppose we'll pop open the champagne. Was it Cliquot Grande Dame I saw in the other room?"

"Champagne?" Crandal grimaced, "I don't drink champagne?"

"Sir," interjected Sharpe," was about to get to that. Agent Osbourne took control of that situation and detained the woman in a coat closet."

Crandal winced, "What the hell are you talking about?"

"Take your vile hands off me!" the face whizzed by, hands slapping General Crandal in the face.

She turned, examining the others--her chest heaved as she collected herself. Clad in a tight top and long flowing pants, noted Tom, the older woman had some plastic surgery under her belt. The most noticeable feature of her tight visage was the majestic, jutting chin which reminded him of Katherine Hepburn.

"Mother?" Benjamin Bronk gasped.

"This bitch is your-" Remy restrained himself, nursing a red cheek.

"This bitch," she pointed to herself, hot and angry, "happens to be Eleanor Bronk of The New York Bronks!

"Ma'am," replied Remy, "if you wasn't somebody's mother, I'd toss your ass right out that damn window."

"Was I speaking to you?" Eleanor Bronk shot attitude back at him.

"How did you get here?" stammered Benjamin.

Her chin jutted high into the air, "I had Lee follow you."

"Lee?" squirmed Crandal.

"Lee's my chauffeur," Eleanor raised a brow, "well he was before I had him tending to the balcony bonsai garden and-"

"And the champagne?" Remy had to ask.

"Well, a woman must have sustenance."

Another voice thundered, "What the hell's going on!" Tom turned to see Agent Dick Osbourne. Clad in a FBI jacket, Dick looked cold and tired. Tom no longer feared Osbourne—he wasn't running the show, "I detained this woman under E.O. 12333," barked Osbourne.

"Executive Orders now, ain't we fancy?" Remy chuckled, "show me the order that says you can stuff a woman in a coat closet. Shit, where the hell are you from?"

"Nebraska," Osbourne fired back.

"Explains his lack of manners," Eleanor stiffened, motioning closer to the General, suddenly her ally amongst two evils, "It was very hot in there. I was practically suffocating."

"Sir," Sharpe added, "the satellite telemetry's in and Secretary Giardino's on the speakerphone for you."

The mood suddenly changed back to business. Crandal followed by his group marched back towards the central chamber to review the telemetry. Eleanor stood still, unsure of what to do.

Crandal turned around, "Well I can't very well let you back on the street now. Might as well follow me."

"Remy, I met with the President an hour ago," Giardino spoke first over the speakerphone, "briefing him on the new developments," Tom could hear the murmur of people on the other end of the line, "he's advised me to inform you that whatever action you feel necessary may be taken.

However, the President feels no attack should be taken at this time--no correspondence with the Arabs should be made without White House approval--no word to the press or anyone else. We would have to dedicate more troops to riot control than in dealing with this situation."

"Wow, Vince," smirked the General, "I can do anything as long as I don't do anything at all. Fuck this! I just hauled my gear in and set up shop! Now am I running this operation or is 1600 Pennsylvania Ave?"

"We're just saying-"

"You can't have specific ranges of authority without specific degrees of responsibility, Vince! Now is the time for action, not reaction," Remy calmed down-- this was his show, mused Grant. All his life he had trained for the big one, thought Tom, and despite all the wonderful acts and arguments he could construct, no one was going to take his moment of victory away from him. The General continued, "ah fuck this! Get the President on line."

"General Crandal," a warm, prosperous voice poured across the speaker phone. It was like listening to an old friend, thought Tom, someone you knew intimately, but had never met, "hear you have some problems?" continued the President of The United States.

"No, Mr. President," Remy leaned over the speaker-phone-

"Hello Marshall," Eleanor interrupted the conversation.

Remy nearly had a heart attack. All eyes fell on her as the President continued, "Eleanor, how are you doing?"

"Not so well, Marshal," Eleanor bemoaned, "a prick is interrupting our General's operation. This bastard locked me in a fucking broom-closet!"

The General stared at the woman, too flustered to light a cigarette.

"A broom closet!" exclaimed the Chief Executive.

Osbourne interrupted, "She didn't have security clearance so Osbourne-"

"Do you know who Eleanor Bronk is!" rumbled the President to no one in particular—but the effect worked.

"Let's cut the shit, Marshal, and talk about just how we're going to get out of this thing," continued Mrs. Bronk, "you've got a good team here in New York."

"Your son's there?" Tom noted a hint of disdain in his voice.

"Yes," Benjamin Bronk chimed, "I'm here."

"I hope we won't have to hear about this on Nightline," Tom didn't get the reference," well I suppose with you there we can consider this is a bipartisan event. But now is not a time for dissension. We need to construct a plan and I think General Crandall is still the man to do it."

Tom could hear Eleanor whisper to her son, "He's such a good adulterer too--never gets caught. Who do you think I keep that Rolls Royce in the City for? Fucks more woman than I can count--a perpetual mongoose in heat. "

"Mother, stop it."

"Well" the President continued, "let's take a look at the telemetry."

The image flashed on both screens. Crandal's staff meandered away from the speaker phones, examining the image. The boundaries of the plant were superimposed over the screen. The background color of the image was purple: three hot points of color glowed red and orange on the screen. Besides these spots, much larger red blobs were dotted through various parts of the plant.

"Is that the hostages?" asked the General, pointing at the red spots.

"No," replied Benjamin Bronk as he scanned the screen, taking note of the superimposed borders, "without the main electric lines, they've routed the back-up generators to contain many of the critical application areas—keeping certain chemicals and operations in their stable temperatures and pressures. Without running those areas, the refinery would explode on its own."

"Yes," Sharpe replied," Sunnyvale reports that the radiant temperatures of the red areas range between 120 and 400 degrees Fahrenheit. They're not people."

A silence prevailed over the line, meaning one thing: if the thermal splotches weren't people, where were the hostages? Candice was right, thought Tom, everything she said was true: they had killed the hostages! He counted only 20 thermal signatures scattered around the plant."

The next close up shot was a series of red splotches surrounded by a superstructure. The splotch was a large dot on the screen.

"That's one fat fellow," commented Eleanor.

"No, it's a group of people," added Sharpe, "looks like they're repeating a motion," commented the General.

"Yes," grimaced Rabb, "like they're lifting something?"

2:32 AM (EST)
Elizabeth, NJ

A cold wind rushed across the open refinery.

Nehemiah watched the three terrorists lift the metal drum on its side. The contents splashed around for a moment, but the drum hadn't been opened yet. They drew back in fear. The biological hazard sticker seemed to glow in the darkness. From a safe distance, they made sure the container had not been breached. After assuring themselves of this fact, the group opened the secured seal, allowing the clear, scentless liquid to pour out.

The liquid poured through the grill, splashing into the stream of drainage water in the tunnel. Snaking back and forth, the liquid had a high viscosity and did not dilute at first. Slowly the long thread of the chemical weaved and turned within the contours of the pipe until it connected with another tunnel, spilling into a larger conduit of almost waste high water.

The network of pipes were designed to drain off melted snow produced from the massive amounts of heat within the refinery. It was also used as a drainage conduit for the reservoir pond on the south side of the plant. The pipeline was pitched at a thirteen degree angle propelling the water foreword.

As it meandered, the diluted chemicals brushed alongside the neoprene waders of the soldiers huddled together. The solution splashed against their waders, tiny transparent droplets landing on the fingers of Rice's gloves. He rubbed his gloved hand along his cohort's back, trying to keep him warm. Then the remains of the stream of hydrofluoric acid continued through the pipeline until it reached the broken grillwork, spilling out into the cold Atlantic Ocean.

A moment later Major Schubert felt a strange tingling in his hand and-

Twenty

Candice Cooperman took a deep breath.

Hidden in the rooftop rafters, she had spied on Nehemiah, waiting for him to leave--to finally step outside of The Meditation Chamber. Skillfully mastering her new world between the roof and the ceiling, she had darted along the steel girder, following him from her overhead vantage point until he exited the engineering building altogether.

Assured she had time, she descended from the steel girder to the office was like slipping through the bars of a tiger's cage. Goose bumps rose on her skin as she dropped to the floor. Staring around at what had been Larry Bagnowski's office, she could barely recall the way this room looked twelve hours before.

She was haunted by something else--feelings of the way she was earlier that day--a lifetime ago. She shied away like a child, her life changing with the slightest occurrence--like Lou flirting with her. She wasn't that distressed woman now. She was-sounds in the hall interrupted her moment of introspection.

She raced to the mound of office furniture and file cabinets, groping under piles of papers to reach Lou's briefcase from which she retrieved two cellular phone batteries stored inside. The moment her fingers touched them she felt at ease-- reconnecting to the sane world thus must exist beyond these boarders--

To Tom.

How had she ever gone on without him? Was this just the result of the pandemonium of the day? No, he cared for her--listened to her--saved her life fivefold! There was only Tom and the mad men and the maddest one of all-

As she was about to climb back into the gap-way of steel beams and pipes, she caught sight of the dark laptop. The screen was dark. She remembered the email correspondence—the other person had spoken of another being alive in the plant. Her heart raced. Everything told her to rush back into her ceiling hideaway--she had the cellular batteries! But wanted to know how such a mad event could have occurred.

Flipping the brightness level up, the screen flashed back to life. Her eyes scanned the remains of Nehemiah's conversation which seemed to have evolved out of E-Mail transmissions. The top corner of the screen read:

INTERNET EXTREME
PENSYLVANIA'S FINEST ISP

Her eyes tracked back along the phone cord. Nehemiah was using the internet to communicate—and this internet ISP line was the go-between. She read the conversation:

Take care of them now, Nehemiah.

I am your Defender of The Faith, but I must ask, should we use the hydrofluoric acid? The drainage pipes are large. It will dilute the solution.

Gummy Bear knows his poisons. He said the chemicals will be potent enough. Flush them out and shall slay them.

Understood, My Master.

Are you prepared for my arrival?

Yes Master, we have begun to create the gauntlet in the parking lot.

**There can be no mistakes, My Defender of the Faith. It is

of no consequence that the money exchange was ruined. It bought us the critical time needed. With this fortuitous interruption by Mr. Bronk, they know the sheer power we wield. Everything is going as planned. If necessary I can now detonate the refinery from my position.

From his position? This person was not in the refinery. Nehemiah's gruff voice echoed outside the door! Think fast! She rushed across the room, crouching behind one of the file cabinets pushed next to the desk. The door to The Meditation Chamber slammed open.

From a crack between the file cabinet and the edge of the desk she watched him enter. How old was he? Late forties, maybe. Then she saw his eyes--gray and dead framed by his cheeks chapped cold air outside. Marching to his computer terminal, he draped his coat over the chair. Then he froze, standing in front of the computer. What was going on? He stared at the monitor. The screen—

She left the screen on.

2:40 AM (EST)
Elizabeth, NJ / 20 ft. below the Union 57 Refinery in the drainage tunnels

Major Schubert felt the tingling again.

He fell into a half sleep while standing up, supported by the huddle of his soldiers-- he dreamed of his pregnant wife. Only a year ago, at the age of twenty eight, Schubert married his college sweetheart. Alice was a Taiwanese immigrant. He met her while doing special training in San Diego. Four months ago they purchased a home on a sprawling golf court in Norfolk, Virginia.

Alice was pregnant with their first child. She refused to get an ultrasound--so they had to be especially careful in buying baby furniture for either a boy or a girl.

Children.

There was one image which burned in Major Schubert's mind: he was sitting on the back porch of their new house, trying to sand the deck while reading the latest copy of *Time* when his wife asked him a question-- he couldn't remember the words or the question, itself, only the image remained. Turning around to answer her, he froze, staring at her thin, little frame with that massive belly so large and distended: it looked as if she was about to explode. It was during that one, singular moment that Schubert realized he couldn't ever love anyone as much as he loved her.

He just wanted to be there one more time-- to sit on that deck and turn around ever so slowly, glimpsing her face in the fading Virginia sunset one more time-

"Ugh, it's cold," someone groaned.

He opened his eyes. Turning to view his companions, he could see their heads hanging, the large protruding night sight scopes extending from their faces in a long, thin line like elephant trunks.

"You guys awake?" the Major asked his men--a sudden euphoric feeling surging within him when he spoke. He felt like laughing.

Without looking up, one of them joked with a poor imitation of General Crandall's gruffness, "I ain't a fuckin' horse--can't sleep standin' up. Hahaha."

Schubert started to laugh, knowing all along that this was simply a stage of hypothermia. He felt the burning within him and wanted to strip the clothing from his body. All he could do was sit tight, conserving body heat.

"Major, how long we gonna stay here?" muttered Rice, "I think my dick froze off ten minutes ago."

"We stay here as long as the boss says so," he was stern--"Ah!" Schubert winced in pain.

"What's wrong?" one of them asked in the darkness.

"Nothing. Nothing," the tingling started again in his fingers, a burning like he never felt before. Was it the hypothermia or frost bite, he wasn't quite sure? The pain hit again--this time so sharp he almost toppled into the water. Wet and cold, he'd have less than sixteen minutes of life if he were totally wet.

"Guys," Rice asked with a queasy look, "you hurting at all?"

Leaning into the huddle, Schubert's hand shook in fierce vibrations. Tearing at his glove in the green light of his night sights, he writhed in pain--this was fucking unbearable!

Rice pulled away from the huddle, "Ah, Jesus--" he tried to whisper, but ended up screaming, "something's eating at my back! Can you see it?"

"Keep it down," another reprimanded.

"It's eating into my back!" Rice fell into the icy cold stream of water, "Jesus Christ, SOMEONE STOP IT FROM-"

Schubert heard others rushing towards the fallen soldier. He could only lean against the cold pipe wall, pulling at the straps of his insulated gloves. The burning moved from his fingers to his wrist. . . as if a rat were trapped inside him, eating out his flesh.

Schubert wanted to act as the leader, but couldn't think--he couldn't do anything except try and get the damn glove off his hand! Finally the glove came off. He could feel the center of his forearm sinking, collapsing, burning.

The glove popped off, falling into the water. Staring breathlessly down at his mangled hand, his fingers were drawn so tight into his palm that his fingertips broke through his skin. The crumpled flesh was purplish green in the tint of the night sites. His thumb was distorted, bent backwards so that the secondary joint collapsed against his hand. Drawing back the sleeve of his coat, his eyes moved up his arm. The pain was so great-- he could feel shooting sensations racing up his biceps! What the hell was going on?

Glancing away, he watched his soldiers laying in the water. His team had degenerated into animals. The scene transpired in slow motion--a movie without sound--men flipping about like a fish out of water. Two of his soldiers cried out in pain--mouth stretched open in pain as they brushed things off their jacket as if spiders climbed all over them. What the hell was going on, thought the Major? They were losing all order!

2:43 AM (EST)
Elizabeth, NJ

Candice's heart raced.

She could feel the blood rushing to her head. She was so stupid. Don't breath--you're in Fiji, watching the sun set over the Pacific Ocean. Nothing can harm you here-

Nehemiah spun around, observing the room. Were her arms tucked behind the file cabinet? He walked towards her, drawing a gun from under his sweater--he stopped in front of the desk. She shut her eyes, expecting a gunshot to her head.

Instead it was creak as Nehemiah stood on Larry's old desk--his feet no more than inches away from Candice as she lay crouched under the half toppled file cabinet. Through a gap, she watched him climb into the ceiling. Then he hopped back down, exiting the room.

Standing on the file-cabinet, she maneuvered into the ceiling. She no longer felt safe here now that Nehemiah had been here! Swiftly, she darted along the steel support beam, her bare feet stinging from the cold steel as she raced to the hatch.

Her heart raced. Sliding the fresh battery into the cell phone, she flipped it on. The familiar green screen lit up. Dancing through the memory call numbers, sweat formed on her brow. She located FBI#2 and pressed 'send'.

Twenty One

2:52 AM (EST)
New York City, NY

Tom's telephone rang!

Grant's heart raced. Could it be Candice? Could she actually be alive? The room was so involved in the satellite telemetry, no one noticed him answer his cellular phone.

"Tom?" he heard Candice's voice.

"Candice," Tom said almost to himself, "you're alive."

General Crandal heard the name and shot around, immediately realizing what was happening, "That's her?"

Grant shook his head. Sharpe plugged a chord into a jack on top of Tom's phone—a moment later he could hear Candice's voice on loudspeakers placed in the room, "I'm in the stairwell in the engineering building."

Crandal and Sharpe rushed to the live satellite feed, trying to place her on LACROSSE's thermal scan of glowing orange spots. The General pointed at the spot where he believed she was located.

Bronk scrambled through blueprints of the building, "That's the fire stairwell."

"Candice," Tom smiled, "I can see you. There's a satellite in space imaging you right now-"

"Damn it!" cried Osbourne, "you don't know if she's-"

Tom quit listening to him. By now they were all barking questions at him--the words mixed into a murky chorus of voices. He concentrated only on Candice's voice.

"Tom, the leader of the group is a blond, Caucasian in his mid 40's--German accent, goes by the name of Nehemiah. He's assisted by an autistic, Caucasian in his mid-thirties, named Runyon, born in Orange Texas, goes by the name of Gummy Bear. Gummy's a chemical genius. He showed Nehemiah how to pour hydrofluoric acid on Polcheck. I want out of here, Tom!"

"She can't leave now," shuddered Osbourne. Tom tried to cover the phone, but she must've heard him because she was silent as Osbourne continued ranting into Grant's ear, "she knows Polcheck's name! Ask her about-"

Tom elbowed Osbourne in the face. The NSC Liaison stumbled backwards, glancing down at his bloody hand. Before either men could do anything, Candice continued, "Nehemiah speaks only to his superior via a computer e-mail link in Larry Bagnowski's old office-- they call it 'The Meditation Chamber'. If you want to strike the leader, hit him there."

"Have you seen any Arabic men?" asked Tom.

"All white guys. They're wacky. One of them has a box taped to his wrist—like a detonator and others are making a geometric shape in the parking lot with oil barrels—The Master calls it the Gauntlet."

"What?" Rabb turned away from the monitors, "have her repeat that!"

There were too many questions being screamed at Tom. He tried to focus only on her voice. Turning back to the screen, he caught sight of the orange blob on the monitor. He was looking at her!

"They killed Polcheck," her voice shuddered, "but not before he told them about Schubert and the strike force in the drainage pipes. Gummy showed Nehemiah were the hydrofluoric acid was and they poisoned the team-"

"Jesus Christ!" Remy rushed back to the computer monitor, "get the strike force on the screen!"

When LACROSSE refocused, the strike team was no longer neatly huddled in the drainage pipes. Orange dots were rushing all over the place. Bronk scrambled through the blueprint sheets and stopped for a moment, his chest heaving, "They're rushing down the pipe to the ocean!"

"What the hell's hydrofluoric acid?" Crandal deferred to Bronk.

The billionaire shivered, "It's a dangerous catalyst used in the synthesis of jet fuel-- bonds with calcium-- runs along your bones, eating you from the inside."

"Is there an antidote?" asked the General.

"Yes," replied the executive, "but I'd bet your men don't have any calcium glutamate on them."

Candice's voice thundered over them, "Nehemiah poured hydrofluoric acid into his eye and killed him--it was awful."

"Get Schubert on the Comlink!" thundered General Crandal.

3:00 AM (EST)
Elizabeth, NJ/ 20 ft. below in The Union 57 Drainage Pipes

Beep-beep-beep-

Schubert's arm was on fire. He kept trying to shut his eyes, to quell the pain, to think. Think damn you, think! You're a soldier--think! He heard a beeping sound and opened his eyes. In various shades of green, he watched his men die.

The beeping continued. The Comlink phone slung over the back of his crumpled sergeant was ringing--the tiny blinking red light nearly blinding Schubert's night-site. Shutting his eyes, he reached for the phone. The tunnel spun as he lifted the phone to his ear, breathless, mist rising from his lips.

"Schubert!" cried General Crandall frantically, "is that you?"

"Uhuh," he winced in pain.

Rice doubled over, screaming like a wild animal, "Schubert, you've been poisoned with hydrofluoric acid!

Its eating through your body. You've got to concentrate--listen to me!"

His arm was mangled, crushed. He would never be able to use it again. He wanted to be back in Norfolk on that deck with Alice. He would never-

"Schubert, we have you on the satellite feed. You've lost order. Your men are fleeing towards the ocean. The terrorists have killed all the hostages-" killed all the hostages? What the hell was he here for, "They're positioned at all the openings of the pipeline. You've got to head inward. We'll guide you with satellite recon! Do not allow your men to be captured, they'll be tortured-"

Schubert drew his gun with his left hand, trying to hold the phone with his lame hand. It fell into the water. Now that he had a goal, he had to focus, to operate within the limits of his pain. He could see his soldiers stumbling ahead of him, twenty feet down the tunnel. His arm burned so much! He drew his pistol, but the silencer mounted on the end of the weapon was awkward--it took a moment for him to loosen the weapon from the holster.

Water splashed around him, "Stop!" he begged them.

They weren't listening, racing towards the manhole cover. The Cowboy's words reverberated through his ears: they'd only be tortured and killed. Schubert gripped the trigger and-

---

3:03 AM (EST)
New York, NY

Too much--too fast!

The room spun in slow motion around Tom. General Crandal and Colonel Sharpe were already on the other side of the table, frantically trying to redial the troops over the Comlink. Eleanor had a hand over her mouth, an astonished look on her face. Benjamin screamed something. . . Osbourne tried to address the General.

"Get me out of here," demanded Candice as if she'd carried out all that could be asked of her.

Suddenly all that Tom had seen and experienced that day seemed to fall away. There was simply Candice. He kneeled down on the floor, trying to speak with a hand over his mouth. He wanted to say things.

So little time and then--

Tom glimpsed the monitor, caught sight of the orange dot: Candice-- resting in the stairwell and another dot entering the stairwell, "There is someone else there," he felt the air leave his lungs, "there's someone else in the stairwell!"

3:06 AM (EST)
Elizabeth, NJ/ 20 ft. below Union 57 Refinery in the drainage pipes

"Aiighhhh!" Schubert raced down the pipe line.

He could feel the animal eating at his shoulder. The tissue of his wrist swelled with fluids causing his chronometer strap to dig into flesh. He bit madly at the strap, but couldn't get the watch off! The nerves in his fingers died away.

Staring through the narrow scope of his night sights, he spotted his fallen companions leaning against the walls, coming to their senses, but two were still racing ahead of them, driven mad with pain. He had to stop them!

He ran past Thompkins, weeping like a child. Schubert wanted to help him, but he needed to chase after two of his soldiers who weaved their way along the curving pipe. In the green tint of his night-sites the Major glimpsed the broken, fenced barrier at the edge of the pipe. He had to turn away from the measly amount of light from the night sky beyond the exit. Tossing the scope upward, the sweat around his eyes stung as he tackled his men.

They would surely be killed by the terrorists. He could see reflections of flashlight beams at the pipe's mouth. The wind howled through the tiny opening. The soldiers were five feet from the exit. He held the gun in his left hand--it felt strange as he took aim at his own men.

"Stop!" he cried one last time.

They continued running, blinded with pain and confusion as the poison ate out their insides. As any Delta Force officer understood, wounding a fellow officer was never an option--it slows down the team and makes the victim easy prey for capture and torture. The question begged from some other part of his mind: what the hell was he doing?

He aimed the gun for a clear head shot and pulled the trigger-

One fell.

Shutting his eyes, he fired again.

Another fell.

He watched the silhouettes and flashlights at the pipe's mouth. The terrorists had been waiting for them-- just as the General claimed. They were being flushed out! Limping backward, he tripped over Thompkins.

"K-kill me, please," the officer pleaded.

Schubert stopped.

Unlike Nehemiah, the Major gained no pleasure in killing and wanted to vomit as he fired on his men. This group was not a random assortment of soldiers. Schubert had trained with this team, forged them together--they were his fellow warriors, compatriots.

Killing his own wounded for the sake of only the mission was the hardest thing he could ever do. An eerie, surreal feeling enveloped him. He couldn't believe this was happening. He tried to think of the Virginia sunset--that was all he wanted--staring at his wife, and her swollen belly--all Schubert wanted was to be back with her, standing on that deck. He'd give both his arms to see her smiling face! Tears streamed down his face.

He fired the pistol.

Thompkins crumpled into the water.

Racing along the pipe he shot his master sergeant, huddled in the corner holding his chest. He found Rice in shock, froth erupting from his mouth. A bullet whizzed by Schubert.

"Stop!" voices of strangers cried out to him. They laughed, taunting him like mad hunters pursuing prey.

He raced up the tunnel in his bulky, neoprene waders, water splashing. Voices cried out behind him-- taunting him like wild dogs at his heels. His pursuers closed in—their flashlights bouncing around the tunnel, but he refused to give up--then a sting!

A bullet struck him in his left shoulder and-

Twenty Two

Candice Cooperman hid in the darkness.

The footsteps continued up the staircase--the sound of heavy boots against cold, metal. Thoughts raced through her mind-- the image of death, a Grim Reaper with scythe in hand--the confidant tone of Tom's voice. She no longer thought of Jordan's good-bye letter because-

Clomp. Clomp. Clomp.

Then the fear fled from her. In the half light of the stairwell, she caught site of the familiar figure. He stood stationary, a ragged plaid shirt and black glasses taped on both ends. Gummy Bear avoided her gaze, twisting a crooked finger through tangled locks of red hair.

"Everybody's outside having fun settin' the babies free ex'ept Gummy Bear," he muttered.   He   must be talking about releasing the hydrofluoric acid, thought Candice.

"Who told you to set your babies free?" she asked.

"Nehemiah. . . an' The Master."

Who was The Master—could it be the caller Nehemiah conversed with over the internet link? "Is Nehemiah the leader?" she asked.

"Nope."

"Who is The Master?"

"The Master's not a person," he babbled on, "he's everywhere."

This Master must be part of some elaborate lie Nehemiah had constructed to manipulate the child man. Then Gummy handed her a package he'd been hiding behind him: a wrapped sandwich.

Pangs of hunger fired insider her. She devoured the sandwich, gulping it down before she realized she'd even been ravenously hungry. She wiped her lips, knowing she looked like some deranged animal, "Thanks you, Gummy."

A tear trickled down his cheek, "You're so kind. No one's been kind to Gummy Bear in a long time," he wept raw tears, "Daddy said he was kind to Gummy Bear, but he'd beat Gummy Bear--that was why Gummy Bear had to use the chem'stry set and make the Babies so that that Daddy'd juss go to sleep."

She stroked his back. She wanted to care for this poor man--the way she would aid any child in need. But he was far more to her now. Gummy Bear was the critical piece in her puzzle-- the leverage she'd need in order to force the government's hand in rescuing her—both of them. She hatched the plan in the confines of her mind, guestimating and planning for the necessary items Gummy would have to fetch her like shoes and a proper coat.

She was getting the hell out of here.

3:27 AM (EST)
Elizabeth, NJ / 20 Ft. under The Union 57 refinery in the drainage pipes.

Major Schubert was bleeding.

He tried not to think of his crumpled left arm, bouncing like dead weight against his side. He smelled the saltiness of his sweat--tasted the bitter iron in his blood. The bullet had pierced his left arm, carving out flesh and bone in its wake.

"Gonna get ya! Yeehow!" the screaming continued from behind him.   The pipe revolved around and around like a twisted funhouse ride. He felt a pressure in his forehead—would he pass out? He triangulated his position from the maps he had memorized during the briefing-- must be under the Catalytic Cracker by now. Shit, it wouldn't take his pursuers long to catch him. From the briefing, he remembered there was an intersection of drainage pipes approximately two hundred yards upstream--still a ways to go.

Most men would've collapsed by now, but Major Schubert was not most men. Still, limping at half speed, his energy ebbed out of him along with liters of blood congealing in his waders. Schubert knew his physical limitations--he would collapse in less than fifteen minutes. In an hour, he'd be dead. . . the Virginia sunset. . . he liked to read history books . . damn it, concentrate!

"First I'm gonna get ya!" a voice cried, "then I'm gonna gut ya!"

He froze.

That voice wasn't behind him, but in front--maybe fifty yards ahead where the tunnel arched to the right. Through his night-site, he couldn't make out anyone. Think, damn it! They must've wedged him between two hunting teams.

He stopped, ignoring the splashing footsteps approaching from both sides. Glancing up, he searched the metal walls of the pipe--no manhole covers--no uncharted intersections--no exits. He was trapped!

Thoughts left him. He lifted up his night-sites. The flight or fight instinct took hold. He wanted only to kill. Crouching down, he glanced back at the men nearing from the rear, the beams of their flashlights lit up the wall only feet behind him, blinding his night-sites. From the bend in the pipe, he still couldn't make out the team ahead of him, but knew that soon the flashlights would converge on him from both sides.

He had only one chance.

In spasms of pain, he lowered himself into the freezing, cold water, covering his body from the neck down. The sudden drop in temperature sent a shock to his system, flaring the racing pain down his shoulder. He thought he would pass out! In a matter of minutes, he'd be dead from hypothermia.

"If you just come out now, it'll be quick," one of them taunted.

The group in front of him cleared the turn in the tunnel. In the green tint of his night-sites, he counted them: five men, their flashlights bouncing around the pipe--the beam grazing an area only ten feet in front of him. Quietly, he swam upstream, his heart racing. Breaking through the water, he spotted five men walking side by side, making sure that nothing drifted past them. That, thought Schubert, would be their undoing.

With his one good hand, he groped for his pistol in the icy water. Aiming the weapon, he chose the figure on the far left. The men were now only six feet from him. Behind him he could hear the other group no more than ten feet away, could feel the pipeline vibrating with their foot-steps then—

He fired.

Schubert didn't have time to watch the figures fall. Spinning around, he fired at the other team before he dropped into the water. Confidant that his silencer quenched his muzzle fire, he pushed forward. Gunfire exploded in the tunnel. The terrorists on either side fired madly, bullets reverberating off the pipe wall—screaming as they shot each other.

Under the cold water, Schubert's heart felt as if it were about to explode. He didn't think about this fact. His mind was everywhere and nowhere at all—he just kept swimming as bodies and guns and flashlights landed with thuds against the pipe floor, arms and hands falling around him, the sound exaggerated through the liquid medium.

Finally, he came up for air.

The burst of gunfire ended. There was only darkness and voices screaming in pandemonium. Through his night-sites he could see the bodies, floating, unmoving in the freezing water and blood. Then he spotted the lone body huddled in the corner of the pipe, weeping.

Schubert drew his knife and slid down his night-sites, studying the figure for many seconds in the cover of darkness. Then the Major rushed forward, the knife held lamely in his wounded left hand. Through his night-sites, he saw the look of surprise on the gun man's face.

"Move--scream," he grunted, the knife pressed against his prey's throat, "just give me provocation to kill you."

Schubert pushed the blade gently into the shaking terrorist's neck, enough to draw blood--like he had to draw the blood of his own soldiers--no--don't kill him yet--as bad as you want to--quell the emotions!

"How many are behind you?" he barked--his voice more wild animal than man. He could taste the feel of the kill.

"Jusssss m-m-m-me, s-sir," from his voice, Schubert could tell the gunman was young--very young--possibly mid-teens. He examined the skinny frame through his night sights--the boy held a dead flashlight in shaking hands, "my flashlight burned out," blinded in the dark tunnel, he must've straggled behind, "how many behind me?"

"Five. . . I think."

"Where're you from?" he asked noting the American accent.

"T-T-T-T-Tacoma--" the boy stammered, "Tacoma, Washington."

What kind of Crimson Fist terrorist haled from Tacoma? What the fuck was going on here? The foot-steps behind him pushed him to action.

"Please sir!" the boy whimpered.

Schubert realized he had dug the knife deeper into his throat. He drew the blade back a quarter centimeter, still keeping it precariously close to the boy's wind-pipe, "This knife," Schubert was hoarse, losing his voice, "is less than an inch from killing you. Give me one reason why I shouldn't do it."

"I'll tell you anything you want, sir," the kid wept, but was careful not to jerk around, the knife resting in his neck; the touch of the cold steel. More blood.

"Who is the leader of your group?"

"The Master."

"Don't fuck with me!" he felt like an old man pursued by infants. Was this whole thing a children's crusade? He carved the knife deeper into flesh.

"Ow--The Master--I don't know his real name! None of us know his name," he whimpered, "we follow Nehemiah. But Nehemiah takes his orders from the Master."

Then he heard the footsteps in the distance behind him--the search party closing in. He didn't have time to complete the interrogation. Schubert glanced up, there was a manhole cover above his head. He didn't have the arms to do it, so he ordered the kid to, "Slide open that manhole cover. Make one wrong move and I slit your throat."

With Schubert's knife still in his neck, the boy lifted the heavy manhole cover. Then Schubert told the boy to give him his own jacket, draping it over his shoulder because he lacked the arm to grab it. The boy followed all these instructions.

"What's your name?" Schubert asked.

"Fred Telly. Please sir, don't-"

Schubert cut straight across the boy's wind-pipe. The boy stood in shock, hands hovering around his slit neck, eyes bulging as his carotid arteries sprayed blood straight into the air, out the open manhole cover. The boy collapsed to his knees.

Taking off his own bloodied jacket, Schubert tossed it through the open manhole cover and put on the boy's thick jacket. Schubert finally reached over, cracking the boy's spine at C4—a hangman's fracture—he'd suffocate on his own blood for another few minutes before he passed out and died.

Such a scene would buy Schubert time. Let them think there was a skirmish, let them think that he'd taken the boy's coat, discarding his wet one on the surface of the plant. . . let them chase him all over the place as long as they stayed out of the tunnels for a while.

He continued up the pipeline, coming to the intersection of pipes. He crouched down, limping in the cramped tunnel. By now he was so disoriented he couldn't tell which way was up. He kept falling over, splashing into the darkness.

Then he spotted the obstacle.

Drawing his gun, he froze. It wasn't a person, but a large pile of sand ahead of him topped off with a few shovels. It looked like some work had been conducted on the pipe. He ran his hands along the cold sand--it was dry! Collapsing, he stripped his cold clothing off and buried himself in the sand, trying to keep warm.

He was dizzy-- floating in and out of a fog. It felt like he was hanging upside down. Instantly, he fell into a deep, dream filled sleep. In his dream he was on the porch of his new home, but each time he turned to see his wife, she darted behind the door. He kept calling out to her, but she wouldn't answer.

4:19 AM (EST)
New York, NY

Tom's cell-phone rang.

Many were huddled around the giant monitors, studying the failed remnants of Major Schubert's advance team. Still, eyes danced across him as he answered the call, knowing all along that Candice was on the other end.

"Listen to me carefully," she spoke first, her strident voice unannounced to her, echoing over the speakerphone. She was different, thought Tom, full self-confidence, "your boss is going to get me out of here and I'm going to give you a blow by blow breakdown of the terrorist's plan and their chief chemical expert."

Tom's eyed General Crandal--the cowboy ran a tongue across a molar.

"And," added Candice, "this has to be kept between us. Nehemiah has a spy amongst your group. He knows all about me—even my name."

The brawny black man looked up from the corner where he spoke on his cell phone. Before Osbourne could object, Remy grunted, "Let her keep talkin'."

Twenty Three

4:33 AM (EST)
Elizabeth, NJ

Nehemiah adjusted himself in his seat.

Alone in the Meditation Chamber, he was excited to speak to The Master. Nimbly, his fingers dashed across the keyboard, continuing his line of communication with his superior who commanded him to--

Speak.

Nehemiah responded, typing out the letters on his laptop keyboard:

They have broken our commandments. They have sent troops into our plant. We must strike--teach them to follow our words! Crash the tanker as we planned. It will buy us time.

A moment passed. Nehemiah rubbed his weary eyes. The responses over the cellular phone lines could be silent and quick, sneaking up on him when he least expected it. He glanced back, surprised at the response waiting for him:

It is not your place to question my actions. Their petty transgressions will be avenged. But not now. There is a grand design and you shall not question it. Is that understood?

Nehemiah's heart sank. His fingers raced across the keyboard.

I never meant to insult. You are my Leader, my Lord, my Master.

Candice is being aided by Gummy Bear in an escape plan. General Crandal has dispatched an agent named Tom Grant to accomplish this task. I foresaw all of this.

Yes, Master, I will slay them both for their transgressions.

No——not yet. Keep Gummy Bear for you may still require his services. Question this woman, find out what she has told Grant. I have a special use for her

Master, your wisdom amazes me more and more each day.

Soon, my son, the stone shall fall. You are truly a Defender of the Faith. The world shall benefit from our sacrifices because-

Twenty Four

4:41 AM (EST)
In Transit Between New York, NY and Newark, NJ

Tom Grant thought he was going to vomit.

More than anything, he hated helicopters. It was from one of his few childhood memories. As a child he had waited for a helicopter tour of The Grand Canyon.

His father let a family cut in front of them while Tom was in the bathroom. The chopper with the family in it crashed into the canyon wall and-

"You gonna puke?" Ice Man nudged him in the arm. He was the plain clothed Delta Force soldier that had restrained Benjamin Bronk in the Cigar Bar bathroom. With a shock of blond hair poking out from all angles, he looked like some deranged Beach Bum, thought Tom, "this is the UH-60A Black Hawk--safest chopper in the world. Cruising speed's 320 clicks--can carry 15 men," he rattled off a few more statistics as if to reassure Grant.

Hell, thought Tom, maybe it wasn't the helicopter, but the mounting tension. Troops were already stationed around the perimeter of the plant, but they wouldn't care for Candice's safety like he would. Or was his sense of duty simply a smoke-screen for nonprofessional sentiment? No, they needed this exchange! But could this Gummy Bear be trusted? Was this a trap?

Benjamin Bronk nudged Tom, "You OK?"

The General had dispatched Benjamin along because of his knowledge of the plant layout. Sitting next to Tom, the billionaire grasped unrolled blueprints of the refinery, "Remember what the General said, "you're not to enter that plant perimeter," he had to stay in The Bob's Big Boy diner across from the main gate.

Tom and Benjamin shared a quick look as the chopper rapidly dropped—heading for the helipad at Newark airport. With the no fly zone currently imposed between Newark and Rahway, they would have to go by car from here.

Strange, thought Tom, despite the fact that the billionaire had stuck a gun to his head hours before, he shared a unique sense of comradery with the man. In all the world there were only a handful of men aware of the threat at hand.

"Why they call you Ice Man?" Benjamin asked the soldier.

He nodded, "Long story."

"Really—why?" pressed Tom.

"The guys claim I look like Vanilla Ice—ya know, Ice Ice baby--pussy."

Tom and Benjamin fought to restrain smiles. They did look strikingly similar, he mused.

"You know this girl real well, huh?" asked Ice.

"As good as you can know someone over phone calls."

"My old man proposed to a woman after one wrong call."

" They got married?"

"Never said married. He just proposed and she said no. Guess she wasn't into pervert callers."

They laughed. The joke cut the tension. Tom now felt more comfortable around this soldier: a man who'd followed him through one hell of a night.

"So what do you think of a real military operation?" asked Ice Man, checking his pistol, "I took your CTJTF tests--those written exams you guys prepared for us. I remember one scenario with a hostage in a pet shop and-"

"I didn't write that one. I authored the nerve toxins in the Delaware--"

Benjamin raised a brow, confused by the comments.

"Oh yeh, nice one," Ice opened the breach of his pistol: a government issue Colt .45 with a special modified trigger and military hammer.

"Ever seen a mission like this?" asked Bronk.

The soldier smiled, his eyes locked on his weaponry as he continued his inspection with able fingers, "General Crandal never escorted us on a mission before. He's the boss, but Colonel Sharpe usually leads the troops to action. He doesn't like the Cowboy always going for the jugular."

"I appreciate Sharpe's reservation," added Tom, "this is a complex operation."

"You analysts don't get it," Ice Man smirked, loading the extra magazines with hollow point bullets, "this is the state of war today. We progressed, creating brilliant weapons with amazing destructive capacities and now everyone's too petrified to use em 'cause they're mutually destructive. So we've regressed past the fucking foot soldier at Waterloo. And left with what? Insurgent groups, the ones small enough to crawl through the cracks of the geopolitical pavement. And to fight em, we've divested ourselves of the bombs, the tanks, the heat seeking missiles and gone back to the first hand to hand combat--ape men going at it. Tell me who's primitive?"

Tom and Benjamin shared an impressed look. Despite his cute nickname and surfer buzz-cut, Ice Man was more intelligent than Tom gave him credit, "So you're saying this thing will be settled in close combat?"

"They're going to blow up the place anyway," sighed Ice, "Let's try to stop it. Worse we do is kill everybody."

"Right," Benjamin smirked. Tom rescinded his previous thoughts on Ice.

Then the helicopter touched down at Newark Airport.

4:56 AM (EST)
Elizabeth, NJ

Candice glanced at her watch, waiting for Gummy to return with boots and a jacket. He'd been gone so long, she thought, had something gone wrong?

4:56 AM (EST)
New Jersey Turnpike, NJ

"Damned traffic," winced Ice Man.

He'd been speaking with the driver of the limousine they were seated in, "a tanker collided with some car."

An accident up ahead stalled their progress. The police escort ahead of them carved out layers of traffic. Tom and Benjamin peered through the windshield, examining the faces of car passengers as they passed. a Latino family in an ancient Oldsmobile. . . a waitress still in her uniform who looked like she was trying to get to bed after the night-shift. What would the traffic mob look like by eight o'clock? He shuddered, all of these people were in the vaporization zone--the fifty mile long black area he witnessed in The Pentagon briefing. A young girl no more than three years old yawned, peering up at him through her car window. It was easier dealing with statistics and graphs in the brain center, but now he was out amongst them--a sampling of the millions of dead--the lucky ones--the ones who would be vaporized, the ones who wouldn't have to have their skin peel off, their eyes weeping with blood.

4:56 AM (EST)
Elizabeth, NJ

Candice heard Gummy Bear returning with the boots.

He clomped up each step as if his feet were filled with concrete. Candice peered down through the metal grating until she spotted fiery red hair and her heart gave a sigh—followed by the urgent instinct to flee.

"Where the hell have you been?" the urge to flee, the urge to finally escape this nightmarish world was so overwhelming--she had to restrain herself.

"Nehemiah's looking for me—says I've been bad," he turned away .

They knew. The spy amongst Tom's group had told Nehemiah. Shit! All was lost—no, calm down, just remain calm.

"They tried to stop Gummy Bear from helping his angel," he sat in the half darkness, taking deep breaths, making the same gurgling sound, sucking his dirty thumb, "I like gummy Snickers and Reese's—"

"What happened?" she asked, her voice failing.

He was no longer listening to her, babbling incoherent statements, syllables strung together into one long word. His shirt was covered in blood! She motioned to touch him, but he pulled away. He opened his palm. In his other hand she saw the glass vial, "Gummy's babies saved him—"

"You released a chemical on someone--on Nehemiah?"

"A guard. We gotta go."

She broke away, putting on the boots, still warm from the man Gummy Bear had killed. They were three sizes too big, like clowns feet, but they would shield her feet from the snow.

"Gummy loves you," he wiped a child-like tear away.

She led them through the heavy iron door, noting the bold orange letters doorway "ROOFTOP EXIT, CANNOT REENTER". You can say that again, she thought to herself.

The wind blew towards the bay.

She walked along the gravel roof, peering over the side of the engineering building. The electricity was still dead, the usual twinkling sea of lights. . . a blackness punctuated only by patches of gray fog.

Her heart raced as she scaled down the ladder mounted to the side of the building, Gummy Bear following close behind. Like Jack climbing out of the bean-stalk, she thought to herself. Then she saw something that made her heart stop-

---

5:08 AM (EST)
Elizabeth, NJ

"Finally," sighed Ice Man.

They pulled into the parking lot of the Bob's Big Boy an hour late. Across the street, Tom scanned The Union 57 refinery. There were no telltale lights--it was dark and quiet. Ice Man lead him inside the restaurant which had been expropriated by Delta Force. The main room was filled with soldiers disguised in plain clothes, inspecting their weapons. Tom was acutely aware of his cell phone practically burning a hole through his pocket. It had not rung yet. He shared a quick look with Benjamin. All the while, neither men could tear their eyes away from the window.

5:11 AM (EST)
Elizabeth, NJ/ The Union 57 Refinery

Candice stared at the scene.

From her vantage point she saw men moving the stiff, frozen bodies. In their hands they held a photograph and without seeing it she knew: it's my photograph. They're looking for me, making sure I'm really alive. Had they been to her house, she wondered?

The wind picked up and she could hear them speaking to each other:

"This is ridiculous. She's not here," one moaned.

"Nehemiah already said she's making a break for the fence-line, what the hell are we doing here!"

Now she was sure of it. They knew she was escaping! Wild thoughts danced through her head. Could she even trust Tom?

"If ya ask me she went to the tunnels. Shit, we'll never find her. They say that nut killed ten men down there. Tough as nails. Nobody'll go in there."

Someone from Schubert's team was alive and still in those drainage pipes. She could head down there, but—the fence-line perimeter was so close! In the distance she spotted the wires of the fence and Bronk Blvd. just beyond. Leading Gummy, they meandered towards it as she dialed FBI#2 on her phone-

---

5:14 AM (EST)
Elizabeth, NJ

Tom's phone buzzed. Seated at one of the diner's long tables lining the front window, he glanced instinctively back at the refinery. Benjamin leaned forward, listening to the call, "Where are you?" he asked.

"Why should I tell you? They know Gummy Bear and me are making a break for the fence-line! You weren't supposed to tell anyone, Tom!" he could hear the sense of betrayal in her voice.

"General Crandal forced me to put the call on speakerphone for his private staff, but I assure you no one told these terrorists anything!" shit, he was yelling, "Gummy Bear must have told them!."

"Listen to yourself!" she whispered angrily, "Gummy's practically a child!"

"What's she talking about?" Ice demanded. Was he a traitor, wondered Tom. Grant's eyes scanned the room.

"We don't have time for talk, Candice," Tom concentrated on controlling his fear, "get the hell out of there. I'm here waiting for you!"

Tom stood up, walking to the front door. Benjamin and ice followed as Candice continued, "They knew you were coming. A van crashed into a tanker," she added, "how could I know that? There are spies amongst you!"

The line clicked dead.

Tom's head spun. He pressed his hand against the door. Ice Man grabbed it, "You can't leave 'till they're across the street." Thoughts raced. They knew her name-- her escape plan! Maybe there was a traitor. Bronk was the only one he could trust—his entire refinery was at stake, how could he ever be part of this? Bronk nodded as if he knew and approved of what was about to happen and said, "What's that?" the billionaire distracted Ice by pointing across the street.

With his elbow, Tom cracked Ice Man in the face. The soldier grabbed at him, his arms catching only air. Clearing the glass door, Tom took off in a mad sprint towards the street. The road was empty.

His feet slapped against the hard, asphalt. Mist rose from his mouth as he tried to sprint faster--using all of his energy. Where were the gunmen? He didn't know and didn't care! In his wake he could hear footsteps behind him. He turned and saw Ice Man and Benjamin racing behind him.

Tom saw a short red haired man teetering on the top of the refinery's perimeter fence—it was Gummy Bear! Below him Tom could see Candice. A gust of wind blew her hair back--he saw the finely featured face. Tom was thirty yards away now--then he heard the sound.

Patatatatatatatatat

Candice heard it too.

She spotted Tom sprinting towards her. Her heart raced. This was Tom--Tom Grant! Suddenly, she looked up, confused by the sound--patatatatatatat.

"Candice!" she heard a voice-- Tom's voice calling out for her! The same voice that she'd heard on the phone. . . the voice that kept her alive, "Candice!"

Everything moved in slow motion. She focused on Tom. . . young face, sandy brown hair, his arms shooting back and forth as he sprinted towards her. Then she saw the source of the noise overhead —the helicopter dropping out of the murky fog--Papatatatatatatatat--the engine roared.

Gunfire erupted!

Tom saw the bullets blast against the asphalt.

"Run to me!" screamed Tom, continuing his mad dash, "run to me!"

"Tom!" Candice yelled, "Tom!"

A bullet struck the asphalt a yard ahead of him. The gunfire was from the refinery. He darted around in serpentine and spotted Candice no more than eight yards away, hands over her head, confused, unsure of where to go.

More gunfire! Tom leaped into a ravine along the shoulder of the road—Suddenly he stared at a ski masked terrorist, hiding in the ravine outside the refinery. The terrorist raised his pistol at Tom when— Benjamin flew overhead, inadvertently crashing into him.

"Holy shit!" Benjamin cried as he saw the ski masked terrorist raise his pistol at Bronk. Tom drew his own gun, unloading two shots into the man.

"I owe you one," a pale faced Benjamin muttered.

No time for words, Tom hopped out of the ravine, darting to Candice! He saw her panicked silhouette at the fence-line--felt his body race forward-gaining momentum. She was so close now, he could see her face—it was so beautiful! Then something struck him in the back-

and the world went dark.

Twenty Five

6:01 AM (EST)
New York, NY

"**W**ake up!"

A sea of darkness enveloped Tom Grant. He had trouble focusing. His tongue felt thick. He smelled food.

His head wobbled to one side, neck muscles giving out, causing him to stare helplessly at the floor.

"Ttrraannqquuiillliizzeerrr" a voice moaned monstrously slow, like a tape recorder in slow motion, "wweeaarrss offffff."

Like swimming in a thick soup--everything had an ethereal quality. Tom felt fatigued and yet peaceful. He just wanted to sleep. But the voice wouldn't stop. He opened his eyes. He was seated next to Rabb in a limousine cruising up the FDR Expressway. He saw the towers of The World Trade Center disappear in a mass of cars and early morning commuters. Dawn's light spread its golden fingers over the cold, damp city. Then reality stung him—where was Candice!

"She's gone, vanished," continued Rabb, glancing at his watch, "you were shot with a tranquilizer. Ice Man risked his life dragging you in from the street."

"Guess I'm off the mission," smirked Tom. Nothing he'd done had helped her, had it?

"You'd be in the clink if they hadn't caught that terrorist alive outside the refinery," Rabb poured a bourbon, "you're going to do something for me. I think I know who's behind this thing," he handed him an envelope.

"What did we learn from the terrorist?" asked Grant.

"Nothing—except he's a teenager and a Caucasian—pretty badly hit in the chest. Remy will be interrogating him shortly. Open the envelope."

Tom opened it, revealing a first class Delta Airlines ticket to Atlanta.

"Because of certain things I've seen, I think the man behind this entire thing," continued Rabb, "is named Bobby Lefrete. He's actually part of an old missing person's case"

Tom's head spun. He'd just jeopardized an entire mission, was berated by the top brass and now was being sent to find a missing person? Maybe Rabb was trying to get him out of there, but why? Did he distrust him? Or was he trying to spare him by sending him out of harm's way.

"Tom, you mean a great deal to me," Rabb turned to him, eyes overflowing with feeling, glistening. For reasons he couldn't articulate, Tom felt that he might never see his mentor again. He examined this figure who was a father to him and yet at the same time, a virtual stranger he could never know, an intellect he would never fathom. Tom wanted to say things. . . one thing at least. But he couldn't. Ever the cold, studious pupil, he was silent, uncomfortable with the intimate moment.

Rabb broke the silence, "I know it's hard to believe, but once upon a time, I used to be young. In my day I did some stupid things that believe it or not equaled your escapades today. You were--" he corrected himself, "you are my finest student. Do you know why?"

"No."

"Because you're smarter than you give yourself credit. You're an agent now--badge and all," he handed him an FBI bade and his own Beretta .40 pistol.

"This won't help Candice-"

"It's much easier to think of saving one than a million. That's fine. Feed on those feelings for her, but you will serve her best by following my directions."

Tom grew hot, "This is bull-"

"I want you to find out what happened to Bobby Lefrete. The clues have been collected, the witnesses deposed, the detectives discharged, all that's required is a little bit of old fashioned deduction."

"What do I say to him when I find him?"

"When you find him, you'll know what to ask."

"This whole thing sounds like crap—like ya want to send me away, spare my life from the danger of the plant and-"

"Here's your phone," Rabb had no time for discourse, handing him a new phone, "same phone number, but it's an encrypted signal. I have someone meeting you at the airport in the frequent flyer lounge. He'll give you the necessary documents and you'll soon understand why you have to do this alone. Study the documents as best you can. If you need, I'll supply help. He'll carry the 'Hail Mary.' Understood?"

"Hail Mary," Tom repeated the password.

It would have been fitting if the car had come to a stop at the airport at that moment, but it didn't. They sat in a peculiar silence, crossing The Triboro Bridge, the morning sky still rich in darkness punctuated by the growing pastel colors of the eastern sun.

Everything was planned so neatly.

At the security check-point, Tom was cleared to carry his fire-arm. Upon producing his one day Crown Room pass, the hostess directed him to a private conference room at the rear of the frequent flier lounge. The nervous looking man sat at a table with two chairs around it. He had curly brown hair, darting eyes as he grasped his briefcase. The hostess shut the door.

"ID please," grunted the nervous man.

Tom produced the badge Rabb had given him. He looked up from it, smiling yellow teeth, "Good to meet you, Agent Grant--" he wasted no time, sitting down at the chair, setting the briefcase on the table. The case was a sleek European design with metal skin, matte black locks. There were no tags of any kind. Tom noticed that it was handcuffed to the stranger's wrist.

"As you know, we would have preferred to have done this through normal channel," the man glanced back at the door, assuring himself it was locked, "you can appreciate the peculiarity of such a meeting."

The man fished out a wrinkled document from inside his jacket. Before handing it to Tom, he rattled off a stream of words at lightning speed, "In taking possession of this brief-case, you agree to the terms of National Security Directive 84 -"

What the hell was going on, wondered Grant? As an analyst, he was quite familiar with the directive the man spouted off. NSDD 84 was set down as an addendum by President Reagan, essentially destroying personal rights at the stake of national security. After widespread public outcry, Congress voted to temporarily block the addendum. Reagan partially withdrew some language relating to lie detector tests against one's will as well as lifetime censorship, but not entirely. Agencies were allowed to fall back on an earlier 1981 Form 4193. Contradictory to the Constitution, top clearance government employees were still forced into lifetime censorship agreements, severely curtailing their rights as well as disclosure under The Freedom of Information Act.

Tom finally spoke, "I'm afraid I can't sign anything without-"

The man snickered, "By placing the case in your presence, you are already governed Form 4193. As for rules of handling, you cannot open the case in public. It can be shared with no one. You can study the case in this room or any other empty room as long as it is devoid of all cameras and all doors and exists are locked. Do you have a sidearm?"

"Yes."

"You must carry a sidearm at all times when transporting the case. The case must be sealed shut and handcuffed to your wrist during transport," he jostled his arm around, purposely exposing the handcuffs, "if you reside in a hotel, the case must be stored in the hotel safety deposit box. Only your fingerprint on the clasps will open the case—we down-loaded your FBI thumbprints. Failure to follow protocol will cause the case to detonate—"

"Detonate!" was this some sick joke?

"Since you'll be flying by air, we've modified the blast range , but suffice to say, you shouldn't have it on your lap at detonation."

"That's almost a joke," smirked Tom.

The man leaned over. Tom smelled the pungent odor of his breath as he whispered, "Let me remind you, we're talking about the worst nightmare our world has ever faced."

"Union 57?" he tested the waters.

"Union 57?" the agent was taken aback. Did he have any idea what Tom was talking about? Perhaps he was bluffing. Tom felt like Alice in Wonderland-- bouncing from one retarded nightmare to another. Exhausted and short tempered, he fired back, "Listen, I've had one hell of a day," he slammed a fist on the table, " give me the fucking case or get the hell out of here!"

The stranger stood up with a final warning, "Follow my instructions or else. We will be watching you, Agent Grant. Oh yes, we'll be watching."

Then he was alone.

Deeper and deeper I go, he mused. What awaited him behind the next curtain in this mad play? Was this really the way to help Candice or was he just moving farther away from her? Then the time for worries was over. He swallowed hard, preparing to take his magic pill, placing his thumbs flush on the clasps and opening the attaché case.

Twenty Six

Tom opened the case.

He wanted to do a thousand other things. . . wanted to rush back to the World Trade Center, to Fort Crandall wanted to help the mission. But there was no role for him anymore in that. He closed his dry, blood shot eyes. . . they burned under his eyelids. All of that work, risking his life, for nothing.

Through the half open case, he examined the laptop computer embedded inside the hard, polymer shell of the attaché. By opening the case, he turned on the computer--the screen flashing to life..

What was he doing here? None of this made sense.

The monitor flashed a subtle shade of sky blue as the unit hummed and clicked, booting up its basic programming. A moment later the logo flashed on screen. Tom pushed away from the table, hands shaking, eyes locked on the three letter acronym:

NSA

The average layman would not be shocked or surprised by the logo, but the average layman would not be well versed in the inner workings of the American intelligence community. As an analyst with CTJTF, Tom knew only enough about The National Security Administration to know that he should fear it. It was difficult to find information on the NSA. . . smatterings of articles—a handful of books published abroad. Typically, the American reporters who attempted to document the organization found that under the auspices of national security, the First Amendment lost its applicability in the shadows of the NSA.

Tom Grant's fear was not one of paranoia. He was a former government employee who believed in the United States intelligence community. Far from being a harbinger of government paranoia, he appreciated that covert operations and intelligence organizations were necessary to maintain the American way of life. Still, he couldn't help but shudder at the mere mention of The NSA.

Formed by President Truman at 12:01 PM on November 4, 1952, the organization was so cloaked in secrecy that even the date of its founding was kept secret for almost 20 years. Never could its birth be found *in The Federal Register* or Congressional Record. For all purposes, the NSA did not exist.

As an intelligence analyst, Tom learned that the NSA's genesis could be found in one, single memorandum written by Truman, addressed to Secretary of State Dean Acheson and Secretary of Defense Robert Lovett. The memorandum was marked with a classified stamp and a code word that was also classified. Despite a failed legal attempt in 1976 to bring the document to public scrutiny, this cornerstone of American intelligence was still as dark and unknown now as the day it was authored.

The NSA was headquartered inside Fort Meade, Maryland. Within the base's fenced perimeter was the town of SIGINT City, population 3500. The city looked like any normal town--had its own restaurants, gym, cinema, even a cute, town square. Yet in order to buy a house, catch a film, or take a walk on its tree lines streets, one would have to pass rigorous sets of lie detector tests, detailed background checks and positive vetting beyond any conducted in the regular intelligence community.

SIGINT City was not a town open to outsiders.

The primary purpose of the organization was to monitor communication traffic-an occupation which proceeded the formation of the NSA, reaching back to the days before World War I when government men such as Herbert Yardley intercepted Western Union telegraphs, searching for encrypted codes and messages transmitted by German spies. The NSA grew over the years, it's computers monitoring all of the most current forms of communication: cellular, voice, phone, telex, fax, wire, radio, optical, and television communication throughout the world. Whole branches of IBM were constructed merely to service the unbelievable needs of the agency!

Of course Truman anticipated the threat of such a powerful institution and in his secret memorandum prohibited NSA's from spying on domestic communication; although this line had to be stretched. Hell, Tom once read that two radio telescopes were actually constructed on the east and west coasts of the US in order to trap stray radio signals transmitted from earth, bouncing back from the moon. The only thing these radio telescopes could have intercepted would have been signals originating from American radio transmitters.

It was no wonder, thought Tom, that in 1975, Senator Frank Church gave his famous, cryptic warning of The NSA's capability which "at any time could be turned on the American people and no American would have any privacy left. There would be no place to hide. If this government ever became a tyranny, the technological capacity that the intelligence community has given the government could enable it to import total tyranny. There would be no way to fight back, because the most careful effort to combine together in resistance to the government, no matter how privately it was done, is within the reach of the government to know."

The NSA was the giant of America's intelligence gathering community. The agency's budget and overall funding was five times greater than that of the CIA, FBI, and NSC combined! Senate Intelligence Committee reports stated that the CIA accounted for less than 10% of America's foreign intelligence funding and information! The NSA employed 68,203 people--more than all of the remaining American intelligence community put together!

Yet as Harrison E. Salisbury, the Pulitzer Prize winning writer noted "If I ask my neighbor what is the country's biggest security agency, he will say the CIA or FBI. He will be wrong. The National Security Agency is the biggest, and not one American in 10,000 has ever heard its name." Within the beltway, people nervously referred to the abbreviated initials of NSA as "No Such Agency."

This was one of the many reasons why Tom Grant was nervous. Suddenly, he sensed that he'd crossed a deep line in the sand. There was no going back. But what the hell was he doing in an airport lounge with a top secret NSA computer briefing? And what did that have to do with Bobby Lefrete?

His heart raced!

The screen buzzed again, the hard drive deep within the protective, plastic case, completed its program boot. The massive acronym vanished from the screen. In its place, Tom saw three headers floating on a sky, blue sea.

CONTAMINATION   **CONTAINMENT**   **THE SUBJECT**

The computer was preprogrammed with a multimedia presentation. Tom had no ability to access the basic computing--typing at the keys had no effect. He could only move the tiny, blinking cursor on the screen with his touch-pad.

This was insane. He pressed the first section titled: CONTAINMENT. The screen went black for a second and then a file materialized. Scrolling with the touch-pad, he began to read.

<u>TOP SECRET UMBRA ALPHA WAYFARER</u>

Part 4.1 <u>(Atrophy of Hypothalamus/ Amygdala/ Limbic System/ Field Study #1)</u>

<u>Early Life</u>

Former FBI Agent Walter Willard was born in Lima Ohio on August 10, 1940. His father was a real estate lawyer, his mother, a home maker. As a student, Walter accelerated in studies, earning his high school degree by age 14. He enrolled Ohio State University in Columbus on government loans, graduating *Magna Cum Laude* in history and philosophy by the age of 18 and earned a legal degree from University of Pennsylvania, graduating with a *juris doctorate* at age 21. After graduation he was employed by the Philadelphia's District Attorney's office for 5 years as an assistant DA before joining the FBI in the Fall of 1965.

<u>FBI Career</u>

Agent Willard was assigned to the FBI's New York City office from 1966 to 1972. He was promoted as head of The Kansas City Office where he served for four more years, 1972-1976. In 1974, he married Anne Watkins Cole and fathered two children (refer to medical background sections). In November of 1977, Agent Willard was transferred to the Los Angeles branch of the FBI where he served for three years. During this time, his superiors noted that he grew restless with the Bureau.

In January, 1981, he was recruited into the Wayfarer Containment Project (CLASSIFIED UMBRA) and underwent the two months special training at Fort Meade. He served on The Watch without complications and was discharged in July, 1982. In March, 1983, Agent Willard requested early retirement from the Bureau, taking a job in the commercial sector as a criminal defense attorney with the firm of "Rosenburg, Walsh, and Baulm" in Buckhead, Georgia.

<u>Medical Background and Personal Profile</u>

During his two months of initiation and examination at Fort Meade prior to serving on The Watch, Agent Willard was characterized by psychological reviewers as "thoughtful, yet easily bored". Polygraph exams proved negative for homosexuality, incest, or major sexual disfunctions. He engaged in *coitus* with his wife an average of once a week, committed adultery only once, and occasionally masturbated.

Agent Willard was allergic to penicillin and had a minor cardiac arrhythmia. He was a cigarette smoker. After a car accident in 1978, he suffered from a limp in his right leg. As of his initiation procedure into The Watch, he was 37 years old, left handed, with 6 cavities, a height of 6"2, weighing 203 pounds, a receding hairline, blue eyes, and a tiny birthmark on his left temple just below the hair-line.

Agent Willard was atheist, but hailed from a Lutheran background. He disliked cinnamon candy and Rosemary herbs. He was addicted to cigarettes (3 packs a day) which he tried fighting. He drank beer, but shied away from hard liquor (his father had a history of alcoholism). He was an occasional handball player and enjoyed cowboy films and war movies. He admitted to occasionally reading pornography such as *Hustler*.

<u>Containment Symptoms</u>

On June 3rd, 1985, Mr. Willard left his law office at 5:14 PM. Mr. Willard had called an automatic time and weather number a total of 286 times between 9:00 AM and 5:55 PM that day.

He was spotted at "The Stop And Shop" grocery store on Highland St. between 5:20-5:30 PM. Credit card receipts indicate purchases of vegetable oil, a carton of packaged carrots, Worcestershire sauce, curry, and ketchup. A neighbor reports Mr. Willard return home between 5:35 and 5:45 PM. Mr. Willard's youngest child, Julia (age 3) was with the baby-sitter, Gloria Restmann. Mrs. Restmann departed the house between 5:45-5:50 PM, leaving the infant child alone with her father. Between 6:00 and 6:10 PM, Mrs. Anne

Willard returned home with her son, James (age 9). Subsequent third party testimony verifies that they attended the boy's baseball game at his school.

The following call was received by the Atlanta 911 operator at 6:12 that evening:

911 Call Transcript:

911 Dispatcher: 911-
Caller: My baby--he has my baby!
911 Dispatcher: I need your name, ma'am--
Caller: The dog-
911 Dispatcher: Just try and calm down. I need your name-
Caller: Mrs. Willard!
911 Dispatcher: Where do you live, Mrs. Willard?
Caller: 401 Pinwheel Drive. Help us!
911 Dispatcher: T-try and tell me in a calm manner what-
Caller: I came home——he had two pots on the stove. He boiled our dog!
911 Dispatcher: Who was boiling the dog?
Caller: He's naked——has a pistol——laughing——
911 Dispatcher: Who's with you now?
Caller: My son and I. We're in the bathroom! He's breaking down the door!
911 Dispatcher: The police are on their way. Who is he?
Caller: My husband-FBI Agent Willard——

Call Terminated-

<u>Reaction</u>

Police officers Reginald Moroder and Bud Halprin of squad car 34 arrived at 401 Pinwheel Dr. at 6:16 PM. The officers discovered the front door ajar and two pots overflowing in the kitchen. They heard screaming, called for back-up and discovered Mr. Willard naked, loading his.38 caliber revolver. Mr. Willard. His wife and son were kneeling in execution position on the floor. Mr. Willard was about to open fire The officers ordered him to stop. Mr. Willard discharged his weapon, firing four shots at the officers. Officer Moroder was killed. Officer Halprin returned fire , killing Mr. Willard–

Tom caught site of his watch. It was almost 8:30. His flight was leaving in fifteen minutes! He locked the attaché and noticed the envelope left behind by the stranger. Tom opened it. The note read:

Transportation will be waiting.
It will take you to 401 Pinwheel Drive, Bulkhead
Mrs. Willard will be expecting you.

Twenty Seven

11:04 AM (EST)
Elizabeth, NJ

Voices!

Candice Cooperman's heart skipped a beat. She heard the sound of metal and opened her eyes. She could feel the sounds of her pulse beating through her head like some massive drum. The sound struck again—clang--distant, but enough to rouse her. She touched Gummy Bear, sleeping in her lap.

They were hiding between two large compressor units in the coker area. The radiant heat from the warm tanks warmed them, drying their wet clothes. Huddled in her lap, Gummy Bear slept like a child. She looked down, noting the cell phone which she'd left on. It was dead and she'd lost the extra battery. But as painful as it was to admit, she could trust no one, not even Tom. The traitor was too close to him. "Anything?" the voice called out—much closer.

They were checking between the twisting pipes and tanks for her. She summonsed the last of her energy and stood up.

"Gummy," she nudged him, "we have to go."

Gummy screamed like a cranky baby, "Gummy don't like to-"she covered his mouth with her hand.

"Shit!" she heard a gunman scream, "it's her! It's her!"

In the far corner of the tiny area, between two snaking pipes she could see the outline of the gunman. She turned around and saw another behind her. They were everywhere! Grabbing Gummy, she negotiated around a compressor and raced along the main storage tank. She could hear her pursuers close behind. Then she came to a dead end!

"She's over here!" one of them cried, "I got her trapped!"

"What's wrong?" asked Gummy, oblivious to their impending doom.

She glanced around like a trapped animal. She wouldn't be able to escape them by climbing around the unit. They were closing in from all sides! Then she looked down, spotted the rusted, manhole cover below her feet—the entranceway to the tunnels. The tunnels, dark and cold, the mere thought sent shivers down her spine. The tunnels where they poisoned and killed Schubert's soldiers—the soldiers that had come to rescue her. More voices, getting closer. She remembered overhearing the terrorists in their conversation hours before:

"If ya ask me she went to the tunnels. Shit, we'll never find her. They say that nut killed ten men down there. Tough as nails. Nobody'll go in the tunnels."

"Gummy," she grunted, "help me move this grill!"

11:25 AM (EST)
Elizabeth, NJ / 20 ft. below the Union 57 Refinery in the drainage tunnels

Major Schubert teetered on the brink of madness.

He stood frozen in the cold darkness, staring at his wounded arm through the phosphorescent glow of his night sights. His mangled right hand had tightened into a ball, the flesh along the arm peeled apart, exposing bone and muscle. A stench filled his nose--a smell all the worse because it was his own flesh rotting.

When he first saw the wound, he keeled over, vomiting in the trickling waters of the tunnel. He was naked, laying there as if swallowed up whole and spit out, dying and cold into this subterranean world. He covered the arm up in the sand and tried to think.

The repercussions of his actions set in. He'd shot his own men—his own fucking men! One by one, execution style, he had walked amongst his team mates, placing the end of his pistol to their temples! Jesus! Jesus! Jesus! He keeled over and dry heaved, coughing air and saliva, bright green in his night-sites, onto the cold, dry sand.

Then he'd think of his pregnant wife staring at him from that porch in Norfolk and he'd turn to tears. Despite his lack of medical training, it didn't take a rocket scientist to see that his career was over. His life was over. He'd never be able to gather his own child in his arms-

Then he heard it—wet splashing foot-steps in the tunnel. His heart raced! They'd found him! Reaching over, he put the night-site on his head, and groped a hand out of the sand searching for his pistol. There wasn't enough time to even get his clothes on. Then he heard--

"Stop running and we won't kill ya!" someone cried. Were they chasing someone?

These terrorists weren't firing at him, but at the two leading the group. Were these members of his own team? Ghosts from out of the darkness? Had he only wounded some of his men? He could see two figures ahead of others in his night-sites. The thought bolted him awake—gave him hope. Schubert felt a bullet whiz by him. Still half buried in the sand and cloaked in darkness, he took aim at the group behind these two lone runners.

"Agghhh!" he heard a voice cry and he watched the smaller figure ahead of him crash into the water almost dragging down the taller one with long hair.

"Gummy!" the taller one screamed, "you have to get up!" It was a woman! She stopped. Schubert watched her lifting the little man up only to trip right over his pile of sand sitting in the tunnel.

"Oh no, Gummy," she pleaded desperately to her associate who laid on top of Schubert, "get up!"

"How ya doin!" a voice cried out of the darkness. There were five pursuers. Schubert could see the terrorists dropping their weapons, taunting the two of them. He could see one fingering a flashlight, "gonna get me some now! Hope ya like ta take turns!"

Quickly, he stuck his lame hand under her shirt, his wrist touching the base of her bra as he pressed her warm body against him. The warmth felt good. She instinctively stiffened in shock, but there wasn't time enough to think. Schubert's first shot killed the one closest to them--the .40 caliber bullet ripping the man's face apart. Before the terrorist even hit the pool of water, Schubert executed four other head shots with seamless perfection. Six seconds later, he could heard only Gummy's whimpering in the darkness of the pipe and then--

"W-w-w-who the fuck are you!" the woman pulled away in fright.

He wanted to answer, but his voice might sound so alien. He rose out of the sand, pointing the weapon at her, "Name!" he grabbed a small penlight from his utility belt, shining it at her exhausted, tear streaked face.

"What are you, fucking Arnold Schwarzenegger!" she cried, "haven't killed enough people already!"

"Name!" he cocked the hammer of his Beretta Centurion .40.

She slapped him across the face. He tried to stop her assault by blocking with his right hand. She stopped in mid swing, spotting the flesh of his arm.

"My name is Candice Cooperman. I'm a good guy!" she cried, "you're not supposed to kill me—what's wrong with your arm?"

"Who's he?" he gestured with his lame hand.

"Gummy Bear," she continued, "Are you one of Schubert's people?"

The mere mention of his name stirred feelings within him. He suppressed the emotion, "We need to leave," he trudged over to the fallen man. It took only a cursory glance to see that the little guy wasn't going to be able to walk. Schubert knew he had to kill him, letting the terrorists capture him would be inhuman.

"Gummy scared," the queer figure sucked his thumb.

The woman—Candice was staring at him. Only then did he realize he was naked. He reached over, trying get his damp clothes on his body. The wet rags sucked the warmth from him.

She asked, "What happened to you? Your arm looks like it's gonna explode."

"Burned," he grunted through the pain, "from chemicals."

"I've seen that kind of wound before—on Polcheck-"

"Y-you saw Polcheck?" he spun around.

"I saw everything they did to him. I was the one who warned Tom and the terrorists about the bastards poisoning the government team. You were one of Schubert's men. . . right?"

"I am Schubert," he grunted, "and if you're who you claim to be, then you must have a phone to communicate with the outside."

"My cell phone's dead. And you wouldn't want to speak to them anyway. There's a spy in the government ranks."

"Nothing makes sense," he grunted, examining the bodies floating all around them, "these aren't Arabs. They're Americans. I just don't get it. We're moving out," he pointed at the little man, "if he can't keep up, I'll shoot him."

"Listen you nut-case," she screamed, "I risked my life to save your ass in these tunnels. I snuck into these bastard's headquarters-"

"You were too late," Schubert fished into his pocket, snapping the handcuffs around Candice's wrist and then Gummy's, "Fine, you drag him," he grunted, "when he can't go anymore, I'll shoot the both of you."

Twenty Eight

1:03 PM (EST)
Atlanta, Georgia

Tom Grant knocked twice at the front door.

Cold air rushed across his face, stinging his dry eyes. He glanced back at the government sedan, running idle in the street as if to assure himself that there was a way out of this place. He was about to turn around when the door opened.

Her eyes were gray like the dead sky overhead, skin taut and pale, hair gathered into a tight bun. She sized him up, the skin around her eyes, creasing and stretching. Although she was alive, breathing and standing in front of him, Tom sensed he was staring at the shell of a woman.

"I'm Annie Willard. Let's make this quick," she turned around.

"As good a place to begin as any," she sighed.

She led him into the cold study. His eyes scanned the room. The walls were coated with framed photographs, awards, and accolades. A handsome wooden desk loomed in the corner, an empty gun cabinet behind it, the felt lining folded and warped with the indentations of shotguns and weapons which had once rested there.

"I'm like a circus attraction now," she sighed, "and this is my tent show—something to scare the bad FBI agents in the night."

The guns, thought Tom. They reminded him of the guns lining the walls of his father's study in a similar room with accolades and awards and-but Rabb was right—better not to think of the past.

"William was so proud to serve in the FBI," added Annie, " I met him when I was at Bryn Mawr. He joined the FBI--wanted to make a difference," she lead him over to a picture of an agent at the firing range. Again, Tom noted a young man almost his own age, "isn't that insane? William Willard at the firing range," she smiled, "an Ivy League lawyer born to run the bureau, running around at a firing range. They sent him to the New York office first—it was a stepping stone. If anything, William was overqualified. I think it was in

Kansas City that he realized he was not going to be accepted by the powers that be. He needed to do something dashing to re-ignite his career."

Tom noted a tennis racquet propped against the desk--left there a lifetime ago. A layer of fine dust covered the desk and yellowing, dog eared papers. This was Agent Willard's living shrine: the mausoleum to a man who had murdered his own child. Why?

Anne shook her head, "I don't know why he didn't just resign. I begged him a million times to do it. The money in the private sector was so much better. But not William. When he set his mind to something, he was so darned determined. Don't get me wrong, he was a perfect agent, a perfect father, a man of God until. . . "

How old was this woman? She couldn't be more than fifty, yet something in those eyes made her look so ancient-- a relic, something that should be stuffed away into mausoleum with the pictures and medals. Then the thought hit him, maybe she was?

"When he went away, everything changed," she whispered.

"Away?"

She flashed another queer look. Was this the first time someone had asked that question? She continued in a matter of fact voice, "He went to that that mysterious place," she paused, "I remember the night he told me-- said, 'Honey, I'm in something now that will put us in Georgetown next year.' I said, 'William, what are you talking about? He mentioned something about a Watch and nothing more. It'd been so many since I had seen him excited.

He left for three months to the day without a single visit. All my calls were routed through some switchboard in Maryland. My mail was sent to Fort Meade, but somehow I knew he wasn't there. When he returned, he was tan. I joked that he'd run off with a girl to the Caribbean, but I never knew where he really went."

Mrs. Willard led him out of the dark study and down a long hall, "After his six month tour, he was withdrawn. Something changed—started drinking--was restless. So he took the private sector job--moved to Buckhead--made the down-payment on this home. We were going to be a real family. No more moving. No more chasing."

She unlocked the door. Tom was shocked for a moment: it was the kitchen. . . cracked linoleum, a stained stove painted in that shade of yellow that screamed the early 1970's. A dust covered silver spoon collection was mounted on the far wall. . . spoons from Colorado, Kentucky, Idaho, New York-

"We had just r-returned home from Jimmy's ball game," Ms. Willard continued, "William's car was in the driveway. When we went inside, " she took a deep breath, "w-w-w-w-we saw the pots."

Tom remembered the 9-1-1 call.

"I ignored the pots. Can you believe that?" she smirked, "I was confused—one of those moments when you're mind refuses to make sense of the situation. I called out for the baby-sitter, but she wasn't there. William was. . . w-well, it wasn't William, Agent Grant," she said his name for the first time, "it wasn't my husband. I don't know what it was. It possessed his shape, carried the contours of his body, even had his scent, but it wasn't him," she began to shake, "h-h-h-h-he was n-n-n-naked and a gash like an x or a cross was carved into his chest. He was c-covered in--at f-f-f-first I thought it was soap? You know w-when you see something and your m-mind just can't make sense of it?

I realized he was covered in blood--blood smeared all over his body. Then Jimmy, my son, screamed. This thing raced by me, grabbing carrots and ketchup and pepper from grocery bags, tossing it into the pots. A-and when he took the lid off the first pot, I saw the dog's skinned paw. I screamed-"

Tom stiffened, trying to control his emotions.

"Thoughts raced through my mind," continued Mrs. Willard, "who was this stranger? I couldn't believe it was my husband. Then I saw him lift the thing out of the pot. It was our cocker spaniel—skinned and. . ." her hands trembled, "h-h-h-he reached--h-h-h-he reached for the other--f-for," she looked as if she were losing her breath, "he--he--"

Tom put an arm around her, a single stream of tears working down his chaffed skin, "Stop."

"I just saw her hand and knew. It was a big pot we used to cook seafood stews. That's all I saw of her, a tiny, innocent hand poking out of the pot--just h-h-her hand," tears came to her eyes, "and I grabbed Jimmy. He was terrified, frozen and I would have froze too if it hadn't been for my son."

Tom tried to control himself. He would have normally thought how unprofessional it was to weep in front of this woman, but he wasn't weeping because of Mrs. Willard. He wept because of his own memories, because of that dark place he never dared to venture towards.

She led him up a flight of stairs.

They entered the walk in closet. The shelves were empty. Her voice had a strange echo in the room, much like the conference room in the airport, thought Tom, "I fled here. He was breaking down the door when I made the 9-1-1 call. Then the door fell away and I was huddled in the corner, arms around my son.

I said--or I tried to say, 'Why are you doing this?' I kept saying it over and over and over. He tossed the knife from one hand to another, toying with us. He cut my arm, right here," she pointed at a long scar running from her forearm to her shoulder, "he just laughed and said--he said--"

"Stop," Tom shut his eyes, controlling his own emotions. These memories struck him profoundly, drawing out his own personal recollections of-

"No, I want to finish because this wasn't my husband, Agent Grant. I don't know what it was, but it was not my husband! His penis was erect and he masturbated," she said it so calmly. Yes, he thought, she didn't believe that man was her husband, " Will was a good man. Will was a kind man. Then the police arrived—gunfire and when it was all over, the creature were dead. I remember its eyes, staring up at me like a wounded dog. Died and died and died and died and died," she stared again into nothingness, "it couldn't have died enough times for me," she rubbed her hands raw as if wiping off some disarming scent.

Tom wanted to put an arm around her shoulder-- the same arm Rabb placed on his shoulder earlier that day, but he couldn't. He stood there, silent and still. The tour was over and yet he still had no idea why he was here.

"I'm trying to find a man named Bobby Lefrete," he asked, "know him?"

"Never heard that name before," she answered through a mental fog, "funny you know, I used to think he'd return. Kept his clothes packed neatly in suitcases so we could leave quickly. I don't think that anymore. I do think that his soul's trapped, fighting to return to me. He must be so alone."

Another long drawn out silence.

She led him downstairs, handing him another envelope. Another pillow for Alice to eat, thought Tom. When he reluctantly opened it, he discovered another airplane ticket. He didn't both to open it.

Then Mrs. Willard added, "After the funeral, I asked his buddies about The Watch. They turned white--told me never to mention that word again. Then the government came, lawyers threatening to sue us, saying that William defied government protocol by telling me things. It was a lie. He told me nothing more than that word. You'd think I would be the one to be consoled. I was a pariah. And they forced me into this arrangement"

"An arrangement?"

"Come now, Agent Grant," she did remember his name, "single mother, no pension. A mortgage on the house and a child who requires 24 hours psychiatric surveillance—you can figure out how I wound up doing this."

A moment passed. Tom didn't know why he said it. Hell, he didn't know why he did a lot of things he did, "He made a series of phone before it happened," he revealed, "dialed the time and weather service 288 times that day. From what they know, he never dialed it before. Do you know why?"

She looked up at him with startled eyes that contemplated points beyond him: scenes long gone, "No idea in the world," she smirked, "but in all my years, you're the first person who's ever offered anything. I appreciate that, Agent Grant."

He bid her goodbye.

He headed back to the airport.

Tom felt like he was on some Disney World guided tour. He feared he'd break down in the car, flooded with his own memories, but he was fine. He opened the briefcase in the taxicab, reading the text as it bounced and jostled in front of him. Again he traced the cursor to the CONTAMINATION icon. The screen buzzed and hummed to life. He could have continued the briefing where he left off: the police bursting into the room with Agent Willard about to attack his own wife and son, but Tom already knew the ending to that story. He began with the second section. It read as follows:

Part 2/ CONTAMINATION   TOP SECRET UMBRA ALPHA WAYFARER
Classification: THE WAYFARER 12 PROJECT (THE WATCH)

Section A: Literal Definitions

Contaminate {contaminus pp. of contaminare; akin to contagio contagion} **a** : to soil, stain, or infect by contact or association <bacteria contaminated wound> **b** : to make inferior or impure by admixture <iron contaminated with phosphorous> **c** : to make unfit for use by the introduction of unwholesome or undesirable elements—

Section B: Project Background

Agent Willard is presented as a case study and was not the first case of contamination. The first 12 patients were transported via the United States Army Hospital at Fort Polk, LA to The National Institute of Health, NIH, on December 2, 1974. The first scientific explanation of the Wayfarer 12 (later to be named The Wayfarer 12 Syndrome Program) was posed on January 12, 1974 by Dr. Ergst Smeilgloke (b. 1920–1993) of The National Institute of Health (NIH), who termed the chronic symptoms as "atrophy of amygdala and hypothalamus, severe blood clotting within the limbic system, Jacksonian seizures leading to a variety of symptoms: schizophrenia, incorrect causal responses, delusional behavior, quasi-religious enlightenment, violent and nonviolent seizures." He classified the chronic behavior as a syndrome on March 2, 1976 in his presentation to the–

What the hell was quasi-religious enlightenment? Tom expected more information about Agent Willard. These events preceded Willard's mutilations by almost ten years. He glanced up and could see the spires of downtown Atlanta silhouetted in the cold, gray sky and pressed the scroll bar, skipping past the more technical information, perusing the next section.

Section 3. Religion and Atrophy of the Amygdala, Hypothalamus, and Limbic Clotting

Dr. Smeilgloke requested a set of psychiatric evaluations to be performed on all 12 patients. Before this was possible, alarm was raised in March of 1974 (4 months after the inception of the project) when 7 of the 12 patients expired: 2 from starvation, 1 from suspected psychogenic shock, 4 from suicide. The remaining patients were restrained in private cells under 24 hour observation and force fed. On March 22nd, 1974, the decision was made by the Secretary of Defense under secret executive order NS32245 to move the Wayfarer Project from The NIH to a secure compound in The US. Army Science and Technological Center in Charlottesville, Virginia.

Psychiatric evaluations were performed by a team of four Army psychiatrists over the course of the next three months. By July 3rd, 1974, seven months from the inception of the study, the psychiatric team requested consultation with various religious leaders. The director of the program, Brigadier General Raymond Bates, resisted such unorthodox requests. However, on August 1, 1974, President Richard M. Nixon completed Top Secret Presidential Order 1004A, redirecting the Wayfarer Project to the jurisdiction of the National Security Agency (NSA).

What?

Tom's mind muddled in confusion. What was so dangerous that The Secretary of Defense and the President were tangled up in it? Why would Nixon direct a medical program to The NSA, an agency constructed to monitor communications outside the boundaries of The United States?

Army Chaplains Jerome T. Solomon (Jewish Conservative Faith) and Peter Taylor (Episcopal Faith) were assigned to the project as "outside religious consultants". No disclosure was made to these men as to how the patients had arrived at their particular physical and mental states. The chaplains were told that the patients had experienced "a loss of religion".

Religious redirection and consultation through the two Army representatives proved unsuccessful. Further attempts at communication with the remaining patients were made via hypnosis, sensory deprivation, shock treatment, and neuroleptic drugs; all proved unsuccessful.

The 11th patient of the Wayfarer 12 died on October 31st, 1975 from starvation. Shortly before the Carter Administration took office, the files of all 12 Wayfarer patients were expunged from all records. There were no visible traces of the project other than secured TOP SECRET UMBRA files stored in the Fort Meade classified archives, to show that all 12 patients were ever employed as field agents for The FBI.

FBI Agents?

Twelve Bureau agents suffering from "religious loss"—whatever the hell that was, starving themselves, hidden away in a secret lab, examined by a sundry assortment of doctors, psychiatrist, and religious leaders? Did this have anything to do with Agent Willard?

Shit. The main question still begged an answer. What the hell did this have to do with Bobby Lefrete? He pulled out his phone, dialing Rabb. The line was busy. Then he saw the airport entrance ramp and remembered the envelope Mrs. Willard had given him. He read the ticket, noting with surprise that it was on a flight to New Orleans. It was another airline ticket to New Orleans.

The aircraft was already boarding. The flight was completely empty. Tom took a row of seats in the rear, eager to open the computer again. Hell, he'd broken protocol and survived this far. He pressed his thumb against the scanners imbedded in the clasps of the attaché case and opened it--just another business traveler. He started where he'd left off.

Then he heard the woman's voice in his ear, even tempered and cold, "Don't even think about reading that brief!"

Twenty Nine

3:05 PM (EST) / 2:05 PM (CST)
In Transit to New Orleans, LA

She loomed over him, standing in the aisle.

She was tall for a woman, five foot eight with a thin, compact frame. In her late thirties with a porcelain like face and elegant, distinct features. Her black hair fell along her neckline as she extended a firm hand, speaking in a crisp, sharp voice that robbed her of any femininity, "Dr. Rebecca Brandt." He shook the hand: cold fingers locked in a firm grip. The flashback of the man in the frequent flier lounge, flashed in his mind, warning him he'd be watched.

"My credentials," she produced the wallet sized badge. Tom took a moment, studying the holographic seal of the National Security Agency emblazoned above her photo. Yes, this was the NSA police, he thought, a minor pang of fear exploding within him. She gestured for him to move to the next seat. He moved, placing the attaché against the fuselage wall and she sat down.

"Wondering if I'm here because you've opened the case in public?" her hazel colored eyes widened, "the answer is no. Rather, Agent Grant, I am here to talk you into abandoning your course of action and-"

So she needed something from him? Then perhaps she was willing to share information in order to get rid of him, he though. Hell, if she only knew that his sole wish was to hop on the next flight back to New York where the real crisis was brewing. How could any of this have anything to do with Union 57? The aircraft began its mad dash down the runway, becoming airborne, rising swiftly into the clouds.

"I don't know who you really are nor do I desire to know," she continued, "I know that you carry FBI credentials and yet your file in the FBI computers have been tampered with—your psychological evaluations are completely excised. I know that you were ordered here by others—people in very high positions. I also believe that you fail to realize the danger your superiors have placed you in."

"Come now," for some reason, he held the upper hand in the dynamics of the conversation, "I love the great unknown--just like Star Trek."

"Who sent you?" she cut to the point.

"What're you hiding?"

There was a tense moment of silence as they sized each other up like two dogs about to do battle. Tom considered blurting out Bobby Lefrete or Union 57 just to see what response it would get. Then he decided against it.

"All right," she sighed, "I'll reveal what awaits you-- even break protocol," all the rules these people created in order to deal with whatever secrets they were hiding, he mused, "you are headed towards the greatest threat ever posed against the national security of your country, your species, your world."

He had one to top her own, he mused. It hit him again! Candice! What the hell was he doing here? There was a real crisis exploding in New York!

"I can see the fear in your eyes," she continued, misconstruing his emotional make-up, "we contain this threat in a delicate balance of preventative defenses. In order to gain entry, we train our agents through two years of psychological and mental background checks and vetting," vetting was background checks and personal profile studies, "a grueling training period that makes the Marine Corp. look like the Boy Scouts. You can see how startled it is to have you coming here, a man who's psyche evaluations are missing!"

"Does this creature have a name?" pressed Tom.

She paused for a long moment as if merely mentioning the name pained her in some way, "Yves— Alexander-- Dussant."

"Nice name. . .for a creature," he tried to hide his burning curiosity.

"Mr. Dussant was the self-proclaimed leader of a religious cult."

"Didn't know the NSA took such an interest in cult leaders."

The tone of her voice, the sudden tapping of her foot, she was nervous even speaking to this individual, thought Tom. No, nervous was not the word, she was terrified, "Yves Alexander Dussant hales from one of the wealthiest families in Louisiana which trace their lineage back to the Confederate General Beauregard and the first families of New Orleans. Yves's father, Barby Dussant, was the inheritor of the family's multimillion dollar oil and land holdings. In 1953 he married Yves's mother, a New Orleans socialite, Jessica Touro. At the time of her wedding, the Dussants were the toast of New Orleans society. Jessica soon became pregnant and gave birth to Yves Alexander-- their first and only child delivered on May 5th, 1955," she rolled through dates and statistics as if she had made his study her life.

"So he's rich," smirked Tom, "there're a lot of rich zealots in the world."

She continued addressing the man by the distanced pronoun, "By its—his--second birthday, strange things began to happen. The family chose to move from their French Quarter home to the family's ancestral estate: The Wayfarer Plantation, located in central Louisiana," The Wayfarer 12, Tom recalled, "yes," she read his face, "you've made the connection. The Federal agents from the second section of your brief bear the same name."

"Were they followers of his?"

He found himself leaning over the seat, craving information, "When the family moved to Wayfarer, Yves Alexander's parents broke off all communication with the outside world. His father sold his companies to his brother via a lawyer's signature. As far as we know, after 1955, upon entering the compound, Barby Dussant and his wife never left Wayfarer again."

"Wealth breeds eccentricity."

She smirked, "That's just on the surface, Agent Grant. The next year, the Dussants relieved their staff of 20 servants and farm hands retained on the 550 acres of land. All 20 individuals committed suicide within six months of their departure from the plantation. Of course at that time, no one was looking for such patterns. So the Dussant family continued their years cut off from the outside world-- no questions were ever raised.

Then on March 12th, 1964 when Yves was only 9 years old, his father took his own life with a revolver. When the police went to collect the body, they found a run-down home in total disrepair. Mr. Dussant's corpse was so emaciated that he was barely recognizable. Mrs. Dussant and her son refused to leave the basement, speaking to officers through a locked door. The attributed cause of death for Barby Dussant was listed as myocardial infarction, heart attack, in order to avoid an inquest under the given circumstances. The Dussants always gave liberally to the political contingencies in power—silencing all questions. The next year at Mrs. Dussant's bequest, an electrified metal fence was constructed around the plantation. It was at this time that the Wayfarer Plantation became the Wayfarer Compound."

"Is that critical?" Tom really wanted to know.

"What's relevant is that everyone who came in contact with Yves Alexander Dussant suffered the same fate. Reading a list of visitors and acquaintances of Yves Alexander's is like running your fingers down an obituary column with only one cause of death: suicide."

"Are you saying that he killed his own father when he was nine years old and somehow caused all the staff to murder themselves?"

She stared off into space, "You'll understand only at the end."

"Well what more could he do? He never left the compound from what you said."

"Actually in 1970 on it's--his 19th birthday, with its mother, it chartered a private plane and traveled to Israel on a 'summer vacation' using a freshly received passport. Subsequent investigations performed in 1977 revealed that the pilots were required to stay behind an artificially constructed barricade inside the aircraft, separating them from their passengers. When they landed in Tel Aviv, the two passengers were spirited through customs and into a limousine. They drove themselves without a chauffeur."

"What did they do in Israel?"

"We do not know. A week later Mrs. Dussant was found dead under the car which had plummeted off a cliff outside of Haifa. Little is known about how it happened. But a week later, Dussant returned to Wayfarer. That was when he formed the cult. At first the members were locals from neighboring towns. He called it The Second Gnostic Church. While he presided as the self-styled leader, he engaged in various criminal activities," her voice took on an air of formality as she continued like a judge reading charges, "molested and sodomized minors—some as young as six years old-- engaged in ritualistic torture. His new religion didn't recognize prior religious bonds of marriage. Males and female followers were required to bunk in separate buildings. All that was important was servicing the wishes, needs, and desires, of their sole master. Then there's the murders."

"Murders?"

"You need to remember that this was the early seventies— Jonestown had not yet awakened America to the horrors of cults. No one knew quite what to make of the compound. The Church left the neighbors well enough alone-"

"So who'd Dussant piss off?"

She flashed a cold smile, "The governor. After a vicious fight, the Governor's wife, a noted cocaine addict, was invited by her former hairstylist and then current member to visit the compound. She went for a weekend trip and never returned. She did, however, call her husband in order to tell the Governor that she had joined the Gnostic Church and was going to father Yves Alexander's child. The next day, the Baton Rouge FBI office got involved. The case was assigned to a seasoned agent named Frank Jacobi and his partner Tom Suller."

"Dr. Brandt," interrupted Tom, "despite your entertaining story, I cannot see how a cult leader, 12 federal agents, a cocaine addicted wife, and a crazy father, despite the curiosity and shear horror of it, pose any threat to the American national security."

"The threat lies in what drew all of these individuals together," continued the Doctor, "you're not connecting the issues. Agent Jacobi telephoned and set up an appointment with Dussant for the next morning. He and his partner entered the compound and were converted as church members."

"What?"

"They called in before entering. So we know that Jacobi and Suller entered the compound at approximately 8:00 AM on May 15th, 1973. Three minutes later, at 8:03 AM they called the Baton Rouge FBI office in order to tell the local bureau chief that they were resigning and joining the Gnostic Church. Each of the men had families, they never contacted them again.

Three more agents attempted to infiltrate the compound in the two months that followed. All of them joined the cult, calmly calling into the central office with their resignations only minutes after entering the compound. By August, the issue reached the desk of the Deputy Director of Intelligence. The Deputy Director thought that it was 'brain washing'. How could he have known? Anyone who interacted with Yves Alexander died or became a mind slave. The Director put ten of his best men on it—each highly trained in resisting brain washing techniques. All followed the same fate as those before them.

By March 1974, the Wayfarer Compound hit the desk of the President of The United States, Richard M. Nixon. Nixon didn't know what to do with it any better than the Deputy Director or Agent Jacobi. Things were getting very surreal and terrifying down in Louisiana. There were more Federal Agents in the neighboring town of Blanche Fields and the woods surrounding Wayfarer than in any other FBI operation at the time. The government had to build a motel to house them all. Nixon issued the order."

"Come again?"

"Top secret National Security Directive 12444.2 authorizing a special forces team to raid the compound and apprehend Yves Alexander on the suspected criminal charges I outlined."

"Did they get him?"

"Of course."

Her words trickled like water out of a half open faucet, "When the agents arrived in the compound, it shocked even the most seasoned men. All of the followers—407 members, 47 of them children, were dead. At first they thought a lone executioner had done it, but each had passed a knife from one to the other, slitting their own throats. The children too young to perform the act were killed by their own mothers and fathers. Dussant commanded them to do this."

"If they died, then how do you know that Dussant ordered their deaths?"

"He chose to keep twelve Federal agents alive: The Wayfarer Twelve."

"Why spare them?"

"They weren't spared. He left them in a state worse than death."

"I still don't see how a man, no matter how charismatic could-"

"Your thoughts on the matter are inconsequential. We're not talking about David Koresh or your run of the mill, used car salesman cultists. We're not talking about minutes, hours, days, months, of strenuous brain washing techniques or torture conditioning."

"So what power does he hold?"

"His voice, Agent Grant, his voice. We're talking about meeting a man and hearing one single word uttered from his mouth-- losing all semblance of self, living only for his wishes, his soul desires, his commands. I'm talking about the loyalty of a janissary, the love of a son. I admit it sounds farfetched, but look at its handiwork--a father who would boil his own child-- such blinding devotion that a rational man on command would rip open his own flesh and pull out his still beating heart," her voice trembled, "that is what caused the Wayfarer 12 to lose their minds. That is what we term 'contamination.'"

"All from a voice?" he scoffed, "come on!"

She remained silent, staring out the window of the aircraft. Either her mind was someplace else or she didn't want to dignify his skepticism with a reply.

"And what is your role in this?" he inquired.

"To look after the creature while he is still alive."

"And you what--freezer tape his mouth shut every morning?"

She stiffened, "I protect the world from itself."

"But surely Yves Alexander," he made a point of stating the name again watching the minute shudder run down her spine—he would not use the distanced pronoun, "had to stand trial for his supposed crimes?"

"Yves Alexander fell under the jurisdiction of a Presidential National Security directive greater than that of the 'Powers Of War Act'. His right to trial by jury was suspended under E.O. 123333. Held due to the exigent circumstances filed in the government's secret pleading of August, 1974."

"So basically, you're holding him without trial?"

"No. The exigent circumstances still exist due to the fact that his powers continue. Thus, we're still in a moment of crisis endangering national security."

"His stay of trial is indefinite?"

She corrected him, "An indefinite stay of trial by one's peers is illegal. The crisis is simply unresolved and still exists."

Tom dismissed the point, asking, "If he's so dangerous, why not kill him?"

She remained silent. The time for answers was over. The pilot came over the intercom, announcing their initial approach into New Orleans, "Looks like we're going to New Orleans together," he grinned, "guess you didn't frighten me."

"You will be, Agent Grant" she probed deep into his eyes, "more afraid than you ever thought possible."

Thirty

"**S**crew you!" the voice howled.

Benjamin Bronk never before witnessed a torture. They were situated on the 67th floor, one level below the chattering control room filled with officers and White House staff. This floor was an absolute shell and their voices echoed off of the outer walls overlooking a fog covered New York skyline.

Benjamin's eyes gravitated to the wall opposite him. This area had once been his father's office. He focused on the secret door his father had constructed for afternoon rendezvous with his countless mistresses. Benjamin had once had this office and kept such relationships, but never used the door, feeling that it would somehow soiled him. Still he had retained it as an emergency egress—still unnoticed in the fine wood paneled wall—one of the few things not stripped out.

"Uuughhh!" the voice cried.

The kid kept trying to move, but his hands and feet were bound to the chair. Every once in a while he would jerk wildly against the restraints, revealing a profound lack of intelligence or excess of aggression, concluded the executive with a distanced intellectualism.

The prisoner had dark hair, a slim narrow face with acne blooming on boyish cheeks. He looked like he belonged at a local baseball game—not the ski masked clad pursuer in that Union 57 ravine that almost shot him in the head. Is this what they were, wondered Benjamin, an army of children?

"Fuck me?" muttered the General. He watched Remy's hand cross the boy's face a second time, knocking the prisoner's head back. They were just as much in the dark as when they began almost a day ago, the billionaire thought in a moment of sudden hopelessness. At that moment, Benjamin Bronk accepted the fact that he was going to die.

And his thoughts returned to Bhopal.

He did not visit that place in India until years after the disaster.

It was like any Indian town, thousands of starving lower cast souls, cows in the middle of the street, the smell of urine and sweat and spices brewed together and. . . the mass graves of those who died years before.

The only mark to indicate that on December 2, 1984, two storage tanks leaked their deadly cargo of methyl isocyanate between 12:30 to 2:00 AM. Nothing to indicate that by 3:00 AM the death toll had skyrocketed into thousands—too many bodies to gather, too many dying to treat. Dead men, woman, children lying next to decaying dogs, cows, cats, horses—all things equal in their finality.

Hell on Earth.

He could imagine the ghosts of the dying, fleeing from Jayaprakash Nagar and the Kazi Camp on the perimeter of the Union Carbide Plant. They laid prostrate on dirt roads and fields as the area of their brains controlling breathing, deteriorated-- like fish out of water—not deficient in the faculties for breathing, but simply unable to remember exactly how to perform the otherwise involuntary act. They rolled on their backs, bodies arched in anguish . . . dry lips pressed against dirt--the conflagrations of bodies, trying to grab hold of precious air. They wept blood, spasmed on the hard ground, tearing at their own skin in a toxicological nightmare.

How would the dead look now? The tristate area would be a pyre of corpses, one great village of the damned. Burned and dying survivors would wade knee high in bodies—mountains of the dead laying prostrate on the streets of Manhattan. The dead hanging halfway out of skyscraper windows, filling the subway tunnels as they clawed their way into the subterranean pits, trying to escape death, overtaken by the gas and—agh!

His family—his children! He felt the burning in his stomach from the bleeding ulcer. Shit. Control yourself. Mueller's out there! He'll find them. Mueller can do anything! He's done the impossible before. He promised you! Jesus, he was making no sense!

"Fuck you!" sputtered the kid.

The General slapped the prisoner again. The slap made more noise than damage -- like a rolled up newspaper to a dog. Benjamin scanned the others. To his left stood the Rabbi with a calm, unrevealing face. Bronk had trouble understanding the calm, studious man. Then there was Ice Man, just returned from their Newark trip with a black eye to show for it. And Benjamin's own mother watching the scene from a distance. How surreal—his own mother was here.

"I told you I don't know anything about what they do?" cried the kid, "I want a lawyer present!"

Well he was definitely American thought Benjamin.

"Not talking, huh?" Crandal turned to Rabb, "do you have the package?"

The Rabbi opened his thick hand, revealing the small eye dropper. The General opened it, saying, "your boss is so fond of this stuff--I had to get some."

The kid's eyes followed him now.

"It's funny you know?" drawled the General, "this nasty little critter killed a team of my best men," he paused, "good men with families and children. But what do you care about families? Hydrofluoric acid, sounds so technical, huh?"

Benjamin noticed the desperate look on the prisoner's face. Was that the look Polcheck had given his own tormentors, wondered the executive? He felt such a surge of emotion rising within him that he almost feared he might attack the bastard himself—

"I'm not saying anything," the kid muttered, "I know my rights. You can't do torture me!"

The Rabbi put on gloves and wedged the boy's head between his two strong hands. The prisoner's eyes darted around the room and tried to shake away as Remy dropped three drops into the kid's right eye.

"Ya know," jabbed the General, "this stuff eats your soft tissue. And it's going to go from your eye to the-"

"Aaiiighhhhhhh!" the kid screamed, lashing around.

"Feel it getting to the calcium in your bones, good. Just wait till it hits your brain stem. That's like the fucking fourth of July--whooyah! Now I happen to have the antidote right here."

"Aiiighhhhhhh! It hurts!" the kid shook in violent spasms. His neck extended, the tendons clear and visible, "stop it!"

"Now you're name and the name of the man running the mission?" demanded Remy.

"James Clancey! The Master runs this mission, but he only speaks through Nehemiah."

"Your home town?"

"Broken Bow, Nebraska! I met Nehemiah at a Freedom Rally there!"

Bronk could hear Ice Man stop scribbling notes on his tiny pad. Strange, they all suspected he was American, but the disclosure stabbed everyone through the heart. Why did it have to be Americans? Benjamin felt empty.

Then the kid pressed further as the General administered the antidote droplets, "We were all in the militia."

Holy shit.

They all knew of the horrors that had proceeded this crisis, thought Benjamin, were familiar with April 19th, 1995: a day of horror. It was the second anniversary of the destruction of David Koresh's Branch Davidians in Waco, Texas. It was also Patriot's Day, the day which first heard the "Shot Heard 'Round The World." Early on April 19th 1995, in an Arkansas penitentiary just prior to his execution for the murder of a pawn shop owner and an Arkansas state trooper, white supremacist Richard Wayne Snell sent his foreboding message to then Governor Jim Guy Tucker, "Look over your shoulder. Justice is coming."

At 9:00 AM in Oklahoma City, a yellow Ryder truck filled with fertilizers was parked in front of The Alfred P. Murrah Federal Building. In the structure's basement level, parents kissed their children goodbye for the day at the day care center. For most of them, thought Benjamin, it would be the last time they would ever see their children alive. Federal employees were sitting down to a long day's work--standing by the water cooler, fixing a cup of coffee, going to the bathroom. Their seemingly random locations within the building would decide if they were one of the few who would live, one of the few that would die, or one of the many who would lay crushed and bleeding to death under a mountain of twisted metal, wire, concrete, and flesh.

Because at exactly 9:03 AM, the Ryder Truck exploded, shattering the building, raining glass shards, blood, and flesh underneath tons and tons of concrete-- enough horrors to last the country a lifetime: 168 innocent people dead, 460 injured. A moment that left its defining mark on every American—each able to remember where they were, what they were doing when they first heard about the largest terrorist attack on American soil.

Yet there was more to come.

Ninety minutes after the blast that shook the world, an Oklahoma Patrol officer pulled over a 27 year old man driving without a license plate. Twenty four hours later in a stroke of sheer brilliance, the FBI connected this individual with the bombing by way of two clues: a scrap from the truck with traces of explosives and the license plate, finally tracing the rented truck back to an witness who recalled the face of the man that rented the vehicle.

His name was Timothy McVeigh.

And what followed was the unthinkable. Benjamin held back a wild combination of emotions. He could never fathom such monsters who used carnage, blood, and bone, in order to make a point, which after the dust cleared, no one really understood anyway. Innocent people dead, people who had done nothing to deserve such a misplaced sense of retribution.

Yet in the end, despite his attempts to understand, all Benjamin Bronk could really focus on were the children—the dead and mangled infants in that day care center in the basement level. For Christ's sake, they were little children! Children who had never hurt anyone. What the hell could a child do to deserve such a fate?

Tears welled in his eyes.

What the hell could a fucking child do? Jesus, he was slipping--so utterly exhausted. How many tortures must he endure! Out there, children, his children were going to die—to die like those children in Oklahoma! What madness worked itself into these terrorists—tears streaked down his eyes.

The logical side of his mind took over. The terrorists of the heartland were back—back to build upon what they had started in Oklahoma. He could feel the anger eclipsing his own silent desperation. That Federal Building was but a dress rehearsal--a prelude to the awesome destruction that would come with Union 57. There was no room for bargaining now. There was no room for discussion. How could you rationalize with an animal who could kill with such impunity, to kill children. There was only one thing to do--kill them—kill them all.

"The solution!" the kid cried, "I need more."

"Tell me more," grunted Crandal

The kid continued, "Nehemiah's a wise man. He's seen the world. Told us about all the nigg. . ." he stopped, aware of Rabb's presence, "the kikes running' all the papers and all. And the way they killed all those people at Waco. Bad times call for patriots!"

Kill them, the words burned through Benjamin.

"Is the Master communicating from a remote location with Nehemiah?"

"He uses a laptop computer to do it. They call the room the Meditation Chamber. He's really somewhere south of us in Pennsylvania—some place called Monongahela—men trained there, but not my group. Look you can't beat The Master—"

Something snapped inside Benjamin.

He lunged forward, grabbing the prisoner by the neck, squeezing deep into the flesh of his throat. He struck the boy so hard that blood and teeth splintered onto the floor. He'd never even hit another man before—had lacked the drive to attack that soldier in the ditch—when Tom Grant saved his life. His battles were waged with the distance of a conference table or the well-choreographed assaults of teams of lawyers. Yet despite all of this, he pulled his arm back. His next move would kill this boy and that was exactly what he wanted!

They were going to kill his children! Then he felt the pain in his shoulder, "Not here. Not now," Rabb grabbed his arms—Benjamin felt his iron grip.

An ecstatic Remy collected the group, moving them to the far corner—away from the prisoner. Benjamin looked away, embarrassed by his show of emotion, but no less sure of his conviction of killing these mad men.

"How did you get that hydrofluoric acid?" asked Eleanor.

"Ivory liquid soap," Rabb smiled.

The General grasped the small dropper, squeezing it into his mouth, "The antidote was tap water. Well Mr. Bronk," he turned to the executive, "now I know what has been lacking on our offensive. Should have juss sent you to reclaim your plant-- sure you would've done a damn good job."

Benjamin was too drained to respond with any witticism.

"Gentleman," the gears of General Crandal's mind spun, "I will issue this report to the President in ten minutes. We're going to Pennsylvania to kill this bastard."

"How do you intend on neutralizing the refinery?" asked Rabb.

"Simultaneous attack--"

"It could take mere seconds to fire their explosives," scoffed Rabb, "you've got no time."

"Well," Crandal screwed his eyes up, "I'm sure you got an idea up ya' sleeve."

"How about a strategic nuclear mortar shell?" suggested Rabb.

"A nuclear bomb!" gasped Benjamin.

"It destroys all organic life," added Rabb for all to hear, "concentrating radiation rupturing virtually every cell in an organism's body while having no effect on inorganic matter—buildings, roads—"

"Great idea! Kill the pricks, keep the Porsches," interjected the General.

"I thought such bombs were outlawed?" interrupted Benjamin, resistant to the idea.

"Any subscriber to the Cato Institute knows the military's been secretly building and researching them for decades," Rabb turned to Remy, "The Carter Administration considered the mortar bomb's use in tank skirmishes, essentially you limit the tritium gas, utilize a Beryllium lining with U-238--well," he simplified his explanation, "you create a bomb with a very tight explosion ring."

"How tight?" asked Benjamin.

"Three yards—a hundred yards—a mile--any range," Rabb continued, "Carter's proposed bomb had a blast zone which was the width and breadth of a tank. Anything outside that range would be totally unaffected. The weapon detonates ten yards above the vehicle and rather than exploding, it implodes, raining massive radiation on the tank personnel, instantly vaporizing all organic matter," another thought hit Rabb, "ya know we'll also pick up EMP."

"Not another government organization!" muttered Eleanor.

Rabb explained "Nuclear bombs release an electromagnetic pulse--EMP. The pulse is a magnetic field which ruptures electric lines, wires --anything electrically based. That's why Carter's plan was fallacious, you can't drive the tanks away. The bomb would fry the electrical systems such as refinery equipment and in our case, the bomb wires and batteries powering those generators-"

"What if the bombs are EMP shielded?" asked Benjamin.

The Rabbi nodded his head, "EMP shielding's not easy or foolproof. They would practically need a government lab to do it. Unless they were actually using bombs from our own government storehouses, they would never have the resources to do it."

"It's our best shot," muttered Remy, "we'll set it somewhere along Bronk Blvd, that named after you?" he asked Benjamin.

"No," only his father was vain enough for that.

"We'll find some abandoned apartment—few blocks away—and fire it from there. So let's go for it. We're gonna kick ass in two states."

4:38 PM (EST)
Elizabeth, NJ / 20 ft. below the Union 57 Refinery in the drainage tunnels

"Uuughhhh."

Major Schubert's screams and moans awoke Candice Cooperman from her dreamless sleep. Flipping on her flashlight, she examined the cold, sweaty walls of the underground tunnel. It smelled bitter here--mildew and sweat.

"Uuughhh," the moaning continued.

She shifted the beam along Schubert's lean frame as he rocked back and forth, murmuring in a feverish sweat. She took a moment studying his arm. . . festering and burned from chemicals. . . muscles wrapped feebly around bone scabby blisters. The limb was infected. The nightmares he languished in were not just dreams, but the product of the fever coating him in sweat.

"No—no—" the soldier moaned like a child.

She flashed the light around at Gummy Bear, twisted red hair framing his tiny, plump face. She faintly remembered reaching this portion of the tunnel where the water was a tiny snake of a stream. She collapsed, rolling over on the freezing pipe floor, instantly falling into a dreamless sleep.

She looked admiringly at Schubert. Around him, she felt as if she could brave whatever challenges awaited. But soon he would be too sick to move. She eyed his pistol, knowing that the time would come when she would have to kill him rather than let him fall into the demented grasp of Nehemiah. Then she would kill herself.

Funny, she thought, that the sight of the superintendent's murder had caused her such grief. That was common-place now. Now such images endowed her with a sense of pleasure. How could she ever explain this sensation to anyone else except by saying that the screaming in her head had finally stopped.

"No. . . no. . . "Schubert tossed his head back and forth.

She put a calming hand on his steaming forehead, cringing at the feverish heat, "You were having a nightmare. Your arm's infected."

"I'm gonna die," the way he said it surprised her. Not fearful apprehension, but a cold acceptance of fact, "I have something to tell you," he whispered in her ear, "we set explosives all over. I have the detonator switch."

"Like the TNT boxes you push down with the handle?"

"I ain't The Roadrunner and Coyote," he instructed her how to use the watch before he had her put it on her arm. Then he turned away from her, mumbling, "I have a son who'll be born in a week," he stared into darkness and so much more, "my head's burning up. I'm not going to live through this fever."

Then a vision hit her—back when she was with Lou in Larry's office:

Larry stumbled over to a large metal medicine cabinet mounted on the far wall, fishing out a packet of antacid pills, "I told you everything I know."

The medicine cabinet was large. . . one of those big ones chocked full of emergency equipment for plant accidents with instructions so that any layman could find the right medicines. Surely she could find what Schubert required! Of course the cabinet was in The Meditation Chamber, the very heart of these terrorists' operation. She wondered if she could really do it?

She looked down, Schubert was wearing one of the terrorist military parkas. She reached into the zippered pocket finding a ski mask tucked inside. Was she afraid? Maybe? Death had become so commonplace in this dark netherworld, thought Candice. It was like breathing or peeing or sleeping—something one took for granted. She wasn't afraid of dying and would kill herself rather than be tortured like Polcheck.

Turning to Gummy Bear, she knew what she had to do. She handcuffed the sleeping, bleeding man to Schubert so that he couldn't wander after her if he awoke. Then she collected Schubert's jacket, giving him her own. She held his pistol in her hand—it was heavier than she imagined. Then his voice echoed in her head: something he'd said to her earlier that day.

"Ya know, those sentiments of yours are a luxury. Give it a little time and you'll think differently."

"If I ever feel like you," she grunted, "I hope somebody shoots me."

She was changing. It was time to visit Nehemiah.

Thirty One

The rain came down in sheets.

Tom examined the gaudy yellow facade of the townhouse—the Caribbean green shudders, noting the crest mounted on the upper cornice: a picture of a unicorn with three stars beneath it. Dr. Brandt led him through a musty basement with biohazard containers up to a second floor hallway. There she asked for his weapons and cell phone. He gave them to her and they entered a compact room with a chair and table facing a rectangular sheet of steel about five feet high, running half the length of the wall. The door shut behind him. He noted two cameras mounted in opposite corners of the room: aimed at him.

She lifted a small remote control from the chair, "There are two buttons on your remote. The first will activate the speaker system and open the blast shield," she pointed at the steel plate covering half the wall, "allowing you to converse with it. If there are any problems, press the panic button, "it was an oversized red button with an exclamation point on it, "that will shut sever all communication?"

"Alright."

"When the metal plate is raised," continued the voice, "you'll see an observation window through which you will be able to view the inner rooms. We call these rooms 'The Suite'. Below the window you'll see something that will look like a bank teller's exchange box. It allows you to transfer items into The Suite. All items, however, are X-rayed and studied before the creature can access any materials from its side. This system allows for absolutely no interchange of air, sound, etc. any of which would lead to immediate contamination. Do you understand the protocol?"

"What's the door for?" asked Tom, noticing a large metal door embedded in the left corner of the cubicle.

"The entrance to the air-lock. You won't have to use that," she retreated to the door, "you're alone from here on in. Last chance to turn around."

Tom remained silent. She shut the door behind her.

Tom sat there for a long moment.

He ruminated upon the fact that he was inside a maximum security, metal reinforced room, being videotaped and recorded. Jesus, they really did take this crap seriously! For a moment he actually entertained the thought that he might be speaking to the modern day messenger of God.

Tom Grant was a modern man of reason with highly skeptical views on religion, the birth of which lay in rumors, exaggeration--delusions of crazed schizophrenics who entertained visions and conversed with hallucinations. Tom Grant's age was a time when all things could be studied, scrutinized, categorized, and explained--when the mysticism of the world could be reduced to basic scientific principles. Then the thought struck him: could science be equally as dogmatic as religion? If science could not reduce through deductive reasoning, experimentation, and analysis, did it simply cast the anomaly into such a prison as this one?

For just one moment, Tom shuddered. Then he thought how foolish he was--he was here to speak to a mad man. He wondered what this cult leader would look like? Inevitably his thoughts returned to the stereotyped image of a tent show healer with homicidal tendencies. He laughed at his own nervous apprehensions. And with that thought, he pressed the button-

and Fred Astaire began to sing.

Or rather Tom caught Fred Astaire in the middle of singing.

The speakers activated first--as the partition began to rise upward, opening the view of the window. The song, Tom realized, was "Dancing Cheek to Cheek, at an obnoxiously high volume causing the speakers in his room to rattle. At first Tom saw Persian rugs and then elegantly appointed furniture pieces, all of them facing opposite the glass window. The room was painted in deep, lacquered shades of red. A burgundy leather chair rested in the center of the room cluttered in high Victorian style. With the bare, white cubicle around him, Tom felt as if he were peering onto a movie set.

Fred Astaire continued crooning...

Suddenly, Tom saw a pale, white hand protruding from the right side of the winged chair. Thin, elegant fingers crept along a small wooden side-table until the hand wrapped around the long stem of a crystal glass. Instantly, the hand and glass disappeared from Tom's view.

"Hello?" he asked. The music in the room overpowered his voice.

A moment later the hand returned the glass to its resting place. Tom noticed the old phonograph sitting on a table on the opposite side of the chair. The record spun around and around. Tom continued to hear the blaring music.

"Hello!" Tom cried loudly.

From out of the side of the chair protruded a waggling finger slowly waving back and forth as if to reprimand him for screaming at the top of his lungs. All the while the music continued at the incredibly high pitch.

"Look, I can leave if you want!" Tom yelled, standing up.

Another pale hand reached over the left side of the chair, fiddling with an ancient record-player propped on the floor. The volume decreased.

"Now," the voice drawled like syrup through the speaker system, "didn't your momma teach ya' not to scream in someone else's home?"

"She also said it was rude for a host to ignore his guest," countered Tom.

He heard the voice on the other end laugh, "That's actually the first attempt at humor I've heard in quite a long while."

"Is that Fred Astaire?"

"Yes," the smooth voice flowed like velvet.

"You like it?"

"Actually, I hate it," he replied, "but it pisses off the guards. Last week we heard the complete collection of Bing Crosby. Ever heard Bing Crosby? Sounds like a dog who got his dick caught in a door."

Tom laughed, "I'd agree with that."

The edge of a face poked out from around the chair. Tom caught a brief glimpse of pale white skin and willowy blond hair, "Is that coffee you're drinking?" the voice inquired.

"Yes," he replied, "want some?"

"My!" the edge of the visage poked a little further out from around the chair. Tom could now see a thin, straight nose, "a joke and a gift all in one day. I should definitely mark this as turning point in my diary," his drawl morphing the last word into 'dowry', "and to whom do I owe this illustrious honor?"

"My name is Tom Grant."

"I suppose I'm being the rude one now."

And with that, Yves Alexander Dussant stood up, turning the chair ever so gracefully around in order to examine his guest. He looked exactly the opposite of Tom's preconceived notions and exactly as his voice might suggest. . . tall and lean with a chiseled, aristocratic face. . . blond hair and sparkling blue eyes like two pools of glistening water, thought Tom. His body carried a feminine touch that lent him an austere grace. Clad in seersucker pants and a loose fitting white oxford, he looked like a Southern gentleman lounging around on some lazy Sunday afternoon.

A warm and inviting smile passed across his face, "My name is Yves Alexander Dussant."

Having turned the reading chair around, he sat down ever so slowly. Sitting cross legged in the chair, Dussant was separated from Tom by no more than two feet and a pane of the thickest glass Tom had ever seen. Through this partition, Tom studied the book laying open in Dussant's lap: The Collected Works of Percy Shelley.

Under this man's guise, Tom suddenly felt disheveled-- a worn hockey shirt and pants stained from his fall that morning at the refinery.

"Do you like Shelley?" asked Tom.

"Yes," the prisoner sighed, "Shelley teaches me what it's like to really live—to be free. He understands the pathetic transience of man. . . bloomin' and dyin' like flower for a day, all the while concerned with his own bloated sense of self-importance."

"When you're a mayfly living but for a day, seconds seem like eternity."

"Indeed, everything's relative."

"So I take it you've been reading *Ozymandias*."

"My my," Dussant clapped his hands, "I'm impressed."

"There are some questions I need to ask you," Tom got down to business.

"That coffee still looks great," drawled Dussant.

Remembering his previous offer, Tom slid the cup into the exchange box. The box lit up for a moment as the coffee was scanned a thousand different ways. On the other end, Dussant picked the cup up, savoring the rising steam for a moment before taking a sip.

"Ah," he sighed, his eyes still closed as he savored the moment, "can't beat the taste of X-Ray's—has a slight glow in the dark aroma to it," he grinned, "we could sell it as brew a' la Three Mile Island."

"You don't get much coffee, do you?" smirked Tom.

"I get K-rations. My, you look a bit shocked. Was it something I said?"

"You must admit, it's a bit difficult to think that I'm here drinking coffee with a self-proclaimed Messiah."

"Self-proclaimed? I believe the NSA's given me their seal of authenticity. Look at you, interrogated and locked into your own room just to speak to little old me. Somebody muss think I'm important," he raised a mocking brow.

"They think you're dangerous. From what I've read, everybody who's come in contact with you proves that point."

"Bah," Dussant threw up his hand with a grin, "don't be so apprehensive. You gave me coffee. You're my part'na!"

"Thanks. . . I guess."

"They're speaking badly of me again, huh? Telling you all those nasty little lies over and over and over."

Tom broke out of his spell of pleasant conversation, "I guess we ought to get down to business."

"Where are you in such a rush to go?" Dussant's blue eyes sparkled, "let's get back the topic of coffee."

"I didn't know Messiah's loved coffee so much."

"Hah!" Dussant drawled, "messengers of God have always been known for their culinary tastes. Christ, you know, never passed up a good meal."

"Never thought about it."

"What did Christ do right before he knew he was going to leave y'all for good? Had a big supper! Everythin' with him revolv'd 'roun' gettin' a good meal—wine out of water and all that stuff."

Tom laughed. He felt so comfortable talking to Dussant. It was almost as if this stranger were an old friend—an acquaintance of many years. Could it be true, he wondered, had this seemingly congenial man slaughtered all of those people?

"I saw that," Dussant's eyes flashed.

Fear struck him. Instinctively, Tom pulled away—distancing himself. This was the man who had murdered and entire compound of his own followers! This was the man who consigned 12 Federal Agents to a place worse than hell—men like Agent Willard, "We're getting a bit too metaphysical for me."

"On the contrary, the conversation was just starting to peak my interest. We were arriving at the politics   of   religion."

"I didn't know religion had politics other than Vatican inner dealings, Borgia popes murdering half the Vatican City and fathering the other half."

"My!" Dussant's eyes lit up, "you're are an interesting one. I took you for one of the regular NSA morons."

"That's OK. I had my own ideas about cult leaders-"

"Cult leader! I've never been a cult leader!" Dussant feigned indignation with a sudden grin, "cult leaders are grimy used car sales men preaching hell-fire, brimstone, and EST."

"So you have no qualms about the government locking up mad men?"

"Mad men? Of course not. What I protest to is the genuine article's confused with the charlatan."

"Sort of hard to distinguish. The asylums are stocked with a lot of them."

"Yes, but how many are locked up in top secret government facilities?" Dussant spread his arms, "but no, you really don't believe I'm God incarnate?"

"I believe that you believe you're God incarnate."

"What a circuitous, roundabout, piece of bull-shit that was," Dussant threw up his hands, "quite to the point of never gettin' 'roun' to a point. That sentence really marks our time, doesn't it? A time when anyone can believe whatever they want and no one infringes on anyone else's beliefs. Tolerance has become so commonplace its dogma-- everyone quits worrying about the truth."

"Mr. Dussant-"

"Call me Yves Alexander, we're friends now."

"Yves Alexander, you're wasting your breath. I'm not a religious man."

"In a plane crash, you might change your mind."

"I'd just be hedging my bets. I've no faith in God or the tooth fairy."

"Don't pick on the tooth-fairy. She's a very old friend."

"Look, it's pretty clear you don't get many visitors. But I don't have time to for idle conversation."

"Don't underestimate the power of the word," the way Dussant said it—almost as if his words had an unspoken significance, "do you know how the world was created, Agent Grant or Tom if I may call you so?"

"You mean in the Bible?"

"Yes, in the Bible?"

"Just—well, He just made it. Took Him a week, I think."

"No," corrected Dussant, "God didn't make it. God said it. You need to understand one of the basic tenets of Judeo-Christian thought. It was the Jews who documented all that stuff in the Old Testament. To a Jew, the act of God saying somethin', creating a word, was an action in and of itself-"

"I've lost you there."

"In the Jewish religion, a word from God is literally a unit of energy. A Word from God doesn't say a thing, a Word makes a thing happen! And thus, the world began when 'God said let there be light' and there was light. Then 'God said let there be light in the firmament of heaven' then God said 'Let the waters abound with blah blah blah" and then God said "let the earth bring back blah blah—God was very hoarse on the seventh day. That's why he rested."

"I never really thought about it that way," replied Tom, "but I'm not a big reader of the Old Testament."

"Well in the New Testament-"

"Missed that one too."

"When John wrote the fourth gospel of Christ," continued Dussant, "he used the Greek term, *logos*, which means The Word. He said Jesus was the *logos* of God—the Word of God. John was trying to convey to future generations the same point-"

"You're saying Jesus had the same ability that you have? That he brain-washed and contaminated his disciples and followers?"

"An ignorant description of a state of being which can only be appreciated by someone experiencing it," interjected Dussant, Tom could imagine the man sitting around a bottle of cognac, pontificating intellectually as only a well-educated, gentile, Southern gentleman could, "this is not contamination. It is blissful enlightenment, undying loyalty and-"

"I guess you Messiahs have to be very careful what you say. I mean if you tell someone to go take a flying fuck-"

"Very messy indeed," he was not joking.

"So you're just like Christ?"

"If you're a Christian, I am. If you're of other faiths, I carry other names. I am The Word and the Word carries to all religions. I am the *logos*," Dussant stiffened. But still he didn't seem filled with self-importance, "I am the messenger. But now a days nobody seems to want to listen. My message conflicts with beliefs of the day. Now if someone doesn't like a message from God, if it challenges the beliefs of this age, then the messenger is silenced."

"So what's your message?"

"I'm afraid you'd have to be on this side of the glass to hear that."

" If you're words are so powerful, why don't you just say you're way out of this prison?"

Dussant's eyes widened, "My power is only over the soul, Agent Grant."

"Is that how you killed all those people?"

A long pause. Tom had definitely insulted the man, "Do you really think I would murder my own followers? Do you think I slaughtered that entire town of Blanche Fields-"

"Blanche Fields?"

Dussant paused for a long moment, "You're not NSA—are you?" he was silent for a moment, "you don't know about Blanche Fields. Who sent you?"

"The Rabbi."

Dussant's eyes opened, wide and confused "The Rabbi," he whispered to himself, tossing the name back and forth across his tongue in whispers.

"He sent me to ask about the whereabouts of Bobby Lefrete."

Something connected inside Dussant's mind. He stiffened in his chair, erupting in uproarious laughter--his face red, eyes tearing. Tom was confused.

"Well how is the old son of a bitch, Rabbi?" Yves Alexander slapped his knee, "thought he'd be dead by now," he dried his eyes, "a pity," he continued chuckling, noting his aging hands, "we have all gotten old, haven't we?"

"You don't like the Rabbi, I take it?"

Dussant looked down at his hands, "He put me here,"

The Rabbi captured him? Tom's mind raced. He'd never read anything about Rabb's involvement in the case. Then he remembered The White House meeting—Giardino's aid—Toblongee had asked Rabb if he was still involved in cults. Rabb had quickly shrugged the question off.

"So he sent you to ask me where Bobby Lefrete was?" asked Dussant.

"What's so funny about that?" replied Tom, "just tell me where he is."

"The more appropriate question," continued Dussant, "would be: who is Bobby Lefrete?"

"I don't understand. Look, I don't know about your history with all this. I'm just an analyst-"

"An analyst," he stopped laughing, "what do you analyze?"

"I author briefs."

"Why not books?" pressed Dussant.

"I've never had much to write about," he returned to matters at hand, "what about Bobby Lefrete?"

"I watched Bobby Lefrete slaughter over three hundred men, women, and children. He's a psychopath. What do you like to write?"

"What?"

"To write? What do you enjoy writing?"

"Can we get back to-"

"Please answer the question."

"Hypothetical test scenarios. Fictitious stories based on plausible situations. So you knew Bobby Lefrete?"

"Did you ever work with codes?" asked Dussant, "codes like in those spy thrillers with lots of numbers and hidden meanings?"

"Yes. Sometimes. Please stay on the subject. What happened to Lefrete?"

"Probably working with militant white supremacists—they were always his favorite."

Could Bobby Lefrete be the Master that Candice had spoken of? Was he the puppeteer holding Nehemiah's strings?

"I knew Bobby Lefrete very well," Yves Alexander raised his brow, "and I could tell you how to catch him. That's obviously why Rabb sent you here."

Tom leaned forward with intense curiosity, "How?"

Dussant glanced around from side to side as if to make sure no one was listening—which was quite ludicrous since everything down to his heart beat was recorded inside the room, "Get me something to drink first."

"What?"

"It's been twenty three years since I had a decent drink, Agent Grant. You have the security clearance to bend the rules, get me some food and some-"

"I'm not a grocery clerk."

"Think of it as a sacrifice to your Messiah. Do you think the Jews just followed Moses around in the desert for 40 years based on Moses' speaking skills and good looks? They stayed because of the manna, very tasty stuff dropping out of the sky three times a day like clockwork. Then again," he sighed to himself, "maybe it wasn't such a sacrifice? I mean Jews love food. Ya' ever see Jews at a buffet? Just like vultures."

"What the hell are you talking about?" scoffed Tom.

"Sacrifice is what we're talkin' 'bout. Don't worry, you don't have to deliver me a virgin—which isn't that easy to come by these days. Just bring me morsels of food and drink and I'll give you precious morsels of information. All the information I have given you so far is in repayment for this tiny cup of coffee," he held up the empty cup, "for our next sacrifice, let's start simple fetch me a bottle of *Pichon-Longueville-Lalande* from *Pauillac*—a good vintage like '70 would be excellent. I've been dying for decent wine."

"Wait a minute, how do-"

"You better hurry Agent Grant—remember Bobby Lefrete's out there, runnin' 'round, doin' bad things. Reminds me of the bible—Revelations, Chapter One, Verse seven, 'Behold He is coming with clouds, and all the tribes of the earth will mourn because of Him. Even so, amen,'" He leaned over with an ominous look, "I can think of some pretty bad clouds."

"What?"

The metal blast shield dropped over the window.

Tom tried to open the blast shield again, but Dussant must have been able to lock it from the inside. Grant left the room, collecting his weapon downstairs and heading out the door. Once outside, he caught a cab to a hotel he was familiar with--The Westin.

The lobby of The Westin was situated high up in a towering skyscraper, affording it a sweeping view of the bend of The Mississippi River. After checking in, he made a direct line for the concierge and from their wine cellar, purchased the bottle of wine Yves Alexander requested.

His mind was a mishmash of anxiety, panic, and confusion. He almost fell asleep on the elevator ride up to his room. Locating the room, he used the keycard and stepped inside. He smelled the cigarette smoke. At first he thought he was in the wrong room. The drapes were drawn. He feared someone might be waiting for him, but how could they? He'd just checked in with no advanced reservation. Then he heard the voice say ominously:

"I have a pistol pointed at your head, shut the door and step inside."

Thirty Two

5:59 PM (EST) / 4:59 PM (CST)
New Orleans, LA

"Don't touch the lights," the voice commanded.

The door closed behind Tom. His right hand was already wrapped around his pistol--the clip was engaged. He spotted the cigarette burning an orange dot in the darkness.

"My eyes have already adjusted," continued the stranger, "quit feeling up that pistol--liable to shoot your pecker off."

A thousand thoughts danced through Tom's mind.

"If I wanted to kill you, you'd be dead already," the stranger remarked as if there was no need for suspicion.

Tom remained silent. After all the twists and turns this day had taken, he knew better than to trust anyone, "I don't like surprises-"

"Just take your hands out of your pockets, that's all I ask."

Tom thought for a moment—the stranger did have the advantage. He'd be dead before he could act. He crossed both arms in front of him.

"Good boy," the stranger sighed as a lamp switched on.

He was in his mid-fifties, guessed Tom, with curly gray hair that receded back over the top of his head—a wrinkled and red brow. Sporting a plaid shirt and tan plants and seated comfortably in the chair, he looked like an Irish man with a glass of beer resting in one hand, a gun in the other, "Your minibar sucks," he took a sip of the half-filled glass.

The glass was almost empty-- he had been here awhile, thought Tom, and how did he know which room was going to be checking into.

The man asked him to toss his gun onto the bed. Under the guise of the gun pointed at his head, Tom complied.

"I don't want you to cringe or do something stupid," the stranger leaned forward, "I am tossing my own pistol onto the bed--strictly an act of contrition aimed at securing your confidence so you'll quit pissin in your pants and listen," he tossed it onto the bed. Tom's noted the weapon: a Smith and Wesson .38—standard issue for government agents, "now I'm disarmed," the stranger extinguished his cigarette in the empty glass, "sorry, a hard habit to beat."

"How did you know I was in this room?"

"I was sent here by the Rabbi, of course," he continued, snuffing out the cigarette.

"Or you might be with the NSA?"

The stranger froze for a moment before looking up, "Listen Sherlock Holmes, I have a password for you: Hail Mary."

Tom's stance relaxed—this was the real thing, his hand fell back along his side, "Do you have a name. . . Mr. Help?"

"Mr. Help," he reflected, "rather like that. . . has a nice ring to it."

"What's so important Rabb sent you all the way down here?"

"What makes you think I had to travel far?" the smoke from the dead cigarette curled and twisted between the two of them. The room stank of stale cigarettes, "you met Dr. Brandt?"

"On the plane flight over."

"Beautiful, but cold as ice. She have anything to say about the creature?"

"If 'it' means Yves Dussant, then yes. She attempted to persuade me from my visit," again these vague references to the prisoner, reflected Tom.

Mr. Help's eyes lit up, "Most unexpected. By now you've certainly moved beyond important, Agent Grant," he lit another cigarette, "lucky I arrived when I did. Dr. Brandt, when she chooses, will eliminate you. The fact that she took time out of her schedule to meet you on a plane only reinforces that point."

"Eliminate me? How would she do that? She's scared of me--thinks I'm here on some official Washington investigation-"

"It will happen like this," he blew smoke rings into the air, watching them rise towards the ceiling, "they will come for you--claim you're contaminated. And before you can reply, you're drugged, strapped to some gurney in the basement of the NIH or Sigint City medical lab, drooling into the next millennium."

"I never took Dr. Brandt for a murderer."

"Agent Grant," he turned away from the smoke rings, "I never said anything about murder. Drugged prisoners don't die, they just drool away. Hell," he pressed his thumb against his index finger, "you're this far from being another cautionary tale for FBI agents who stick their necks out too far."

"That's why you're here—to protect me?"

He tapped the ash on the table, I'm here because the Rabbi asked me and Rabb and I go back a long long way. I am here to educate you," Tom noted the razor sharp eyes behind that jolly, face. Yes, wondered Tom, how many men have you killed? There are no innocents amongst Yves Alexander Dussant.

"By now you've spoken to it?" he asked. "Yes."

"Can't believe a single word it says."

"Why?

"It may come off as a soft spoken Southern gentleman right off the plantation, slaves picking cotton and all that shit, but let me tell you, that creature is as evil and dangerous as they come."

Doesn't leave a lot of room for Bobby Lefrete, thought Tom.

"Anything he tells you must be scrutinized and guarded," cautioned Mr. Help.

"He didn't seem threatening at all-"

"He's locked away at the cost of countless good men going insane, killing their families--horrible, insane, acts!"

There was a cold moment of silence. Mr. Help took such things personally, thought Tom, he must have worked on the program.

"I read the brief," replied Tom, "but I have to admit, he's locked in the tightest prison, but Dussant knows things that he could never know-"

"This ain't Psychic Friend's Network."

"Then what is it? A man who's voice can control your mind? How do you explain that?"

"The medical team suspects many causes. For a while they thought it was a chemical enzyme—a pheromone—which might emit an odor that caused some primitive reaction in the primal center of your brain—just an enzymatic thing."

"You makin' this shit up as you go?"

He huffed indignantly, "In the postmortem autopsy's each of the agents exhibited the same medical symptoms—the hippocampus and amygdala were—oh never mind, we're not here to talk about that now. This creature is a very dangerous thing—a con-man—a mutant—a master manipulator, a liar, but definitely not the next coming of Christ."

"You all need to make up your mind. One minute he's an inhuman creature and the next he's just a con man with a special enzyme in his sweat. All this fence sitting is awfully confusing."

"He's just dangerous—is that good enough?"

"I have a question for you," replied Tom, "Rabb sent me here to ask Dussant about the whereabouts of someone," he made it a point to call the "it" by his real name and felt a certain degree of power in the action, "I think Dussant knows where this person is. Now tell me why Rabb didn't come here himself?"

"Think about that brief you read. It spoke of the Wayfarer Twelve--said they were all deceased. If you're careful as I am and count the patients' names, you'll realize that the fate of the twelfth member is never mentioned."

"Rabb?" Tom was thunderstruck, "the Rabbi was one of the Wayfarer Twelve?"

"Rabb spent nine years locked up at The NIH like a damned," Mr. Help suddenly became emotional., his hands shaking, face red. He took a moment to calm down, "let's just say that your good old Southern gentleman did some very bad things to our friend, The Rabbi. Turned a grown, rational, kind man into a stark raving lunatic. He is the only one to date who has been able to recover from the Wayfarer Syndrome."

"What exactly happened?"

"I'd have to take you to Wayfarer to see that," he smiled.

"You're dancing around the point."

"I like to dance and there are so many points to cover."

"Tell me why the government never killed him? If he's so dangerous why didn't they just blow its head off?"

"That creature is a dangerous weapon and the United States government would like to know just how to harness that energy—to put it to their own use. But even that power eludes them after all these years. And Dr. Brandt fears they might cut the program--"

"But Dussant knows things that he could never know—"

"Listen to yourself!" Mr. Help scoffed, "that bastard's been locked in the tightest prison in the world! When he farts there's a medical team bottling it. His feces is under tighter security than half the prisoners in the country! It's guards are the cream of the crop, watched 24 hours a day by third party medical teams. How could it ever be involved in anything outside of the suite."

"I don't know? Maybe he contaminated someone on the inside?"

"C'mon. Do you think if he were contaminated he'd stay there," Mr. Help stood up, walking to the door. Tom noticed a slight limp in his gate—perhaps a cause for early retirement? "every visit you make with it, you risk your life. If you don't believe how dangerous it is, ask it about the little jaunt to Israel with its mother—ask him what he did to her there."

"What?"

"Ask him," he shut the door behind him.

Tom stood up, walking over to the door. Yet when he opened it, the long hallway was empty. Glancing down at his watch, he realized that he was late getting back to Yves Alexander.

On the way out of the hotel, he tried to ring the Rabbi again on his phone. The line was busy. It was strange, thought Tom, he wanted to help Candice--if she was still alive, he wanted to believe in Rabb's words, that in finding Bobby Lefrete he would somehow solve the crisis, but more than anything, he just wanted answers to a puzzle that grew deeper and darker with every passing moment.

It was time to get back to Dussant.

6:15 PM (EST)
Elizabeth, NJ

Candice Cooperman was dying of thirst.

Snow fell in thick, silent clumps, covering the familiar landscape of the refinery. The constant hum of the refinery had turned to an eerie stillness. The two sentries guarding the engineering building stood twenty yards ahead of her, warming their hands like winos over an oil barrel burning with hot coals. They smoked cigarette after cigarette, laughing, talking, oblivious to the pile of frozen corpses, arms and legs rigid from *rigor mortis* and ice, stacked behind them.

It should have seemed surreal to Candice; instead, it was commonplace. Commonplace that she had buried herself under the snow , spending the past hours studying two more men she would kill. Commonplace that she spent even more time mentally planning where she would drag the bodies.

Then it was time.

She pulled off her glove, holding Schubert's cold pistol with her bare hands. Stealthily, she crawled on her belly through the snow bank until safely behind the twisted metal pipes of the Coker Unit. Only then did she stand up in the shadows, brushing snow and ice from her clothing.

Her teeth rattled.

She couldn't feel her toes anymore. Her eyes were raw and wind-burned. She pulled the oversized sleeve of the parka over her right hand, revealing only the very end of the pistol. Ever so carefully, like a climber scaling some precipitous cliff, she motioned out of the shadows and into the light, forcing her freezing feet into a natural gate, looking relaxed, like any of the other guards who walked by these two sentries.

Through the mist of her breath, she spotted them eight yards away. The details of their faces came into focus. They were much younger than she thought. . . the one closer to her was fat. They were still warming their hands over the barrel and laughing when she lifted her right arm up and fired.

The silencer muffled the sound--like a gentle sigh in the night. The first man fell back. The second was about to scream when she squeezed the trigger again. She fired at his face, aiming between the eyes, just like Schubert had done in the tunnels hours ago. He spun around, falling on his back.

Her hands shook, but inside, Candice felt surprisingly composed. She dragged the skinny one around the building before retrieving the fat one. When she touched him, his eyes opened, startling her.

He was still alive, but weak, barely able to whisper, "Don't hurt me."

She rolled him around the side of the building, letting his overweight frame sink into the snow bank. His lips moved in gestures of deprecation, but she couldn't hear the words. She fired a shot into his left eye—blood poured out of the open hole. Then she turned, walking right through the front door of the engineering building.

The warm air inside the building brought tears to her eyes. Her nose began to run--her cheeks hot. Her feet were so cold that if she hadn't taken great pain in looking normal, she would have had to crawl from the sudden pain. With the hood still covering her head, she knew to be cautious.

In a strange way, it was like returning home. Finally able to walk on the floor level of the building again, she thought it would seem different now, but beside the blood streaked floors, she could almost imagine Lou speaking to her only three paces ahead.

She saw the water fountain—thirst stung at her and she was unable to stop herself from lapping up sip after sip of water. As she drank, she didn't care, let them shoot her. Nothing can hurt me now, she repeated the words again and again. But no one harassed her.

Motioning to the door of The Meditation Chamber, she knocked. A voice grumbled from the other end. This is how I end the madness, she thought to herself. A moment later, the door opened. She shoved the end of Schubert's pistol into Nehemiah's face, "Step back," she grunted--the cold air making her voice raspy.

He silently stepped backwards, arms in the air.

Thirty Three

6:30 PM (EST)
Washington D.C.

All Candice Cooperman could think was that she was hungry.

"Hello Nehemiah," she finally sighed. Eyes locked on him, she groped with her left hand, making sure the door was locked behind her.

In a way, the bastard looked different—only because she had built him up in her mind as some superhuman creature. Having seen more of his boots and the top of his balding head than his face, it was strange to finally stare eye to eye. The sweat forming on his brow surprised her.

"So we finally meet, "my 8 ½ B," she didn't know what he was talking about. He continued, "the shoe was yours."

She'd forgotten about the shoe—the one she left at the water fountain. She recalled watching him through the grill of the door as he examined it.

"We don't have a lot of time," she barked, "stand against the wall and continue facing me."

Surprisingly, he showed little resistance. His voice was calm—the beads of sweat continued to from on his forehead, "I know much about you. Wouldn't you like to know how?" he was stalling--fishing for a way out of this mess. Gun pointed at his head, she weaved around the desk, opening the medicine cabinet. With her eyes still locked on him, she managed to stuff as many medical supplies into her coat pockets as possible.

Then something caught her eye: Lou's cell phone battery laying on the floor. He must have had an extra one. She grabbed it, stuffing it into her pocket.

"I underestimated you," he smirked, "I applaud your aggressive gesture."

Only then did she notice the laptop computer. Nehemiah watched her--she realized he'd been talking to draw her attention away from it. She turned up the computer screen's brightness level, perusing the last entry of a conversation from the Master.

They must not find out about Monongahela!

She watched as the next sentence typed out before her very eyes.

I require a response, Nehemiah.

Oh no, she thought, the fucking Master is on the other end of that line--right now—right here!

"You should concentrate on getting out," added Nehemiah.

Glancing up at Larry's clock she knew she had very little time-- her mind screamed that they were going to find the dead guard outside—they were going to find her, but she had to know more! She reached down for the scroll key on the computer in order to move back and read the whole conversation.

"I know everything about you, Candice," Nehemiah babbled, "you and Gummy Bear can't survive alone for long—"

"Shut up," she winced as she read on from the beginning of the segment, starting with The Master.

Nehemiah, I cannot believe that you would have allowed this Cooperman woman to hide in a broom closet. I thought your men swept the entire building.

We did, Master.

She was able to climb in the rafters, able to hide in a stairway corridor, on the roof, all without notice? She witnessed Polcheck's execution, your own secret conversations with staff members!

I tell you Master, she is not the civilian you claim.

What are you claiming?

I think that she's with the government, sent here to foil our plans. She did come with Lou Pauzpolis-

You fool! Don't you realize that in my position I would know if she were with the government! I have been with the government's team since this affair began! None of us had any idea who she was before this mission began. I gave you everything you needed to know to catch her. They must not find out about Monongahela!

There was a knock at the door.

"Ask him what he wants or it'll be a real short conversation," she spun around, whispering, the end of her pistol at his head.

"W-w-what?" Nehemiah's voice was feeble and weak.

"We're about to flush the tunnels, sir! Should we go ahead without you?"

They were going to flush the pipes, thought Candice. Probably reroute the massive drainage pond, run it right through the pipes and into the harbor. Jesus, they'd certainly capture Schubert and…she'd handcuffed Gummy Bear to him!

"What are you going to do now?" Nehemiah turned with a smug grin, "if I tell them not to flush, they'll be suspicious."

"Sir," the voice on the other end of the door pressed for an answer.

"Tell them you're meditating with your master," she whispered, "and can't be interrupted. You'll contact them with instructions in a few minutes."

He did as he was instructed.

The person left the door. Candice sighed a breath of relief. Nehemiah spoke in a soothing voice, "I know your story, Candice. I've read your file. My men have searched your apartment. I know you sleep with your ex-husband's photo under your pillow. I know you're weak, alone, tired. You don't have the strength to kill me. Just give me the gun."

She held the gun up, "If you'd seen all that you did then you should know that I've nothing to lose. You can't take anything else from me. But you everything to lose. Ya see, I'm gonna do the worst thing I can to you," she grabbed the laptop computer , "after you're gone, your plan dies. Because nobody's gonna talk to The Master," she folded the tiny laptop up, stuffing it under her arm.

Nehemiah's expression changed-- as if someone were cutting his lifeline. His heavily perspiring brow revealed his thoughts. He made his move, leaping forward at her, arms stretched wide, fingers arched like claws.

Pop.

When she pulled the trigger he was more astonished than surprised. She heard the puff of air muffled through the silencer--watched as he was kicked backward against the wall, head slamming to the floor, blood splattered everywhere. His arms flailed upward, he tried to scream, unable to utter any sound. The bullet had ripped through his face exiting right under his ear. His jaw was hanging, teeth scattered across the floor-- chin was gone. He made a strange gurgling noise, blowing blood and bubbles out of the space that had just seconds ago been a mouth.

She spun around and exited through the door. Pulling the hood over her had she walked down the hall. Two terrorists, white with blonding hair, walked by. She continued walking. Once out in the snow, she trudged safely behind the coker unit. In her wake she could hear screaming—they had discovered Nehemiah.

They were going to flush the line—she would never have enough time to get to her friends. What had she accomplished? She had medicines and couldn't give it to her friends. She might not even have killed Nehemiah. Her head pounded. Then she glanced down at the computer resting under her arm. She did have that.

Slowly, she opened the laptop computer. Her eyes danced across various files and folders. . . each title confounding her even more. She read the titles over and over in disbelief. . . CANDICE COOPERMAN. . . TOM GRANT. . . GENERAL REMY CRANDAL. . . DR. BRANDT. . . CONTAMINATION. . . TIME SEQUENCE. . . ALTERNATE PLANS. . . MONONGOHELA—she stopped on that one. What the hell was a Monongahela?

Turning the arrow to the electronic file, she opened it.

The screen projected words and letters across her windblown cheeks. Her eyes raced as she peered through the mist of her own breath, reading the file line by line. What she read terrified her--she snapped the battery in and dialed speed dial on her cell-phone. She had to risk talking to Tom and only hoped that the pipes overhead wouldn't disturb the cellular signal.

Thirty Four

Tom Grant pressed the button.

The sound came first, the speakers flooding the tiny, white observation room. This time Tom heard the sorrowful sounds of a classical piece. After a moment, he realized it was the weeping Tomaso Albinoni's *Adagio*.

As the blast shield retracted into its recessed housing, Tom was surprised to observe that Yves Alexander had not moved from his previous position. . . his body draped across the red chair, one foot resting against the glass partition. He flipped through the end of Shelley's work, utterly absorbed in the prose.

Tom slid the bottle of wine into the feeder box, "I have-"

Without looking up, Dussant shot a finger in the air: indicating silence. Tom listened as the feeder box scanned its contents. His feet tapped against the floor-- he demanded answers. Dussant must know how to help Candice—Rabb would never have sent him unless it was true!

Then he saw the vision—the back side of Agent Willard's head, bloody and clammy, turning ever so slowly so that at any moment Tom would be able to see his face and--

"Well, what do we have here?" Dussant folded the book in his lap. Stretching his arms wide, he squeezed out a yawn, "I hope you weren't too inconvenienced. I didn't bother to think if wine stores would be open at this hour. In here night and day have no real meaning."

"Now you have your wine, tell me about the clouds you spoke of when we last met," it was strange— he'd just met this man earlier today and yet felt as if he had known Yves Alexander Dussant for years. . . as if he were one of his closest friends. He struggled to combat the man's unbelievable charisma.

Dussant breezed over the comment, "You know Agent Grant, God never liked to burden any of his subject with complicated sacrifices," he retrieved the bottle from the feeder box, examining the aged white and gold label, "marvelous," he drawled, "and you managed to get the '70! Ah, how I do adore Chateau Pichon Longueville Contessa De Lalande. Did you know most of the great French vineyards were actually founded by the Romans two thousand years ago? They boiled their wine in lead-- gave em pretty nasty headaches indeed!"

"Didn't know that."

"The Romans claimed that the great Roman wine of Opimius," pontificated Dussant, "could be drunk 125 years later. Strange, doesn't seem that long from our present day perspective, does it? I always fancied the fact that wine seemed to withstand the transience of time, but-"

"Sooner or later everything rots," interjected Tom, "can we get to the questions now?"

"Where's the fire? Way you're actin', must be a damn big fire. And need I remind you that this is a sacrifice, not an exchange. Of course you did bring the corkscrew, right?"

"A corkscrew!"

"It was a joke," Dussant laughed, "you're so damn edgy. I believe I have a corkscrew somewhere. You better hope so," he sauntered over to an antique étagère returning with a small black device in his hand, "it uses compressed air. They would never give me a real one—voila!" he opened the wine, pouring a taste into a crystal glass on the side table.

"Do we really need these theatrics?"

He took great pains sniffing the wine, "You have to smell the wine! The scent is called the nose. You can smell 3,000 smells--yet you can taste only four things. It's the nose that makes the wine so divine."

Tom always calmed down when he was near Yves Alexander. The prisoner's charisma and charm were infectious, "I suppose," he joked, "God drinks Pichon Langwhatever too?"

"Of course not," Dussant grimaced, "He drinks *La Tache*," he took a sip of the wine and his cheeks glowed red and satisfied.

"Good?" asked Tom.

Dussant poured a half glass, "This bottle is very reminiscent of the "61. My father has one of those ancient wine lockers in the basement of The Rib Room—oh, I keep forgetting you're from around here. Of course you know that's just across the street from here. You should go there. The key's hidden on the mantle above the locker. The Dussant family has bottles of wine dating back a century—all stored in the cool room. You should visit it. Wine holds many answers to your questions, Agent Grant."

Tom tried to control himself. Out there Candice Cooperman might be in the throes of unspeakable torture! Mad men controlled the lives of tens of millions of people! His compatriots and allies had few clues! And here he --entertaining an eccentric prisoner, and it truly didn't bother him?

"You look very tired, Tom. Didn't you catch a nap at The Westin Hotel?"

"How did you know I was at The Westin!" he jumped out of his seat.

"Calm down," Dussant pointed the wine label with a smaller sticker reading: Westin Hotel Wince Cellar.

If Dussant didn't want to talk about the clouds he hinted at or Bobby Lefrete then perhaps they could pursue other questions, thought Tom, "In Israel," he pressed, "you must have stayed in a hotel--I mean while you were on vacation with your mother."

"Vacation?" Yves Alexander raised his brow, "is that what they said? That I was sunning myself--drinking too many Mai-Tai's with little umbrellas?"

"The brief said you took off in a jet from an air-strip near Wayfarer-"

"In the town of Blanche Fields to be exact," Blanche Fields, thought Tom, Dussant had mentioned that place before, "the brief probably discussed the strange sound proof wall installed in the aircraft," continued Dussant, "dividing my mother and I from the pilots. I suppose you can now understand why. Couldn't have the pilots in the back with me, caught in sycophantic spasms, and I didn't want to sit in the cockpit for fifteen hours."

"Same reason for the limousine?" asked Tom only to quickly answered his own question, "you slept in the back of the limo because you couldn't go outside and interact with people."

"My," Yves Alexander face almost touched the glass as he muttered sarcastically, "but let's get back to wine."

"Your mother was probably deluded too," he jabbed, "thought she'd probably bring you to Mount Sinai to converse with the burning bush."

"Burning bushes are quite passe'," the smile was gone from Yves Alexander's lips. He didn't want to talk about this topic, "anyway I could have lit a bush on fire at Wayfarer."

"Then why go halfway around the world?" pressed Tom.

"Every man must have a few secrets," he declined to offer more information, "if I didn't have them, you wouldn't keep coming back, would you?"

So Dussant intended on seeing him again, thought Tom. Why? The creature outlined in that brief and Mr. Help's testimony didn't thirst for companionship—he slaughtered indiscriminately, treating humans like pawns.

"Did you wreck the limo?" Tom stabbed into the darkness. He didn't have time to play games. If Dussant wanted idle conversation, he was not the one to give it to him, "was she suddenly overtaken with sycophantic euphoria while at the wheel, steering the car off the cliff? Or did she intend on killing both of you?"

"You are correct in only one point. She did kill both of us," Dussant tried to smile. The gesture was unsuccessful.

What the hell was Yves Alexander talking about? "So you're dead."

Silence.

"Nuff'bout me. Let's talk 'bout you, Agent Grant," Dussant broke the silence with a smirk, "let's talk about your mother, shall we? I'm from Louisiana and did read the newspaper with great interest when I was a free man—you were little more than a boy when it happened."

"What?" asked Tom, shielding his trembling hands. His stomach churned. He felt totally visible—his entire past on display to this monstrous mutant who seemed to have powers beyond anyone's control, "what did you read?" he feigned invulnerability.

"Tragedy, Agent Grant," Dussant's eyes probed deep inside him, "Greek tragedy."

There was a long moment of silence. Tom sat perfectly still, his eyes locked on Dussant's.

Finally it was Tom who spoke, "I suggest we find a new topic of conversation. Shit, you may be a messiah. But I'm not here to commune with you. I'm not here to be your pal," he sputtered—the raw uncontrollable anger seeping through to the surface, "I really don't give a damn about you --locked behind that glass wall! You can rot there for all I care!" a rush of emotion was very uncommon for Tom. He funneled all of his energy towards quelling the fit.

There was another tense silence.

"I'm sorry if I was cruel, Tom," continued Dussant reproachfully, "you were driving home some personal points, yourself. Think I wanted to say all that? Don't treat me like a lab rat and I won't treat you like a prison guard. As for your comment about my desire to be on your side of the glass, it's short sighted.

I would give my body, my very soul not just to be on your side of the glass, but to be in your body. Do you think there was a time when I didn't want to be like everyone else? You think I enjoy the solitary confinement that is my life—speaking to people, never able to hear a single a sincere reply. Either they're lost in sycophantic exhalation like a drug addict or they're my prison guard spitting at me from your side of the glass."

Yes, in certain ways, thought Tom, they were similar—putting on their cold, airs, flashing apathy, when all along there was a huge soft spot in the armor, susceptible to the slightest jab, "I didn't mean to--well-"

"What color is my skin, Tom?" interrupted Dussant.

"Pardon?"

"My skin. . . what color is it?"

Tom studied Yves Alexander's face, taking note of his milky white skin, "Pale. . . you look pale."

"Ghostly pale, Tom. Rarely has it been that I've stepped outside in the sunshine or moonlight--my entire life spent in prisons of one sort or another. From the first moment I could speak," continued Dussant, "nannies refused to leave my bedside. They had to be removed with brute force and then those that removed them became—well you can see the vicious cycle it created. That was why they hid me in Wayfarer before I was even two years old.

Even my own beloved parents weren't immune, trapped by an uncontrollable obsession to constantly be near me. Do you know what it's like to see your own father weep because you want to play alone or use the bathroom without constant eyes upon you? Do you know what it is like to have to hold your mothers hand while she showers? And yet you can't bear to command your parents—your prison guards, can you? So you let them continue their obsessions and compulsions. Tom, I'm the consummate prisoner."

Tom focused on the brief, reminding himself how dangerous this person was—repeating the stern warnings from Mr. Help and Dr. Brandt. Every person who ever came in contact with Yves Alexander was dead: Agent Willard, the nannies, Dussant's parents, the followers of that commune, and 12 federal agents, all consigned to hell.

"Why didn't you just stop talking?" he asked, "you could have made yourself a mute."

"Don't you get it? I'm the voice of God! A voice that can speak words, or just grunt or sigh or merely breath. All of these thing carry a divine force and energy. In the context of the outside world, I'm imprisoned by my own body."

"I can imagine that the obsession, the constant neediness of others must have driven you mad. I might have even wished them dead."

"Now you see why Jesus was so controlling of his emotions. He had to be very careful and reserved. If Jesus ever called someone a mother fucker," grinned Dussant, "well you can see the problem. I learned very early on to be careful with words."

"Sounds like *Invasion of The Body Snatchers* to me."

"Science can't explain me, so it locks me up and throws away the key. I don't fit into the current generation's view of the universe. But the desire for me still lingers—people need beliefs and idolatry- teenage fans dying to touch a rock singer's body? Old women writing their home away to some creep who preaches on TV? Soldiers dying for a crazed dictator. It's idolatry—the craving for communion--the hunger for spiritual unity, ridding yourself of the emptiness."

"Not everyone's a rock and roll fan or watches TV preachers."

"People still need beliefs."

"You're pontificating."

"Look at me, Tom," he threw out his arms, "I am the voice of God! Don't you get it? What more proof do you people need before you admit it? How far do I have to go before the parallels open your eyes. Only a few generations in all the millenniums have ever been fortunate enough to witness such a thing. I am the meaning--the alpha and the omega and everything in between."

"You do that very well, but-"

"Have you ever felt weak?" persisted Dussant, "maybe for only the passing of a moment, weak like a child? Ever longed to speak to your dead father or mother—just once, for one single moment to hear the sound of their voice, see their eyes upon you, speak one last sentence to them, smell them near you? I offer a divination of the most simple sort. I can complete you. That is what Dr. Brandt calls 'contamination.' That is what she and your government and the Rabbi fear so much: a society allowed to attain its true purpose. A society where each individual is one with the will of The Creator—where no one is alone, no one hungry, no one sad, no one afraid-"

"And no one is an individual," added Tom, "and all serve you."

"You're speaking in tiny terms. Think upon how many generations have prayed for the chance to sit alone with me in a room. God chose this point in time, not I. God dispatched me here. And I have his voice to back up and quell all skeptics who might disbelieve. *Every knee must bend, ever heart give homage.* God is not discretionary amongst his followers. Do you want to know what I can say to make all the wrongs of the world right? Just open that airlock door over there and I'll tell you."

The metal airlock door had a numerical key pad next to it. Beyond the reinforced glass window of the door Tom could see another inner door. He felt himself falling away. He was disoriented. For a moment he worried and actually fingered the panic button on the remote control without pressing it--finally appreciating the option. Then he collected himself, realizing that he was still inside the observation room and a glass partition still protected him from Yves Alexander Dussant.

"If you have all of this then why can't recordings of your voice carry the same power?" Tom turned away.

"Unfortunately, I'm fashioned for a simpler age. A hundred years ago, nothing would have stopped me. Who could have ever envisioned Walkmans and Dictaphones and phonographs?"

"Guess God doesn't keep up the new technology, " he turned to the next topic, "did you inadvertently cause all of those people to kill themselves?" asked Tom with brutal bluntness, "or did you command them to do it?"

"You tell me."

"I don't know, but you seem intelligent—too intelligent to be a slave to mere primitive impulses or plain madness."

Dussant clapped his hands, "Let me tell you a short little anecdote to warm your heart. As I said, my parents were constant escorts of mine since my birth—I think I've illustrated that point already. One day when I was twelve, I was masturbating when my parents walked in the room weeping. They couldn't stand to be away from me, behind a closed door. I told my father in childish anger that I wished he was gone. What child hasn't at one time or another? Except my father, without a thought or moment's hesitation, leapt out the second story bedroom window to his own death. That is also the only time, Agent Grant, that I have ever voluntarily caused anyone harm."

"How did all of your followers die?"

"Rabb never told you how he slaughtered those innocent families in Blanche Fields."

"Rabb never killed anyone!"

Dussant was lost in quiet rumination for a long moment before looking up, "Tell me, do you like soup?"

"No more culinary runs!" countered Tom.

"But turtle soup from Galatoire's would be marvelous!" he drawled—his eyes took on a dreamy state as if he were staring through Tom, through the cubicle walls, at images of the past, "the soup would mix well with your extraordinary wine: true symbiosis," his lips moved, but his eyes did not, "we used to get their soup delivered to Wayfarer in their own white China. Galatoire's serves it piping hot with a cup of Sherry."

"It would take hell freezing over to make me get it."

"Hell's out of my jurisdiction. Though I love the notion of freezing hell over for a little Galatoire's turtle soup. There's a certain *je ne sais quoi* about it, But I think I can motivate you without freezing anything. Examine the front of this townhouse, you will find my family seal. Go the Marigny District of the French Quarter, look for the same seal. There you will find a clue to Bobby Lefrete. Once you see what awaits you there, you'll be back with soup in hand."

In the blink of an eye, the blast door closed shut.

8:39 PM (EST)
In Transit from New York to Pittsburgh

They were going to crash, thought Benjamin Bronk.

The billionaire dug his knuckles deep into the arm rest. Lightning flashed white across the officer's cabin of the Lockheed C-141 StarLifter. The military aircraft, roughly the size of a 747 dropped like a stone out of the sky.

"Heads up!" Ice man cried.

The overhead compartments opened--olive green blankets and pillows showered the room. The frame of the aircraft rattled. I'm going to die, thought Benjamin, never expecting it would be in a nose diving military transport with ten special forces soldiers in the rear hold.

Benjamin glanced at Rabb, seated next to him. The black man had an utterly bored and composed look on his face-- he actually yawned. It was as if Rabb didn't mind dying, thought Bronk, he just didn't want it to interfere with the mission. If Benjamin's family were safe, he might have entertained such a distanced, intellectual fascination with the moment. But this wasn't the case.

Under any other circumstances, thought Benjamin, the plane would have been grounded. But they had to press on. This was the second stage of a quickly developing operation. They were catching up with the FBI lead team already in Monongahela. Benjamin, Rabb, Ice, and a handful of special forces soldiers were to be the eyes and ears for General Crandal who remained in the New York headquarters to oversee the Elizabeth refinery attack.

"Boys," he heard the General sigh, "I know it's bumpy up there. But we've got some damn good news.

We just found out who this Nehemiah character is. It's downloading on your laptop right now!"

Thirty Five

8:39 PM (EST)
In Transit from New York to Pittsburgh

The laptop computer downloaded.

The plane continued to shudder. Benjamin shut his eyes, gripping the side of his chair when he heard Rabb say, "Alright, where were we?"

"Jesus, do you ever lose your composure?" Bronk opened his eyes, smirking.

"I follow Delta Force philosophy, when you're ticket's up—it's up" Rabb turned to Ice who was looking green, "you losing your philosophy?"

"Just dinner," he burped.

Benjamin liked the Rabbi from the first moment he met him—which was a strange moment because he was pointing a loaded pistol at the man's head. Rabb was one of the most objective and clear thinking individuals the executive had met in a long time. The sagacious black man didn't mince words or waste time with small talk. It was all business and Benjamin now appreciate why Tom had showered such respect on the man.

"Look" Rabb tired of waiting, "just tell us about Nehemiah."

"Oh you can grandstand in that cigar bar bathroom with guessing games," jibed Remy, "but I gotta' spill the beans. Hell, you're on a plane with nothing better to do but wait."

"I'd like to know before we plummet to the ground," replied Rabb.

Benjamin glanced at his laptop computer he was still clutching. A file now rested on the screen—the data had downloaded via the satellite link-up, "I got it!"

Rabb opened the file, quickly perusing it as Colonel Sharpe came over the line stating, "Berlin CIA headquarters has a file on a man matching Nehemiah's description. The picture was taken outside of Ruse, Bulgaria in 1987." he slid the computer around so that the entire group could see the emailed photograph.

The figure in the photo stood in the foreground with a knife in his hand and a beer in the other. It looked like he had been cleaning a slaughtered animal which hung from a tree behind him. Benjamin's eyes focused on his children's' possible would be murderer with distaste. The man looked Aryan with a square face, receding blond hairline, and tiny eyes spaced wide across flat cheeks.

"Hans Zimmler is his actual name," continued Rabb, "born August 10th, 1958 in Sentencer, East Germany. He was religious, went by the nick-name Nehemiah. Zimmler's record shows three prior arrests in his early teens for child molestation-"

"Wouldn't put it past the twisted bastard," grunted Benjamin, "he's a sicko."

"Curiously, he was never convicted," Rabb read from the electronic report, "at the age of eighteen through a cousin who was a high ranking Comintern official, Zimmler attended Furstenburg," gasped Rabb, clearly unhinged, "are you sure about this, Sharpe?"

Colonel Sharpe's voice broke over the speakerphone, "It's the only reason Berlin CIA had a dossier on him. After German reunification, based on prior arrests and extensive training, the police gave him a plane ticket and booted him the hell out of *der fatherland*."

"So they punted the asshole over to us, great" Ice interjected.

"Slow down here," Benjamin hated all this private jokes and quips, "can someone explain to us layman what the hell is Furstenburg?"

Rabb sighed, "Before the fall of the iron curtain, Soviet special forces were trained and housed in a compound at Furstenburg, East Germany. Jesus," Rabb ran a hand through his short cropped hair as he realized the implications of his own explanation, "do you remember the Russian primary objectives for a full Western European assault?"

"You mean *Spetsialnaya Razvedka*?" General Crandal answered in perfect Russian—a crack in the façade of the redneck idiot he so carefully constructed for himself, noted Benjamin.

"Remember some of the eleven goals of the plan?" Rabb shivered.

The General barked out a grocery list of items, "Clandestine communications, physical incapacitation of NATO warheads, interruption and disruption of NATO political commands, oh shit--total destruction of key power stations, military electronic industries, and oil refineries."

"Of course," chimed Rabb, "the Soviets viewed a breach in Western European oil consumption as a massive advantage in a first strike winter attack. They would effectively stop the flow of gasoline to enemy tanks and the flow of oil for heating and power to much of central Europe."

"A-a-are you telling me," stumbled Benjamin, "that this bastard has been specially trained in destroying my refinery?"

"Not specially trained," replied Rabb, almost to himself, "with Furstenburg, he'd have a doctorate in it. Damn! Most unforeseen."

"Unforeseen!" cried Bronk , "it's fucking unbelievable that you people would instruct men in this kind of madness!"

"He still couldn't do it alone," Rabb ignored Benjamin, addressing the General, "he'd probably need someone who knew his way around the unique catalysts and chemical elements of that specific plant-"

"How many chemical engineers are gonna go along with blowing up the northeastern seaboard," bantered the General.

"Gummy Bear," added Benjamin, "someone autistic enough to master the art, but deficient enough to understand what's going on."

Rabb nodded his head, "If what Candice said was correct, Gummy Bear could explain what and where the most volatile chemical combinations were. That's why Nehemiah faxed his bogus ransom demand letter to The White House and set up that first exchange at the cigar bar. He was exposed--vulnerable for the first few hours until he stabilized the—shit we should have attack then. We need to hit these guys hard and fast!"

"Well we're gonna nuke his ass now," grunted the General over the speakerphone.

"Wait a minute!" Benjamin held up his hands, "if this guy's so good. Who's to say he hasn't factored the electromagnetic pulse into his plan? I mean, with every hour these guys are sounding more like pros—what if they EMP shielded their bombs. We blow the place and the bombs blow on some backup timer."

General Crandal chimed in, "It's not like you go out and EMP shield your garden shed. He'd practically need a week at the FBI Nevada Test Range to do the job right."

The plane suddenly slammed its nose upward, causing the computers and papers to fall into Benjamin and Rabb's laps. The faces of his children passed through his mind, but he tried to concentrate on the upcoming raid. Let him land in Pittsburgh! He would do everything differently from now on. He'd gladly give his life to save his babies. . . no more than that-

To save them all.

9:49 PM (EST)
Elizabeth, NJ

It was snowing again.

The three black, Lincoln Town Cars arrived at the fluorescent orange barricades lining Bronk Blvd. A smattering of press reporters were huddled outside the area, but most fled after the government claimed a toxic leak at Union 57 and sealed off a six block radius around the refinery.

The guard opened the barricade for the convoy of Lincolns. They proceeded down the icy street full of refineries, topless clubs, and abandoned buildings. The contingent of cars were transported via a Lockheed C-130 Hercules to an airfield just outside of Princeton, New Jersey. Each automobile was armored with bullet proof plating, Plexiglas, and counter tactical weapons.

Garbed in a dark, black suit, the lone escort in the second car glanced behind him, knowing that a contingent of special forces troops were all around him-- his car sandwiched between them. He checked his watch ever few as the car pulled in front of the condemned apartment house.

A team of soldiers with night-sights and heavy weaponry piled out of the second and third Lincoln and searched the building. Then the escort in the Town Car was instructed to proceed. He opened a secret safe under his seat producing a small case which he handcuffed to his wrist. Flanked by escorts he marched up to the attic of the apartment house, full of men and mortar cannons.

Through the window the escort studied the multicolored lights--a sea of chemical plants spread before him. He had no idea of the target, only the mortar cannon operator knew the coordinates and even then they were just numbers on a plotting map downloaded by satellite.

"Ready to receive the package," the mortar operator stood to attention.

From the far side of the room, the escort noticed his counterpart already standing there, holding his own attaché case, having come through another entrance, arriving his own separate convoy of three cars with his own group of armed escorts, flying into a separate airfield. Only now at that single moment, were they in the same physical location.

Crouched down, the escorts opened their cases, revealing half of 2 separate mortar shells. They screwed the threaded pieces together producing two full ones. The mortar cannon operator scanned the shells with a Geiger counter which chirping lightly. The nuclear package was not hot, the Uranium 238 and 235 and the Plutonium 239—in the military, they called this *a hot pickle.*

"Permission to proceed is granted," replied the mortar cannon operator.

"Packages are mounted and armed," the escorts replied simultaneously.

The mortar cannon operator placed the two shells at his feet, reaching inside his jacket for the Comlink phone. The air was cold and his breath misted as he spoke into his communicator, "General Crandal, the physics package is prepped and ready," he continued, "awaiting final launch authorization code."

9:38 PM (CST)
New Orleans, LA

"Stop here," Tom Grant muttered.

Riding in The United Cab, he fought hard to stay awake. He opened his eyes and yawned feeling a throbbing exhaustion. Every cell in his body wanted to go to sleep. He had gone for almost 48 hours without it. He stared out the window at the lower Quarter which was more residential and sleepy with peeling paint and great limbering oak trees. The cab crossed Esplanade Avenue.

He was now in The Marigny, a smaller district of homes and shops with a more funky feel. . . Latin dance clubs and soul food kitchens. Tom remembered an old bar from his distant past where an amateur band played ragtime songs on Sundays. The cab had been cruising up and down the streets for almost an hour as Tom searched through the streets for the Dussant family seal.

Then he saw it—a unicorn with seven stars. The house was what they termed "shotgun shacks"--rooms stacked one in front of other so that you had to cross every chamber to get from the front to the back door. The windows were boarded up—a condemned building in a bad neighborhood.

Tom asked the taxi to wait for him. He screwed up his eyes and simply laughed. Grant paid him. As the taxi pulled away, Tom drew his gun, approaching the rotted balcony. He had to kick through the boards blocking the door before he ripped enough out in order to climb through. It was the smell that hit him first and then-

10:47 (EST) 9:47 PM (CST)
New Orleans, LA

Tom gasped.

The living room smelled putrid. Drawing his pistol, he scolded himself for not bringing a flashlight. Stumbling in the darkness, he found himself in the first room of the shotgun house. Old boards creaked under his feet. The smell was working on his nerves. . . a mixture of feces and urine? He spotted fingers of streetlight creeping through a boarded window on the left hand side of the room. He ripped away the planks-- meager light pouring into the room, illuminating curling wallpaper and syringes. He stopped, spotting a rat scurrying into a distant corner. Then he realized that the curling wallpaper he noticed was actually a design. . . some geometric amalgamation of lines painted on the wall opposite the window. He neared, his eyes adjusting to the light. He was about to touch the pattern when he caught a whiff of the smell, strong and unmistakable.

The design was a cross painted in excrement. Along the borders of the cross were scribbled a series of numbers:

1*7-10,18   3*10-12   18*10,21   1*19
22*18   6*11   18*24   21*3

Taking out his notepad, he jotted down the numbers.

Then he heard something in the next room. In shock, he almost dropped his note-book . Drawing his gun, he motioned towards the next doorway. The smell ravaged his senses before he even entered the second room. Bending over he grabbed at his shirt tale, shielding his nose. He thought he'd vomit and had to stop, dry heaving before he could continue.

Terrified, he took a moment to fight his instincts to run. With controlled steps, he entered the room and found himself standing inside a dilapidated bathroom. . . crusty molding and cracked tiles. Discarded beer cans crumpled under his feet as he swung the gun to either side, scanning the room. A tattered curtain fluttered into the air—the source of the sound he heard.

He was alone. Then he spotted the two cracked marble columns in the tub. His mind took a moment to realize that they were legs littered with veins that bubbled to the surface like cracks on a broken vase. The corpse laid face down in the tub—the skin along the spine was desiccated, shriveling and curling with a spinal column which seemed to rise up, out of the body. Tom took a moment collecting himself. Searching the floor, he grabbed an old beer box, using it as a shielding and lamely flipped the body over.

With a heavy thud, the head crashed against the ringed wall of the tub. The dead man's expression was horrific. Tom knew he had drowned in water which had long ago evaporated from the ringed tub. The corpse's nose and eyes were gone. . .its flesh green and stiff like dry leather. He was almost naked--Tom noticed the cross etched in the body's chest: a probing knife wound who's lateral cut ran through the man's rotted genitalia, almost slicing the penis from the body! Be strong, he thought to himself, covering his nose. You can do this. Standing up, Tom realized the man's pants were dragged down to his ankles.

Gathering all his strength, he groped around the ancient pockets of the pants, searching for some type of identification. He discovered a wallet, opening it under the floodlights. It was an FBI badge. He strained in order to read the name in smudged ink, making out only the first name: Thomas Gr-.

Thomas Grant? That was his fucking name. No, he couldn't make out the last letters on the badge. He dropped it on the ground. Fear surged through him—a childlike fear of the darkness.

Unable to catch a cab from The Marigny, he walked down Royal Street, heading back to his hotel. A thick New Orleans mist hung in the street. . . the air was silent. He cut through the large stone alleyway between St. Louis Cathedral and The Cabildo. I could be in another century, he mused. His feet echoed on cobblestone. . . the streetlights faded away.

He heard a voice chuckle demonically. Tom spotted shadows on the peeling wall of the Cabildo. Like some bizarre shadow puppet show, comically proportioned figures moved back and forth engaging in acts of sex and violence.

Then the source of the shadows made himself visible--a midget street vendor clad in a tattered Jester's costume with Mardi Gras colors: gold, blue, and green-- the ends of his oversized hat and shoes tied with bells that jingled across the cobblestones. The performer extended his hands in front of an antiquated light projector—a box with a candle inside it. The queer little man bowed, "Good to see you, sir. Shall it be the usual?"

Tom silently smirked, trying to get around him.

"Do you pretend not to know me," he grew indignant.

Tom was not going to chat it up with some deranged dwarf in strange clothes. The Jester was nimble, blocking his path, "Come now," his voice carried an accent, "was not Yorick a fellow of infinite jest, of most excellent fancy? He hath borne me on his back a thousand times I've heard it said."

This strange little man was quoting Hamlet. That in itself was probably worth a few cents. Tom tossed a quarter into the tip jar.

The Jester's eyes lit up, "A quarter for a poem--a poem for a life--a life for a secret--and after ya hear it--ya get ta' keep it."

"No poems tonight, buddy. . .it's fine."

"Please," the little man begged. For a moment the light projector hit the Jester's face just right and Tom could see the vendor was eyeless! He jumped away, walking briskly towards the faint lights of Jackson Square, still able to hear the Jester reciting a poem in Tom's honor:

"Twenty Five cents is not a great number-
for a life twisted by fate,
Ya must know that truth is in the numbers-
if you're to acquire eternal faith."

Tom continued walking.

11:17 PM (EST)
Monongahela, PA

"Not you!" moaned Benjamin Bronk.

"And what's surprising about my presence?" Agent Dick Osbourne blasted. Behind Dick stood the entire White House entourage, "Secretary of State Giardino dispatched us by Lear jet directly to Monongahela."

"Took you long enough," cracked the FBI Field Commander with very little love. He was a tall, lean man with a neatly trimmed, gray beard which framed a large, hawk-like nose sticking high in the air with more than a touch of arrogance.

The FBI Filed Commander and Osbourne both sported blue jumpsuits emblazoned with the gold FBI logo. Benjamin's group sported black Delta Force jumpsuits with hip holsters—so as to distinguish friend rather than foe.

They looked like a handful of auto mechanics, mused the executive in rare moment of sarcasm. He glanced around what had once been a travel agency— perhaps only hours before. Posters of far off lands like Tahiti, Orlando, and Cleveland hung precariously off the walls. Suspended from the ceiling, a cardboard model of a Singapore Airlines 747 spun in slow, lazy circles, propelled by the opening and closing of the front door. All the windows were covered with black plastic sheets. Soldiers buzzed everywhere.

"I head up the FBI counter-terrorist team," continued the FBI Commander without disclosing his name, "as I explained to Agent Osbourne, we didn't need you guys. So just stay back and shut up—"

"What have you learned from the thermal scans?" Rabb had no time for petty bravado.

"I've reviewed the situation," Agent Osbourne grandstanded, "it's fine."

Rabb exploded in a thunderous voice, "Both of you shut up and speak to me or I'll get General Crandal on the phone!"

The Field Commander visibly shivered, "We found them in the abandoned church across the square. We've been listening in on their conversations with fiber optic sensors drilled through the roof. There's a congregation of 28 humans inside."

"What are they doing?" inquired Benjamin with little fear of the man.

The commander turned to Osbourne, "Do I have to answer questions form someone who's clearly a civilian?"

"Come now Commander," smiled Rabb, "I think we would all like to know the answer to his question."

"To the best of our knowledge," the Field Commander rolled his eyes at his own revelation, "they're praying."

"Come again?" Rabb was startled.

"It's already been disclosed to us," the Field Commander shouted, "that they're clearly part of a Christian militia group—one might expect prayer. We ran the tapes eight times--digitally verified five minutes ago with voice and speech pathology at FBI Crime Lab-"

"All to figure out prayers?" Benjamin jabbed. He hated this jerk. Then he felt Rabb's eyes upon him, telling him to cool down.

"Not to identify a prayer," the commander fired back, "to figure out Latin--they're speaking in Latin. Not exactly what you expect to hear through a fiber optic sensor? Sound's like the devil talking."

"What are they reciting in Latin?" asked Ice as he checked his pistol. He was always fooling with his weapons, noted Benjamin, must be a nervous tick.

"Crime lab hasn't come back with that yet. I mean we aren't really trained to deal with terrorists speaking ancient languages."

"Any fiber optic surveillance?" asked Rabb.

The Commander dug into his oversized military satchel, a moment later tossing a handful of photographs across the unrolled blueprint. Benjamin took a photo, each wrapped in plastic with the label: EYES ONLY/ FBI EVIDENCE. The quality was poor--angles and colors stretched out over a bird's eye view of a series of men gathered in rows. He handed the photo to Ice Man.

"I have a very bad feeling about this," winced Rabb. He couldn't make out anything in the photos.

"Well Secretary of State Giardino disagrees. We were given verbal authorization ten minutes ago," the Field Commander addressed his men in a loud, thundering voice, "gentleman, we attack in two minutes," he turned back to Rabb, "some of my men will have cameras on their helmets. You can watch it on TV-learn how the real FBI handles a raid."

11:32 PM (EST) 10:32 PM (CST)
New Orleans, LA

Tom's cellular phone rang.

He found himself on Chartres St., staring at his reflection in a shop-front window--a full beard blossoming on his face--his hair was greasy. Hell, he hadn't brushed his teeth in two days. He was cold, hungry, thirsty, and disoriented from being awake for 48 hours straight, still he fumbled for the cell phone as it rang.

"Tom," it was Candice! His heart raced, "you have to listen!"

Was she being tortured, forced under duress to mislead him? "This line may be tapped," he warned.

"Thanks for believing me. So much has happened. I may have killed Nehemiah, "but I know who the Master is--his name's Bobby Lefrete! "

The street spun around him.

"He's operating under a covert identity," she continued, "within the government group--Lefrete knew everything I ever told you—where you were, what you were doing! He even considered killing you. He knew what I was doing when I was planning my escape!"

"How do you know this?"

"I can't explain now. Your friends are racing to the terrorist's headquarters, but there's something wrong in Monongahela!" and then she proceeded to explain.

Thirty Seven

Benjamin Bronk stepped out into the cold, wet air.

Under a thin sliver of moonlight, he could see the old church--triangular cresting roof with rotting wood sides and an overgrown front yard framed by a small iron gate. Only the church had electricity . . . dim yellow lights showering out of old stained glass windows—then that died.

He could hear tiny clicks as the soldiers adjusted their night-sites. Benjamin watched in detached curiosity as the FBI crept out from behind cars rushing across the street--an army of forty men in full battle gear, slowly converging on the abandoned structure. Behind Bronk, Ice was dialing a number on his comlink phone. The rest of Rabb's small Delta Force contingent groaned, eager to attack, but held back by their leader.

"Dramatic," he whispered to the Rabbi.

"Quite," Rabb peered through field binoculars.

Benjamin caught a quick look at the prick, Agent Osbourne. He completed a call on his cell phone and signaled to his agents. Rabb watched with a quizzical look as they packing up, shuffling back along the street and out of sight.

"Do you have General Crandal on the line yet?" Rabb asked Ice Man.

"No sir, we have an incoming call-"

"Must be trying to contact us," added Rabb, "take it."

Then Benjamin heard tear gas canisters, breaking glass as the men on rappel lines swung into the building. The entire force of men burst through the front doors of the church. Rabb took the call. Benjamin, only a few paces away, could hear the voice on the other end when something strange happened which caused them all to freeze:

The bullets stopped.

"Holy shit," someone muttered.

The smell was noxious--the room dark. The FBI Field Commander peered through his night-vision goggles, examining the room drenched in green light. The site defied logic, "What in the hell is going on?"

His team burst into the dark building, screaming, yelling--firing warning shots--still the people inside did not move. What he hadn't been able to see from the fiber optic vantage point was that they were all kneeling, chanting in Latin, oblivious to his men's' presence.

The sight defied logic. The terrorist crouched on long church benches, eyes forward, lips chanting in whispers. The Field Commander struck one of the figures on the shoulder, but the man was oblivious to him, knees pressed together, hands in a praying position as he chanted in the dead language—some were dead, others half alive.

"What the fuck's going on?" the Field Commander wondered aloud.

Then the inhuman stench was too much for him. He pulled the collar of his shirt to his nose. It did little to help. His stomach churned—he began dry heaving and collapsed on the wet floor. One soldier with a video camera attached to his helmet scanned ghouls—there was no other word to describe them. Then he noticed it. In the haze of his night sights, he touched his wet clothes--held his fingers near his nose, smelling the distinct scent.

"Oh no."

"Get out of Monongahela now!" screamed Tom Grant.

Even Benjamin could hear him screaming over Rabb's phone. Too many thing happening at once, thought Benjamin. The gunfire stopped! What the hell was going on in that building?

Rabb stammered. "Tom, h-h-how did you know I'm in-"

"Your hunch was right!" cried Tom—Benjamin could still hear him, "the Master is Bobby Lefrete!"

"That's impossible," interjected Rabb.

He created Monongahela as a trap for you! Candice read this all on Nehemiah's computer—Lefrete is operating under some alias, but he's part of the government team—he's the spy!"

"Fall back!" ordered Rabb.

Benjamin and the Delta Force team retreated away from the street, negotiating around cars, heading back to the travel agency headquarters. He saw Rabb out of the corner of his eye, fiddling on his phone, muttering, "C'mon Remy, answer the damn phone!"

11:52 PM (EST)
New York, NY

"Looks like Monongahela's secured," added Colonel Sharpe.

General Crandal glanced around his headquarters in The World Trade Center. Thick snow fell on either side of the massive glass windows.

"We are ready with the secondary attack preparations!" added Sharpe.

"Sharpe," ordered Crandal, "prepare the mortar crew. We're about to-"

His personal phone rang. He picked it up, hearing Rabb on the other end, "You've got to call off the attack! It's a trap!" screamed Rabb, "do you hear me, a trap! They know what we've been doing all along!"

11:53 PM (EST)
Monongahela, PA

The horrific chanting wouldn't stop.

The Field Commander looked away from the coating of syrupy coating on the floor. He lifted up his boot—making a sucking sound along coating of blood, feces, and urine. Most of his men were hunched over, vomiting. A few escaped the pool by fleeing onto the elevated alter.

"Half the people in this room are dead!" cried one of his men.

The Field Commander's eyes scanned the seemingly endless rows of men, all chanting in harmony, all bleeding. pushed over one of the ghouls. The man toppled to the ground, eyes dreamily staring at the ceiling, lips still moving in chorus with the others.

He scanned the sweaty, pale faces, sunken eyes, emaciated limbs—had they been here for weeks? He looked around at the windows and doors sealed tight, catching sight of the air vents on the far wall stopped up with freezer tape and cardboard as if this place were meant to be. . . to be a tomb?

Then he saw a face he recognized—how could he ever recognize someone here. Then he noted the pattern on the suspect's neck. With the muzzle of his rifle, the Field Commander pried the man's shirt lose-- buttons flying into the air, sticking to wet sludge coating the floor. The vertical incision ran from the base of the neck to the lower abdomen, the horizontal incision slicing across the left and right breasts: the shape of a cross. It was an old cut, the area around the wound bruising yellow--swelling with purplish dots of bacteria.

"Sir," cried one of his officers, "y-y-you need to look at this!"

The Commander walked over to him and froze. Positioned under the wooden alter, hidden from the view of their overhead fiber optical cameras, were two metal canisters labeled in black print: "RDX, PROPERTY OF THE FBI."

The field commander knew the substance well. His team had deployed identical canisters, using only a fraction of the amount blast the rear of a jet plane in hostage extraction drills, or a wall in mock terrorist situations. It was a combination of C-4 explosives, hexamethylenetetramine, and nitric acid. Then he realized how he recognized the ghoulish man, but--

"Look at this!" the soldier pointed at a fishing line attached to the tank. The snapped line was secured with a clothespin: a mousetrap detonator! Someone had tripped it—Oh no--there was enough explosives here to-

"GET OUT!," The Field Commander cried, "GET THE HELL OUT OF—"

11:55 PM (EST)
New York, NY

General Crandal winced.

Rabb screamed over the phone, "It's a trap! Do you understand! I can't tell you all the details now, but the Master is the mole! The Master is the mole!"

Crandal glanced around the control center, "That's a load of shit—"

The line clicked suddenly died.

11:55 PM (EST)
Monongahela, PA

Benjamin gasped!

The sky lit up--as if the sun had crashed into Monongahela! Instinctively, Bronk threw his body across Rabb's, attempting to push them through the doorway of the headquarters when the explosion lit up the sky!

He and Rabb were in mid-air when the shock wave impacted them, flinging their bodies through the glass window of the command center. The executive caught sight of Ice Man tumbling through the air, a wall of glass howling close behind—glass and metal—he was flying through the air-- an automobile rocketed by-- ringing in his ears—couldn't even hear the sound of his pulse—then alone in darkness. . . and he thought. . . this is the end. . . all things stripped away. . . naked and alone—and he could think only of his children.

11:59 PM (EST)
New York, NY

Chaos.

"Rabb," whispered General Crandal.

"We have major thermal readings in Monongahela!" screamed Sharpe.

Every sensor and alarm in the entire brain center of Fort Crandal exploded into a raging cacophony. A warning light blared from the corner of the room. Colonel Sharpe danced around the computer banks, calling in other soldiers to assist him with the equipment he usually let no one else touch. The monitors were going hay-wire, the computer systems chirping, printers printing.

"That isn't just Monongahela," Crandal muttered to himself.

A line of phones in the far corner of the room rang simultaneously. Remy rushed to them, dodging Eleanor who held a champagne glass as she stared at monitors. He stopped, catching sight of her expression--raw, naked fear--the masterful chin began to shake, tears welling in her eyes as she whispered, "My son." The champagne glass crashed to the floor, shattering into pieces.

Spinning around, the General glanced at the television monitor and felt the air in his lungs escape him. He could see LACROSSE following the spread of endothermic reactions outward from the refinery. Without warning, every gas sensor alarm around the refinery fired up.

"Gas sensors firing in the northern perimeter," screamed Sharpe.

"Has there been an explosion at Union 57?" asked Crandal.

"No," the General let out a sigh only to hear, "LACROSSE confirms Union 57 is dumping gas straight to atmosphere. We have readings of hydrofluoric acid! Phosgene! Sulfuric acid! Oh no, twenty times the levels of Methyl Isocyanate than Bhopal—headed right for us!"

"Scramble the Comlink to the White House," grunted Remy in a mad rage, "tell em we got a big fucking problem!"

part four
THE GRAND DESIGN

Thirty Eight

It sounded like a snake hissing.

At the northwestern perimeter of the Union 57 refinery—beneath dark towers of pipe and steel sat tank #546. From its open control valve rushed an invisible gas with a mild scent of almonds called hydrogen cyanide—a chemical so lethal that .6 grams administered to a rat caused instant pulmonary edema: fluid buildup in the lungs exploding outward, choking the victim.

Thirty yards away, tanks # 456 and #457 housed two other lethal gasses under great pressure and at very low temperature: methyl isocyanate or MIC and monomethylamine—two equally lethal chemical compounds.

By 12:10 AM Wednesday morning, tanks #456, #457, and #546 were empty— the final whizzing sound of pressurized gas escaping. Over 176,000 lbs. of gas climbed with the cold updrafts seventy feet off the ground. The body of vapor was stroked by a strong northeasterly wind, carried out over the shipping pier towards Jersey Bay. The refinery was ghostly at that moment, devoid of all humans who temporarily fled to the hermetically sealed security/ engineering building. Then it wafted over the bay—an invisible angle of death.

The MIC tripped the remote sensors which the Delta Force had set days before. The second cloud of Monomethylamine, thirty yards south, had not yet registered--the true magnitude of the threat was still unknown. By 12:13 AM, while General RM Crandal and his staff sized up the situation, the poison cloud had killed all of the Delta Force soldiers on their attack boats still moored in the harbor. The gas continued, swirling and spiraling towards the glistening lights of Wall Street and the southern tip of Manhattan.

12:11 AM (EST)
New York, NY

The world spun around General RM Crandal.

He saw Eleanor Bronk, face frozen in shock. Even she had lost her calm demeanor: the jutting chin freezing in nerve chilling fear.

"Sensors are tracking the cloud!" cried Colonel Sharpe.

Because of the temperature differential of the gasses, LACROSSE registered the cloud on the monitors. The twisting lines covered most of the shipping channel as it moved across Newark Bay to Bayonne, working its way to the northeast. Jesus Christ, Remy thought to himself, this fucker was at least three miles wide, "I need reports!" he barked.

Sharpe tried to remain calm, "We've lost contact with our attack team in the shipping channel!" his fingers pointed towards the center of the cloud on the monitor, "she's juiced full of gasses. Should we evacuate?"

Evacuate? This was his moment. When the odds were stacked against you—Chamberlain at Little Round Top, Patton in the Ardenne. When on the defensive, one must strive for the offensive, "Sharpe, is the physics package in place?" he referred to the neutron bomb.

"Yes sir."

Shit, at least one thing was working. He would take out that plant right now, he thought to himself, before they leaked any more crap into the world! Crandal would stay, but he couldn't ask his men to do the same, "Sharpe, you and I will stay to the last minute--download our computer banks to The White House Situation Room and oversee the bomb," commanded the General , "I want everybody else evacuated now."

Although General Crandal was months from mandatory retirement, he was eager to take one last charge. He wasn't leaving--to retreat in total ignominy after such a long and glorious career, unthinkable! Hell, he'd rather be dead than chasing a white ball across fairway greens.

"We are ready with bomb!" Sharpe yelled.

He prepared to give the order. Fuck it all, he was going to nuke those sonsofbitches straight to hell. Then his Comlink rang. "General Crandal, I presume, " the caller spoke in a foreign accent.

"Who is this?"

There was heavy breathing on the other end, gasping--spitting, "I am the one that sent this gift to you." He knew the caller was Nehemiah. Crandal's expression must have revealed his own shocked surprise because Eleanor focused on him. He turned, facing the window, "How'd you get this number?"

"Let's not waste time with details. The wind is blowing northeast tonight."

"Thanks for the weather report, bozo. What'd'ya want?"

"I hope you're not getting any ideas with bombs—"

Bombs! How the hell would he know anything about that, thought Crandal. Hell, how did Nehemiah get his own private comlink number. Sharpe gestured to him--just ten seconds before the bomb launched!

"My explosives," continued Nehemiah, "in the refinery are encased in lead lined chambers protecting them from the EMP of your bomb," General Crandal's head spun--he couldn't believe what he was hearing. These terrorists were impervious to nuclear attack, "I wear a detonator box on my wrist which must be pressed every ten minutes. My detonators are set up on an automatic feedback system. If I'm killed, the bombs will blow with or without me."

The line clicked dead.

Shit he remembered Candice telling them about a box taped to that bastard's wrist! He really did have a mole—as Tom claimed, "Stop the attack," Crandal's voice was weak.

"What?" Sharpe stammered, "we're about to-"

"Stop it now!"

Colonel Sharpe and others stared up at him. The General turned to the LACROSSE monitor—the poison cloud meandered towards Bayonne, New Jersey. Was there nothing he could do?

12:16 AM (EST)
Monongahela, PA

Benjamin Bronk found himself lying next to a Ford pickup truck.

The Ford was upside down. He tried to remember where he was--what made him lie down in shattered glass. Slowly he sat up. His right elbow blazed with pain--shards of glass sticking out of his flesh. The room was illuminated in shimmering orange.

He took a deep breath. He was alive—actually alive! He cocked his head to one side, but could only see only a large chunk of rock or asphalt teetering precariously close to him. Pushing back on his forearms, he tried to sit up. The pain in his chest was excruciating. He fell backwards, rolling to his side in a strange choreography of pain.

Through what had once been the front wall he could see a massive crater in the center of town—all things wiped away. He stumbled to his feet, he noticed bodies scattered and still. One man looked awkward--Benjamin stopped for a moment, realizing the figure was missing his lower torso. The former headquarters was filled with broken people--blood and limbs—fingers, boots, hands, feet.

Then he saw the Rabbi.

The black man lay on top of a collapsed wall, Ice Man's sprawled alongside. Rabb was awake, muttering feebly, "You alright?"

Tears welled in Benjamin's eyes. To see this pillar of strength so weak, it made him feel so empty—they were never going to win this. Then he remembered his children—waking him up like a bolt of lightning.

"This has got to be part of a double attack. Something's happened at Union 57," grunted Rabb, "they've done something horrible."

12:27 AM (EST)
New York, NY

General RM Crandal felt helpless.

He watched the trail of gas on the television monitor.

The winds blew it north along Newark Bay until a cross wind pushed it gently to the east. Not enough time, thought Remy, not enough time to evacuate or do anything, "Jesus Christ," he whispered in disbelief, "it's making landfall."

12:27 AM (EST)
Jersey City, NJ

The dog was the first to notice.

He barked madly, growling at the strange smell which he sensed in far greater proportion than his human masters. Tugging on his chain, he fled into his dog house, paws scraping madly against the dirt. The gas was attracted to the warmer dog house, seeping insidiously through the cracks between wood and earth. The dog felt a moment of twisted fear and rushed out, snapping his chain. With his nose as a guide, he leapt over a fence onto the cold, icy street.

The gas flowed upward from the dog house, curling around power lines—then caught in a cross-flow current between two homes which led it to the attic of the second home where it seeped through the ventilator grill. Once inside, the pressure differentials drove it forward. . . tiny fingers swirling through coatings of insulation, working its way down through the cracks of a light fixture in the ceiling.

It sank to the floor of a dark bedroom, but a current coursing under the closed door lifted the finger up, spreading it wide along the covers of the bed. The woman in her mid-thirties rolled on her side as the subtle hint of almonds danced in her nose. She took a breath, sucking the vapors deep within her lungs. The MIC and hydrogen cyanide rushed down her throat and she experienced a horrible sensation.

The outer layers of her lungs burned away, filling the respiratory cavity with dead, flaking tissue. His respiratory system instantly reacted by pumping copious amounts of mucous into her lungs, bathing the damaged tissue. Then the hydrogen cyanide worked through her body--she gasped—unable to breath!

Reaching for the bedside lamp, her husband inhaled the scentless gas. By the time the lamp was on, he grasped his throat, choking on an invisible source. Her motherly instincts kicked in, her first thought was for the infant child in the next room. She leapt out of the bed—legs tangled in the sheets and blankets as she clawed her way towards the door.

From the corner of her eye, she saw her husband: shaking, convulsing, foam rising from his mouth. She blocked out the image--her entire being focused on getting to her baby's room!

Her husband crashed to the floor--the lamp and bed-stand falling on top of him. His hands cupped around his face, blood pooled around his body. She had to get out of this room! Then she felt her intestines cramp up-- as if someone had sliced her body in two with a machete.

Her bowels evacuated--mind numbing nausea rushed up her spine. When her head hit the floor, she saw foam rushing out of her mouth, foaming onto the carpet. A moment later she heard her baby screaming from the other room. Every ounce of her energy tried to employ itself to get up, but she could not. She lay there, prostrate--trapped—her body became a living tomb.

Her baby continued to scream from the other room. She could only lay still, entombed—choking on the sea of mucous insider her. The baby continued screaming. She could no longer breath—the room went dark and--

Her baby stopped screaming.

The dog ran down the cold, lifeless street.

Wind rustled the limbs of leafless, winter trees. Windows were thrown open, heads sticking out, screaming for help. A few jumped out of the upper stories of their homes! At the far end of the street, a young couple stood in their yard, flashlights in hand. The husband wore a puzzled look, staring curiously down the street, hearing faint voices crying out in the dark. The dog barked once as he passed—perhaps a canine warning? But it was not understood. the couple felt the burning in their throats. The couple collapsed, cupping their throats.

The gaseous body infected a square mile radius around the street. . . coursing through homes and bars and bus stops and offices and diners like a silent angel of death. There would be no alarms. No one had time to call the authorities. Out of this entire street with fifteen homes, only the dog survived. Even then, the dog was getting tired. He continued running along the cold street. If he had bothered to look up, he would have seen the massive New York skyline rising in the distance. . .less than a mile across the harbor. Perhaps the dog even understood the futility of his own escape. For the wind was still howling-

And no animal could outrun the wind.

12:35 AM (EST)
12,000 FT. Over Monongahela PA

Flashlights bounced around the destroyed building.

Rubble and shards of broken glass illuminated in the faint gaze of light. Benjamin could see soldiers prowling the streets and heard the choppers landing. Then a soldier was standing over them, the bright yellow letters of his shirt reading DELTA FORCE.

"Benjamin," Rabb whispered now, barely conscious.

"I'm here!" Benjamin reached out, grabbing the man's hand—his fingers seemed as wide as Benjamin's whole hand. Rabb gripped him tightly, "get their phone."

"What?"

The soldier continued to muddle around, afraid of journeying too deep into the building, his flashlight falling upon them as he scanned the room for survivors.

"I just realized it!" the black man swallowed hard, "Remy has the answer," he winced, "it's so elementary. I know how he can stop whatever they've done!"

Thirty Nine

"The download is complete," replied Colonel Sharpe.

Sharpe, Eleanor, and Crandal were the last to leave the control room. Everyone had already piled into the choppers waiting on the roof. Eleanor glanced at him. He could tell from her look that she knew he wasn't leaving.

Remy liked this woman—in some distant scenario, he could have seen falling for her. Although she hailed from a different world, she was a fighter and would never give up—which is why he let her hang around. Still they weren't here to have a garden party, "It's time for y'all ta leave."

"What!" she gasped, "you're not coming!"

"Get out!" he barked, turning back to LACROSSE's video monitor.

"I'm not leaving! Where do I have to go, Remy?" she pleaded—the hint of naked hopelessness in her voice, "I told you already, one of my son's is probably dead. My grandchildren are practically dead," for the first time exhaustion and anger and frustration showed on her face. The tight, puckered cheeks turned red, the jaw moving back and forth in slow piston like motions, "and I have no life without my town--I won't leave! I'm staying with you and that's that!"

"Fine," General Crandal sighed, "you're old enough to make that decision-"

"Well, I'm not that old," she quipped.

And the General actually laughed.

"See," she grinned, wiping the tears from her face, "what would you do without me? Death would be a real bore," the tears seemed so out of place, like water on steel, thought the General.

He didn't hear her. His mind focused on the greater problem: how could you destroy a three mile wide cloud spreading its lethal fingers and branches across homes and highways? Damn it, he wished Rabb were here! Rabb always had the answers. How could you kill something you couldn't touch?

12:53 AM (EST)
The Upper New York Bay

The poison cloud sought the path of least resistance as it flowed along the New York Harbor, towards the skyscrapers and office buildings of the lower financial district, shielding the wind from its vaporous body. The cloud zigzagged like a drunken sailor to the shore.

It was less than a two hundred yards south of Manhattan.

12:59 AM (EST)
The Upper New York Bay

Benjamin Bronk took a deep breath.

The soldier had escorted them by jeep to the only cellular phone left in town. They were their massive Starlifter jet, back in the conference room they had met as they blindly headed to Monongahela—except now the rear hold was stuffed full of wounded men about to be air-lifted out of town.

The whole plain smelled of sweat and death. Benjamin helped a wounded Rabb to the phone built into the wall of the cabin. Bleeding, unable to hear, the burly black man dialed the number—leaving blood and dirt stains on the buttons of the phone.

"C'mon!" screamed the Rabbi, "connect damn you—connect!"

1:00 AM (EST)
The Upper New York Bay

Another cross wind spun one of its arms out a hundred yards. The cloud was now less than eighty yards from the shores of Manhattan.

1:02 AM (EST)
New York, NY

Think, damn you, think!

General Crandal searched his mind for any solution, but all escaped him. Was this the end, the way he'd die, choking on some toxin? Sharpe remained standing—he wasn't leaving either.

Remy was about tell his second in command to get the hell out when he noticed it on LACROSSE's monitor-- the cloud touched the southern point of Manhattan. Where was there to go now? He would not give up! He peered out the window, now able to watch the victims of the cloud.

Then his comlink rang. He picked it up—

"REMY, WHAT'S HAPPENED?" it was Rabb!

1:03 AM (EST)
The Bay Just Opposite The World Financial Center, NY

The edge of the invisible cloud crawled along the shores of Manhattan, circling around The World Financial Center across the street from The World Trade Center where Remy Crandal stood watching.

The cross wind pushed the gas past windows-washers who instantly keeled over, coughing and foaming. The gas rushed through the ductwork, turning and pulling and seeping out of the grills, emptying out into the adjacent parking lot where two lawyers, who had been burning the midnight oil, climbed into their respective cars.

1:04 AM (EST)
New York, NY

"Rabies," General Crandal held the phone firm, "I don't have time to review the-"

Eleanor's ears peaked. "Is Benjamin alive?"

"DAMN IT, TELL ME!" Rabb demanded. Crandal glanced through the window at the street far below him, "Well they released a bunch of toxins—"

"Where's the cloud now?" asked Rabb.

"'Bout a block away."

"Damn it you blockhead," scolded Rabb, "use the damn bomb!"

A millisecond of thoughts--what a fool he'd been! The bomb! The nuclear implosion would vaporize anything organic—including organically combined chemicals! The implosion would concentrate all the remaining gas into ground zero and blow it straight into the stratosphere! But wait? The physics package had been modified for a tiny blast zone, barely a square mile long—the dimensions of the Union 57 plant!

"Sharpe!" he turned to his second in command, "use shell on the cloud!"

"What? It's not large enough. The shell was sized for the Union 57 plant," replied the Colonel.

"What's the blast range on the second one?" screamed Crandal. Sharpe took a moment to think, "damn it, think man!"

"I-I d-don't know," Sharpe screwed his eyes up, running a mental calculation in his head, "maybe two and a half--three miles?"

"Fire the fucker!" cried Crandal.

"What?" the Colonel looked surprised—then his head swung back as if someone hit him from behind, the idea striking him like a lightning-bolt, "I w-well I need proper coordinate!" he rushed to the computer consul.

"Ask him if Benjamin is fine!" screamed Eleanor.

No time, thought Crandal, "It's done Rabb. Get off line! I have to call The White House!"

1:06 AM (EST)
Upper New York Bay

"Aaighh!"

Two lawyers in The World Financial Center parking collapsed onto the ground, mucous erupting from their moths. Beyond the garage, the upper vector of the cloud covered everything from Whitehall to Coenties St—the gaseous body was over six hundred feet high.

It enveloped everything from the tip of Manhattan to Bayonne, New Jersey. Another minute or so--with the current wind conditions—it would be carried over the towering skyscrapers, falling upon Tribeca, Greenwich Village, and Midtown—areas filled with people sleeping through the cold, winter night.

1:07 AM (EST)
New York, NY

"You got those coordinates yet?" cried Crandal.

"I just need a moment to calculate the drop point," Sharpe grunted, "One wrong coordinate and we take out Brooklyn or the island!"

"Just blow the fucking thing out the back door!" cried the General.

"What?" the voice echoed in his ear. It was the Razorback.

The comlink had connected with The White House Situation Room. Remy's hands were so sweaty, he had to grasp the phone with both hands, "I need authority to launch the mortar shell—"

"What!" raged the Razorback from the other end—

"Fuck it," grumbled the General. He tried to get permission, but he had no time for talk. He slammed the phone down, glancing back at the television monitor. The cloud covered the financial, "Hurry Sharpe! Hurry!"

"A moment longer!"

"This is killing me!" groaned Eleanor Bronk.

"Just do it now!" ordered the General, "I'd rather fry from a bomb than-"

"Got it!" screamed the Colonel, typing the final launch coordinates into the email file, "we are go!"

The Colonel pressed the button. The data file was emailed at the speed of light from The World Trade Center to an Army communication satellite hovering 236 miles above the earth which bounced the signal to the Pentagon ground satellite tracking station in Washington DC which routed it to a separate satellite over the Midwest, transmitting it back down to the mortar crew in Elizabeth, NJ.

1:09 AM (EST)
Elizabeth, NJ

"We have launch authorization!" the mortar cannon operator spoke, mist forming in the cold air.

There were only two of them in the old, abandoned room. Three sentries stood guard just outside the door and the rest of the platoon were positioned in various points around the condemned structure.

The cannon operator grabbed the second shell, loading it into the mortar cannon. Then he turned around, facing the large, black box resting next to the cannon. From the box two stereoscopic video cameras flashed a vivid infrared light into his eye. At the speed of light, the computer scanned his inner cornea, verifying a pulse and 22,000 ID points within the corneal vessel. With authentication confirmed, the device sent the infrared code to the missile's computer chip. A microsecond later, the strategic neutron bomb was armed.

"Fire!"

It happened in terms of milliseconds.

The mortar shell shot through the air at the speed of sound. The room disappeared in a fiery wake— the entire city of Elizabeth streaming behind the mortar shells' bullet-speed wake. The shell skirted the low cloud cover, spiraling down, the force of gravity drawing its cylindrical body to the earth. The bay rushed under—a flash of black—it was a thousand feet above the New York harbor--placed between The Statue of Liberty and The World Trade Center—six hundred feet--two hundred feet.

Something clicked in its metal innards.

The inner workings of the shell was composed of separate, individual compartments holding different elements. By breaking down the outer compartment, the individual elements in the first layer mixed, setting off a reaction which broke the next layer down until all the elements percolated in one organic soup. The reactionary soup pierced the beryllium lining, collapsing into the next layer of uranium 235. The soupy reaction caused the uranium 235 to collapse into the next compartment housing plutonium 239 which then cavitated into a core of tritium gas. A millisecond later, the chemical cocktail reached critical mass.

The atoms comprising Uranium 235 were cut in half like a knife slicing an apple in two. Uranium 235, a heavier element, transformed into Uranium 234, a lighter one. The splitting of these uranium atoms unleashed an amazing burst of energy and for one incalculably short moment in time, a single, solitary point over the New York harbor reached the unique state of being naturally found only within a star.

No sound was produced.

A quick flash of white, hot light was emitted over the center of the bay, reflecting off the glass windows of The World Trade Center. The invisible forces of the explosion raced outward, vaporizing the lawyers dying in the parking lot—the cleaning team inside The Financial Center. The lights and electrical system of the entire structure shorted out, all connective wires fried by the EMP pulse.

Every plant, human, animal, rat, virus, bacteria, insect, and carbon based life form from the Financial Center to The Statue of Liberty were instantly vaporized and for a single, solitary moment in time, this two square mile area was the cleanest, most sterile place on earth.

The blast burned up half of the poison cloud-- everything from the financial district to the lower New York bay. A millisecond later, the implosion force sucked the remaining 45,000 lbs. of the gas back to ground zero—where the mortar shell fired.

To an observer, one would have noticed two curiosities. First, all lights and electrically operated items from The Financial Center to Bayonne, New Jersey went black from the EMP, dousing New York harbor in darkness. The second was the thick, winter clouds parting in a wide, dark circle, funneling back towards the stars--as if someone had pulled the plug in an upside-down drain.

The hydrogen cyanide and Methyl isocyanate were sucked straight into the upper atmosphere, rising 47,000 ft. into the air. What little gas left, was blown into the stratosphere, breaking up and diluting with the ethereal solar winds of outer space.

2:02 AM (EST)
New York, NY

Remy's hands shook.

Colonel Sharpe stared at the monitor with a blank expression—sweat pouring down his face. In the passing of single moment, the cloud had vanished off their screen.

"Oh dear," Eleanor gasped.

"I don't believe it," Colonel Sharp whispered to himself. Remy winked back at his second in command wiping beads of sweat from his face. His clothes were soaking wet from perspiration.

Crandal looked down realizing his shirt was also soaking. Then he smiled, full of bravado, "Well ya better believe it. Remy Crandal don't ever die and he don't ever lose!"

2:03 AM (EST)
New York, NY

Benjamin Bronk examined the inner cabin of the aircraft.

The aircraft shuddered as it crossed through turbulence. Rabb was enraptured as he watched the videotape linked to the FBI strike force agents just prior to the blast. Benjamin reviewed the tape with him, but had no idea what he found so interesting.

The aircraft shuddered as it crossed the thick cloud cover still locking in the east coast. Benjamin walked into the second rear office. This was his moment—he reached over picking up the bloodied phone, dialing send. It rang for a moment and then-- "Mueller here," his head of security replied from the other end.

A shiver passed through Benjamin's entire body. He wanted to speak, but tears flowed down his cheeks, "Did you find my kids?"

"No, but Jesus Christ, Benjamin—you could've called. I have something I have to show you," Mueller sounded visibly shaken. What could be more important than his own children, " come to your apartment alone. And whoever you think these terrorists are, I have the proof to show you're completely wrong!"

Forty

2:45 AM (EST) 1:45 (CST)
New Orleans, LA

Tom Grant walked quickly.

He couldn't get Rabb on the phone. He had sat in his hotel room, dialing the Rabbi's number over and over—craving any info as to what happened in

Monongahela. Then he remembered Dussant's turtle soup. There was none on the room service menu. He dialed Galatoire's--no one answered. So he decided to go down there, find a late night employee and talk his way into some soup.

He crossed Decatur Street. . .the tacky tourists and smell of stale beer vanishing behind him--he could hear his footsteps echo off the ancient streets. The cool, winter bite in the wind vanished, replaced by a thick, wet humidity that coated everything in dampness. The temperature would be in the eighties tomorrow, mused Tom, then it might freeze the next night. One never knew what to wear for winter in Louisiana.

He spotted Bourbon St. in the distance—The moon came out from behind the clouds--milky light bathing the wet street. Then something grabbed him, spinning him into darkness.

The figure slammed him against the alley-wall, ramming a forearm against his throat, "You didn't heed my warning!" the figure grunted between clenched teeth. It was Mr. Help.

Tom reached for his pistol but Mr. Help got to his first, placing the cold end of the barrel against Grant's forehead, "Don't even try it," he grunted, spinning him around at gunpoint, dragging him deeper into the alley.

Tom felt his pulse thump so loudly that he had to strain in order to listen. He smelled the musky scent of "Old Spice" on Mr. Help mixed with the scents of decaying garbage all around them.

"You're an amateur, Agent. Grant," Mr. Help spun him around--he could now see his aggressor's face in the darkness, "you fool! Two plain clothed men have been following you for almost two hours!"

Tom heard a sound at the end of the alley. He turned and saw two men mulling around at the alley's opening.

"We best get back to your hotel," Mr. Help continued, "there are things I need to tell you."

Tom followed him because he craved answers. He noticed the slight limp in Mr. Help's leg and the fact that it didn't slow down his gate. As he weaved through the alleyway, Tom wondered what Mr. Help's real name was and a how a man could wind up in such a secret and dark world? Everything to do with Yves Alexander Dussant seemed unreal--men with alias's and too many guns, crazy NSA reports, and then the culmination of it all. . . Agent Willard turning ever so slowly around, blood covering his face-

"Did you ask it about the Israel excursion?" asked Mr. Help as they exited the alleyway on the next block, jogging towards Decatur St.

"Yes," Tom took in deep breaths as he ran, "but Dussant said that he and his mother went to Israel and then she-" Tom took another deep breath, they were practically sprinting, "she steered the car off a cliff killing them both," he scoffed.

Mr. Help just nodded his head.

"What?" Tom stopped, "you saying Yves Alexander died!"

The headlights of cars on Decatur St. reflected off Mr. Help's pudgy, red face before he crossed the street.

"Y-you said Dussant was a con-man," gasped Tom as he followed, "c-con-men don't rise from the grave. That stuff's reserved for religious parables."

"I did not say Dussant was a con man--I said 'it' was a con man. There's a difference."

They entered the hotel, hopping into one of the elevator's. They were now alone as the lift delivered them up to the massive lobby many stories above.

"If I'm being followed," continued Tom, "shouldn't we avoid the hotel?"

"Doesn't matter now.

The elevator doors opened. Through the far lobby windows, Tom saw the sweeping view of the city—twinkling lights of ships and barges headed through the Batavia Delta into the open waters of The Gulf.

"We need to talk in your room," barked Mr. Help, stepping out of the elevator, heading to the other bank of lifts leading up to the hotel rooms.

Tom stood stoically in the elevator. If Mr. Help intended on killing him, he thought, then his hotel room would be a perfect place. A suicide case. . . a gun planted in his open hand or perhaps he'd be thrown out the window—would look far more real than a murder in a back alley. No, thought Tom resolutely, he would converse with Mr. Help here in the lobby: where he was safe.

Mr. Help realized what he wanted, "We can't actually talk out here in the open lobby," his eyes darting suspiciously around the room.

"I'm not gonna speak anywhere else," Tom strolled to a couch in the center of the room. Even at this hour, a few drunk revelers were scattered across the sprawling couches, queerly looking at him. The red faced stranger finally acquiesced and followed him, sitting down in a chair.

"Was Dussant killed in Israel in 1970?" asked Tom. First Dr. Brandt had breezed over the point and then Mr. Help had discounted the entire affair. What was so damn important about that moment in time?

"It's true," muttered Mr. Help, "from what we can understand, on July 12th, 1970, Mrs. Dussant drove her Mercedes limousine off an ocean-side cliff just outside the city of Haifa, killing both herself and her son, Yves Alexander Dussant," curiously, noted Tom, it was the first time that Mr. Help called the man by his true name. He continued, "the Israeli authorities recovered both bodies that afternoon."

"Wait a minute," Tom kept his voice low, "who could I.D. the bodies? Yves Alexander wasn't yet under observation by the government. And anyone who had ever seen him on The Wayfarer Estate had killed themselves-"

"They both had dental records," he shifted his eyes around, uneasy in the open lobby, "Israeli officials demanded an inquest. The coroner discovered water in the lungs of both bodies confirming that they drowned. Bruises on Mrs. Dussant's breast and sternum confirmed she was behind the wheel during the point of impact. More curiously, Yves Alexander's blood levels held three times the lethal dose of a sleeping drug called diazepam."

Yes, he recalled, Dussant had hinted at that fact.

"A more detailed physical exam was performed. The coroner discovered traces of sperm in Mrs. Dussant's vagina-- she'd had sex a few hours prior to death. Even more alarming were scars on the inner lining of the uterus suggesting an E&D device employed in abortions. Yves Alexander's mother and he were connected at the hip for as long as anyone could remember. You don't need Freud to put those two together."

"An assumption based on circumstantial evidence. She could have aborted fetuses from her husband years before? She could have engaged in sex with another man shortly before her death? There was no electrophoresis or genetic testing at that time."

Mr. Help pressed on, "As Mrs. Dussant's will spelled out, Yves Alexander's aunt chose to bury them on The Wayfarer Estate. Three months after the burial, the creature, claiming to be Dussant, started up the Cult on The plantation. It claimed it awoke naked in the cemetery on Dussant's exhumed coffin. At the time, the IRS had frozen all Dussant assets for back taxes-- trapped in a court succession, no one was eyeing the place. He set up house--fostered his cult."

"Where is the body of the dead Yves Alexander Dussant?"

"We do not know. What we do know is that we suddenly were faced with a very dangerous creature--"

"Why not stick him up in the North Pole if he's so dangerous—where he could harm no one?"

"It was believed that isolated environments would be the worst place. Separated from the outside world, the guards and personnel could be even more susceptible to the creature's powers. Ironically, it was, therefore, placed in a populated area where prison personnel could be grounded in reality. The government felt it more palatable to hold him in his own home in case word of the affair broke out."

Tom had enough of all this double talk. Rabb might be dead for all he knew. Candice's life was in jeopardy. He finally said it, "What the hell does this have to do with Bobby Lefrete?"

Mr. Help was thunderstruck by the name, "Bobby Lefrete," the gears of his mind shifted into overdrive as he placed a firm hand on Tom's arm, "had no idea. . . if you're looking for Bobby Lefrete you have to go to Wayfarer with me—now."

"What? Wayfarer's hours from here!"

"You have to!"

Tom pulled away. Others were staring at them now. He was careful to whisper his reply, "There's only one place I'm going and that's back to Yves Alexander."

4:01 AM (EST)
Elizabeth, NJ / 20 Ft. under The Union 57 refinery in the drainage pipes

Schubert's lungs were on fire!

Darkness everywhere. The cold water rushed around him. He had no sense of direction, slamming into the sides of the tunnel, dragging Gummy Bear behind him by the handcuffs. Where was Candice? His body was on fire—craving a breath of air.

He tried to hold on as long as he could. For a while, they were on some type of metal bar cutting across the roof of the pipeline. The water was rising and they were running out of air. Finally letting go, he took a deep breath and surrendered to the torrent of water.

His eyes felt like they were bugging out of his head. No more air. . . nothing. Then he caught site of gray sky, so starkly different from the surroundings of the past hours. He took a deep, violent gasp of air. He felt himself shot out of the tunnel into the freezing waters of the shipping pier. Then darkness again, silence punctuated by the gurgle of air bubbles. Gummy kicked him the head, jolting him awake. He fought and clawed his way to the surface for a single breath of air.

He shot out of the water, mouth arched wide as he breathed. A moment later he dragged Gummy's head up. The little man was barely coherent. Schubert breathed again and again and then scanned the pier trimmed in early dawn light. Then he heard it.

Baannnggggg.

It sounded so slow and exaggerated—as if someone had taped the sounds of gunfire and then played it back in slow motion. The sound shuddered through him.

"Gummy want to go home now!" Gummy chattered, refusing to go any farther, "Gummy don't like this."

I agree, thought Schubert as he felt hands on him. Then they lifted him onto the rocks—hands upon him and a taunting laugh, "Well well well," someone laughed, "looky what we got here."

Forty One

4:39 AM (EST)
New York, NY

Benjamin and Rabb took the lift up.

The flabbergasted doorman watched his billionaire tenant, weary and tattered as he stumbled into One Sutton Place looking like two homeless derelicts. Inside the antique elevator, the familiar smell of the place caused a rush of emotions in Benjamin. For some reason he thought of the night he ask for Amanda's hand--after three years of casual meetings and occasional dinners. Using his mother's table at *La Grenouille*, his proposal was ever so Bronk, the art deco Van Cleef & Arpels ring waiting on the table upon their arrival.

"Well, what will it be?" he asked, the scent of flowers all around.

"Jesus, Benjamin," she took a deep breath, "this isn't a stock option."

"Will you be my wife?" he fuddled for words, "will you bear my children?"

"Is this an invitation to breed?" she smirked—that quizzical little half smile.

"Shut up and answer the damn question."

"Well, let's see--Moslems always introduce the second wife to the first one when proposing. Let's go see that one."

That night she made love to him atop his father's pool-table size desk. He remembered the scent of sex and furniture polish. Afterwards, she stood naked in front of the wall of windows overlooking the harbor. She would never be as beautiful to him as she was at that moment. . . the subtle curve of her back sweeping into the graceful, thin legs.

"What do you love about me, Benjamin?" she traced circles around her nipple with her index finger. And he thought love you but have no idea what's going on in your head. And how beautiful it was. How had they strayed so far away from that moment of intangible perfection?

The elevator doors opened.

Mueller bellowed, "What the fuck happened to you!"

The elevator doors opened onto his penthouse apartment. The smell of Christmas pine needles filled his nose. Mueller stood in the green marble foyer, leaning his bulky body against an antique Blackamoor.

His chief of security stepped forward. In his mid-sixties, Mueller cut a harsh, square figure-- square head, square shoulders, square body--a human rhomboid. With his trademark tan overcoat slung over his shoulder, he looked like a hard-boiled New York detective.

"What the fuck happened to you?" he repeated loudly.

Benjamin caught site of himself in the mirror-- his face was black with soot and cuts and blood that covered the tattered jumpsuit. He had left the aircraft without even seeing a doctor.

Then Mueller saw the Rabbi, still standing in the lift. His chief stiffened.

"It's alright, he's a friend," the executive slumped forward, pushing against the wall to stabilize his balance. He needed to sleep. . . just for a few minutes. . . shut his eyes, "he's with the government."

Mueller's eyes changed. He drew his pistol on the Rabbi. Benjamin trusted Mueller. When he took over Union 57, Mueller was the only old employee faithful to him. Together, they fought one of the bloodiest corporate battles in history—but what the hell was he doing?

"Put that gun away!" barked Benjamin.

"Just hear me out, kiddo."

"It's alright," muttered Rabb.

At gunpoint Mueller led Rabb into the living of the apartment. It had been the former Annenberg Hooker residence. Amanda took great care, refashioning the rooms in *Trompe l'oeil* so that the living room with neoclassical chairs, sponged walls, and ornate woodwork, resembled a Pompeian *Villa Of The Mysteries* with a view of the East River in lieu of Mount Vesuvius.

His Chief turned on the stereo-- a child sing song from his daughter's collection blared over speakers. Then he turned on the television and VCR. The security surveillance ape played--the camera was mounted in a corner of the Union 57 entrance post. Benjamin caught of the top of a man's head.

"He signed in at the security gate as Robert Fallow," Mueller coughed, "an outside contracting engineer for the turnaround on the Cat Cracker."

"And?"

"His real name's Jerry Kinder."

"How would you know that?" Benjamin didn't have time for games.

"He worked with me in the New Mexico FBI office for four years."

Bronk froze for a moment, turning back to the frozen image of the sixty odd year old man. Deep bags sweeping under his eyes, the character looked more like a janitor than a retired FBI agent, "Are you sure that-"

"Served with me for four years," continued his chief of security, "retired from the force three years ago. We're not good friends or anything, but I keep up with him--mostly at funerals and christenings now a'days. The guy retired to Clearwater, Florida to fish and fall apart. And guess what his specialty was? Explosives," he pushed fast forward, "there's more. Voila' Curtain Number 2."

The tape paused on a Latin American looking man--late forties. He was signing a log sheet--the walls and floor around him were different. This was taken from another guard shack.

"Logged in as Johnny McGhee," continued Mueller over the childish singsong, "look at that face. You'd have to be certifiably blind to pass that guy off as

Johnny McfuckingGhee! He should be sellin' hot tamales on the street!"

"So he anglicized his name."

"His name is Juan P. Reinota," continued Mueller, "head of the FBI's Carson City, Nevada office. I called around--guy's attending his mother-in law's funeral in Monterey, Mexico. He supposedly flew out of the country the very same morning he signed the log sheet at Union 57!"

Bronk studied the face, "This doesn't make any sense?" They'd just spent three days figuring out the real identity of this terrorist group—and now this?

"I couriered the tape to a buddy of mine," interrupted Mueller, "works in personnel at the Bureau--we went through Quantico together. He identified seven other FBI agents from the tape: their names are Terrence Stewel, Richard Martin, Carl Cotter, Roger Pzolsky, and James Reed, and Lou Pauzpolis.

All the agents entered Union 57 between 12:30 and 1:30PM, Tuesday afternoon. The complex was taken over between 1:43 and 1:50 PM that day! But that's not everything," Mueller's eyes flashed, "my buddy tried to look up backgrounds on these guys and found only Lou Pauzpolis's file. Of all the men signing in that day, only Lou Pauzpolis was officially dispatched there!"

Lou Pauzpolis. . . Benjamin remembered the name. Candice used Lou's phone to contact Tom.

"When my buddy went digging," continued Mueller, "the files for these men were deleted from the FBI data banks—not just expunged, but wiped clean! You need to be very high up—higher than even the Deputy Director's office. You'd practically need to be in a serious position of power in The White House to accomplish that!"

Oh no, thought Benjamin. He hadn't even begun to think about the Master since Monongahela.

There was ample evidence to suggest that the Master was part of the government team, but it'd never occurred to that The Master was working with the President's team!

"I have to make a call," muttered Rabb.

He strolled into the kitchen. Mueller didn't want to let him. Benjamin studied him for a long moment—of all the people around him, Rabb was the only one he trusted. Then he and Mueller were alone.

"I haven't found her yet," whispered Mueller.

"This is good work, but focus on Amanda," he sighed, "I don't know how she ever became such a whore."

Mueller whispered in his ear before stepping away, motioning towards the door, "I believe you were the first to check into the Drake Hotel, kiddo" he sighed making reference to his numerous mistresses, "I'll find Amanda. You find out what this means," he pointed a finger at the frozen image of the agent on the TV, "How can I communicate with you when I need to?"

"Remember my father's secret door on the 67th floor--leave a note for me there when you need to. Now get back to work."

With a nod, his Chief of Security was gone, spirited back down the elevator. Benjamin turned back to the freeze framed photo image of FBI Agent Juan Reinota a.k.a. Jerry McGhee. Just what the hell was going on? FBI Agents walking through his gates on the one day that his refinery was taken hostage?

In the reflection of the TV tube, Benjamin saw the Rabbi reenter the room, his voice deep and grave, "Benjamin, remember the tapes of the FBI strike force in Monongahela?"

"Yeah," Benjamin remembered Rabb's keen interest in them.

"I recognized ten of those ghoulish men, they all were or had been agents of the Federal Bureau of Investigation."

The FBI thought Bronk! That plus this tape, what was going on.

Rabb headed for the door as he muttered, "And I know the identity of The Master. It's--"

5:29 PM (EST)
Elizabeth, NJ

"Why haven't you killed me yet?" asked a worn Peter Schubert.

Someone administered a shot of some type into his arm, discarding the spent syringe in the trash can. With warmth and plenty of Tylenol in him, the fever began to clear and some form of rational thought manifested itself within him. He no longer had to focus on the figure standing before him in order to bring the shapes and colors into focus. With the heat of the room and water they'd given him, his strength returned.

He tried to fight, but the leather restraints held him to the gurney. As if to mock him, they left his withered burned hand outside the restraints, knowing that he couldn't move it—the dead flesh hung off the bone. His pants were pulled down and electrodes had been placed on his shaved testicles. Dumb fucks, he thought, he'd been forced to resist such tortures.

Then he smelled the sweat and grime and looked up. From out of the darkness appeared the figure, his face wrapped in bandages, two cold, gray eyes poking through torn holes in the gauze.

"Who are you, The Invisible Man?" he smirked—yes, even with his destroyed arm, his senses were coming back to him.

The character gurgled—Schubert saw a spot of red blood forming where the man's mouth should be. Had someone blown his jaw off, he wondered. Gurgle—gurgle—the character loomed over him, "Where is—gurgle-- Candice Cooperman?"

"I told you the truth, she left to get me medical supplies."

"And then she returned?"

"Yeah," he would go along with it, if that's what they believed. Why not set them farther off track? Just what was this bastard fishing for? What was so important about Candice and this computer? "I lost her in the tunnel."

"We would have found her. We will make you talk," the bandaged figure clapped his hands. A moment later the door to the break room swung open. The bloodied body was tossed onto the floor. Schubert fell into a soldier's trance, hiding all emotions as the bloodied and beaten face stared up at him. Gummy Bear folded himself up in a fetal position at his feet, sucking his thumb like a child. The little red haired man crawled to him like some wounded animal—gashes and cuts covering the man's body. They had burned the right side of Candy's face with cigarettes--like torturing a child, he thought.

"Unfortunately," gurgled the bandaged character, "for him, we no longer require his services—gurgle—now where is she!"

"Go fuck yourself," muttered Schubert, "whoever you are."

"The name is Nehemiah," he threw a switch on the box. And Major Peter Schubert screamed like he had never screamed before

---

5:37 AM (EST)
Washington DC

Agent Dick Osbourne sat in his White Office.

Since being called back to Washington by the Razorback after the Monongahela raid, the White House was trying to distance itself from the impending fiasco. He had no problem with that—waiting, biding his time. His phone rang. It was a private White House line, "I thought I gave orders not to be disturbed," he barked.

"This is first position operator. There's someone calling in regards to Union 57?" He said if I relayed his message to you that you'd want to speak to him."

"Well what's the message?" his pock marked cheeks turned fiery.

"He says he can generate a great deal of trouble for The Master-"

He shot to attention, beads of sweat gathering on his forehead. His left eye began to flicker as it die when he was nervous, "I'll take the call on my private line."

Forty Two

5:01 AM (EST) 6:01 AM (CST)
New Orleans, LA

The blast shield opened.

Tom Grant was exhausted. Sitting in the cramped, white cubicle, he realized just how much he wanted to see Yves Alexander Dussant—not just for the sake of his mission: but was something more.

Again the images boiled out of the depths of his mind: Agent Willard turning ever so slowly--face bloodied and wet. . . the numbers scribbled in excrement around the cross. . . the dead corpse's FBI badge. . . something bothered him about these surreal visions. . . was there a pattern to be found?

"Well, well, well," Dussant grinned through the partition--his legs sprawled across the red reading chair. Lost in thought, Tom hadn't realized the blast shield had opened. The prisoner's eyes brightened, "got my turtle soup?"

"No, but I do have something," from the floor, Tom produced the small cardboard box, placing it into the feeder booth.

A moment later, Yves Alexander opened the box on the other side of the partition, "A Lucky Dog!" he studied the hot-dog.

"It's barely dawn, Yves Alexander, believe me--I tried every place—no turtle soup around! We're just running out of time and—" restrain yourself—he focused on Mr. Help's warning, repeating the words over and over like a mantra chant: he is deadly, deadly, deadly--

"Let me see your shoes," demanded Dussant.

"What?"

"Your shoes. . . hold 'em up to the glass."

Tom lifted his foot up, allowing Dussant to examine the sole of his cross trainer like a doctor diagnosing a rash, "Bubble gum and shit," he winced, "you have been walkin' up and down Bourbon Street—and all for little ol' me?" he seemed flattered.

"Yves Alexander," Tom cut to business, "what did those numbers mean on that wall?"

"What numbers?"

"You know what I'm talking about! Answer me!"

"Did the corpse have a wallet?"

"An FBI badge."

"What'd it say. C'mon, the suspense is killin' me."

"I could only make out the first name. . . Thomas."

A long pregnant pause—then, "What hangs on your walls, Agent Grant? In you apartment or home, wherever you live--what hangs on your walls?"

"What does that have to do with anything?

"Look at my room," sighed Dussant, "maps line my walls--ancient maps of far way places like Khartoum and the harbor passage to Madras. Quite ironic for a man who's been practically nowhere. A man who's never seen the big skies beneath Kilimanjaro or smelled the succulent mildew of an Amazonian jungle. But then again, most of the people beyond these walls never bother to live life--to see such things. Our lives are cartography. And as every explore knows, Tom, the only way to find your way is with a good map. So what hangs on your walls?

Military lithographs and books of war, thought Tom. Then he righted himself. Dussant was doing it again—drawing him off course, "I need answers Dussant--you've given me nothing but half-truths--riddles."

"Perhaps you're asking the wrong questions. You still don't realize that the puzzles to unlike lie in the past and, "he bit into the hot dog with a wince, "you get what's ya pays for in sacrifices--my goin' rate for Lucky Dogs isn't much. So make us friends and I might tell you for free."

"Friends? Yves Alexander, you could never be a friend. The voice I use to express myself is the weapon you employ to control men's minds. You're an emotional island."

"C'mon, lighten up. Tell me about the strange episodes in Tom Grant's life that led him here. Why is he single and alone? Why does he aim for such difficult hurdles? Why government service? Or was it the mentor father figure of the Rabbi that inspired him?" his eyes probed into Tom like a laser beam, "or was there a single episode, a fundamental moment, that shaped him? Something he refuses to come to terms with?"

The hallway—control yourself, thought Tom. He felt nauseous and didn't like where this discussion was going, "I-I don't talk about my parents," he looked away, fingering the panic button on his remote control.

"I never mentioned your parents, Tom. But since you've said it-"

"Leave it alone!"

"Touchy. Touchy," Dussant was leading up to this point, dropping little allusions, identifying Tom's weakness. Were people that insignificant to him—simply toys for his own petty amusement? "Time's running out, Agent Grant! I can hand you Bobby Lefrete. Just let me get comfortable with you."

The desk—Tom remembered hiding under the desk—he turned off his mind, "My parents are dead. You know that."

"I read that in the papers long ago," continued Dussant, "tell me something I don't already know."

The sounds of a struggle. . . Tom lashed back like a wounded animal, "How did your parents die? Let's see, you murdered your own father!" he swung his hands through the air, screaming, "then you fucked your mother until she tried to kill you—you fucking incestuous bastard!"

Silence. Dussant pointed at droplets of saliva on the partition, "Now look what you've done--spit all over the partition-- my window on the world."

Tom collected himself his breath--messaging his temples, feeling the weight of many days on his shoulders. He regretted the venomous attack--he needed Yves Alexander as an ally, but he wanted to know, "Is it true?"

"I told you Tom, my life is not like yours or anyone else's. A child only knows what he's taught. My parents were affected by my powers. I hinted at these anomalies--told you that my mother could not bear to shower without my hand upon her. I simply failed to elucidate, stating which exact place on her body it was that my hand was placed. I intimated that we slept together. . . you could have gathered what you wished. "

"Now who's withholding information?"

"She seduced me when I was eight years old," he stared into nothingness, "I didn't know about taboos or social doctrine. I was raised in a virtual prison of my parent's creation. She bathed in amazement--that her loins had produced me. She claimed I wasn't my father's child. Did you know she was diagnosed as infertile-- prone to hallucinations and spells. . . claimed to have been impregnated by a shining angel who-"

"Give me a fucking break. The Jesus parables are really tiring."

"HOW MANY MORE PARALLELS BEFORE YOU PEOPLE BELEIVE ME!" he screamed before taking a deep breath, repasting Southern gentility across his face, "Tom, she wanted me all to herself, beckoning me to kill my father. One day I simply lost patience and I regret it."

"Well fucking bravo for you! You murdered your father, ya sonofabitch! You should feel bad about it. And if she was so enthralled with you, why did she drug you and drive you off the cliff in Haifa?"

"You want answers?" he jabbed, "tell me about your parents?"

"Shut up!"

"Make up your damn mind! What'll it be?"

"Are we like ants to you: inconsequential and small or worse yet, did you get some sick, perverted amusement from it all?"

"I could construct miracles and you still would feebly try to explain it all-blaming it on weather balloons and mirages. Why is it that everyone preaches tolerance except for me? I was born in a prison--a Skinner's Box-- well educated indeed, read every book in the family library twice, knew my Shelley from my Swinburne, my Cliquot from Crystal, salad fork from dinner fork. Imagine if Pip had lived his entire life in Mrs. Havisham's wedding banquet--solitary—ignorant of any social morays beyond those rotting walls?"

"Don't quote Dickens to me. You could have escaped-"

"I jumped the fence as a child. You can imagine what happened--little girls, vagrants, old men, all who met me, couldn't part. Suicide! Suicide! Suicide!" he sputtered, his own turn to fling saliva onto the partition.

"The NSA says you're not even Yves Alexander, but some charlatan."

"With my teeth broken and all?" he ran a finger along his perfect white teeth, "strange that the government after all these years of study should not perform the one, obvious test, comparing my sperm sample with the one they found in my mother? But if they performed that test," continued Dussant, "the government would be forced to accept the fact that I rose from the dead. That I can't be killed. A notion which practically everyone accepts about a day laborer who died two thousand years ago, but not me."

"What the hell is your message. Is it just controlling men's minds--is that what this boils down to—some kind of blind faith?"

"Refer to the bible: *every knee must bend, every heart give homage.* "

"Some refused Jesus's will. Judas betrayed him!"

"C'mon Tom, Judas did as he was told. Jesus was destined for crucifixion from the beginning. He struggled with it, fought it, but ultimately surrendered to God's will."

"But your mother must've had a second thought when she drugged you and drove off the cliff? Why would a faithful murder you?"

"You don't know everything yet, Tom. Ya don't appreciate that I'm the victim here-"

"You're not the victim, Dussant!"

"I'm the one who's been wronged! What did I do that was so evil? I built a quiet, humble following in the woods of central Louisiana. And they came and killed the only woman I loved."

"A follower whom you seduced—"

"She wasn't a follower. She was my lover. Then a man obsessed with her, tracked her down to Wayfarer. You're entering the third act of a very long play--an epic tragedy set into motion decades ago. Your beloved mentor, your great Rabbi, slaughtered her and all my followers. When he was finished, he killed the entire town of Blanche Fields," he stammered, "I w-w-watched that son of a bitch blow her head off!"

Tom shot up out of the chair pointing an accusing finger at Dussant, "You're lying!"

Dussant wiped a tear from his face and tried to chuckle, "A liar, huh? I've made up these fascinating stories for the amusement of The National Security Agency and I'm just an eloquent *monitor*—is that it?"

"As crazy as it sounds, I believe it all—the power, the resurrection. With all my training and my preconceived notions of the world," his lips trembled, "it took a little more than twelve hours to break down my universe and I didn't even have to hear your voice. But why? Do I have to self-deprecate myself for the answer-- the only one who showed you respect and compassion. Do you want me to grovel over my woes? We all have tragedy in us—things better left alone."

"You want to know what has caused all of this?" Dussant pressed the flat of his palm against the Plexiglas partition. Standing up, Tom leaned against the partition—only an inch and a half of Plexiglas between the two men. Dussant mimed the words as he said: Go to Wayfarer.

Then the blast shield dropped from the ceiling.

Tom Grant opened the door to his hotel room.

He left a message for Rabb with the Pentagon and hoped he'd get it. As he expected, Mr. Help sat waiting for him in his room. a half empty beer in his lap. The red faced man looked up at him, "Figured you'd want to see me."

Smoke curled and twisted in the stale air.

"Yeah," Tom sighed, "think I'm ready to take that little ride in the country."

Forty Three

It was the muskrat that did it.

Or maybe it was beaver? What was the name of that big rat—well shit, it was some furry rodent. How the hell did she know she'd be allergic to it? Should have taken allergy medicine, he said—his accent practically spelled Valle d'Aosta—real northern Italy. Ugh, she abhorred the Valle dastans—didn't quite know if they were German or French or Italian—on the verge of being rude or pleasant. She told him to take the jacket off, but he was ever so snooty and turned up his nose—with oversized tweed pants, mandatory European pot belly, and tacky Sulka shirt—who in their right mind ever wore a print design on their collar?

But Martine was ever so French. It was a party after all. Her lover *de jour* asked the little prick ever so nicely, *en francaise* of course, to please take the jacket off, indicating she was allergic to the fur. Then the little barbarian from the north peaked his nose and grinned one of those sincere smiles as if to say: from one European to another: well I would have taken it off if she had asked civilly.

Fucking little prick.

She was so tired. . . vagrant tired, like she could lay down in the street and people would toss pennies at her—haha—that was very funny. She rubbed her nose—it burned with that exquisite pain—like a brush fire—no, like an eternal flame in some war memorial that didn't want to die. Fumbling through her purse, she groped around for the vial of cocaine and realized how foolish she was being. After all, here she was, standing on a street corner in broad daylight—where? Where the fuck was she? Her hands and eyes fidgeted about. Where was a street sign when you needed one in New York City?

Motioning towards her sister's apartment house, she remembered that cold, shrill feeling she experienced when the taxi dropped her off at her own apartment a few minutes before. She imagined seeing the old bastard with his scowling look, reprimanding her for being oh so modern.

She would get some rest and pick the kids up around noon. Fumbling through her purse for the keys to her sister's apartment, she felt the hand wrap around her mouth!

She screamed and bit into thick fingers.

"Ow shit!" the bloodied fingers groped lower, wrapping around her long, thin neck. Shit, the bastard was bleeding on her—she was going to get AIDS!

He spun her into the alley The cocaine confidence vanished. He tossed her into the alley, the gun poking at her back. She shut her eyes, afraid to look at him. He was going to rape her—sodomize her! She stiffened. His breath smelled of mustard as he spoke-- then the biggest surprise! She recognized the voice and knew who sent him. Fear ebbed, anger filling the void. The fucking nerve of the brute. She swung her hand to slap him--

He caught her hand, "Your husband's been looking' high and low. I'll give you this," smiled Mueller, "you are one hard woman to find Mrs. Amanda Bronk."

5:58 AM (EST)
New York, NY

Benjamin Bronk's heels clicked against the cement floor.

Fort Crandal was a tomb. Silently they walked into the brain center they'd left almost 12 hours before. Rabb and he looked like concentration camp survivors in their tattered jumpsuits--faces blackened and burned. He caught sight of his mother and realized how much he'd changed. She rushed over to him, trying to nurse him. But there was too little time.

"We don't have a lot of time, Remy," the Rabbi dropped the surveillance tape on the desk, "we have proof that the men that took over Union 57 are FBI agents so far identified as Terrence Stewel, Richard Martin, Carl Cotter, Roger Pzolsky, and James Reed."

General Crandal didn't seem shocked. Only then did Benjamin notice that the Sharpe, Remy, Eleanor, the hand full of soldiers were all ghostly white. A tape played on the monitor in the far corner. On the TV Benjamin made out jostling camera angles of ghoulish men and vomiting, panicked soldiers.

Crandal pointed at the TV, "Well I'll be a sonofabtich. That's the Monongahela raid tapes. The camera was attached to some young buck's helmet on a satellite feed. So far we've identified twenty one of those ghostly looking chanting guys-——they're all FBI agents—ten field officers, three chief deputies out of Washington—"

"I know who the Master is," added Rabb, "and this cannot leave this room. As of right now, we are on our own—no White House—no President—nobody. Because the Master is FBI Agent Dick Osbourne."

"What?" gasped Crandal.

"Osbourne can connect the links in their organization," continued Rabb, "we have the militant, East German special forces officer Dick could met through intelligence contacts, a ragtag team of militant middle-class crazies he met through FBI surveillance reports. Osbourne is also the consummate outsider: unhappy, passed over for promotions, much of it because of the stigma I placed on him in his early career because of his general incompetence in the Bureau. So he included me in the ransom note and now he's in a perfect position of control as NSC advisor to The White House."

"I hate him too," added Crandal, "but—"

"The Master was able to wipe out records, to create cover-ups, to report on our inner workings to Nehemiah and his henchman. Dick is the only one."

"What do we do?" asked General Crandal.

"We can't show our hand yet. We need to have a legitimate reason to call him back here—the trip should take a few hours. Then we interrogate him on our own—learn more about how to stop them. It's our only hope."

Forty Four

"It's not really that bad a drive."

"I know. I grew up not far from here," responded Tom Grant. Peering out the window of the car, he watched rain drops streak along the glass, casting awkward shadows through the automobile.

Mr. Help lit another cigarette. Tom's eyes danced along the dashboard of the rented off road vehicle, wondering if Mr. Help owned or rented it? He hungered for any clue he could find about this strange man sent by the Rabbi.

The Rabbi.

How strange to see your mentors fall and your enemies rise. Yves Alexander Dussant was imprisoned, charged with the crimes that the Rabbi had probably perpetrated. How twisted everything had become. Tom actually began to think that Yves Alexander, behind his ten ton cement walls and bullet-proof partitions, was the only one he could actually trust.

Here he was traveling to Wayfarer, Louisiana—to the place where Rabb Bobby Lefrete stood side by side—and he still didn't know the true identity of the latter. Mr. Help fiddled in the duffel bag between them, dropping a thick brief it into Tom's lap.

"What's this?"

"Postmortem reports on the contaminated FBI agents—hard brief to come by these days. The first is the coroner's examination of Agent Willard who's--"

"I know who Agent Willard is," Tom glanced down at the photo, noting the gaping incision in Agent Willard's head—yellowish brain matter and a block spot-

"That thing," Mr. Help pointed at the black spot, "should be six times as large. It's Agent's Willard's limbic system—the primitive center of his brain."

"I'm not too familiar with human physiology."

"Think of your brain as a tree stump. Back when we were all lizards, the center rings of the tree were formed. With each advancement in size and capacity, more rings were added, one outside the other. You're looking at the most central ring on Agent Willard's tree stump. Understand?"

Tom nodded his head.

"All of the agents in postmortem examinations displayed massive metabolic changes in their limbic system," continued Mr. Help, "Dr. Brandt theorized that there might be some basic programming that the creature's voice was able to trip."

"You saying we're all preprogrammed with these codes?"

"Dr. Brandt thinks so."

"How did these men exhibited perfect behavior until they went mad?"

"Flip the page and I'll try to explain."

Tom examined another photograph: a woman laying prostrate on a long, metal table. She was dark skinned, slim and naked, eyes frozen wide like dead fish in a market. The right side of her head was sawed open and a second photo revealed a close up shot of the point of incision, revealing brain matter.

"Do you see how the tissue in her brain looks like it exploded under some compacted pressure?" continued Mr. Help.

He nodded. It looked like an overblown balloon, exploding outward.

"That's the medial temporal lobe—the hippocampus and Para hippocampal cortex of her brain. Little background--schizophrenics' hippocampus and Para hippocampal cortex are smaller than normal patients. This anatomic change causes people to experience hallucinations--"

"And his voice does all that?"

"Dr. Brandt believed at first that it was a pheromone emission. Later theories revolved around the voice frequency. When I drag my fingers along a blackboard, you experience a shrill, shooting sensation.

That frequency is the same signal emitted by a chimpanzee when a lion breaks through to the baby chimpanzees nursery. It's like a basic language that we don't need anymore, but we still carry it around in our head. Dussant is able to re-ignite those old codes."

"A Godly code," Tom thought out loud.

"Hold on Tonto. A physical curiosity maybe, but not God almighty thundering down from the heavens."

Or was it, wondered Tom? Did Moses part The Red Sea, did Jesus turn water to wine—or were they simply mass hallucinations? After all the things you heard in your life, how could a mere voice alter you like that. What went through Agent Willard's mind when he boiled his child? Was he undergoing some hallucination? Did he think he was doing something completely different? Tom wanted to think so. Or did Agent Willard cease to exist during that period of madness—as his wife so violently wished.

Or was the truth far more sinister? Was Agent Willard so devoted to a higher being he had not a moment's hesitation about killing his own child--like Abraham with Isaac. Was this "contamination"--the force to make a father slaughter his son? The car veered off the road, cruising down an exit ramp.

"Need to gas up," grunted Mr. Help, "ain't no more gas stations where we're headed."

Tom gassed the car up.

He watched Mr. Help hobble out of the vehicle, that faint limp in his walk as he entered the small convenience store. Tom peered down at the duffel bag on the driver's seat. Curiosity got the better of him. He groped inside, pulling out the first thing he felt: a manila folder. Opening it, credit card receipts spilled across the floor. He quickly stuffed them back in and caught sight of the Penthouse magazine, dog-eared and weathered.

Out of the corner of his eye he saw Mr. Help exit the building and enter a nearby port-o-let. Tom dragged the bag closer, fishing further inside, he spotted a clean undershirt, a biography on Clint Eastwood, and a dog-eared back issue of The New Republic. At the bottom of the bag was an old tennis ball. He held the tiny, ball in his hand. These items stirred something deep within him, an answer on the tip of his tongue, but--

The gas dispenser clicked off. The tank was full. His stomach grumbled and he decided to get something to eat. As he neared the station, he noticed the Vietnamese woman, probably the proprietor of the family store, glaring at him through the glass window.

He entered the small store. A wall of photographs of hunters with their fresh animal kills and prized catches of the day lined the wall and cabinet beneath the cash register. Behind the counter, the Vietnamese woman eyed him. He grabbed a Coke and Fig Newtons and dug into his pocket for a few bills.

"You gonna pay gas?" asked the Vietnamese woman.

"Didn't my associate pay?"

"No," she scoffed, stuffing the items in a paper bag, averting his eyes, "no one pay."

Tom reached into his back pocket and pulled out a larger bill.

"Thought you drowned," Tom ate the Fig Newtons as Mr. Help climbed into the car, starting it up, "I paid for the gas too."

"Well you should," Mr. Help drove them out of the gas station, "this's your expedition."

Tom let it drop, "How did you get that limp?"

"How'd you get such a big mouth."

Tom sipped the Coke.

"Car accident," replied Mr. Help, "long time ago."

They didn't turn back on I10, but raced down a winding, country road. The sun broke through the clouds—light broken by the limbs of oak trees. He was not very far from his own home, thought Tom, barely an hour to the west.

"Here it is," grunted Mr. Help. He veered off the road, weaving between oak trees, the vehicle bouncing along a steep expanse, crashing through low lying bush. Tom had to hold on to the door in order to keep from being thrashed.

"Where the hell are you taking me?" asked Grant.

Mr. Help puffed on his cigarette with a calm expression, "I told you, the government destroyed all the roads leading to even Blanche Fields."

Thundering through the creek, they rose up on the far side of the hill. Ahead of them, Tom could see more brush and then a long wire fence. Spaced at every ten yards were signs in bright red letters:

NO TRESPASSING!
GOVERNMENT PROPERTY!
VIOLATORS WILL BE PROSECUTED TO THE
FULL EXTENT OF THE LAW!

Mr. Help careened through the fence, tossing the sign across the top of the off road vehicle. Smoking his cigarettes without a care or regard for government property or his rented truck.

It began to drizzle. The windshield wipers smeared fallen leaves across the glass: a conflation of yellow and orange. Negotiating large pecan trees, they entered into a steep ravine, riding it for what seemed like an eternity. Then--

"There it is," grunted Mr. Help, "that's Wayfarer."

Far off in the distance, storm clouds gathered around its edges. Tom could see the dilapidated old house, its frame crumbling and falling in. It vaguely reminded him of the stark Victorian mansion in the film *Giant*. . . a rundown antebellum plantation surrounded by sapling trees and weeds for as far as the eye could see.

This was Wayfarer.

The place was in total disarray.

The front salon was ghostly silent. Tom and Mr. Help stepped across rotted boards. Ancient curtains blew in the breeze, the stitching and shards of fabric hanging off of them. . . the last remaining pieces of a dusty chandelier clanged hauntingly like wind chimes.

"This is where it all happened—the Mouth of The Beast," Mr. Help spread his arms wide, "back in "74 when the Feds raided the place, nobody knew how Dussant contaminated people," he pointed through a broken window at the muddy field behind them, "it rained hard the day Rabb decided to enter the compound——he 28th FBI agent to do so. With the ground muddy he stood far away from the house with a bullhorn."

"Is that relevant?" asked Grant.

Mr. Help led him up a rickety stairway. Tom noticed bullet holes in the rotting wood walls. He carefully made each step, afraid of falling through.

"He didn't make it within ear-shot of Dussant, but spoke over a bullhorn. He used an alias so Dussant wouldn't figure out he had leverage with her. Then the idea struck Rabb--that it might be the man's presence that did it. So he retreated and ordered the house be shelled from afar."

"Then what?"

"Dussant complied. He had no choice. Rabb readied a biohazard transport truck for him and ordered from afar for Dussant to enter it. As ordered Dussant went alone. Once contained in the truck, Rabb ran up these stairs."

Mr. Help led him along the second floor hallway, opening the door at the end of the hall. Pigeons settled in the rafters and ancient droppings coated the floor. A cobweb covered bureau rested near a rotting sleigh bed. This was Yves Alexander's room—Tom knew it. Dussant had consorted with his mother here--he imagined Dussant's father leaping to his death—and could only guess at the thousand horrors that happened here.

"This is where Rabb originally discovered her," pointed Mr. Help.

"Who?"

"The woman. . . Tabatha Granger--the Rabbi's lover. The reason he left the Army to join the operation," Tom remembered Dussant speaking of her. The woman that he in love with who was murdered by Rabb.

"She was in bad shape. You have to remember it was the first time anyone had ever seen a contaminated person before—she shivered, clawing at her flesh, poking out her eyes. And while Rabb toiled with his contaminated lover, Dussant was transported to a cordoned off holding cell in nearby Blanche Fields. No one still guessed it was his voice. Within an hour the contaminated Sheriff and FBI agents were firing at non-contaminated forces.

There was a real panic because now--Dussant might be on the run. It was a December Sunday--ninety percent of the town was in the gym for a Christmas play: 332 people in all. The creature fled heard the singing from the gymnasium and entered," Mr. Help's voice petered out--his hands sweaty.

Tom was silent for a moment.

"When Rabb and the government forces arrived," he continued in speechless breaths, "t-they found something meant to divert the soldiers from their pursuit. He had them engaging in acts—I could tell you," he took a deep breath, fumbling for another cigarette, "but the words would mean nothing. They were doing things to each other. . . women, children, mothers, fathers--having sex, eating each other's flesh. They were mad animals—too many to cover up. Rabb gave the order to kill them all."

"Then what?" pressed Tom.

Mr. Help led him out of the study, down the huge spiraling staircase. The strange man negotiated the steps with his limp, finally standing in what must have been the front parlor, "They found the creature here in the front parlor," he was breathless from his climbing, "it returned."

"Why go back?"

Mr. Help led him down the rickety staircase, back to the front parlor before answering, "Why does anyone go back?" Mr. Help ran his fingers along the dusty banister of the staircase, "I guess in the end, Yves Alexander went back for her."

It was the first time Tom heard him call Dussant by his name, "Rabb was over there," Mr. Help pointed at a dusty old corner, "he tried to talk her out of her spell," Tom imagined that Tabatha must be that dead woman from the medical photos he had just seen, "when Dussant returned, the soldiers went into a panic—some firing on each other. And in the mud his former worshippers howled and joined him—some gunned down—other racing into the house, looking for their master, ripping out their eyes and teeth—unable to live without him. Dussant made it here. Rabb grabbed his woman and forced her downstairs to the spring cellar. Come downstairs and I'll show you how it ended."

Tom smelled the rich dirt-- beer cans littered about. It was a cramped and dingy basement level with a dirt floor, "This is the surprise?"

"You'll need to climb in the trench. Here, get in first."

Tom hopped into the six feet deep trench. His eyes were now level with Mr. Help's shoes. The red face agent turned his flashlight so that Grant could see that the trench extending under the home, ending at a small door on the far end.

"Rabb fled down here. Dussant followed. Eleven non-contaminated officers fought their way down—then the light burst happened."

"A light burst?"

"Soldiers and eyewitnesses all claimed the same thing—the sky overhead opened and a column of white light shot straight through the house. All electrical systems were rendered immobile. Everyone was found unconscious including Dussant who was transported to The NIH before he awoke two days later. Later they began to realize the damage. Whatever these twelve agents witnessed, it drove them all mad—including the Rabbi who was the only one to recover."

"What did they see?"

"That secret's locked away in some NSA vault where-"

Tom's Comlink phone rang. He brought the phone to his ear. He heard the Rabbi whispering on the other end, "Listen to me, Tom. I never sent anyone to meet you in New Orleans. Osbourne never touched Dussant. He wasn't personally at Wayfarer, never knew what was actually happening. You're in grave danger! You are in-"

"Put the phone down," commanded Mr. Help.

Tom turned it off. From his vantage point in the trench, Mr. Help's feet were at Tom's eye level. He watched as the man limped towards him. Fear gripped him. Tom didn't need to glance up to know the man was pointing his pistol down at him. The limp. . . of course. When had he began to suspect it?

"We didn't really need that little interruption," he aiming his pistol at Grant.

Tom tried to find a solution as he said, "I just have one question for you. Why'd you call the time and weather service 286 times that day?" .

"How long did you know?"

Arms outstretched, Tom Grant looked up, "Are you going to answer my question or just boil me in a pot, Agent Willard?"

Forty Five

11:20 AM (EST) 10:20 AM (CST)
Restricted Government Area #32AB , South Central
Louisiana

How had he known?

Perhaps it was just gut instinct. Then again, the image haunted him--FBI Agent Walter Willard turning towards him, blood covering his crazed face. Tom recalled the words from Dr. Brandt's computer brief:

Agent Willard was characterized by psychological reviewers as "thoughtful, yet easily bored, responsible, and extremely self-assured". Subsequent psychological--

Agent Willard stared down at him, the gun in hand--red cheeks, glaring eyes, receding hairline, an appearance all the more sinister in the half light of the flashlight—just as Tom had imaged. Then he shuffled his weight from one leg to the slightly lamer one—another burst of thought--

After a car accident in 1974, he suffered from a slight limp in his right leg. . .

Tom searched for a plan. Buy more time, he thought, buy more time! "Agent Willard, are you going to answer my question?" he pressed, "why did you call the time and weather service over 286 times on the day you boiled your baby daughter in a pot?"

Did the question disturb Willard? Tom sensed conflict in the man's eyes--like two pools of fire. What was going through the bastard's mind? How had he managed to survive? Why had the brief lied? Why had the government claimed he was shot dead years ago? Tom positioned his hand closer to his sweat pants pocket, to his own pistol. Then he remembered opening the man's satchel: the Penthouse and New Republic Magazines. The book on Clint Eastwood--

drank beer. . . favorite actor was Clint Eastwood. . . subscribed to Playboy. . . The New Republic. . . on field trips admitted to occasionally reading . . . Penthouse.

Agent Willard smiled, "The answer's so obvious, Agent Grant. Had to make sure the time was right," Willard gestured, moving the gun an inch or two—taking the line of sight away from his head.

That was Tom's chance! He swung his pistol up, firing twice! The bullets ripped through Willard's chest, throwing him backwards—out of Tom's view. Grant raced along the trench--he had to get through that summer door! Behind him, bullets struck the mud a few paces behind him as Agent Willard discharged his weapon. Tom slammed his weight against the locked door. It wouldn't budge!

He was trapped! More gunshots! Then he felt the frame of the house overhead rattling—shaking dirt and wood all around him. He threw his body into the wooden door again--it gave a bit—hinges stretching--creaking.

"Stop!" he heard Agent Willard screaming from the cloud of dust.

The frame continued to shake above him--a whole segment of floor came crashing down! Then he could see him. The bullets had torn through his Agent's Willard's chest—he was bloodied—bloodied like Tom had imaged him in his head. Agent Willard lunged for him. Tom flung himself forward-

The world fell away.

A rattling resounded through his head.

He spun around--the door gave way. Then he was laying on soft grass, weeds all around, a gray winter sun shining meager light. The house shook as if an earthquake had hit—it was going to collapse, thought Tom! Then he identified the cause of the shaking.

The three helicopters circled over the house, spraying bullets all around-- shattering wood and glass. They were bombing the fucking house! One of the choppers zeroed in on his location--gunfire exploded again! He tried to run, but a cold, bloodied hand wrapped around his ankle.

"Damn you!" it didn't even sound like Agent Willard. His voice was evil—bone chilling cold, "I've waited too long for this!" from the other side of the sunken door, Agent Willard attacked him. With his free foot, Tom kicked him in the face--cartilage and bone shattering beneath the sole of his shoe.

Then he was up.

More gunfire! Sprinting across the field, he ran in a zigzag motion—as his combat scenarios suggested—making a dash for Agent Willard's parked truck. Flinging open the door, he spotted the keys in the ignition. Then more gunfire-- bullets tore through the side windows, showering glass across him.

Glancing through the dirty windshield, he counted three choppers— Boeing Sikorsky RAH-66 Comanche's—he could tell by the streamlined shape of their tale rudders. He knew these crafts from training manuals—armed with 20 MM cannons, Hellfire ATGM's, and Stinger AAM"'s in side weapon bays—shit, they were circling to a safe distant from which they could fire their missiles! He had to get to thick underbrush and--

"Damn you!" through the open door, Tom saw the bloodied figure of Agent Willard lurching only ten yards away. . . nose hanging like limp flesh.

Fear overtook caution. Hopping into the driver's seat, Tom turned the ignition and threw the car into drive, slamming hard on the accelerator. Agent Willard disappeared out of the view as he raced desperately across the field.

Choppers zeroed in! Glancing around, he knew his only hope was to drive into the woods. The forest would slow his speed down, but hide him from choppers overhead—another bullet hit the hood--it severed the radiator line, a cloud of steam covered the cracked windshield. He spotted the tree a moment before impact, hitting it head on-- thrown forward, head crashing against the shattered windshield.

For a moment he laid there dazed, the engine running, the tree wrapped around the front of the truck, horn blaring. He could see the distorted lights of the choppers as they raced overhead treetops. Blood trickled in his eyes. He threw the car into drive again and bounced his way down into the steep ravine.

He wasn't sure how long he raced along it. His mind floated in an ethereal fog—Agent Willard turning ever so slowly towards him. . . Rabb—Rabb wanted him dead. . . Dussant—Jesus Christ, was Dussant the only one he could trust?

Then more gunfire and—

11:56 AM (EST)
Elizabeth, NJ

Candice awoke.

She fell asleep while reading the laptop. Instantly her thoughts returned to Gummy and Schubert. Huddled on the landing a hundred feet in the air, she crouched between heavy equipment and metallic pipelines, shielding her from the view of those below.

How long had she been here? She'd fallen asleep. The pumps hummed far below. From her frequent visits to the plant, she knew the sound of the pipeline being flushed. They could flush the lines for almost two days before they ran out water. Already, the water bubbled out of open manhole covers, freezing to ice along the grounds of the refinery.

She ached to call Tom, to hear his voice. But The Master was entrenched in the government team. Was she stalemated. The snow stopped, but the gray clouds did not relent. She wanted to keep reading the computer—to keep going.

Because in an inexplicable way, she didn't want to leave this refinery—she knew that sounded mad, but this was home now. She didn't ache to return to the outside world, she only wanted to return to that younger woman--to go back to that moment when she began taking the safe road, making the compromising decisions—she wanted to go to that solitary place and stop the entire cycle of events which occurred after that point. Of course, she mused, some might say she was experiencing some kind of crazed mania with its jagged peaks and plunging valleys.

She took a deep breath.

With the realization that she probably wasn't going to see her friends ever again, she opened Nehemiah's laptop computer again. She scrolled back-- far before the few correspondences she spied in Nehemiah's office, taking the cursor to the very beginning. She came to the sentence and stopped—she went back, rereading it again.

Only then did she realize the enormity of what was happening. She held her face in cupped hands, rocking back and forth. It couldn't be true. She now understood. It was all here—spread out across files of data. This was the connecting point--more horrible and unbelievable than she ever imagined.

Because she now knew who the mole—who Bobby Lefrete really was. The others were wrong—no one would ever have guessed this!

12:12 AM (EST) 11:12 AM (CST)
Route 17A, two miles west of I10, South Central Louisiana

Tom saw the same gas station up ahead.

He'd finally escaped the choppers--ripping out of the woods, racing back along the oak covered country road. The engine was overheating—the radiator line hit. He had to get back to that gas station to plug up the hole and fill the contraption with water.

Crouched over the hood, Tom dropped the radiator cap. As reached down to retrieve it, his cell phone fell out of his pocket. Slamming against the concrete, the power button turned on. Instantly he heard it ring—had he turned it off?

Frantically, he picked up the phone, "Rabb?"

"Tom!" she cried, we're in this together--you and I," she continued in a gentle tone, "you must trust me—listen," was she somehow involved in a trap? Were they triangulating his cell phone signal, vectoring in the choppers? "something's happened to you--you're being pursued by choppers, right? But none of this is real."

"Right? Tell that to the choppers," damn it, she was captured! He fingered the power button, eyes searching for airborne pursuers.

"This will be hard to hear. You think you met someone named Yves Alexander Dussant. You think you had various conversations with him. In fact, you met Dussant only once and for 2 minutes," how the hell did she know who Dussant was? "you asked him about Bobby Lefrete, he laughed and told you to get the hell out of there. Then you incriminated yourself on the video, confessed to taking over The Union 57 Refinery and aiding the terrorists in--"

"What!"

"You think you've met with Dussant numerous times, right? You brought him food and wine and stuff. But it's a lie, you never did any of that. And you think you met someone named Agent Willard who called himself Mr. Help and brought you to Dussant's home called Wayfarer," Jesus Christ, he shuddered-- how could she know this, "Agent Willard's been dead for over a decade! The Wayfarer estate was razed to the ground eight years ago. There is nothing in Wayfarer except plowed dirt."

"W-what are you saying?"

"Everything you've been experiencing for the past day is an illusion-"

He stomach tightened in knots "No! You're lying!" this was part of the trap. Another way to catch him!

"An integral audiovisual hallucination that—" he shut his eyes afraid to hear what she was about to say—hearing the last word as if it were shot through his head "because you are CONTAMINATED."

He heard his heart beating, pulse throbbing. He didn't feel different—no, this was a lie—he shut his eyes and finally saw Agent Willard's face as it turned to face him—no longer just hints of cheekbones. It was his own face! No—no—he felt the same—was the same. This was a lie—a lie!

"Tom there's more, "Candice continued, "much more. And it's frightening. Bobby Lefrete is--"

Tom dropped the phone and vomited on the bumper of the automobile. The world spun. It was a lie. It had to be a fucking lie! His mind searched for some other explanation. Wait, he thought to himself, there was a way to prove it all—a simple, easy way! He looked up at the Vietnamese woman staring at him through the window of the run down convenience store.

"Get out! Get out!" the Vietnamese woman screamed at the sight of him. He saw children rushing to the back of the store.

"I was here," Tom grabbed her from across the counter--

"I call police!" screamed the woman, reaching for the phone. Tom ripped the phone out of the wall, "I was here with someone else. Remember?"

"You come alone!"

"He used the port-o-let around the back--"

Her frail body shook, "You sit in car-- sit for minutes--talk to yourself-- come inside and buy things! You crazy!"

Thoughts--Willard met him in his hotel room-- then in an alleyway--secluded, private areas. In the lobby of The Westin Hotel, the red faced man wanted to go upstairs—somewhere they could be alone. And the eyes—people staring at Tom in the lobby just as they had stared at him in this rural convenience store. As if he were a lunatic speaking to himself. But how had Willard known Rabb's password: Hail Mary? Of course, Tom knew the damn pass-word so he was able to hallucinate it!

Ring.

Tom jerked back, releasing the woman. He stared down at the severed phone he'd just pulled out of the wall—it was ringing—

Ring!

The Vietnamese woman stared down at the phone then back at him.

"Do you hear it?" asked Tom.

Ring!

"W-w-what?" she stammered, her eyes tear streaked and frightened.

"The fucking phone is ringing!"

Ring!

She exploded in a wave of emotion, "Phone no ring!" she pointed at the severed phone wire, "you pull phone out wall!"

Tom picked up the receiver, his arm couldn't stop shaking. He heard the cool, gentile voice on the other end, 'Tom, good to hear from you, old boy—"

He shut his eyes, "This isn't happening. This is just a hallucination—"

Dussant laughed on the other end of the phone, "Tell that to the poor woman you juss scared the shit out of. I'm afraid our little field trip's been ruined."

"What have I been doing for the past 3 days!" he exploded.

"Juss come on over," drawled Yves Alexander, "and grab me a Baby Ruth while ya' there—I got a real sweet tooth today."

Forty Six

"They want you now," the voice beckoned.

Major Peter Schubert was carried down the long expanse. . . . a hallway of fluorescent lights and cheap wood paneling. Barely able to walk, two of the terrorists carried his limp body wracked from torture.

His right arm must be dead, he thought to himself solemnly, because he couldn't even feel pain in it anymore. His head swam again in a thick fog. It took him a moment to place himself in the Security and Engineering building. How long had they tortured him? He winced again at the thought as the bandaged fucker kept throwing that switch.

They tossed his limp and shaking body through the open doors--into the cold, winter air. Someone draped a jacket over him and snow began to fall on his face. His testicles raged with pain. In front of him, he saw the congregation of people collected in the parking lot. The crowd parted as the terrorists carried him into the center of the group. There stood the bandaged Nehemiah. What the hell was going on?

He fell onto cold asphalt.

Trying to stand, he found himself too weak to do so. A moment later, hands grabbed him, forcing him into a crouched position which moved his testicles, sending roaring pain up his back and along his legs. Glancing to his side he could see Gummy Bear, no more than a few inches away from him. He heard the cock of a pistol and looked up to see Nehemiah, a cell phone in one hand, a gun in the other.

"Gummy unhappy," the scarred little man whimpered.

"For once, I agree with ya, buddy," the injured soldier winced.

"Candice Cooperman!" cried Nehemiah at the top of his lungs—as if addressing the entire plant, "I know you're out there in the plant and can hear me! Candice, it's time to make a deal!" he placed the pistol at the base of Gummy Bear's neck, "I call it 'Who Do You Love?'"

"Gummy scared," whined the little man.

His frizzy red hair blew in the wind. Rizzuti held the pistol to his head. The little man turned to Rizzuti with sad, pleading eyes. . . the eyes of a child, "Schubert help Gummy. Schubert good!"

Despite his cold facade, Schubert felt tears trickle down his cheeks, "Be strong, Gummy. Everything will be alright," Gummy focused on Schubert's face, patting one trembling hand with another.

"Candice!" Nehemiah screamed at the massive towers of the refinery all around them, "I'm going to do it!"

Schubert whispered to Gummy, "Shut your eyes, Gummy."

Nehemiah chambered his pistol.

"Gummy n-not liking this," the little man shook.

"Gummy, shut your eyes." Schubert begged. He followed his orders.

"It's alright," Schubert coaxed him, "don't be afraid. Don't be--"

Baannnggggg!

"YOU SICK SON OF A BITCH!" Schubert saw Gummy Bear fall to the ground, blood spouting from the open wound in his head.

1:28 PM (EST)
Elizabeth, NJ/ high in the metal scaffolding

Candice Cooperman watched in shock.

The fucker killed him! She saw Gummy Bear collapse. She turned her head away as blood poured out of his head. Gathered between the base of Coker tower and The Security/ Engineering building, the terrorists were gathered directly below her—but unaware of her presence. This was ludicrous! She knew they were desperate for Nehemiah's computer, but did they really think that she would give herself up after this fucking lunacy?

Pressing her body near the warm metallic lines running along the tower, she stared through a crawl space at the men which seemed as small as ants.

"Candice," she could hear Nehemiah screaming, "Make it easy on everyone and we won't kill Schubert. Give me the computer and you can walk right out of the plant."

Did these sick bastards really think she was so stupid?

1:33 PM (EST)
Washington D.C.

Dick Osbourne took a deep breath.

The Situation Room buzzed around him. How strange, he reflected once again, that fate had thrown him alone into such a position of power. How strange that it had been he who received the call in the early morning hours. He remembered picking up the phone, the first position operator speaking to him in a frightened tone:

"He said to tell you that. . . " she paused as if reading a scribbled note, "he can generate a great deal of trouble for The Master-"
"I'll take the call."

The decision was made.

The terrorists made contact with him of all people—boosting his own power. In the end, their demands were mundane and it would be a deal—a deal the government had to take—hell, they had no other choice. Nehemiah wanted only two things and both were easy to do.

"I have a bad feeling about this," muttered Secretary of State Giardino.

Osbourne knew if the plan failed—he'd be made the scapegoat. But he had no choice now—he was tied in for the long ride.

"Sir, one of the technicians turned to him, "I think we've got the vector."

Dick grabbed the scribbled coordinates and picked up the telephone. Shit, he didn't really start all of this, but he was damn well going to end it. Everything was transpiring just as he planned:

"Are you there?" he asked over the line.

"Yes," Nehemiah answered on the other end of the line.

"She's on the Coker tower. Seventy five feet over your head."

1:50 PM (EST) 12:50 PM (CST)
New Orleans, LA

Tom Grant felt like he was dying.

He opened the duffel bag that had belonged to Agent Willard, pouring through the receipts for the rental car, for the back-issues of The New Republic, Hustler, and The Clint Eastwood biography from a used bookstore—another receipt for the duffel bag from a used luggage store—ALL SIGNED BY HIM!

He wiped the sweat from his brow. He was going to throw up again--was he contaminated? Just like Agent Willard? f he lived, would he one day rise up and murder his own children sleeping in their beds? He longed for the drab life he'd endured before this—when he had a soul.

That creature with his grins and smooth drawl had taken his life from him and he wanted it back. He didn't want his hippocamp—whatever the hell it was, sucked up--his limbic system exploding outward. He didn't want to be like those people in that medical brief—like those mad bastards in the—Jesus, he wasn't making much sense, was he?

Chills ran down his spine.

He stopped for a moment at the head of the alleyway, examining the townhouse. Storm clouds gathered in the distance—the crackle of thunder. . . rain drops sprinkled his face. He stood there, feeling as if this would be the last time he would ever see the sky and the rain. He took a moment to search out the spires of St. Louis Cathedral and the stone façade of the Cabildo, but in the mist and winter fog, he couldn't see them. Then it was time.

In the dark alley, he was about to press the ringer next to the iron door when it swung open revealing Dr. Brandt: her dark hair falling around her neck. What struck him most was the seductive black, floor length evening dress she wore. Only then did he notice the make-up giving her a feminine touch. She smiled and he realized just how beautiful she was.

"How do you do this afternoon, Tom?" she spoke gingerly, ushering him inside, "he's has been waiting for you."

The door shut behind them.

Forty Seven

2:16: PM (EST) 1:16 PM (CST)
New Orleans, LA

The cubicle was in total disarray.

Tom glanced at the furniture stacked chaotically in the cramped room. Staring down at his feet, he could see boxes of antique books and smelled the scents of dust and old furniture—four men hauled an etagere through the cramped airlock door.

"Tom old boy," drawled the familiar voice of Yves Alexander Dussant, then he cried, "watch the cornice work!" a shard of wood broke off from the top of the antique piece.

"Sorry sir," one of the men groaned.

"Not your fault," Dussant sighed, "something's gonna break when moving," he glanced at Tom, "can you believe they make these damn doors so small!" Then Dussant ushered him to a group of chairs in the center of the room.

Tom remained standing, spouting out, "It was a lie—all of it."

Another figure ambled by, hauling a box filled with paperweights and a tall, brass lamp. Dr. Brandt appeared before him with a silver tray and two tumblers of bourbon—one of which she offered to him. He hesitated.

"Well, don't be rude," Dussant drawled.

He took one with shaking hands and sat down before he collapsed, "Where are you moving?"

"Can't tell you that yet," he sipped his drink, "would ruin the surprise. I hope Agent Willard was a good guide--though I must say--never cared for him."

"He's dead been dead for a decade—it was a hallucination."

"Come now Tom, remember Moses and his burning bush? These were all private affairs, but I can assure you, not hallucinations. Now try that bourbon."

"This room wasn't sealed. That's how you contaminated me," Grant looked around, "so why stay? Why keep up the façade in a prison?"

With a rosy smile, Dr. Brandt set the tray on the table, curling into Dussant's lap, her fingers playing in his fine hair, "Had to let the government think they were having their way," he turned to Brandt, "go ahead, tell him."

"Project Alpha Wayfarer 12 formed under NSD 12444.2," she spouted, "to use and study the test subject claiming to be Yves Alexander Dussant, for us as a weapon in the Psyop group for said secret termination assignments."

"The power of God, Tom," winked Dussant, "the Romans wanted to kill it, but The United States government had to control it! Imagine the power the divine word could yield for a nation! When Catherine arrived, we were having contamination outbreaks. She stopped it—or so she thought."

"How'd you break free?"

"She got really good, sealed up all the security protocols—but you can't avoid the will of God. Hell I should know, I tried. Back then I was slitting my wrists—the only escape I had—then finally I gave into his will. I offered myself to carry his message and then it happened.

God gave me a gift—far too many things to be a coincidence. One careless guard enters the room to fix the relay camera over there," he pointed to a surveillance camera in The Suite, "the sound door mechanism was faulty--the door didn't lock. When the alarms rang he tripped on the chair you're sitting in now and ripped his biohazard suit with a device that tumbled under the couch. A minor tool that wouldn't be classified as a weapon—but could poke a tiny hole in the caulking around the observation window."

"What was it?"

Dussant produced the tiny devise: an orange handled Phillip's head screwdriver, tapping the pointed end into the flat of his hand. This thing, thought Tom, had started all of this.

"It happened ten years ago," continued Dussant, "that day Catherine interviewed me in this very cubicle--one pick up line was all it took. Like I said," Dussant winked knowingly at Tom, "you know how woman are."

"Stop it," she cooed.

"The hardest part," continued Dussant, "was conning the government into keeping the operation going long after they realized they wouldn't get anything out of me. Catherine gave some wonderful oratories on the subject."

"I'm in love. What do you expect?"

"I suppose in the back of all those government bureaucrats minds," sighed Dussant, sipping the bourbon, "was the fear—the possibility, that I might survive an assassination—like Jesus rising from the dead. After all, they knew it had already happened once in Israel," he winced, breaking his speech, "Tom, it's rude not to drink at a friend's home."

Anger surged within him, "Order me to sip the drink," countered Tom, "or order me to run my fingers through your hair-"

"Blame me if you want, but this is God's will."

2:19 PM (EST)
Elizabeth, NJ

They were upon her!

The first one dropped down from the overhead deck. By the time Candice raced to the outer deck, the pursuer's hands tugged at her parka, spinning her around. With her pistol, she shot one through the chest, lunging outward for the ladder. They were like flies, jumping down from the deck overhead, climbing up the ladder beneath her.

How had they found her? Her hiding place was so perfect—she'd told no one not even Tom! The sky spun around her. The whole theatrical piece transpiring beneath her was a damn ruse—a trap to keep her in one place! She rushed forward, but trapped!

2:20 PM (EST) 1:20 PM (CST)
New Orleans, LA

"I sick and tired of hearing about God and the parallels between you and Jesus. He preached peace and goodness to all men-"

"Maybe Christ wasn't so good? The disciples never knew him—had heard everything through second hand. Maybe they were afraid to write what he really said. Maybe Christ made the masses hallucinate about water turning to wine just to quell a rebellion? Maybe their bellies felt full, but they were really starving, chanting in Latin in some abandoned building, or raping their children—perhaps that's what bothered Judas so much-"

"All you have are questions without answers. Hell, all that stuff happened 2,000 year ago. We're talking about now—today!"

"The parallels slap you in the face, Tom! The NSA as the Roman Occupational Government of Israel. President Nixon as Regional Prefect Pontius Pilot. And in the starring role," Dussant swung his arms wide, "Yves Alexander Dussant as Jesus Christ!"

"If all this is true, the question still begs an answer: why?" then it hit Tom, "Israel! It goes back to Israel, doesn't it? You and your mother saw something there—a burning bush, a vision, a sign-"

"Isn't she beautiful?" Dussant stared at Dr. Brandt, "a regular Mary Magdalene."

"Stay on the subject."

"Darling," Yves Alexander prodded her off his lap, "show Tom what gifts you possess."

Dr. Brandt pulled the straps of her dress away, allowing it to fall away. She wore no underwear, staring before him naked with firm, rosy breasts, a trimmed patch of pubic hair framed by seductively curvaceous hips. The fact that she was so cold and now stood before him like some sultry vamp made the moment eerily erotic and haunting. Fingers crept along her breast—another hand finding its way down between her legs. She moaned.

1:00 PM (EST)
Washington DC

"Sorry it took so long," Secretary of State Giardino plopped the VCR tape into the machine. Breathless from his run up to The Oval Office from The Situation Room, the Secretary took a moment to gather himself. The tape just arrived—he'd seen only a few seconds of the footage electronically transmitted from Fort Meade and encoded on the VCR tape.

The President shifted in his seat as it began. On the TV, they saw that the camera was mounted in the upper quadrant of the small cubicle, the picture fuzzy—they saw Tom Grant address the occupant on the other side of the glass:

Tom Grant: **"You have to come to Union 57! It is the only way to appease us!**
Dussant: **"How many people in the government are involved?"**
Tom Grant: **"More FBI Agents than you can imagine--all are acting for you.**

Dussant: **"This is wrong!"**
Tom Grant: **"You must come to the refinery now or else—**

The name Tom said sent a shudder through the room.

"Turn the fucking thing off," the President shifted in his seat, rubbing sore eyes. Then he glanced up at Secretary of State Giardino, "Looks like Osbourne was right—the kid's no good."

"We still know nothing about this Dussant character," replied the Razorback, "all files are expunged. We think files may be in some archive—"

"They must exist—find them! Accept their deal, transport Dussant--do everything they specified in the telephone conference with Osbourne."

2:33 PM (EST) 1:33 PM (EST)
New Orleans, LA

"Something erotic about the moment," commented Dussant like a spectator watching a play, "when you know that you can really have someone."

Dr. Brandt fondled herself--hips fluctuating back and forth—a hand messaging her breasts--fingers creeping between her buttocks—like an brain-washed animal, thought Tom.

"Agent Roberts!" Dussant called.

From out of the airlock, stepped a tall, black FBI Agent. Dr. Brandt rushed to him, unbuttoning his pants, reaching for his penis. Without enough time to get erect, she brought him deep into her mouth, forcing her head back and forth as he stiffened.

"Stop it!" cried Tom, trying to ignore Dr. Brandt--head rocking back and forth. The FBI Agent arched his back, wrapping his dark, firm hands around her black hair.

"Come now Tom," smirked Dussant, "I've seen her take four or five men at once—and with a fervor—loves that dark meat!"

She pulled away for a moment, wiping saliva from her lips "Does Tom want to join us?" The black agent grunted, drawing her back to him.

"Is this what you get off on?" asked Tom, "are we really so insignificant in your eyes—so little? Or do you join them?"

"Tom," winked Dussant, "how do you know you didn't join in?"

He shivered, "Am I going to kill my children like Agent Willard?"

"I'm like the wind or rain. You're not supposed to predict nature—to know what you're gonna do—when you're gonna die. Tell me, have you ever heard of The Ballet of Chestnuts—but of course you would."

It was party thrown by Pope Borgia and his sister Lucretia in the 1400's, recollected Grant. The Pope had chestnuts spread about the floor--invited his guests—formidable clergy and upstanding citizens to engage in sex acts with female courtesans. There were special gifts, silks and such, for those that could perform the task with the most women.

"Tell me Tom," added Dussant, "where was the Pope?"

"Sitting at a table with his sister Lucretia, watching. What's your point?"

The Agent looked like he was about to climax. Dr. Brandt took the agent deep inside her, rocking her pelvis back and forth. Dussant studied them like a horse owner at a stud breeding farm as he continued, "Maybe when you strip away the repression, the true nature of man is spread out across those chestnuts? I don't pervert people--I bring out what's inside them. And you're good, Tom. I always said I liked you. You're not contaminated like the other-"

"Oh yes! Yes! Yes! Yes!" the FBI Agent ejaculated across Dr. Brandt's face. She grabbed his penis, sucking madly until the agent had to pull away.

"Keep it down, we're trying to talk," chided Yves Alexander with a smile.

Ever so gently, Dr. Brandt wiped her face clean of ejaculate, groping for her black evening dress. She looked so happy, thought Tom, and yet was she even alive? Or were they zombies? How tiny he felt in Dussant's eyes. And he had actually bothered to defended this man--against hallucinations!

"The most difficult part was the live surveillance cameras that patched our little home back to Fort Meade where other researchers studied the tapes," continued Yves Alexander, "she devised a backup tape feed and then Catherine mandated all new agents enter this cubicle—after that it was New Year's Eve every night. Hell, she mandated all new agents would enter the cubicle to look with me—the party juss' kept goin."

"You've been biding your time for seven years?" pressed Tom, "why?"

"Just making friends."

Tom answered his own question, "The NSA would've nuked New Orleans--hunted you to the corners of the earth. Were you biding your time for escape? Does this have something to do with what you saw in Israel?"

"Why should I share my pain if you won't share yours," pressed Dussant, "tell me and then I'll make it go away."

Tom gasped, hearing the awful screaming of his mother from the Suite. Peering through the partition, it now overlooked his father's study lined with guns and hunting paintings. The room was dark—still he saw the small child hiding under the mahogany desk.

"Make it go away," he turned away. His mother continued to scream. His mind floated back to that night--*from the bedroom, Tom heard the sound of glass shattering, sounds branded into his mind. . . the struggle*--he shut his eyes but could hear the weeping inside the suite in synch with the weeping inside his head—his memories plastered up for all to see.

"Tell me what you saw?"

"You know!" he screamed, "he broke in! An intruder without a name. A man they never caught--raped and murdered my mother!"

"You were seven years old, Tom. What could you've done?"

"Nothing!" a wave of emotion swept over him, "something! Nothing! Nothing! Something--I don't fucking know!" he rubbed his throbbing temples. He peered through the partition, unable to escape the imagery--seeing the sandy haired boy in striped pajamas curled up, shaking, weeping. The door through the study was open and Tom saw her shadow as his mother fell to the floor. Then he saw the shadow of the attacker--he shut his eyes.

"A burglar broke in your home and killed your parents," narrated Dussant, "or that's what you told the authorities—the sole survivor."

"I should have done something!" tears rushed through him.

"Because you were in a study filled with guns? And what would you've done? The guns were bigger than you. If you'd acted, you'd be dead with your mother and father. But then, I guess you are dead, aren't you? Agent Willard shouldn't have been any surprise to you. . . you've been living with ghosts all your life. War, killing, slaughter is your occupation—yes, you refine it with trappings of government titles--called analytic skills--statistics, but you're just a spectator of the game. Maps line my walls and military lithographs line yours. You're like me," he sighed sadly, "your life's empty and you're incapable of love."

But you're wrong, thought Tom—he focused on Candice. If you know me so well, why don't you know about Candice? How could you not know about Candice! He anchored on that thought bringing him a semblance of sanity.

Focus was regained. Israel was the key, he thought. What made Yves Alexander's contaminated mother, a woman unable to display anything but love for her son, murder him outside Haifa? "What did you see in Israel?"

"God made clear my destiny. I was to enlighten every soul on the Earth. To achieve such a goal, I would shut off the engine of the world."

The engine of the world, he thought, "So you mastermind it? And don't fucking pretend you don't know what I'm talking about—say it!"

"Yes, Tom," he smiled, "I am involved in Union 57. I'm not conjuring this from your own mind. I orchestrated the Union 57 take-over from the beginning."

"But they'll never let you out—" he grasped the plan, "but they won't know who you are. All those files are stuffed away in NSA archives. You're going to force The White House to get you out of here and deliver you to the refinery. No one will have a chance to get to the files."

"Bravo."

"What are you going to do—blow the place up?"

"Can't give everything away just yet," smiled Yves Alexander.

The thought struck him, they were never meant to have this conversation here in this room. He wasn't supposed to know these things yet—Candice had foiled Dussant's plan, "What happened in Israel? Damn you, tell me!"

"The same thing I saw in that basement in Wayfarer when that blast of light parted the clouds and shook the house!" Dussant glared at him. "the same thing that put your mentor in a mental hospital for six years. As Rabb proved in that hospital, some things you people aren't ready to see."

"Then who's Bobby Lefrete? Tell me that!" Grant gritted his teeth.

Dussant glanced down at his watch, "They're coming soon. You need to do this on your own, but I promise the answers are right under your nose."

He knew who the mole was! He wanted to vomit, he wanted to crawl into a hole and die. The truth stung him--the worst thing he could ever imagine. Kicking back the chair, he raced to the door.

"Tom!" Dussant screamed as if he reading his thoughts, "it's too late!"

Everything flashed chaotically across his eyes. Agents blocked the staircase down. Turning left, he raced along the hall, pushing open the next door, entering a larger room that looked like a space shuttle mission control with computers and equipment-

---

2:47 PM (EST)
Elizabeth, NJ

"You OK?" Benjamin asked the Rabbi.

"Yeah," Rabb answered, "I'm just worried about Tom—it's a long story."

He should be concentrating on the matters at hand, thought Benjamin. What the hell was Tom doing for him that was more important than this?

Through the window, he spotted Dick Osbourne's chopper resting in the bricked atrium of The World Trade Center. General Crandal requested Dick's return from The White House—asking for a White House liaison. The request worked on the NSC agent's vanity. Now he was unknowingly escorted up by a tiny cadre of troops to his own enemies—and he didn't even know it.

"We ready?" General Crandal asked his weary companions: Rabb, Eleanor, and Colonel Sharpe, Rabb, and himself, "we need to extract a confession quickly. Sharpe is that tape recorder running?"

"Yes sir--whole room's bugged."

The doors swung open, "What the hell's going on!" Dick chewed on a pen. With his pock marked face, the White House Liaison agent possessed a perpetual scowl, thought Bronk. Dick sported his trademark FBI jacket despite the fact that he wasn't an FBI agent anymore.

Sharpe shut the door behind the man, blocking the only exit with his body. Eyeing the room, Dick looked scared. The old General aimed his pistol at Osbourne's face, "Games up! We know you're the Master."

The pen fell out of Osbourne's mouth, "Is this a joke?" his pock marked cheeks turned red, "you think I-I'm The Master? That's f-f-fucking crazy!"

"You're the one stuttering, Dick," groaned Crandal.

"I'm s-stuttering because you've got a damn gun pointed at my head!"

"Speak!" cried the General, "OR I'LL PUT A BULLET IN YOUR HEAD!"

2:52 PM (EST) 1:52 PM (CST)
New Orleans, LA

Tom locked the iron door, tripping over equipment. The room was filled with computers--a massive window overlooking the now vacant suite. He fumbled for his cell phone. Someone shook the doorknob! He dialed the number to the number on his cell phone--with his other hand he drew his pistol, firing shots at the door. It was giving in. The line connected and-

Forty Eight

2:55 PM (EST)
New York, NY

"I DON'T KNOW WHAT YOU'RE SAYING," screamed Osbourne, "I'M NOT THE MASTER!"

The Rabbi felt confidant. Dick was The Master--there from the beginning—he knew about Schubert's strike force—he fled Monongahela right before the explosion—he fled—he repeated the thought again.

Fear and anger laced itself into the agent's pock marked face, "Get that gun away and quit kidding around!"

"Why'd you leave Monongahela right before the explosion," the General shook the pistol as he made his accusation.

"Giardino recalled me to Washington!" screamed Osbourne.

Rabb's cell phone rang. With the screaming, no one except he and, only a few feet away, heard it. Entranced by the interrogation, Rabb brought the phone to his ear, hearing Tom Grant on the other end.

"T-Tom?" he pulled the phone away for a moment. Tom was alright. He'd been trying to reach him for hours, the day you apprehended Dussant, you used an alias over the bullhorn didn't you?"

"Yes."

"You called yourself Agent Bobby Lefrete."

"Yes," whispered Rabb, turning away from Crandal's interrogation, "but it was just a code, to tip Dussant off that I might suspect—"

"Rabb, you visited Dussant in the New Orleans compound, didn't you?" screamed his young student.

"What are you talking about?".

"Did you visit the compound in New Orleans?"

"Yes, years ago, I requested an interview," he remembered visiting Dussant, only once—ten years ago.

"Rabb   you   were   CONTAMINATED!" screamed Tom on the cell-phone—his words making no sense to the Rabbi, "he had you quit the FBI—to start CTJTF, a terrorist think tank. It allowed you to look for a terrorist scenario that could get him freed, to read up on terrorist groups such as The Crimson Fist and The Brotherhood of Freedom, to author the ransom letter requesting your involvement. Because you knew Delta Force would be called in and Remy would pull you into the center of the action--"

No—this was madness, thought Rabb—pure madness.

"Bet you still have that cell phone with the keyboard on the back side for emails, huh?" pressed Tom, "you contacted Nehemiah the whole time--masterminded the money exchange to buy you time--revealed Schubert's strike force to Nehemiah—and oversaw the bombing of Monongahela."

Rabb shut his eyes, all emotion flushed away. His mind continued processing, "This is crazy," he muffled his words.

"But Candice screwed up your plan—she was the unknown variable! You would have to stay in New York. But you might need a physical go-between with Dussant—someone to take care of the odds and in's—so you dispatched me down here to ask a meaningless question. Don't you see? We've been speaking continually since I left New York! I've been executing your orders in the field because YOU ARE THE MASTER!"

Gunshots-the line clicked dead.

The thought took hold and spread.

All those phone calls he thought he'd been making to Tom when the line was busy—had they really spoken? He made phone calls from the very beginning, in the control room, in Monongahela—had he called Nehemiah.

No—it couldn't be—*he had enough connections to purge those FBI agents' records*--he was exactly who he had always *been—why did you leave the FBI*—he hadn't changed—*if you really suspected Tom, why not go to New Orleans yourself*—no, he was the *same*—*of all the analysts, why did the terrorists request him*—he was—*with a brilliant career, why did you become an analyst.* . . no. . .yes. Stupid! Stupid! Stupid!

His logical mind worked it out at lightning speed. Dick was too much the fool to create such a conspiracy. Giardino was too rough to carry it off. That was why he knew those FBI agents in Monongahela—they were Dussant's former bodyguards—gathered before him— following his orders. He had ordered them to Monongahela once he no longer needed them. Why? Why would he do that? To destroy all the eyewitnesses who knew of Yves Alexander Dussant.

But why?

Then he realized the plan—a plan he had unknowingly concocted for this mad man. How could he have ever been so stupid? He searched anxiously around the room, but all attention was on Osbourne. Rabb's eyes pleaded--every ounce of his energy begging for someone to turn towards him! Now that he knew, would he be able to say anything or would he simply blow his brains out?

Then Benjamin flashed a quick look at him. Rabb shook his head at him--Bronk looked utterly puzzled. He had to act quickly! He tried to say the words, but his voice escaped him and only his lips seemed to move, his voice barely a whisper. But Benjamin understood the message.

Rabb knew he did. Then he noticed that snow was falling, coating the windows of The World Trade Center in a white haze. The Rabbi prepared to address the room: Remy, Eleanor, Sharp, Dick—

But before he could open his mouth to speak, something happened--like a thousand pin pricks working their way up his arms, back, and chest. He saw a light so deliciously bright that it made him feel empty as it wrapped its electric arms around his body. He was so weary—suddenly so tired. Then the jolt—a pain—things happened too fast and--

There was only light and--

Benjamin Bronk was blinded.

He slammed into something hard-- heard all the glass windows in the room shatter. Then he realized that all of the windows in the room were shattered. He felt a cold, howling wind rushed across his, face--placed a hand to against his brow--realized it was snowing in the control room-

"Aaiiighhhhhhh," someone moaned in the distance.

Only then did he realize there'd been an explosion. Gathering his senses, he discovered himself laying underneath the shattered conference table. Rolling over, he realized he was lying next to Colonel Sharpe. They were under the conference table. His ribs dug into his lungs-- could barely breath!

Then he thought of his mother. Scrambling to his feet he almost fell through the blasted window of The World Trade Center, "Mother!" he screamed.

"I'm here Benjamin," replied Eleanor. She motioned out of the smoke, using his voice as a guide. She appeared almost unscathed. She peered over her shoulder. General Crandal tried to get up, a wide gash ripped across the Texan's brow—his jumpsuit was tattered and charred in certain spots.

"You alright?" Benjamin asked.

"Where's Rabb?" the General searched for his friend, "Rabb!"

Then Benjamin saw the motionless body lying in the far corner-- precariously close to the shattered window ledge. The Rabbi lay motionless.

Benjamin moved closer to him, but the General was up, stumbling and to his fallen comrade—his best friend. Everything would be fine, Benjamin told himself, it had only been a small blast.

He sounded like a wounded animal dying in the night, thought Benjamin, There were no words, only the intangible of emotion in General Crandal's voice. Still the out of character nature of it all, made Benjamin want to turn away as if he were glimpsing something so private that he should not see it.

General RM Crandal wept. He crumpled over the Rabbi, his arms and legs wilting like a flower in the sun. Benjamin didn't know what to do. Everyone knew they'd lost something precious not only to the mission— but for the world? Rabb was the genius who'd save them!

"Noooooooooo," Remy screamed, his back arched in painful pose—he was alone, oblivious to everything else. His leathery face red and strained, his lips parted wide, he was unable to conjure sound now from his anguished lips.

The Rabbi was dead.

Crandal tried to lift his dead friend in his arms. As Rabb's torn shirt fell away, the General and everyone could see it—freezer tape wrapped about his chest as if he were a mummy. And taped to the freezer tape were shards of former explosive packages and wires. The detonator switch fell out of his dead hand, the button dangling by the tiny wire running up his sleeve. The room was aghast. The Rabbi had blown the explosives attached to his body.

"No!" screamed Crandal, pulling back, not sure of what to make of this. Then Crandal noticed blood trickling from his open chest wound. A large shard of metal had sat on his lung—finally puncturing it. General Remy Crandal collapsed, dropping Rabb's corpse with him. Dick Osbourne instantly took control—ordering Eleanor Bronk to be restrained—he wanted no civilians. Then he barked a seemingly endless list of orders. Everyone was so shocked—no one realized Benjamin had left minutes before any of this happened.

He stumbled towards the elevator. Osbourne would probably be running the show. He didn't care. Weaving around the soldiers, he took the elevator to the lower floor, knowing soldiers would not be guarding the floor below.

The smell of sheet-rock filled his nose. He didn't want to think about who had set the bomb—he didn't care about the world—about even Rabb. The entire lower floor was empty. Bronk heard his feet tap against hard, concrete. Benjamin had tried everything—gave his body and life to the fight, but the sad truth was that they weren't much farther along now than when they began 72 hours before. The only truth was that in less than ten hours Union 57 was going to explode—if not by terrorists, without electricity the place would blow on its own.

He ran his hands along the far wall still fresh with sheet-rock—through a child's eyes he remembered the opulent office of mahogany and ivory that had once been here. He was now appreciative of his father's excesses. Benjamin pressed the tiny electric button still untouched by the construction.

The secret door swung open. Benjamin saw the small, white envelope at the top of the metal staircase. Carefully, he opened the letter written in Mueller's furious penmanship. The note read as follows:

HAVE YOUR WIFE, BUT NO CHILDREN. SHE WILL NOT SPEAK. MUST COME QUICKLY TO THE PLACE WE MET BEFORE.

His apartment. Mueller had his wife at his apartment. On the small landing was a cell phone, a clean suit, shoes, and underclothes-- Mueller forgot nothing. There were many times in men's lives, thought Benjamin Bronk, when they had to make critical decisions, choosing not only a course of action, but defining their own convictions—their morality. How strange that the millions of people, the billions at stake, didn't matter now. There was only his family—his children.

He knew what he was doing before he even saw the note. He would have dragged his mother out, but he knew she wouldn't have followed. He shut the secret door behind him, stumbling in the cold darkness of the cramped staircase. They might kill him over this-- say he was a traitor—but he'd return to face the penalty, if it was of any value, he'd die with them. But only after he saw his children and wife take off from Teterboro on his Falcon 50 headed to Zurich. Then the thought hit him and he realized the full magnitude of the crisis—something he'd failed to grasp earlier. Still, as he escaped the impending crisis which had enveloped his life for the past 72 hours, he remembered the Rabbi's last dying breath—he'd whispered it to Benjamin alone, recalling the words:

Trust Tom. Trust Tom and no one else.

Forty Nine

3:23 PM (EST) 2:23 PM (CST)
New Orleans, LA

The needle touched the record.

The hand moved away from the gramophone. Frank Sinatra began to sing "New York New York" over the aging record player.

Dr. Brandt raced up the stairs.

The music followed her up the tiny, winding staircase. By the time she made it to the second floor, agents stood in the open doorway in surprise. When she arrived in the control room, she almost fell over. How could it be?

The image conveyed a thousand words. Through the Plexiglas partition, she observed Yves Alexander Dussant sitting cross legged in his burgundy reading chair as he toyed with the gramophone playing the song. Besides those two items, the room was empty.

The moving truck backed into the alley lining Dussant's townhouse. The rear door of the truck opened and from out of the darkness they came, looking surreal in the old alleyway of The French Quarter. The old bricked alley walls reflected in the polarized faceplates of their space suits. The man in the astronaut suit, turned away, the environmental system strapped to his back feeding fresh oxygen into the pressurized suit, as he helped the other ten men in astronaut suits out of the truck.

"Turn it off!" screamed Dr. Brandt.

"Come on Dr. Brandt," shrugged Yves Alexander, his voice coming over the speakerphone, "always thought the place needed a little mood music."

Her employees fiddled at the control switches, but were unable to silence him and his music. How was he over-riding the speakers? Where the fuck had his furniture gone? Agent rushed by her.

Agent Roberts, a tall, wiry black man screamed at the top of his voice into his headset, "Fort Meade, we have a security breach! I repeat, a Level 1 Breach!"

She glanced back through the partition. Ever composed, the bastard reclined in his chair on the other side of the glass, yawning as if he tired with this spectacle before him.

"We're dead!" another agent sobbed, "we're fucking dead!"

"Why Dr. Brandt, I think I've shaken you?" Dussant grinned.

She reached forward, her palm looming over the large green button which could release the lethal amount of Sarin nerve gas into the suite of rooms, "Shut up and tell me what you've done or I'll gas you, you stinking bastard! I swear, I'll gas you."

"How can you do anything," he scoffed, "you barely even know yourself,"

Simultaneously, the television monitors in the tiny room flashed on. The screaming and yelling ceased. Men shook in terrified fear, eyes locked on the monitors like deer caught in headlights. Only then did Dr. Brandt hear her own voice moaning. A hand still held precariously over the phosgene switch, she glanced up at the monitor.

She watched a tape. . . a ghastly tape of her crawling to Agent Roberts, unbuttoning his pants, reaching for his penis! This had to be a fake—her mind struggled to make sense of the tape. Without even enough time to get erect, she brought him deep into her mouth, moving back and forth as he stiffened-

The men were on the roof.

They finished checking the vacuum seals. This was the first time they ever worked with such equipment in such civilian areas—in the middle of The French Quarter! "Ready?" the team leader grunted through his headset, snapping a cartridge into his short barreled, silencer mounted MP-5 rifle.

If anyone spied the scene, they wouldn't have known quite what to make of it all: four space men crossing from one roof to another in the middle of The French Quarter! They stopped ten feet from a semicircle of plastic explosives.

A flash of light. The black tar roof collapsed in a circular pattern as the explosives were blown. Wood, timber, and tar splattered across the roof. Each of the men took the rope and lowered themselves down.

"We've got an intruder alert in the attic!" someone screamed.

Dr. Brandt couldn't turn away from the TV. Let it not be true—let it not be true. She turned away as Agent Roberts fucked her on the TV screen. The horrible thought took hold. She was contaminated! Contaminated!

"I just wanted to say goodbye in my own special way," Dussant chimed over the intercom, "by now The White House has come to fetch me and has no time for the obstinate NSA who still has not claimed this program exists. By now the President's been forced to take drastic action."

Someone farted. Others dry heaved—stress affecting each of them in a different way. Some stood about, cradling their guts or temples—all eyes on her and the television monitors. The music rumbled through the room. She was so scared. Scared like a lost, little girl. Scared beyond anything she ever imagined--a trickle of urine streamed down her leg.

"We're gonna die!" another agent turned away from the video tape, screaming insanely, "they're going to kill us all! I-I'm making a run for it!"

There was still one option open to her, "Go to hell, you bastard!" she pressed the Sarin nerve gas switch.

Dr. Brandt was stunned.

Nothing happened—except Dussant's laughing, "Did you really think it would be that easy, Catherine?" sighed Dussant.

"Shut up!"

She pressed the button again. Nothing. Turning to watch, she noticed that her hand did not actually touched the switch! She pressed it again and again--feeling the switch depress under her fingers and yet her arm and hand never moved! It was true, she was contaminated--she couldn't kill him. All the power and strength escaped her. Then she heard distant gunfire beyond Frankie's crooning voice.

The space suited men took the four agents out simultaneously with shotguns and machine gun fire. The astronauts, in their Biohazard 4 suits, clambered down the rickety staircase to the second level. Satellite recon, projected on the inner face of their helmets, identified the location of the life-forms in the building. They rushed towards the control room.

"You are Satan!" screamed Dr. Brandt.

Dussant yawned. Why the hell couldn't she press the damn button! What the hell was happening? On the TV she was fucking three of her subordinates, taking them in various orifices—it made her want to vomit.

"No. No. No," tears streamed down her cheeks.

Bang! Bang! Bang! Agent Robert's head exploded on the partition glass. She saw another tech fall over his console, two gaping holes in his back sending smoke curling towards the ceiling. A female tech lay spastic on the floor, a bullet hole between her eyes, pouring blood across her face--

"Don't press that button!" a new voice cried.

She turned to see seven men in Biohazard IV suits holding shotguns and machine guns. Two other men held a large metal capsule—like a sleek coffin. She knew what it was—a Biohazard IV transport capsule. A final astronaut held an empty space suit and a sign, presumably for Dussant, which read:

PUT IT ON AND GET IN THE CAPSULE.

Men poured gasoline over the dead NSA agents and computers and briefs. Then she fainted--

---

4:07 PM (EST)
29,000 Ft. over Meridian, Mississippi

That damn song still played.

"Can you hear me?" the voice inquired. At first she thought it was Old Blue Eyes. . . then things connected.

Dr. Brandt awoke to find herself tied naked, spread eagle on the bed. She felt the entire room vibrate--caught sight of the Presidential seal brandished on the far wall. The entire room shook like an earthquake. The man in the space suit braced himself against the wall to hold his stance.

"Do you know where you are?" Dussant asked—no eyes, no mouth, just that copper colored face plate reflecting her own bound body.

She was on an airplane. What she just felt was turbulence. Her eyes darted about the room. The door was covered in freezer tape--everything looked like the Press photos she'd seen of the executive bedroom of Airforce   One.

Dussant smiled—sensing she knew her surroundings, "I'm letting you feel the panic—as if this is all happening again for the first time," his thick, gloved fingers ran up her thigh, stopping between her legs. She clenched her teeth tightly--felt the thick, horrible gloved fingers entering her vagina and anus. He pinched them together—two fingers pressing through the *cul-de-sac*—the posterior vaginal wall and anterior rectum wall. It hurt so much--she saw stars!

"Tell me, how does it feel to be the prisoner?" he asked.

"Why don't you untie me and I'll tell you." she knew judo and could escape—but where would she run?

"Alright," he unstrapped one of her arms. She cracked his faceplate so hard she thought she might've broken her hand. Rolling over, she struggled to get her other hand free. She noticed he was taking off his helmet. She lunged forward just as the crack in the helmet showed and then the world fell away.

A surge of energy.

Inner peace? Wholeness? Fullness? Words couldn't describe the sensation. . more tingles. Then no words. No thoughts. She was beyond that. She realized how incomplete Catherine Brandt had been—so lacking, so wanting, so needing. The entity that she now comprised was so much more—the way she'd forgotten—when she was an infant child—at one with her mother.

All the darkness in the room turned to indescribable joy and then a massive orgasm rushed through her—it was indescribable--like being a little girl and a grown woman all at once. No fear. No hatred. Only love.

"You know what I like," Dussant sighed, pulling off the top of his suit.

She wrapped her arms lovingly around his head, bathing in ecstasy for until now, she'd forgotten how much love she possessed. The feelings and emotions wracked her body, bringing tears of joy to her eyes.

Her lips raced along his flesh as fast as he could disrobe. She was so moist between her legs as she pulled his spaceman pants down to his knees—how cute, a space suit! She was a dog, a whore, a bitch, mere excrement on a wall, nothing, small and insignificant and she didn't care. So secure was she in her love. She would give her life without thought to bring him an ounce more pleasure. Such love, such thoughts, such beliefs needed no proof—pure faith—with no room for question or reasoning. Of course she didn't perceive these thoughts because—

Faith does not allow thought, but only belief.

"Oh baby," sighed Yves Alexander, rubbing the back of her neck.

Laying back on the Presidential sheets, kicking his feet about, he was happy. Therefore she was happy. She knew where they were headed—the song filling her ears. And as Yves Alexander ejaculated in her warm throat, she heard him singing the final bar in a gingerly voice along with Frankie.

Fifty

Sounds rushed through him.

He heard the clink of glass--opened his eyes, pupils taking time to adjust to the low light. He looked down at his two hands casually resting on the polished table-- turned to his right, startled by two Japanese business men who stared at him as if he didn't belong here. He remembered the bandage covering his cut forehead. Fans spun overhead. . . cold, brick floors flowing out of the room towards windows overlooking The Wildlife and Fisheries building.

"Another drink?" the voice inquired—the bartender loomed, , fat and pale.

"N-no," he stammered. Moving his hand forward, he noticed the clothing tag hanging from his sleeve, reading 'Perlis's Clothing Store'—an uptown store across town. He was wearing a white linen suit. Only then did Tom spot the elegant open grill in the far corner of the room, elegant tables and chairs of The Rib Room Restaurant. He glanced at his watch, he'd lost two hours of his life.

What had he been doing besides buying a white linen suite? The thought hit him again: he was contaminated! He'd lost his soul! Shit, was this real? Was he really here or was he imagining this situation? It hit him, Rabb was dead.

The sounds of conversation vanished. Three days of hell took its toll on him. His arms hurt, his forehead was cut, eyes weary. And all he could think was that the greatest men he ever knew, his surrogate father, was dead. Tears came to his eyes, he must look like some derelict drunk. Had he killed him?

"What a fucking fire," a customer pointed at the crowd of firemen and spectators through the window. Tom knew that Dussant's home was on fire. He remembered Candice's warning—he had revealed himself as a terrorist during the first videotaped conference with Dussant. FBI agents were looking for him.

He fled into the bathroom on the lower level.

What could he do? Couldn't take a plane to New York to try to stop Dussant. Shit, he didn't even understand Dussant's plan. Too much—he broke. Tom Grant was not an emotional person, but he was worn to nothing. Tears rushed—emotions strong, paralyzing him. Dropping to his knees, he huddled against the door, pressing legs against flushed cheeks--he wanted to travel back to three precious days before--when he had a soul and Rabb, a life.

Candice was all he ever had. . . a woman he never met face to face. He focused on Candice and the panic ebbed—had to be strong for her. He returned to the stairs, hearing the chitter chatter up above of businessmen finishing their five martini lunches. He couldn't go up just yet, he wiped tears from his wet cheeks. Then he remembered Dussant's advice--

"My father has one of those ancient wine lockers in the basement of The Rib Room-

The Pipkin Room.
The wooden sign hung ominously from the ceiling, calling him down a deeper, subterranean staircase. He followed the stairs to the bottom, groping around for the light switch. When he turned on the lights, he noted the red velvet case with shiny keys hanging below small embossed plaques with family names—the Dussant key was missing.

Wine holds many answers to your questions, Agent Grant."

He pushed open the door to The Pipkin Room.
The air was cold—must filled his nose. He glanced around the stone chamber--pictures of Napoleonic battles dotted the walls--against the far wall

underneath a family crests sat a wall of wine lockers devised out of fenced gratings. He ran his hand along the cold metal grills of the wine cabinets--each labeled with engraved copper plaques.

Peering through the ironwork, he observed bottles of wine racked one atop the another. . .new bottles in some cabinets while other bottles were so ancient, their labels pealed and rotted—many hadn't been touched in this century. Then he came to the Dussant plaque--

"The key is hidden on the mantle above the locker."

His hand slid along the cornice until he found the key. He opened the cabinet, discovering the following parcels: One bottle of Pichon-Longueville-Lalande 1970 from The Westin Hotel, one "Lucky Dog", and a note.

He grabbed for the note, the paper cold and damp. The lead top of the wine bottle had oxidized against the paper, eating out a corner--these parcels had been here some time. Tom broke the wax seal on the letter, a unicorn with seven stars beneath it, spreading the damp paper on the table. The letter was US postmark August, 1973—a month after Dussant's Israel trip—addressed to the his wine locker at The Rib Room. But under the spell of contamination, thought Tom, he could've constructed the forgery in the past two days— after all, the hot dog was still fresh. He read the note:

August 10th, 1973
Dear Tom Grant,
Bravo! If you are finally here then you are all I ever hoped you would be. Try the wine and food. In the end it all adds up.
Yours truly,

-Yves Alexander Dussant
P.S. Just kidding about the "Lucky Dog", they're made out of pigs lips and assholes. Wouldn't touch em with five foot stick..

Tom moaned.

Every puzzle led to another one. If this letter were genuine, Tom was only three years old at the time! The letter clearly was a fucking forgery. Shit! He didn't have time for this crap. The government was looking for him! He had no time for codes. Then he remembered something from one of his conversations with Dussant—another conversation from a hallucination.

"Do you ever work with codes?" asked Dussant.

Codes?

He recalled the gnarled, little French Quarter dwarf of a Jester, laughing and eyeless. Nothing he had seen since he was contaminated happened serendipitously—they were all hallucinations—clues to Dussant's puzzle! He remembered the Jester's poem— putting the pieces together.

"Twenty Five cents is not a great number-
for a life twisted by fate,
Ya must know that truth is in the numbers-
if you're to acquire eternal faith."

Truth is in numbers? He searched his pockets— finding the tiny notebook, studying the numbers written in excrement on the wall of the abandoned building— another vision!

1*7-10,18	3*10-12	18*10,21	1*19
22*18	6*11	18*24	21*3

Perhaps the numbers were part of some alphabetical code?

He examined the first number set: 1*7-18. Could each number represent an alphabetical symbol? If 1 was the letter first letter of the alphabet: A—then 7 would be G—8 would be H—I0 would be I—J would be 11—he worked out the rest of the sequence: AGHIKL

That made no fucking sense. But there was a star after the number 1. Perhaps the 1 was to be added to the numbers following it in the solution set? He worked out a solution along those lines. It read as follows: AHIJKL

Gibberish! He threw the pencil against the far wall-- rubbed his eyes. Damn it, he didn't need this Sherlock Holmes bull-shit! If Dussant wanted him to know, why was he making it so damn difficult. Or was it supposed to take time? If Candice hadn't called him-- interrupted his hallucinations, would his grand tour of illusions end in this room? Probably, but long after Dussant finished his tasks.

Stuffing the note in his pocket, Tom turned around. He had no choice now, he had to get out of The Quarter before the government agents found him here-- before he was killed or spent the rest of his life chained to some hospital gurney.

"Yee Sinners go to hell!" cried the preacher.

At the man's feet, a makeshift amplifier blasted his words down Royal Street. Wielding the microphone in emaciated arms, the awkward road side reverend marched along the pedestrian street, ranting and raving at passersby's who would listen, "Burn in hell, shall you all!"

Tom turned away, having enough bible babble to last him a lifetime.

"Let us not forget The Book of Zephaniah," cried the preacher as Tom turned away, "I will utterly consume everything from the face of the land—"chapter one—verse 2—"

Tom froze.

Verses. Books, chapters, verses. . . could it be? He pulled the sheet from his pocket again, unfolding it in his hands.

1*7-10,18	3*10-12	18*10,21	1*19
22*18	6*11	18*24	21*3

The stars could be colons? Could 1*7-18 denote Chapter One, verses 7 through 10 and verse 18? He felt his pulse race--knew he'd unlocked a secret. Spinning around, he grabbed the bible out of the preacher's hand--flipping through the pages, oblivious to the world around him. The preacher ranted even louder, calling on heavenly intervention and when that didn't come, calling on the police. The FBI were looking for him. Bible in hand he raced away.

There were so many books in the testaments. What would Dussant refer to? It hit him--Dussant would cite the book that dealt with the second coming of Christ: John's Book of Revelations, the final pages of The New Testament. Darting into an alleyway, he flipped through pages until he found Chapter One, verses 7 through18—the first code. A queasy feeling set in as he read:

Behold, He is coming with clouds, and every eye will see Him, even they who pierced Him. And all the tribes of the earth will mourn because of Him. Even so, Amen. I am He who lives, and was dead, and behold, I am alive forevermore. Amen, And I have the keys of Hades--

Then 3*10-12. Tom located Chapter 3, verses 10 through 12:

Because you have kept My command to persevere, I also will keep you from the hour of trial which shall come upon the whole world.

Tom felt as if Dussant were speaking to him through these ancient prophecies. He pressed on:

For I testify to everyone who heard the words of the prophecy of this book: if anyone adds to these things, God will add to him the plagues that are written in this book:

He continued--

Write the things which you have seen, and the things which are, and the things which will take place after this--

That was why he had been led around by a ghost walking him through the gates of hell. He was to see all of it-- then go to the wine cellar.

Oh no.

Tom Grant was to be the chronicler of the last book of the Bible: The Gospels Of Yves Alexander Dussant. That was why Dussant asked him if he was a writer, asked what he enjoyed writing about. But what did he intend to do with Union 57? Tom pressed on, locating verses-- drawing them into one cohesive paragraph. As he read, he felt his knees go weak:

A white robe was given to each of them, and it was said to them that they should rest a little while longer, until both the number of their fellow servants and their brethren, who would be killed , as they were, was complete. Standing at a distance for fear of her torment, saying, 'Alas, alas, that great city Babylon, that mighty city! For in one hour your judgement has come.

Then a mighty angel took up a stone like a great millstone and threw it into the sea, saying, "thus with violence the great city Babylon shall be thrown down, and shall not be found anymore. And in her was found the blood of prophets and saints, and of all who were slain on the earth. Behold, the tabernacle of God is with me, and He will dwell with them, and they shall be His people. God Himself will be with them and be their God."

Oh no.

Rabb hadn't just formulated a threat for Dussant. Dussant always planned on destroying the east coast. Why? The trip to Israel! He rose from the fucking dead already. Dussant must intend on contacting the press. He would destroy Union 57 only to rise from the ashes—to be reborn. Tom would be his Chronicler, a third party to document his rebirth, his unholy resurrection.

Words?

Why words? Why wouldn't Dussant use a TV or movie producer for the chronicler? Did he believe that through the destruction of the east coast he could wreck the world? Did he hope to set back the planet, so that there would be no more electricity, no technology, no voice recordings, no method to filter or control his power? Would he then import total tyranny on mankind: a Godly messenger king who contaminated all indiscriminately. . . a new age when God and man would walk together, hand in hand?

Of course.

Rabb laid the plan out so well. First their henchman took over Union 57, initiating the greatest terrorist threat anyone ever witnessed. The terrorists led the government in circles, culminating in the Monongahela trap, demoralizing the government's strength and killing all the former agents—anyone who knew anything about The Watch. Then the government would see the tape of Tom and Dussant where he claimed the terrorists would surrender only if Dussant were brought to the refinery! Anyone who knew anything about Dussant-- who understood his horrible powers-- would be dead or as in Tom's case, blanketed by suspicion. There would be no one to warn the government.

Only then would the demand be made for Dussant's immediate transfer to Union 57. Dussant warned him of how little time he had. Dussant would allow the government a few hours to get him to New York, not enough time for anyone to find the time-sealed files tucked away in some top secret government archives.

Tom was a scholar of terrorist scenarios. He knew that the government would go for it. They would escort Dussant to New Jersey. It took ten years of planning, but Yves Alexander Dussant had returned, forcing his own enemies to aid him in their own destruction: every knee must bend, ever heart give homage.

What could he do?

Shit, he couldn't even get within a mile of an airport. Dussant was going to blow Union 57 sky high! He focused on Candice because he couldn't really fathom the murder of millions of people. Candice. Candice. She rattled his nerves. He had to do something! He rocked his weary had back and forth, searching for an answer.

In the heat of the moment, the answer came to him. Pressing his face deep into the phone booth, he dialed the toll free number. The line connected:

"Thank you for calling," the operator answered gingerly, "this is the Union 57 Corporation. How may I--"

"I want to speak to Benjamin Bronk," screamed Tom.

Fifty One

5:17 PM (EST)
Elizabeth, NJ

Candice Cooperman regained consciousness.

"Where are my friends?" she tugged at the restraints holding her to the chair. She didn't need to look beyond the bloodied floor to realize she was back in the breakroom—where it all began.

The man before her was bandaged—gauze stained with blood and grime. Beyond the bandages, gurgling sounds were her only reply. She knew it was Nehemiah—knew her bullet had hit his jaw and not his face. His hands shook as he tried to restrain himself from strangling her—but why?

He drew something on her forehead and then held a mirror in front of her. She glanced into it, studying her wearied, dirty face—like the face of a stranger with the words scribbled in black grease pencil:

MYSTERY. BABYLON THE GREAT,
THE MOTHER OF HARLOTS AND
OF THE ABOMINATIONS OF THE EARTH

"Just fucking kill me, you fagot," she moaned, trying to push him to the limit. A quick death would be so much easier than torture and she knew Nehemiah was impetuous enough, callous enough to simply put a bullet in her head. What the hell was going on in this sick fuck's head?

Nehemiah fought to control himself.

Through the slits of his crude bandages, he examined the little bitch tied to the chair--had to remind himself that he couldn't kill her yet. No, The Master had designated her for a special purpose now.

To restrain himself, he fed on memories—what he'd been before his transformation: the lonely East German soldier exiled from his homeland because he tasted their tight innocent bodies of boys, felt their warm openings wrap themselves around him—a love he could not control.

He remembered the bone chilling cold nights in New York City as a vagrant—cast out of Germany--a drifter speaking a handful of English-- remembered the hollowness--days of hunger—meager change in his pocket from sucking old men's dicks, swallowing the bitter semen--nights too numb to masturbate to angelic children's faces that danced in his mind. He was so alone.

Then they came for him as he slept in an alleyway in the meat packing district. It was the Rabbi who greeted him. Rabb knew his name-- what he'd done before-- as if he'd read his dossier. Rabb offered him food--clothing. At first he was suspect, he hated grubby niggers and kikes--Rabb was both. Then he realized that the Rabbi was special—like a wolf in sheep's clothing.

"Why are you doing this?" he asked in broken English.

"Because, you are special," smiled the Rabbi--his Master, "the Messenger of God has seen you in visions. You are meant to do great things."

"What things?"

"You shall bring about God's work. Then you shall die and enter a greater world because of it. Because you are The Defender of the Faith," Rabb patted his head and baptized him into their following--gave him his one true name: Nehemiah. Of course he had never met the Messenger of God in person, only Rabb—The Master had met him, but Nehemiah was promised the opportunity before all the others. What ecstasy that would be!

The Master had showed him a photo of Yves Alexander Dussant--the image bored into his very being as Rabb promised, "One day you shall walk through the portals of the world with him."

"What will it be like on that day?" he asked.

"All desires will be fulfilled," replied the Rabbi, "you will have youthful angels--as many young boys and babes as your heart desires," and Nehemiah loved the Rabbi and never thought of him again as a nigger kike.

His pulse raged. Drawing out his serrated knife, Nehemiah slit the front of Candice's jumpsuit—cutting bra and panties until she sat exposed in front of him— soft breasts and a tuft of sandy brown pubic hair in front of him. He imagined a penis in that pubic hair—his erection formed. But he couldn't sustain it for long and once again realized he was looking at the bitch who shot him.

With the edge of the knife, he lightly cut her right breast, flesh opening—she flinched, hiding a scream, gritting her teeth--blood trickling toward the tuft of pubic hair between her legs.

He wanted to hurt her--wanted to take that fucking knife and spread her legs wide, entering her in the painful way—serrated steel against soft, pink flesh-- the way he entered those little boys—tearing--widening them. That was power—brand them with the knife--let them carry the pain forever—and when you're dead and gone they'll still know who owns them--ohhhh—he ejaculated in his pants.

When he opened his eyes he saw her staring at his pants leg, wincing, "You are one sick fuck."

He rubbed her cheek into his jism stain, pressing the knife against her throat—no, restrain yourself—tell her, "This is the last act of kindness you'll get. Because, Candice Cooperman—slurp--Mother of Harlots and Whores, you will await His arrival. In ceremonial fashion—

6:01 PM (EST)
Washington D.C.

Havoc.

Secretary of State Vincent Giardino saw The Secret Service agents piling into the room—a bald headed officer stating firmly, "We have to go sir!"

No time to talk--Giardino and The President hurried through the chaotic west wing--a hurricane of confusion--people racing everywhere. News of the impending crisis had broken—he knew it was a matter of time. It couldn't have been a White House leak—they had clamped the lid of secrecy on the whole place—had the terrorists done it?

The balding agent turned to the President, "Need to get you out of here, sir. Your wife and daughter have been evacuated from the other side of town. We've patched through a call from them to Marine One," Marine One was the Presidential chopper.

Over the heads of agents, the President turned to the Razorback with a disappointed look, "Get to Fort Crandal and oversee Osbourne's delivery," or it'll be your ass—you believed in this deal—you better be there. The last part wasn't said, but clearly visible in the President's expression. And Vincent was hustled down another hall to another chopper. Because he was going to New York.

7:26 PM (EST)
New York, NY

"I just don't want to talk about it and that's final!"

"Amanda," ranted Benjamin Bronk, "have you listened to anything I've said?" it was like talking to a dog, he thought to himself.

He arrived back at his apartment only fifteen minutes before. Mueller had locked his wife in the bedroom until his arrival. Disheveled and tired they had argued in the living room—she refused to tell her where the kids were. Mueller had tried to get a chopper, but could get a limo in far less time—it waited downstairs for her.

Amanda Bronk brushed back her long, dark hair, tossing it over her shoulder as she so often did. Seated on the oriental divan in the center of their Pompeian styled living room, she struck a plutocratic pose, "Look at yourself, Benjamin--a complete mess. Take a shower or-"

He grabbed her arm, twisting it--one more ounce of pressure and I'll pop it out the socket. He had withstood too much—his wife would not stop him—

Her screaming woke him from his spell. He released his grasp. She leapt away, nursing her wrist, "You've gone mad! And you send your little henchman, Mueller, like some hit-man to rough me up."

"For the love of everything, get the kids, go to the jet, leave New York. This is bigger than you and I and our petty little problems—"

"That's the problem," she turned away, "you think my issues are so petty."

Damn he thought he'd made headway, "These are our children's' lives we're talking about. I am giving up my life for you—what so petty about that!"

Silence. Her eyes wide--yes, he thought, I've made contact. She screwed up her finely etched nose, "This isn't a joke--a plot to get the kids from me?"

He nodded his head, sweaty, tired, exhausted.

"The kids are at Susan's," one of her sister in laws who lived in the Village, "we can pick them up now."

Benjamin searched for the words—holding back his emotions, "Amanda, I'm not going with you to pick up the kids. This is the last time I'll see you," his eyes watered, "the kids won't remember me—tell them how much I loved them."

"I don't understand what you're talking about."

"And I don't have the time to explain."

For the first time in years, Benjamin Bronk's held his wife-- pressing his nose to the small of her cheek. How he loved her smell--light and sweet. For years he thought the woman he married was dead. Maybe that was when his trips to The Drake and hers to the Village began. He breathed in her scent again, feeling as if time and space bent for him, drawing him back to when they were younger. . . when their lives were more ahead of them than behind.

He felt her tremble in his arms, "Benjamin, you're going to make me cry."

"I didn't mean any of it," he said, "I didn't mean any of it."

Then Mueller was standing in the doorway, tapping his watch. Benjamin was squandering time. She fought, beckoned him to go with her. If Union 57 was going to be detonated, he had to die too. He knew— even back in *The Petrossian*, he always knew this would happen. Then Mueller collected her and told him, "the kid, Grant, is on his way. Just got choppered in from the jet. Should be here in five minutes," he turned--

"Mueller," this wasn't the way Benjamin wanted it to end.

"Yeah?" his boxy chief of security never turned around.

"Make sure you're on that plane too."

"Can't do that kiddo," Mueller shook his square head, "I'm afraid it's out of character for me. If that refinery blows, I got a bottle of Scotch for us to share."

You'll be dead before we see each other again, thought Benjamin. He wanted to say goodbye to his old friend, but simply turned around, staring out at the lights of the East River, watching the reflection in the window—his Chief of Security vanishing into the foyer. Benjamin felt so alone.

7:59 PM (EST)
New York, NY

Dick Osbourne was nervous.

This was his grab at power—his fucking moment in the sun. The hundreds of soldier surrounding him, the countless jeeps, vans, trucks parked on the tarmac, were his glorious escort to victory.

He glanced up. The sleek lines of Air Force One's reflected the gray skies overhead. The prisoner almost cleared the long flight of stairs, his limbs restrained to his Biohazard IV suit--legs chained--arms cuffed to a restraining eyeholes at the base of his space suit helmet. As he approached, the helmet turned-- drops of rain water on the copper colored faceplate.

Approaching the prisoner, Dick felt sweat forming on his brow despite the cold wind. He wondered who this man really was. Giardino's men were still unable to locate the sealed documents on this joker and Dussant wasn't apt to disclose anything about himself. He just knew that the NSA thought this guy was carrying some kind of wild disease—maybe leprosy?

"I'm FBI agent Dick Osbourne-- dispatched as the representative of The President of The United States to offer you our humble thanks and gratitude for your services. The President wanted to me to confer to you that despite whatever medical condition you have-- your case has shocked his administration. As a token of our sympathy, we've dealt with your jailers and as soon as we know more will punish those who've—"

"Did you bring the items I requested?" the syrupy Southern voice drawled over the speakers mounted to the helmet.

Dick held up the large duffle bag, "It's all here." Dussant opened up his hand concealing a tiny package wrapped in waxed paper, "If you could kindly put that in there—we can get going."

8:12 PM (EST)
New York, NY

"What's so damn important?"

Benjamin Bronk greeted Tom Grant in the limo waiting just outside One Sutton Place. Since the government was after both of them, Benjamin felt it best to keep the car moving. The tiny limo TV was playing a sitcom--Benjamin turned down the volume.

Tom didn't look good-- a bandage over his forehead--clad in a ghastly white suit, huge black bags ringed his eyes. Benjamin wasn't in much better shape. Still the beginnings of a quiet satisfaction filled his soul-- his job was almost done. He glanced down at his watch. Forty five more minutes and his family would be safely away.

Tom slid up the partition as he spoke first. Benjamin noticed a Bible in Grant's lap—apropos reading material, he thought to himself, "I'm gonna tell it you exactly as it happened. Rabb sent me to New Orleans on a hunch to meet a man he suspected was behind the hijacking of your refinery named Yves Alexander Dussant. He aims to blow up your refinery and thinks that in doing such he will 'stop the engine of the world'."

A pregnant pause. Benjamin's mind returned to the Rabbi's last words: *Trust Tom. Trust Tom and no one else*. In this strange world of guns and bombs and killers, he trusted Rabb and Rabb told him to trust Grant, "Well your story does fit into a biblical theme."

"What do you mean?"

"Your Dussant guy wants to stop the engine of the world? I can't believe it-- took me so many days to see it. It just struck me earlier today-- blowing up Union 57 would not only kill 27 million people-- it would lead to a global meltdown of financial markets: stopping the engine of the world."

"How?"

"In 1929 a 30% drop in the New York Stock market initiated a worldwide depression for 10 years leading to global fascism, and the eventual death of roughly 30 million people by war," elaborated Benjamin," if Union 57 blows we're going to kill the majority of top CEO's in the country, the staff of the most powerful corporations, trading houses, brokerage firms, banks, and the fucking exchange itself. The US dollar isn't supported by gold or silver--it's value's derived from the mere faith in our government and economy. When those markets crash, the US dollar's going to go bust in a matter of hours."

"A meltdown of the US market. But we could stop all trading—"

"It's beyond our control. You know what sits in the bank vaults of the world--backing up their currency? It's not gold, Pounds Sterling, francs, or yen."

"It's treasury bills," added Tom.

"Exactly. When we go bust the world goes bust with us. A mass panic. Every financial market from the Nike to the CAC will crash. Currencies from the Indian rupee to the Bundesbank's deutschemark will devalue to nothing in a day."

"A global meltdown," added Tom, "breakdown of capitalist systems—"

"Food crops rot," elaborated Benjamin, "because there are no trucks to transport the goods because there's no gas because there are no freighter because, because, because. Think of what will happen! The loss of all regional and global transport, famine, starvation, outright war, suicides, famine, revolution, utter and total chaos. In one day, we're set back a thousand years. Who will invest their money? If money is the fuel that powers the world, your little prophet is about to take that religion away."

"A day of revelation," whispered Tom.

Benjamin took a deep sip of his Gin and Tonic, the liquor burning the back of his throat, "So I'd like to know how you intend on achieving in a few hours what the entire force of The US government couldn't achieve in three days and--"

"I have to get near Dussant and kill him," grunted Grant.

"That's the stupidest plan I've ever heard," smirked Benjamin, "there is no way in hell that I'd ever agree too—"

The car came to a smashing halt--liquor flew out of Benjamin's tumbler, spilling along the carpet. The limo driver honked the horn. Traffic came to a stop. Something caught Benjamin's eye--his tumbler rattled atop the wooden minibar.

The rumbling grew. Benjamin never before experienced the sensation. It wasn't an explosion--lacked the intensity of a bomb—of which he could now write dissertations. It was like an earthquake--the tumbler vibrated louder--it fell off the mini bar. Bronk saw people running, weaving between the limo and stopped cars.

Benjamin glanced back to the TV—the entire screen was blue. He turned up the volume. A gingerly voice said, "WE INTERRUPT THE FOLLOWING

PROGRAM TO BRING YOU A SPECIAL REPORT FROM THE EMERGENCY BROADCAST SYSYTEM. PLEASE REMAIN CALM. PLEASE--"

"What the hell?" Benjamin opened the door--what he saw defied words.

9:23 PM (EST)
New York City, NY

Something was wrong.

Dick glanced at Dussant, seated in the row in front of him, flanked by armed guards. Beyond the prisoner and over the tops of the Army jeeps and armored personnel carriers in the window, he studied a sea of red lights--traffic was grid-locked all along FDR Drive.

One of the soldiers nodded to a voice in his head-set, turning to him, "CNN just broke the Union 57 story--city's panicking. It'll take a while, but we can get a small chopper in here that can transport just three people, you a guard and Dussant. You'll rendezvous with a chopper convoy at The World Trade Center."

"Ooh good," cooed Dussant, "I juss love chopper rides."

"Can somebody shut him up?" Dick sighed nervously. Shit the news was out—the city was going to go absolutely hog wild.

8:47 PM (EST)
New York, NY

Exiting the limousine, Benjamin Bronk stood in total awe.

The rumbling grew louder--a sea of stalled automobiles for as the eye could see—the sound of metal against metal—a sea of car horns rushing like a wave down Broadway, rattling his body.

Then he saw it--clothing, suitcases hitting the sidewalk--possessions falling out of open windows as if the heavens had opened up. People rushed out of apartment houses: men, women, children swallowed in the maze of gridlocked traffic. A fire hydrant exploded on the corner. New York was rioting.

He glanced back at a pale faced Tom and wondered: has it happened? He tasted the air for the scent of phosgene--like freshly mowed grass. The thought hit him--he pulled out his cell phone, dialing Mueller's number. All lines were busy and he knew Mueller was stuck somewhere in traffic and would not make the jet with his wife and children. Benjamin tapped the phone against his forehead—he should have waited to send them in a chopper! He hopped onto the trunk of the limo, realizing he'd never be able to find them.

"Well!" Tom yelled over the noise, "one thing's for certain: our little prophet isn't getting to Elizabeth by way of car. I bet they'll construct a flotilla of helicopters as escort. They'll need a place to store Dussant while they gather those kind of helicopters and men."

"Why would you be qualified to figure out what they're gonna do next?"

"It was my job to create hostage scenarios just like this."

"They'll regroup up at The World Trade Center," added Benjamin.

"That's where I'll kill him," grunted Tom. Benjamin could only look at him as if he were mad, prompting Tom to say, "we're going to save your children. Rabb had a football play for this—when you've nothing left-- throw the Hail Mary."

"This isn't football, Tom," sighed Benjamin.

"It's alright, I have a plan."

9:47 PM (EST)
New York, NY

"Well gentleman," the Razorback entered the control room.

So this was Fort Crandal, he thought to himself. A black officer, introducing himself as Colonel Sharpe, briefed the Secretary of State on the current situation and then asked what the Delta Force role would be.

"There is no role," huffed the Razorback, "you've had your chance. The White House is taking over this operation directly," yeah, right, he thought to himself—he didn't need to be here. But he had supported Osbourne's plan to transfer the prisoner to the refinery so he was now in charge and properly distanced from The White House.

10:11 PM (EST)
New York, NY

Where was he?

He tried to set his mental bearings. . . had a sticky metallic taste in his mouth—the worst headache ever. Was he dead? Was he in heaven? Then he saw the wall of medical supplies and the skinny medic reading a book. It took General Remy Crandal a moment to realize that he was in an ambulance. The gurney he rested upon had restraints which someone loosely tied to his arms. Had he passed out? Damn, they were taking him to a hospital--Dick must be in charge now. The General glanced at the man reading his book before reaching for his gun. Damn, his holster was empty. He reached for his ankle holster.

Outside he heard sirens. The ambulance wasn't going anywhere. He identified two individuals in the front seat. Beyond them—through the windshield lay an endless sea of stalled cars and people running in the Manhattan street—people panicking—screaming—rioting. News must have broken.

"Huh?" the medic put down his book and realized his patient was awake. The boy had a round angelic looking face—must be a fairy, thought the General. Crandal grabbed his gun, pointing it threateningly at the boy.

"He's got his gun!" the kid screamed in a high pitched-- feminine voice, tossing the paperback into the air, fleeing to the driver's compartment.

Shit. Remy pulled the restraints away just as a second, larger figure bounded at him, "Now Pops, just calm down-"

"Who the hell you calling' Pops?" his voice sounded slurred. He looked at his chest wrapped in gauze--IV lines hooked to his arm. He pulled them out.

"I'm the medic whose job it is to get you to the hospital. You're sick," he spoke slowly as if he were addressing a hunting dog, thought Remy, "as soon as traffic clears, we're gonna-"

"Traffic don't look like it's moving. Now don't come any closer," he threatened. Shit, if he didn't make it back to the headquarters, Who knew what horrors would happen? The world rested on his shoulders.

The man lunged at him. Remy fired his Glock 9MM, tearing into the man's shoulder. The figure was blown back into driver's compartment. Crandal heard someone else screaming over the ringing in his ears from the gunfire. Weak and dizzy, the General hobbling to the door--barely able to stand on his own.

"Aaaighhhh!" the effeminate tech was screaming at the top of his lungs.

Blood splattered everywhere. Shit, sighed the General, the bullet ripped through the big one and hit the driver in the head. He glanced back at the thin, wiry orderly, his face cupped between two hands: yelling all the while.

"Shut the fuck up!" barked the gruff General. There was too much at stake. He pointed the gun at the kid's face--his own head woozy, "How far are we from The World Trade Center?"

"F-f-from w-w-w-where?"

"The World Trade Center, you fuck nugget!"

"You've got a gun pointed at my head! How am I supposed to think with all this violence going on!"

"Alright," Remy sighed, continuing in a sweet, affected tone: like a Dad addressing his newborn child, "how far are we?"

"A good bit?" the kid couldn't tear his eyes from the bloodied dashboard.

"Open that door," the General barked. Outside, people rushed through the narrow channels of cars. They'd never be able to drive. It was hard for the kid to wrestle the door open. He looked up, "What are you gonna do to me?"

Remy wrapped an arm around the boy's thin shoulders—couldn't walk on his own, he thought, "We're gonna take a little walk."

Fifty Two

Benjamin Bronk chambered a bullet in his pistol.

Like trying to find a needle in a haystack, the thought to himself. He knew the mortar crew was tucked away somewhere near the refinery. Glancing around at the Union 57 helicopter, he wondered if his little convoy of men and guns weren't just fooling themselves?

As if to answer him, the chopper jerked forward. Benjamin glanced up and saw the row of helicopters lined up in front of him. Shit, he remembered the government imposed no fly zone between Newark Airport and Union 57. How could he have forgotten? The pilots panicked, chattering into their headsets. He glanced at his panicked guards with weapons in their hands. Beyond them—through the chopper window he saw Army attack choppers zeroing in around him. They were being surrounded!

His pilot screamed into his headset. Benjamin saw the flare of light under the landing leg of the aircraft hovering a hundred yards ahead of them. They were going to blow them out of the sky. The missile fired and-

---

10:20 PM (EST)
New York, NY

Destiny waits for no man, thought Dick Osbourne.

The tiny McDonnel Douglas MD-500 hovered high over the brick atrium of The World Trade Center. The compartment was cramped with Dick, Dussant, his restraints poking into Osbourne's thigh, and an armed FBI agent.

Through the window, barely visible above them, Dick spotted the blinking lights of the chopper convoy waiting to take them to Union 57 where Dussant would call off the mad men in exchange for government sympathy to his cause—whatever the hell kind of disease he had—they didn't need to shut him up in some tiny ass townhouse. So the twit goes to a larger prison and

for Dick Osbourne—savior of the East Coast—maybe the Presidency—who knew?

The FBI Agent listened through his headset, "The Secretary of State has requested we go up to Fort Crandal until the choppers are properly—"

"Fuck that!" Dick had purposely disconnected his headset to the Razorback waiting upstairs—always easier to get your way when you don't have to speak face to face. He tapped his watch, "we're behind schedule."

Already he could see the outline of the two chopper convoy landing alongside them in the bricked atrium. Ground crew squirmed below. From his pocket, Osbourne produced the handcuffs locking himself to Dussant.

10:26 PM (EST)
6,000 FT. Over Newark Bay

Benjamin was alive.

Chills ran down his spine. His pilots sat frozen--palms pressed white against the controls of the helicopter. The missile was a warning shot, weaving between two of his three choppers. He spotted more Army attack choppers gathering--blinking lights illuminating their missiles and rocket launchers. Through his head-set he heard the Army pilot say, "you've entered restricted Airspace. In sixteen seconds, if you do not comply, we will fire-"

"Keep going," Benjamin gritted his teeth.

"Those are fucking Huey Attack chopper!" cried his pilot.

Benjamin placed his pistol against the pilot's head, "KEEP GOING!"

10:27 PM (EST)
New York, NY

"Let's go," Osbourne screamed over the wind.

The FBI agent aided Dussant out of the chopper. Wind whipped Osbourne as he charged across the bricked atrium—handcuffs connecting him to Dussant. He could see the convoy of helicopters fifteen feet away—a large Boeing Vertol Ch-47 Chinook—a large craft with two helicopter props on both ends.

The chopper door slid open. The FBI agent and Dussant clamored in first—Osbourne followed. The ground crew shut the door. The aircraft lurched upward. Only then did he see it, but it was too late to--

---

10:28 PM (EST)
New York, NY

Benjamin winced.

The government pilot demanded, "You are to land at the Hudson River landing pad! You are not to deviate from—do you see that?" the government pilot spoke to his own crew.

The inside of Benjamin's chopper was flooded in white light. He turned to see a wall of white--blinding his view of the sky. What the hell was it?

10:28 PM (EST)
New York, NY

The Razorback watched the helicopter convoy disappear.

Blinking lights headed off into the foggy darkness. He glanced at his watch—they were late, but would make it before the midnight deadline. He was about to dial Osbourne's headset when Colonel Sharpe drew his attention away:

"Sir, we have an unidentified craft requesting landing in the atrium."

"What?" barked the Razorback.

He turned to see a group of helicopters descending alongside the twin buildings of The World Trade Center—a squadron of attack choppers and cargo carriers marked with US Army insignias.

"W-w-who," the Razorback fumbled for words, "just left?"

10:28 PM (EST)
In Transit To The Union 57 Refinery

"Nice to see you Dick," Tom pointed the gun at Osbourne

He had to keep swinging the weapon between Dick and the FBI agent, standing the corner, hands in the air, his weapons already at Tom's feet. Grant was amazed that he actually pulled it off. He knew the time constraints—the confusion—Dick's arrogance would play into his hand.—hell, the only order he'd given to his pilot was to fly towards the Union 57 refinery and then stay once they landed on the marked field.

"What do you want?" asked the pock faced agent.

"To stop you," grunted Tom. He turned to Dussant and--

10:29 PM (EST)
6,000 FT. Over Newark Bay

Benjamin squinted as he watched the sea of light.

Like an ocean of stars, thought Benjamin, he saw spotlights sweeping through the sky-- a wall of white light. The voices scream over the open radio channel on his speakers above his head:

"WE ARE ARMING OUR GUNS!" screamed the government pilot.

"Go ahead!" a woman thundered back, "shoot us--let all American see-"

The Attack Hueys buzzed like bees in front of the close formation of thirty choppers, "Identify yourselves!" he demanded.

Over the airwaves they came—each identifying their chopper. There was Affiliate Weather Chopper 12--Pilot Richard Praxton with Fox News 23--Traffic Center 120 Alpha--CNN News One--ABC SkyCam reporting in--MSNBC number 3-and much more—voices rolling into one confusing harmony--

The press.

Everyone with a camera who wasn't fleeing New York city was headed to Union 57, thought Benjamin in stunned amazement. He almost fell out of his seat. There had to be at least thirty five choppers in the air and-

"STAND DOWN--UNDER NATIONAL SECURITY DIRECTION 4.222-"

"Freedom of the Press!" another cried, "this is Jersey Bay!"

"I WILL FIRE! I REPEAT, I WILL FIRE!"

"Are we getting this on tape?" a new voice asked over the line.

"I AM FIRING!"

A flash of light. Benjamin knew it was just another warning light, but the news chopper panicked, swinging his craft upward into the hovering formation—an explosion as the two helicopters collided—setting off a third--the sky lit up--

---

10:30 PM (EST)
New York, NY

Tom tried to separate them.

The handcuffs connecting Dick and Dussant were locked. Tom didn't have time to search Osbourne for the key. He stared at the copper colored face plate—the speakers mounted to the helmet--noticed Dussant's hands were cuffed to a neck harness mounted around the suit.

"Well Yves Alexander," he shook his head, "almost pulled it off. They were going to bring you right there. They still have no idea who you are."

Dussant was silent. Tom saw the volume switch on the breast plate of the suit--thought of increasing the volume, then decided against it. There was little time to waste on conversation. Tim to end this crap.

"Something," smirked Tom, "tells me this isn't a hallucination."

10:30 PM (EST)
6,000 Ft. Over Newark Harbor

Explosions lit up the sky,

Benjamin saw metal and fire showering upon the other choppers—more aircrafts colliding together and exploding. There was so much screaming over the line, Bronk could no longer make sense of the babble. The concentration of crafts broke apart-- Cobras trying to chase those determined to across the no fly zone.

"Move on," Benjamin ordered his pilot, "if we fail, everyone in a three state area is dead! All of your families--all of your children--friends! I will not be stopped by some political no fly zone. I know where they are!"

10:32 PM (EST)
In Transit Between Manhattan and The Union 57 Refinery

It was time to kill him, thought Tom.

Placing the pistol at Dussant's face-plate, he winced—pressing the trigger, knowing he'd blow a hole through Dussant's brain. He only hoped that this creature was not some prophet who would rise up from the dead. It was time.

Tom pulled the trigger.

Click.

The gun must've jammed--then something struck him in the head and he saw stars. He fell backwards. Osbourne was on top of him, struggling for control of the pistol, dragging the handcuffed Dussant to the floor with him. Blood poured down his forehead--Tom saw the FBI agent charging at him and Osbourne struggling with him for his gun!

10:33 PM (EST)
6,000 Ft. Over Newark Harbor

"Look out!" cried his copilot.

High above Benjamin, Cobra attack choppers swarmed, circling in for the kill. His chopper veered onto its side. Benjamin and the guards were thrown against the side wall. This time everyone had their seat belts locked in.

Benjamin watched in amazement at the pyrotechnic show of death dancing high above them—choppers exploding—metal and fire falling in the cold, dark night, punctuated by Huey attack choppers chasing off those that had survived. No one noticed his little convoy streaking only a hundred feet over Bronk Blvd.—I could reach out and touch the cars below, he thought to himself.

His eyes scanned the street. There were so many abandoned buildings here. This street, named after his father, was a real dump. This was useless—fucking useless! He would never find the bomb site.

10:40 PM (EST)
1,000 Ft. Over Patterson, NJ

Tom kicked Osbourne in the crotch.

Spinning around, Grant fired two shots into the charging FBI agent's chest. The man fell back—blood spewing from open holes in his chest. Then he saw Dick lunging for the FBI agent's discarded weapons on the floor. Tom shot Dick twice in the chest. The agent looked stunned, eyes glassy as he fell back, floundering on the metal floor.

Without pause, Tom swung around, aiming the weapon at Dussant. It wouldn't misfire this time. He pulled the trigger and—

Nothing.

Tom Grant pulled the trigger again. Nothing. He pulled it three more times. Had the pistol jammed? No, the breach was secured—the weapon was in perfect firing condition. He examined his hand. It was bizarre.

He could feel his fingers drawing the trigger, but his fingers never moved.

The massive space helmet rocked from side to side. Only then Tom realize the volume switch on the suit had been turned up all along. Yves Alexander chuckled, his voice floating through the cabin like that archaic music he was so fond of playing:

"Try as he might,
and try as he may,
little Tom Grant,
ain't gonna kill nobody today."

Fifty Three

11:06 PM (EST)
11,400 Ft. Over The Atlantic Ocean

President Cormon watched his political life pass before him.

Seated in the plush conference room of Airforce One, The President of The United States felt his stomach boil with nausea. He'd just been given an unconfirmed report that Osbourne and Dussant may have been kidnapped. What the hell was going on in New York! The world collapsed around President like a Cuban Missile Crisis gone awry.

He'd just gotten on board and was going to change his sweat drenched shirt, but there he'd had no time. Walking into the office adjacent to the board room he turned, looking at the live CNN feed. The TV was muted, he winced, looking at the explosions and helicopters raining out of the sky.

"What the hell's that?" he neared the monitor.

11:08 PM (EST)
1,000 Ft. (and descending) Over The Union 57 Refinery

Tom Grant tried to focus.

"That's a really nice outfit you got," Dussant drawled from behind the copper tinted face-plate of his space suit.

Tom rushed to the pilot's cockpit door. He tried to knock on it, but couldn't. Jesus Christ—no matter what he tried he couldn't knock on the door. He secured his headset, dialing the number on his cell phone Benjamin gave him—he couldn't get a signal. What a fool he'd been. He was contaminated, he should have sent Benjamin to carry out this task. But he thought since he had the power to challenge Dussant, he'd be able to kill him. After all, if this creature was so omnipotent, why did it not sense Candice's presence in Tom's mind? Why did it not order him around right now and--

"You can't stop the will of God," he imagined Yves Alexander smiling behind that copper face plate.

He had to act! He pulled the trigger again--nothing. He looked down. He could feel his finger pressing the trigger and yet his finger never moved—as if paralyzed by some invisible force--think!

The chopper hovered over the New Jersey coast line. Through the window, Tom noted the endless sea of twinkling lights--the petrochemical complexes spanning off into the horizon. Tom felt the craft swaying from side to side—they were descending! He reached over, dialing the number again--

"Untie me," griped Dussant, "we don't have time for theatrics."

His cell phone connected. Tom heard chopper props and gunfire over the phone., "Benjamin," Tom screamed into his headset, "contact my pilot and tell him to turn away from Union 57!"

11:15 PM (EST)
1,000 Ft. Over Patterson, NJ

"What!" cried Benjamin, "I don't have time for that!"

Around him buzzed Army Attack Cobras, firing off missiles at choppers high above. It was pure pandemonium.

"Have you found the physics package?" asked Tom.

"No luck," Bronk braced himself as the chopper swooped down, barely scraping the cars and people gridlocked on the Bronk Blvd. below—AN EXPLOSION came from below—from a building--Benjamin felt cold air--mind numbing swirling as the chopper spun. Through the window the world flipped upside down, then they were plummeting--

---

11:17 PM (EST)
11,400 Ft. Over The Atlantic Ocean

"Oh no!" gasped President Cormon.

Around the President buzzed aides, interns, air force men, froze. The President looked down at the CNN live feed—helicopters being destroyed in mid-flight against a dark night sky. A reporter screamed, "That was the CNN news helicopter that just got shot down! Agh! We've taken up live coverage for most channels since most of the press choppers have-"

"You shot down CNN?" President Cormon screamed at The Razorback.

"Osbourne must've given the order," cried the Secretary of State, "look, I just arrived here. It's all confusion."

"YOU SHOT DOWN CNN!" the President sputtered, "GET YOUR MEN TO QUIT SHOOTING THOSE FUCKING CHOPPERS!

11:19 PM (EST)
600 FT. Over The Union 57 Refinery

"Will you talk to me?" moaned Dussant.

Tom rushed around the interior of the cabin, searching aimlessly for something that might aid him. Fear and panic were his enemies. Rabb always said there was a solution to every problem—the answer was always right under his nose.

"Just talk to me," moaned Yves Alexander.

Tom spoke without turning around to address the prisoner, "We don't have anything to talk about! Our talks never existed in the first place!"

"On the contrary Tom, take off my helmet and we'll talk for a thousand years."

Thousands of conversations that never existed nor will exist, thought Grant. But I haven't taken off your helmet, have I, and you want that, don't you? I'm not totally contaminated. If I were, even a filtered form of your voice might control me, wouldn't it, shouldn't it? He hoped so, "You affected me in a different way, didn't you? You weren't looking for just another drooling, idolizing fan. You needed someone with a vestige of free will to tell your story."

"Keep telling yourself that and you might juss believe it."

Distant explosions cast orange and green blasts of light into the cabin of the chopper, lighting up Osbourne's prostrate body, making the blood on the floor appear black. Bound and chained in the corner, Yves Alexander continued, "I see you've been to *The Rib Room*. The wine was good I hope-"

"Shut up about the damned wine. You had me put the wine there myself. You conned me--led me on a deluded merry-go-round."

"You know what this story's about, Tom? God sent a messenger who possessed a power that proved his authenticity. But nobody wanted to hear it—so the prevailing forces stuffed him in a dark corner--ignored the religious parallels-- tried to study the power, to deconstruct it and—"

"Spare me this lecture! This is about a mutant who can control men's minds--steal their souls!"

"It all boils down to faith--believing in something without question, without a need for proof. For thousands of years, people prayed such a thing would happen again—well it has! My voice is the microphone of God . You've been designed to receive such powers. You want your free will—well, GOD

DOESN'T CARE ABOUT YOUR FUCKING FREE WILL! HERE I AM—YOUR MESSIAH!"

I created the wine note, thought Tom. This is about people and he is just a mutated human being people—the chopper continued descending. Tom searched for a solution to the crazed terrorists, the government snipers and imminent danger which awaited him on the ground. He almost tripped over an open duffel bag filled with white linen.

"Tom," drawled Dussant, "quit digging. It's over. You can't stop me. When that chopper lands, I will hobble out, bound or unbound and embrace my flock and begin a sequence of events that no man or nation can stop."

Tom pulled the white robe out of the garment bag and saw a stone and another item—it made him gasp--

---

11:25 PM (EST)
Elizabeth, NJ

They came for her quickly.

"It is about to begin!" one said with a zealous smile

She'd been locked away so long –looked at Schubert's watch still on her wrist—trying to see the time. Lights flashed overhead as they dragged her down the long hallway. Terrorists rushed out of doorways--all wearing white robes. Then between the people she glimpsed a weary looking Schubert's, being dragged, head bobbing—a door burst open and she was being dragged through the cold parking lot.

It was snowing again.

Massive floodlights drenched the parking lot in harsh, bluish, white light. She saw a large walkway or gauntlet—a hundred and thirty yards long-- carved out through the plant. It ended in a geometric circle of people in the parking lot—the design she'd seen them working on days earlier.

The winter wind blew through the dress, freezing her body. Her feet were damp and burning against the icy ground. She caught sight of an open manhole cover, water bubbling out of it. Were they still flooding the tunnels? Then she heard the propellers. A large chopper was landing at the end of the gauntlet--

A hand wrapped firmly around her throat. Nehemiah stood behind her, holding a knife to her breast. She turned to see Schubert standing next to her. He was badly beaten, black eyes and swollen cheeks-- almost unrecognizable as he turned to her to weary to even whisper. She fought to hold back tears.

Nehemiah's hand shook with excitement as he whispered in her ear, drops of saliva falling on her, "It's time! It's time!"

11:28 PM (EST)
300 Ft. Over The Union 57 Refinery

Tom held back the urge to vomit.

It was a severed human heart, bloody and round, resting on a sheet of waxed paper. Jesus Christ, what the hell was this about.

"It belonged to Catherine. You should've seen Dr. Brandt—pulled it out of her own chest—I didn't want it, but you can't just leave it--"

"You sick, fucking bastard!" he wanted to shoot him, hit him—anything! But he knew he wouldn't be able to! He was forced to just stand there, body shaking in anger.

"There is a reason for everything," sighed Dussant.

"Let me hear the reason from those genteel lips. I want to know what it sounds like when the devil explains himself to me."

"Devil?"

"Why the killings--the mutilations, eviscerations, families raping each other—this fucking heart. What could justify all of this?"

"It is God's will-"

"Don't give me that stuff! If He existed He'd never allow this!"

"We've already covered your fallacy of a kind-hearted God."

"Shut up about the bible! This is about people. I don't see God here. I see a man—a mutant—but a man all the same!"

The helicopter touched down in Union 57.

"And you, my friend," drawled Dussant, "have reached the end. I wanted a scribe to write my Gospel, but there won't be enough time for you to escape the inferno now. Guess I'll write it myself and I hate writing. . . this is check-mate"

11:30 PM (EST)
Patterson, NJ

Benjamin Bronk woke up.

Hands were upon him. He was still inside the helicopter. Around him he saw wounded metal shards, broken glass and injured men. The craft had crashed. Blood? He looked down--his hands covered in it. A soldier lifted him out of the chopper.

"What happened?" he asked, mist rising from his cold lips.

"They shot us down from the ground," someone grunted.

Shot him down? Only the bomb crew would arm their building with such weapons. He looked up, getting his mental bearings—seeing the building a block away, silhouetted against gray clouds.

"We have to attack," he muttered, pushing away the soldier's hands.

He counted his remaining contingent at eight—eight measly men to fight Delta Force trained officers! Jesus.

"Let's go," Benjamin grunted.

They raced forward in a spread pattern, guns drawn. Two guards were standing perimeter, face to the sky, watching the blazing battle high overhead—

Pop—pop—

Benjamin felt awful shooting American soldiers, but there was nothing he could do. The front door was wide open, boards ripped away. This was too easy, thought Benjamin, too fucking easy. The smell of stale wood and urine wafted through the air, striking him in the face as he raced up the stairs.

They made it to the second floor without incident. The lower floors were empty. Benjamin feared they might be in the wrong building or perhaps these floors were laced with some type of infrared security system like something out of a James Bond movie--one of his guards gestured silently to the others. They creeped up to the third floor as quietly as possible.

"Benjamin?" Tom suddenly whispered over his headset.

"Yes," Benjamin forgot he still wore the headset. He stopped to talk--his men continued up the stairs.

Tom screamed so loud, Bronk pulled the speaker from his ear, "I've left the chopper! We have a problem. I couldn't kill him!"

"What?" Benjamin fought to restrain his voice. Up ahead, his guards were almost at the top of the staircase to the third floor--something clicked in his head.

"Benjamin?" Tom asked, "you there?"

Bronk looked up speechlessly at the dots of red light all over his men, moving and curling along their bodies. At first he thought it was his imagination, suddenly realizing it was laser beams--

"Get back!" screamed Benjamin, leaping back along the staircase.

Gunfire exploded!

The room spun around as he soared backwards through the air. Some of his men were sawed in half by the onslaught—others returned fire at point blank--sending splinters of wood, flesh, and chips of sheet-rock into the air. Four men escaped to the lower landing, firing up at the attackers.

Benjamin hit the landing, slamming into the rotted walls. It was an ambush! A fucking ambush! Down below him, gunfire rattled up the steps. In front of him he could see the doorway to the second floor. Delta Force soldiers charged up the staircase from the first floor.

They were trapped!

11:35 PM (EST)
45 Ft. over The Union 57 Refinery

"Unlock my cuffs. The key's in Sullivan's pocket. Let's be rid of this bitter charade--you've no options left. This is God's will--you've all strayed so far from the proverbial watering hole. This is not the way He wanted it-"

But your mother knew what you planned, Tom's mind raced. She willingly drove that car off the cliff. How could she summons the power? I can still win--just have to think—fucking think!

"You can't win this. Even if you did stop me--I'm the one that wakes you eight years from now, prompts you to the kitchen to get the knife and whispers in your ear as you creep ever so quietly up the staircase to where your little babies sleep soundly-"

"Shut up!"

"I'm like the wind or rain or death—you're never really supposed to know when I come. I'm nature—I'm God's will—swift and unmerciful. What I saw on Mt. Sinai--what Rabb and I saw in that basement, do you want to know what it was?"

What could he do now? Tom dropped to his knees, staring at the white robe--then he figured it out! He glanced at the stone.

A white robe was given to each of them. . . then a mighty angel took up a stone like a great millstone and threw it into the sea, saying, "thus with violence the great city Babylon shall be thrown down, and shall not be found anymore."

He couldn't kill him, thought Tom--but he could damn well be him.

"Tom, what are you doing?" Tom heard the first trace of panic in Dussant's voice, "you're not that child in your father's study. You can't right those wrong through a suicidal act—"

"I'm gonna die anyway," he draped the robe over his body--the arms were too long—good, he tucked the gun up his sleeve. He retrieved another pistol from the floor—discarded by the FBI agents, tucking it into his pants waste.

Yves Alexander screamed from behind the faceplate of his biohazard suit, "You have no idea what you're playing with-"

Tom approached the door.

Dussant screamed at the top of his lungs--rattling the speakers, "You're meddling in things that are beyond you! This is God's will!"

Tom switched on his cell phone again, adjusting the head set. The line rang. He pressed the latch on the chopper door. It opened revealing a corridor lined with floodlights for sixty or so yards ahead—he couldn't make out any more.

"If God wants this," Tom turned around, "then fuck the both of you. Tonight, Yves Alexander, it all ends--twenty years of killing and horror and manipulation. I didn't start it, but I damn well am gonna finish it. Tonight this tale comes to a conclusion!"

"No!" screamed Dussant, "stop it! Stop it!"

Tom Grant stepped out into the light.

part five
COMMUNION

Fifty Four

Tom Grant stared down the makeshift walkway.

It was as if someone had swathed a fifteen foot walkway through the refinery. Flood-lights lined the linear path to the parking lot of the Engineering/ Security complex—over a hundred yards ahead.

Tom felt his feet sink into pools of ice and slush. He noticed water bubbling up through a manhole cover. The terrorists were flooding the place. Ahead of him he saw a crowd of people gathered under blue flood lights which nearly blinded him.

The wind tossed his robe upward. He grabbed the hooded cloak, making sure that it covered his face, knowing that the terrorists and government snipers might be watching him through their binoculars. He was a hair trigger away from death—from both sides!

"Benjamin," he muttered into his head set, "now I've got a real problem."

11:41 PM (EST)
Patterson, NJ

"I've got problems too!" Benjamin huffed.

He bolted through the door to the second floor. Gunfire erupted in the staircase--they'd shoot each other to hell. They were losing time!

"I'm out in the refinery, sixty yards or so from these terrorists-"

"What!" cried Benjamin.

"My plan's not great," Tom rumbled in his ear, "I'll try to locate the trigger man and kill him. You need to launch that bomb!"

11:42 PM (EST)
11,400 Ft. Over The Atlantic Ocean

President Cormon tried to control his diarrhea.

"Someone's exited the chopper," the Razorback echoed over the speakerphone, "the figure's wearing a hooded robe. It's could be Grant. Our snipers could fire."

Cormon felt his intestines cramp. He looked at his handful of aides and the Joint Chief of Staff, General Prolog, who'd managed to make it onto Airforce One, "Hold your fire," the President wiped the sweat from his brow.

11:43 PM (EST)
Elizabeth, NJ

Tom walked.

He was forty five yards away from them now—moving as slowly as he could without drawing attention to himself. He focused on the sound of his feet slogging through the wet snow.

11:43 PM (EST)
Elizabeth, NJ

"Huh?"

Dick Osbourne felt hands reaching into his pockets, a slight tickling sensation near his waste. He opened his eyes. The astronaut was sitting right beside him on the floor, fumbling to get a key inside a pair of handcuffs. A moment of confusion and then all things returned to Sullivan, jolting him awake.

Dussant unlocked the handcuffs.

Dick tried to move. Painfully he lifted himself to a sitting position, eyes wide, gazing down at an open hole in his side. His body was covered in blood. A nausea like none other he had ever felt, swept through his body.

"W-what are you doing!" muttered a wounded Osbourne.

 Dussant wiggled his wrists out of the cuffs. White light poured in through the open doorway, bathing Dussant's space suit and the other agents in subtle shades of gray. Osbourne tried to stand, but lacked the strength. The helmet came off and-

Ecstasy.

An immense orgasm like none he ever felt-- wracked his body in tingles so strong they hurt. The pain in his chest fell into a sea of pleasure. The dark walls of the chopper brightened. He took a deep breath, like breathing electricity. He arched his back, ejaculating into his pants——the sensation didn't stop and he didn't want it to. It was the most pleasurable thing he ever experienced.

Dussant tried to peal the bottom part of the space suit off. His pale, naked flesh was exposed to cold lights shining through the open door. Dick couldn't turn away from this brilliant man—more than a man. . . more than a father. . . more than a mother. . . more than a lover——

Dussant's lips didn't move, but a thousand words were said in the passing of mere seconds. In the end, Osbourne understood that he had to exit the chopper--had to stop Tom Grant from reaching Nehemiah and the others. The pleasure faded back to a dull tingling—he needed more!

Dussant handed him the pistol. Then he grabbed at his own cell phone, slippery in his blood drenched hands as he stepped through the payload door.

11:44 PM (EST)
Elizabeth, NJ

The gun felt cold in Tom's hand.

Grasping it by the barrel, he pushed the stock up along his forearm, concealing the weapon deeper beneath the cloak. Wind ripped across him, it was difficult to listen over the headset, but he thought he heard gunfire and Benjamin Bronk's heavy breathing. Tom winced, trying to focus on the faces silhouetted in the sea of light ahead of him.

What the hell was he going to do? Nehemiah awaited with detonators switches and bombs and an eschatological apocalypse! Was there a routine or a ceremony Dussant was going to perform? Was Dussant supposed to utter words? Or was his approach supposed to signal the men to detonate the plant? In his other hand, Tom grasped the rock. He'd almost forgotten it. The rock must be the key. The biblical passage floated through his mind:

A mighty angel took up a stone like a great millstone and threw it into the sea

Dussant was going to toss the rock onto the wet ground and signal the explosion--defined figures were now visible in the sea of floodlights.

11:45 PM (EST)
Patterson, NJ

Benjamin Bronk was losing his mind.

Where the fuck was the second staircase? He rushed frantically through rooms. The hallway was long and dark. His foot fell through a rotted hole in the floor. Steadying himself, he took a breath, regaining balance. His body ached.

"Benjamin, how close are you?" whispered Tom over his headset.

"Shut up," Benjamin gasped between breaths.

Gunfire echoed down the hall. Benjamin pushed open another door and saw the set of stairs leading to the third floor!

11:45 PM (EST)
Elizabeth, NJ

Dick Osbourne dialed the number on his cellular phone.

Wind whipped across his face. Each time he breathed, energy surged through him, powering his limp, dying body. He brandished the pistol in his right hand. White hot floodlights coated his ghostly white skin.

He was delirious.

Holding a hand over his gaping, bleeding wound, he tripped, falling on the cold, wet ground. But he felt none of that. Only one thought filled his very essence: kill Tom Grant! The phone connected, ringing and-

---

11:45 PM (EST)
Elizabeth, NJ

Tom walked.

He could see faces coming out of the darkness now--noticed one man with bloodied bandages wrapped around his head. He spotted Candice, her blond hair blowing in the wind—something black on her face—

maybe writing? How strange to see her now just before they would die one way or another.

"Benjamin," he grunted into the headset, "I'm almost there!"

"Then walk slower!" seethed Bronk.

11:46 PM (EST)
11,400 Ft. Over The Atlantic Ocean

"Snipers confirm a second person is out there, " cried the Communications Officer, "he has a gun!" his words reverberated in the cabin of Airforce One.

The President shuddered—eyes tearing. What should he do? What could he do? How would it look if the terrorists saw the robed figure gunned down.

"We have a call coming through," another officer stated. He patched it into the loudspeaker.

The room rumbled with the voice of Dick Osbourne, "Grant is trying to blow up the refinery!" his NSC liaison screamed, ""MR. PRESIDENT, YOU MUST KILL HIM!"

11:46 PM (EST)
Elizabeth, NJ

Candice studied the robed figure in the distance.

She was so exhausted-- the faces of the dead— the superintendent, Lou—all seemed so near to her now She would soon be joining them. She remembered Tom's voice. If only he were here--he could save her. But he wasn't, was he? The man who approached was a mad man who would gut her in some perverted ceremony. She gathered her strength, forcing back tears. She would not cry. Screw them all—she would not cry!

11:46 PM (EST)
Elizabeth, NJ

"Stop him!" Tom heard someone screaming behind him.

Turning around, he spotted Osbourne racing towards him. How was that possible? The man was on the verge of death, bleeding and—Dussant had contaminated him! No telling how fast that bastard could run now, throwing all of his life's energy into the action. Tom sped up his pace.

He had to get to that trigger man!

11:46 PM (EST)
Patterson, NY

Benjamin Bronk raced up the rickety stairs, his feet snapping through rotting wood as he held on to the banister. He heard gunfire erupt on the other side of the abandoned building.

"Benjamin!" screamed Tom, "you have to hurry!"

11:47 PM (EST)
Elizabeth, NJ

Dick could see Grant moving quickly ahead of him--his white robe fluttering in the wind. Dick was close now. He raised his pistol, trying to take aim.

11:47 PM (EST)
Elizabeth, NJ

Tom sped up his pace.

He noticed another figure in the ring of people ahead of him—a man in a torn Delta Force jumpsuit—that must be Schubert. Behind him, Dick screamed something incoherent, but louder now. Tom's feet moved faster, sloshing through the freezing ice.

11:47 PM (EST)
11,100 FT. Over The Atlantic Ocean

The President's mind raced.

"SHOOT HIM!" Osbourne screamed over the speakerphone.

The President trusted Dick, but he didn't want to startle the terrorists by ordering his snipers kill Grant. Then again, he couldn't allow the wacko to shoot the terrorists! A decision had to be made.

"Have the snipers shoot," he barked at General Prolog.

"Shoot which one?" asked the head of The Joint Chiefs.

"The one pointing the fucking gun! DO IT NOW!"

11:47 PM (EST)
Elizabeth, NJ

Tom shuddered.

Osbourne was too damn close. He knew the terrorists could hear the bastard's screaming. He turned so that the terrorists at the end of the gauntlet couldn't see as he drew his gun on Osbourne--

---

11:47 PM (EST)
Elizabeth, NJ

Osbourne aimed his gun at Tom's back.

The wind howled around him. The old Osbourne was alone--weak and worthless. He was so much more now. This was his moment. Wrapping his finger around the trigger, he repeated the words in his mind as he drew back the trigger: this was his one true mo—

11:47 PM (EST)
Elizabeth, NJ

Tom shuddered as he saw Sullivan's head explode.

The bullet tore through the agent's skull, tossing him forward into the cold, wet ground. That bullet was for me, Tom thought to himself. He was supposed to be that bloodied corpse lying in the snow. He watched with a sickening feeling in his stomach as the dead man jerked and spasmed on the cold, wet asphalt. How long would it take them to figure out that they shot the wrong man?

He was almost running now as-

11:48 PM (EST)
Patterson, NJ

Benjamin Bronk hadn't found the bomb crew.

He'd failed. The third floor was empty! Tears rushed to his eyes as he collapsed on the cold, wood floor, bloody, tired and--glancing down through rotted floor-boards, he saw gun men gathered around a mortar cannon. In the other corner, three soldiers rushed out of the room, leaving one soldier to guard the cannon. Benjamin thought of his children--summonsed all his courage and leapt through the hole as--

---

11:48 PM (EST)
14,400 Ft. Over The Atlantic Ocean

"Sniper team one confirms a kill!" replied General Prolog.

"Who's down?" the President's knees wobbled.

The speakerphone was no longer filled with Osbourne's screaming over the open communication line. He heard only the open chatter of the snipers—a lot of confusion.

"He did shoot the one with gun, right?" asked The President.

"Sniper team one cannot confirm identity," the sniper spoke over the speakers, "the target was shot in the head—but both had guns drawn."

"WHAT!" cried The Executive and Chief.

11:48 PM (EST)
Patterson, NJ

Benjamin Bronk hit the ground hard.

Rolling, he swung his pistol at the soldier. The Delta Force officer scuttled to the corner shielding the mortar cannon and two shells on the floor—his gun was on Benjamin's side of the room.

The soldier produced a hunters knife which he held to his throat, "Come any closer and I slit my throat. You need my pulse to fire that shell."

Benjamin recognize the voice--it was Ice Man.

11:49 PM (EST)
Elizabeth, NJ

Tom was only 20 yards away.

The wind ripped through him. He wrapped his finger around the trigger of his pistol, safely concealed under the robed sleeve. The bandaged figure cocked his head, looking at him--

---

11:48 PM (EST)
Patterson, NJ

Ice jabbed the end of the blade against his flesh as he fiddled with a tiny box behind him--

"Stop!" screamed Benjamin, "just calm down, Ice!"

The surfer was shocked—took him a moment to recognize him, "Benjamin? W-what the fuck are you doing here?" then he broke out of the spell, treating Bronk as if he were a stranger, "You need my live retinal print on that pad," screamed Ice, " to arm the mortar shell."

"Listen for one moment," pleaded Benjamin, "we must launch the shell."

"Too late," Ice moved his hand. He had switched something on—something built into the small computer that rested next to the cannon, "I just turned on the comlink to headquarters. They're listening to us right now."

11:48 PM (EST)
14,400 Ft. Over The Atlantic Ocean

The Razorback shuddered.

The conversation flashed over the open comlink for all to hear. Colonel Sharpe and Fort Crandal were in a panic. Then he heard The President screaming to him over the open channel, "Vince, he has the neutron bomb!"

"No one panic!" screamed General Prolog in the background—his voice rumbling over the speakerphone, "Mr. President, we have computer fail-safe codes embedded in those shells. We can beam them via satellite transmission and disarm them."

11:48 PM (EST)
Elizabeth, NJ

Tom stared at his feet.

He continued walking—twenty yards to go. He glanced up--eyes focused on the man with the bandages. Why would such an injured man be here unless he were important? The wind blew back the figures long overcoat. Tom spotted the detonator wires concealed underneath. This was the trigger man.

This was Nehemiah.

11:48 PM (EST)
Elizabeth, NJ

Major Peter Schubert saw it too.

As the wind swept past them, Nehemiah's overcoat was blown back. Without sleep, tortured to end of his stamina, Schubert focused on the detonator package the bastard had wired to him! Schubert fingered the syringe he'd lifted from the break-room trashcan—wait until the moment is perfect.

Turning to Candice, he mimed the words. It took her a moment to realize what he was talking about. She reached down for his watch on her wrist.

11:48 PM (EST)
Elizabeth, NJ

From out of the chopper door, he stumbled.

It had taken him many minutes to extricate himself from the leg cuffs. He was naked from the waist down, clad only in the space suit top and gloves. His legs were freezing. In a strange way it was pleasant—the first time his body felt the cold wind in over twenty years. He was blinded momentarily by the spotlights ahead. Yves Alexander Dussant slipped, falling onto the icy asphalt, before getting up, racing towards Tom Grant and the others.

11:48 PM (EST)
Elizabeth, NJ

Candice remembered.

Schubert told her about the detonator inside his watch. Setting the inner face to midnight would blow all the incendiary bombs his team hid in the plant. Gently, she slid her hand along her opposite wrist, drawing the winding arm out of the chronometer--setting the arm on the smaller face of the chronometer.

11:49 PM (EST)
Elizabeth, NJ

10 yards to go.

Tom wrapped firm fingers around the stock of the gun. He could see the trigger switch in Nehemiah's hands, connected by a long wire up his overcoat.

"Benjamin," he muttered into the headset, "I can't stall much longer!"

11:49 PM (EST)
14,400 Ft. Over The Atlantic Ocean

The President cringed.

"Whoah!" the sniper exclaimed over the comlink, "a half-naked man just exited the chopper! Looks like he's got half of a space suit on!"

He and his staff had focused their attention on down-linking the over-ride codes. He heard the comment, but was unsure as to what to do.

11:49 PM (EST)
Patterson, NJ

"On the lives of my children," Benjamin pled, "we have to blow up Union 57."

"Have you gone ape shit? I can't fire that bomb without a direct order from my commanding officer!" retorted Ice Man.

"Soldier, a voice screamed over the speakerphone. Benjamin placed the identity of the speaker, "we are aware of what's happening—this's the President of The United States. Under no circumstances are you to fire that bomb."

"Disregard that order," another voice cried out.

11:49 PM (EST)
New York, NY

Colonel Sharpe stiffened.

He felt the eyes of Secretary of State Giardino and others on him. But he had enough. This was madness—a fucking mess stirred up by White House imbeciles. His man was there with the mortar cannon. They had to fire that bomb now and take their chances that the EMP shielding wouldn't work. If he hesitated any longer, the down-load codes would disarm the shells and who knew who the hell this half naked mad man was, charging across the gauntlet.

"Dick," he heard the President of The United States scream over the open line, "order Colonel Sharpe to rescind that order."

The Colonel stood firm, "Ice Man this is Colonel Sharpe. As your direct commanding officer, I order you to fire that bomb."

11:49 PM (EST)
11,100 Ft. Over The Atlantic Ocean

Who the hell was this bastard Colonel, wondered the President.

What the fuck was he pulling? Marshal saw his men preparing the over-ride codes. He fumed with anger, ""Vince," thundered The President with all the anger he possessed, "SHOOT THE COLONEL!"

11:49 PM (EST)

Elizabeth, NJ

Tom was 7 yards away.

The plan was simple. He would shoot Nehemiah first, then take out the one with the ball cap. In his left hand, he raised up the stone.

All eyes turned to it.

11:50 PM (EST)
Patterson, NJ

Benjamin Bronk was startled.

Did his ears deceive him? Was he actually hearing Colonel Sharpe giving an order to fire? Ice was in shock--cocking his head to one side, mentally reviewing what he had just heard.

"Ice," Sharpe barked again, "don't make me repeat myself, soldier, fire that damned shell!"

11:50 PM (EST)
New York, NY

Colonel Sharpe didn't flinch.

With glee, Giardino pressed the end of the pistol against the officer's head. Sharpe scanned his men--his soldiers--he didn't know what they were thinking and didn't care. This was it—the edge that Remy had so often spoken of. He would do his duty as he saw fit. Too much had happened to back down now.

"Fire that bomb," barked the Colonel.

"SHOOT HIM!" raged the President.

Sharpe didn't even shut his eyes as Giardino prepared to kill him. He wondered if the bureaucrat could summons the courage to do it?

11:50 PM (EST)
11,100 Ft. Over The Atlantic Ocean

The room spun around the President.

On the LACROSSE monitors, he watched two thermal images racing from the chopper to the terrorist cluster. He turned back to his soldiers who had gathered the over-ride codes for the shells.

"Override codes on the bomb!" screamed General Prolog, "are coming through in just a second!"

11:50 PM (EST)
Elizabeth, NJ

Tom was 4 yards away.

All eyes were on the stone. He drew his right arm up, preparing for a clean head shot. Without a head shot, Nehemiah would have time to press the detonator. He had to make this one count!

11:50 PM (EST)
New York, NY

Sharp shut his eyes.

Click--he heard a pistol chamber and opened his eyes to see Giardino standing prostrate with a gun pointed at his head. The assailant grunted, "Nobody fucks with my boy!" he heard the familiar voice of General Crandal, himself. Crandal looked on the verge of death, pale and withered, a shaking hand holding the pistol, his body supported by a young medic.

Sharpe tried to control his shaking knees.

"Good job there, Sharpe," grunted his commanding officer as he turned to the speakerphone to address Ice Man, saying, "the way I see it, we got one hope, Ice--show me some fuckin' fireworks."

11:50 PM (EST)
Patterson, NJ

"Let's do it," grunted Ice Man.

Benjamin watched as Ice dropped the knife, hopping to his feet--preparing the mortar cannon. His fingers danced across the keyboard, programming codes into the launch computer. He gestured for Benjamin.

Bronk helped the soldier load the shell. The intensity was killing him-- could barely breath! Outside in the hall he heard his own men still firing on The Delta Force-- there wasn't enough time to stop them—

"Benjamin," he heard Tom on his headset, "I've got no options left—"

"Just another few seconds!" Bronk cried.

11:50 PM (EST)
Elizabeth, NJ

It was time.
Tom raised his pistol.
A gust of wind pushed back the hood of his robe!

11:50 PM (EST)
Patterson, NJ

Ice Man placed his eyes on the scanning pad and-

11:50 PM (EST)
Elizabeth, NJ

Nehemiah studied the face of the man who wore the robe—it was not Dussant--the savior's face he'd seen in Rabb's photograph. He was about to reach down for the detonator—he'd blow this place straight to heaven--

---

11:50 PM (EST)
Patterson, NJ

The neutron bomb ran through its self-test.

11:50 PM (EST)
Elizabeth, NJ

Candice pushed the winding arm of the chronometer.

The watch was set to midnight-- white light filled her eyes! A blast near the Coker unit set off a flare blast. Another blast--the side of the engineering building blasted across the parking lot. Terrorists collapsed from the debris. Other terrorists ran, scurrying. Nehemiah paused for a moment, about to press the detonator when--

---

11:50 PM (EST)
Elizabeth, NJ

Schubert slashed Nehemiah's neck with the syringe.

He grabbed the terrorist's hand, forcing it back. The detonator switch fell away--still tethered to Nehemiah by the long umbilical cord. The Major and Nehemiah hit the icy ground. Nehemiah slammed his elbow into the Major's face.

Schubert could only think of that sundeck in Norfolk—his baby, his wife—everything he did, he did for them. Nehemiah grabbed his Glock .40 from his waste holster—Schubert managed to knock it away as the Major jabbed the syringe into Nehemiah's throat--cutting into his carotid artery. Then he looked down to see Nehemiah reach for a pistol in his ankle holster as--

---

11:51 PM (EST)
Patterson, NJ

The mortar cannon aligned itself to the predesignated coordinates.

11:51 PM (EST)
Elizabeth, NJ

Baaaannnggg!
"No!" Candice screamed.
Nehemiah fired his second gun at Schubert's head--blood splattered everywhere. Her eyes strayed away--she spotted his other pistol at her feet! In one motion, she dropped, grabbing the weapon, spinning around to face the robed figure. If it was the last thing she did, she would blow this antichrist straight back to hell. Then she saw something which shocked her--

The robed man was being attacked by two of the terrorists—why? Then she heard his voice--how could she ever forget that voice that kept her alive the past three days, "Shoot Nehemiah!" he screamed, "shoot Nehemiah!"

It was Tom!

11:51 PM (EST)
Patterson, NJ

The bomb was armed.

11:51 PM (EST)
Elizabeth, NJ

Baaaannnnnggggg.

Candice spun around—shooting Nehemiah in the neck, spinning him back to the wet ground. He was still alive, grabbing at the umbilical cord connecting him to the detonator switch-- only inches from the detonator button. Candice aimed her weapon at Nehemiah when-

"Move!" Tom lunged for the detonator switch!

11:51 PM (EST)
11,400 Ft. Over The Atlantic Ocean

"We've ready to down-link the override code!" screamed the White House communication officer.

The President pressed his hand against the palm --beaming the codes to the bomb site in Patterson, New Jersey.

11:51 PM (EST)
Patterson, NJ

The override signal was received by the mortar targeting computer-

---

11:51 PM (EST)
Elizabeth, NJ

Tom gasped.

He tried to stop him, but Nehemiah's pressed his thumb down on the detonator button. Tom ripped the umbilical wire out of the switch—Nehemiah was about to shoot him in the head when—

Bbaanngg!

Candice shot Nehemiah through the chest. The terrorist rolled over, gun falling out of his hand as--

---

11:51 PM (EST)
Patterson, NJ

Ice pressed the firing button.

Nothing.

Benjamin froze, "What?"

"Override code!" screamed the soldier, racing over to the tiny computer, "I'll stop it," he tossed the firing switch to Benjamin. Bronk dropped it. The firing pin rolled along the floor.

"Fire the pin when I tell you!" screamed Ice. Benjamin clamored towards it.

11:51 PM (EST)
Elizabeth, NJ

Tom laid face down in the water and snow.

He heard laughing. He turned around to see Nehemiah oozing blood out of two bullet holes in his chest and neck. Nehemiah gasped one last breath and went still. But he'd been laughing? Only then did Tom see the blinking lights underneath Nehemiah's half open overcoat.

11:52 PM (EST)
Patterson, NJ

Baaaannnnng!

Ice fired his pistol into the computer, "Benjamin, press the firing pin!"

Benjamin held the firing pin in his hand.

11:52 PM (EST)
Elizabeth, NJ

Tom Grant pushed open Nehemiah's overcoat and gasped.

The detonator transmitter was freezer taped to the dead terrorist's abdomen--switches covered in blood--the timer switch still blinking: 15 seconds 14 second 13 seconds--shit, there was a failsafe reroute on the detonators!

"Benjamin!" he screamed into his mouthpiece, "you've got to-"

11:52 PM (EST)
Patterson, NJ

"—blow that fucking bomb!" Tom screamed into his head set.

Benjamin wrapped his fingers around firing pin.

"STAND DOWN!" the President yelled over the comlink speaker.

"FIRE THAT FUCKER!" ranted General Crandal over the same channel.

"I'm tryin'!" Ice fiddled at the launch computer.

11:52 PM (EST)
Elizabeth, NJ

Tom turned to see Candice.

Clothed in a white dress stained with mud and blood, she looked back at him--writing scrawled across her face. Her eyes were soft and inviting. So this is it, thought Tom. No escape. He laid on his back, staring up at the gray sky. This was the way he would die. This is the end. He looked back at Nehemiah's detonator box reading--10 second--9 seconds—

11:52 PM (EST)
11,400 Ft. over The Atlantic Ocean

"Have we inputted the override command?" screamed the President.

"The codes were received!" the communication officer cried.

11:52 PM (EST)
Elizabeth, NJ

7 seconds—

Tom reached out, squeezing Candice's hand firmly, "Don't be afraid."

11:52 PM (EST)
Patterson, NJ

"Blow it now!" screamed Ice Man, looking up from the computer, "NOW!" Benjamin wrapped his hand around the firing pin-

---

11:52 PM (EST)
Elizabeth, NJ

"How can I be afraid?" Candice squeezed back, "I love you."
6 seconds-

11:52 PM (EST)
Patterson , NJ

Benjamin pressed the button.

11:52 PM (EST)
Elizabeth, NJ

5 seconds-
Water splashed in Tom's face. He turned to see the water rushing out of the open manhole a few feet

away. No, the thought hit him! There wasn't enough time to speak. He flung Candice towards the open hole--

---

11:52 PM (EST)
Patterson , NJ

The room lit up--
Benjamin shut his eyes as the mortar cannon fired

11:52 PM (EST)
Elizabeth , NJ

The skies overhead parted.
Tom saw a solid shaft of light aimed directly down on him—the hint of a figure racing at him--he leapt head first into the manhole.
0 seconds.

11:52 PM (EST)
Ground Zero and Surrounding Areas

Light.

Light searing through the windows of the command center--as if all the suns in all the universe were simultaneously ignited. Remy, Sharpe, Eleanor, Giardino, soldiers--all turned away. The LACROSSE TV screens flared to white-

Benjamin Bronk turned away from the open window of the abandoned house. He caught sight of Ice Man. It seemed as if all the lines in the room had suddenly become sharper and crisper—light bluish and radiant like cold metal-

Crowds of rioting New Yorkers stranded in the busy city streets saw the skies light up as if dawn had come early--casting a brief luminescent shadow across Greenwich Village, spreading fingers of light between the skyscraper windows--a Metropolitan eclipse all the way down to Central Park--

High above Elizabeth, NJ helicopter pilots were blinded. . . other crews simply vanished from their choppers now rendered ghosts ships, snarling back and forth, swathing a blazing path through the sky—their occupants now gone--

It was as if God had opened up the very heavens, thought a government sniper as he turned away, leaping backwards off the roof of a nearby building. His eyes were frozen with light--watching in shocked amazement as the illumination engulfed him and then instantly, without warning-

Darkness.

11:53 PM (EST)
Elizabeth, NJ/ 20 ft. under The Union 57 Refinery in the drainage pipes

Tom Grant felt like a rag-doll.

Tossed from side to side in the freezing rapids of the tunnel, he tried to steady himself. The water was so cold he thought his heart would explode. Caught in the dark, raging subterranean river, he lost all sense of direction. His bandaged head slammed into the wall of a pipe-- he twisted and turned through the rapids. How long could he hold his breath? He hadn't had a chance to breath before he made it in--don't panic. The pipes had to lead out the bay. Then he felt a hand reach out for him—Candice! He grabbed it, surprised.

The thick gloved hand locked around his shoulder--the other wrapping around his neck. He heard the words—muted by the rapids-- blowing bubbles in his ears-and realized he was feeling the glove from the space suit--

It was Dussant!

Fifty Five

Tom Grant screamed.

In the confines of the raging subterranean river, his breath escaped him in bubbles racing along his face.

Dussant's fingers wrapped around his shoulder and neck, pressing his face to Tom's ears. The bastards was about to speak! Tom squirmed, kicked--managed to loosen Yves Alexander's grasp, sending his own body spinning into the darkness.

Then the thought hit Tom: escape was not possible. Once Dussant and he were spit out of the pipeline, he was done for! Would his brain simply fry to a crisp? Or did Dussant have something far more sinister for him? Would Tom be ordered to rape and kill in order to buy the evil creature time to escape just as he had done in Blanche Fields or would the sick fuck chose to contaminate Candice—rage--Tom would never let the bastard touch her!

He pushed backwards through darkness, moving closer to the creature. He had to somehow kill him before they exited the tunnel--Dussant wrapped a hand around him--arms locked on his face, pulling him closer to his mouth. The creature's lips brushed against his ears! Tom fastened a hands around Dussant's neck, using all his might to squeeze off the creature's wind pipe—to keep him from speaking.

They crashed into another pipe! Like two wild animals, they fought in the darkness. Tom felt a surging pain—like none before. Dussant pushed his fingers into his fractured skull! He shut his eye—pain lighting up the darkness. Tom pushed himself off of the pipe, trying to launch himself to the opposite side of the pipe wall. The arm would not release its iron-clad grip from his neck.

He still saw light beaming through his closed eye lids. He opened his eyes in the water—he still saw the light and was able to discern a fork ahead of him in the pipeline. From one side of the pipe, the brilliant light flickered.

They tumbled towards it.

Tom caught sight of Dussant's face as he pressed close. It wasn't the face of a man. Through the swirling water, the eyes were red--demonic. Yves Alexander's genteel, pale skin was pinkish green, his smile now fanged with jagged, demonic teeth--a frightening sight. Tom kicked and struggled to break free. The creature pulled him ever closer--snarling lips parting to release its horrific voice! Dussant was only an inch from his ear. Tom screamed: a conflation of bubbles and fear streaming across his eyes. The lips pressed against his ear.

This was it-

Suddenly Dussant's head shot backwards.

Tom looked down and saw the arm cross his line of vision. Another arm wrapped itself around the creature's throat. Was it Candice? Only then did Tom notice the dark skinned flesh, catching sight of the back of his savior's head as he struggled with the evil creature.

The strange figure cracked Dussant across the face, locking his arms around his neck. Only then did Tom see other hands coming out of the light, tugging and pulling at Dussant's monstrous body-- fingers wrapping themselves around the creature's arms and legs, pulling him towards the light. Now it was Dussant who screamed, bubbles rushing headlong past Tom as they flipped and spun with the raging current.

Through the blurring waters, Tom saw faces emerging from the light. . . children. . .Agent Willard. . .old men. . .Catherine Brandt. . . Peter Schubert. . . all of them grappling in a tug of war with the creature-- dragging him into the light.

Its arms flailed and lunged, securing clawed fingers around his ankle! Tom was being pulled into the light! He kicked and shook and fought, but Dussant would not let go of his tenuous grip. The tunnel spun as they all flipped and turned into the light which enveloped him, wrapping its energy around him. He felt his body slow down, resistance flagging. Tingles ran up his body. He didn't want to fight anymore. He wanted to be swallowed hole in the light.

Then a figure lunged out of the crowd of faces and wrestled with Dussant's clawed hand, prying back the fingers: one by one. Tom caught sight of the back of the man's head--the same person that pulled the creature off him before. The figure glanced up at him and for a single moment they were face to face in the blurring water. It was the Rabbi. Rabb took hold of Dussant's last finger, pulling the hand off Tom.

Dussant's lost his grip and was sent screaming into the light. The current was so strong! Tom was spun around and around, entering the light—he wanted to enter it! Then he felt Rabb's hands, thick and strong, wrap around him. For a moment they were face to face-- the light just beyond.

Rabb shook his head: no.

Tom tried to speak: so many things to say. The lightness in his head was enormous. He felt dizzy and empty. Rabb pressed both hands against Tom's chest. He could see Rabb emitting all his energy as he pushed against his former student, his friend as he said, "go," the voice carrying through bubbles.

Rabb sent Tom flipping backwards--then the pipe was spinning around him. He saw the fork in the pipeline again and was swung around, streaming out the other artery. On his way down the pipe, the light faded-- darkness filled his eyes. He struck the side of the pipe wall and—

"Tom?" the voice broke the darkness.

He opened his eyes to fog and smoke, black and gray, rushing across his line of vision. He took a deep breath and coughed up salty water. Then he saw the face hovering over him, beautiful in the reflections of red and green lights. It was Candice.

"Oh," she whispered, "I thought I'd lost you."

The light. Dussant—"Where's Rabb and--" he spasmed with coughing, clearing his lungs of water. He felt her cold, shivering flesh against his face.

"What?" she was puzzled.

"The Rabbi," he gasped, "w-where is he?"

"What are you talking about?"

"I-" he coughed up more water.

"Take it easy," she stroked his wounded head, "you've suffered a concussion."

"The tunnel. There was a light. Dussant was there! Rabb was there!"

"You were spit out of the pipeline seconds after me. You were unconscious. You look like you got pretty bashed up in the tunnel. Must have gone in head first."

She helped him up. His brain felt like a bowl of soup, rocking and rolling around inside his skull. He felt for his leg, drawing up the pants of his wet Union 57 security uniform, examining the flesh underneath. Indeed his ankle was bruised and scarred, but he could see deep parallel scrapes that looked like claws marks.

"You did it, Tom," Candice hugged him, "you did it!"

For the first time, he could hear the gentle surf. The waters of Jersey Bay splashed up against the rocky coast line. Tom could see that they were beneath the massive shipping piers of the refinery. Above him he heard choppers.

"We did it," he mumbled to himself, "people, not Gods—people stopped this."

"What?" she looked more puzzled.

"I thought I witnessed something that would've made me believe that there really was something so much greater, but—"

"Tom, you're not making sense. Look, pretend we're meeting for the first time," she extended a hand, "I'm Candice Cooperman and you are?"

He smiled, "Sean Connery."

"What?"

"You asked which Bond I was—I'm Sean Connery."

"I told you, I don't want to be Moneypenny, she never—" Tom drew her close, kissing her long and hard, taking in her smell, her feel. Finally she drew away opening her eyes as if to regain balance, "never gets her man."

"But Moneypenny, there's no other woman for me, but you," he drew her close again—their passionate embrace illuminated in the countless choppers and helicopters now circling around them, lighting up the shipping pier as if it were center stage in some Broadway play for all the world to see.

Fifty Six

Eleanor Bronk forced back tears.

"We did it," smirked General Remy Crandal.
He collapsed on the floor of the New York
Headquarters. Most of the power grubbing politicos,

thought Eleanor, had left. She heard that Osbourne died on the way to the hospital. So many dead men, she thought to herself, enough to last her the rest of her life.

Vince and Osbourne were probably vying for the first chopper to Union 57. All around her-- soldiers collected, walked in silence. Eleanor Bronk could tell the veterans from the new arrivals. The new arrivals were clapping and applauding. The veterans were simply in shock—shock that this crisis could actually be over.

Kneeling over Remy, she ran her hands along his pale, sweaty face. She shut her eyes and tried to recall the moments, the situations which constituted the past three days. But Eleanor Bronk was not a nostalgic woman: people imparted to memories, qualities that they never really possessed in the first place. Yet beyond the cold marriage that was her life, the endless parties, dry and hypocritical soirees and get-togethers which comprised her unique and surreal existence, this week by far topped them all. In the past 72 hours, she had felt more alive than all the years of her life.

"What'ya thinkin' 'bout?" drawled the leather faced Texan. Extending a rough hand, Remy brushed it along her cheek. His flesh was cold and clammy.

"I was thinking about you, you crazy old goat."

"Ya know," he sighed, "from down here all I can see is that big ass chin of yours, Eleanor."

She smiled.

Remy smiled too. His eyes carried a distant gaze now—distant in a way she had only seen once before: when her husband was on his own death bed. She looked up, examining the men that stood around her: the loyal soldiers of Crandal's Delta Force.

"My young Turks," Remy acknowledged their presence, but didn't look at them, "Stonewall's last words were 'strike the tents and we shall cross the river to the other side'," he coughed, "or some shit like that."

The soldiers motioned away from them, widening the circle. No one made any pretenses. Hell, thought Eleanor, Remy knew he was a dead man when he escaped from whatever ambulance or hospital he was in--to return to Fort Crandal. He had given his life so that millions could live. What grander thing was there.

"Is there something you want?" asked *La Grande Dame* of New York.

"A beer," he replied, "throat's parched."

She grabbed the bottle of champagne in the cooler beside them. She had been taking ice from it, cooling Remy's burning forehead, "bubbly's all I have. I know you don't like it."

He coughed again, "Beggars can't be choosers," his voice weak and distant, a dying man sprinkling on pretenses of humor.

Although she didn't tear up, her hands revealed her thoughts. Colonel Sharpe had to help steady the champagne flute as she poured the Cliquot. Then ever so carefully she tilted the flute, allowing a thin stream of the champagne to flow into Remy's mouth.

Among the toughest soldiers in the United States, there was not a dry eye in the room. Colonel Sharpe broke down so badly he had to step into the other room. This old bastard does command the respect, she thought to herself.

He sipped half the flute before motioning for her to stop, "Damn good stuff," he licked his lips, pronouncing the word mockingly, " Dom. . . Perigg. . . Nonn?"

"Dom Perignon's shit. If you weren't such a stubborn old dog, you might have tried champagne long ago," she smirked.

"You weren't there to talk me into it," his voice was weak and trembling.

The emotions hit her and despite her best attempt, she broke down, tears streaming along her wrinkled cheeks.

"That's a rarer sight than me sipping champagne," Remy joked. But his face had a stillness to it now, "would have liked to have taken' ya down to Harlingen for deer huntin'."

"I wish I could have gone."

"Damn," he winced, taking in a deep, desperate breath, "I wanted my place in history like Patton or McArthur. Ain't nobody's gonna hear about this old dog. . . promise you that. . ." his voice trailed off, his eyes closed, "covert op.'s sucks. People only hear 'bout. . . our. . . fuck. . . up's."

General Crandal died.

1:59 AM (EST)
Kennedy Airport, NY

Tom Grant met him in a public place: JFK airport.

Of course, JFK Airport was shut down for hours with the riots and was such a zoo that no area was private. People fled to the airport--others stranded as all aircrafts in the Triboro area were grounded. Bodies filled the hallways, people sleeping on benches, scraping up the last of the food that the restaurants had to offer, watching the flight screens filled with backlogged flights just beginning to depart. The place looked like Thanksgiving Day in hell, thought Tom.

Flanked at a distance by secret service agents, Candice and Tom wandered down the Delta concourse. Tom told her not to speak. Only an hour ago they were blindfolded and separated. When they were reunited in a car on its way to the airport, Tom knew some deal had been made, but they were still in danger.

Flanked at a distance by secret service agents, they walked cautiously in a sort of shock, silent and wary as they walked. The government offered a private room at the Delta First Class International lounge, but Tom refused. He wanted some place public with a lot of witnesses.

They discovered a tacky little bar with Caribbean décor and a juke box that refused to play anything except *Mack The Knife*, stealing two seats at a corner table. With the disheveled and exhausted travelers, the two of them barely stuck out. In the hall, the plain-clothed FBI agents, claiming to be merely escorts, eyed them cautiously.

Tom kept swimming in and out of consciousness. Normally a man in his condition would be in a hospital, but this was anything but normal conditions. The rapid announcements of flights and immediate boarding calls echoed in his ears. With the overrun of customers drinking, eating, and sleeping in the place, the bartender had run out of glasses. Tom bought a bottle of Jim Beam and watched CNN on the television overhead, taking slow sips as he waited for his guest to arrive. When he saw Benjamin standing in the far corner, he sat up.

"I need to talk to him for one minute," Tom whispered to Candice.

Her arm grasped his. She didn't want to let go.

"That was a great show," Benjamin Bronk looked like crap, bandages covering half his face, his arm set in a cast and sling, "CNN huh? You're quite a celebrity now."

Tom realized how different Candice, Benjamin, and himself looked from the other people. He stared at

Benjamin's swollen face, the tattered suit, ripped tie, ankle air cast. He looked like he'd been caught by surprise in the wrestling ring. People must think they were injured in the riots.

"How ya doin?" smirked Tom, adjusting his own bandages.

"Just had an earful from some of the most powerful men in the country," Benjamin sat down at the bar, "beyond that, I'm fine," he looked at Candice, "let's take it to the bar for a minute."

They weren't able to get a spot at the bar. So they leaned against the wall in the corner, talking and sipping from the bottle. *Mack the Knife* played over and over in the background. Tom positioned himself so that he could see Candice at all times. She stared back at him, longingly. The bar smelled of buffalo wings. His stomach ached with hunger.

"Remy's dead," continued the executive, swigging back the liquor. By his tone, Tom sensed that the comment required no reply.

"You come all this way to tell me that?" Benjamin glanced back at Candice, changing the subject, "So that's her?"

"Want to say hello?"

"No."

"Why you so concerned about Cormon?" asked Tom, "did I fuck up your little deal?"

Benjamin winced, "Who the hell do you think saved your ass? I got you freed and you try to screw it up by not negotiating-"

Tom restrained himself, realizing just how edgy he was from lack of sleep, "They didn't ask me what I wanted. I figured you cut the deal for me, my freedom and willing participation in exchange for whatever lie devise. But they just brought me here. The thing bothering them is that they don't know how to approach me. So they send you."

Benjamin said nothing. Tom smiled. He recalled the moments he had spent with this man over the past 72 hours. Benjamin was a puzzle, but more importantly, he was a friend. Tom was just too tired, lashing out at anyone. *Mack The Knife* continued playing over the jukebox.

"I'm sorry, Benjamin, that was pretty cynical and cold," he sighed, "just need a week's sleep and I'll be fine."

"You were wrong. It's not just your freedom they're offering."

"You know," Tom grinned, taking another swig of liquor, changing the subject "I was just sitting here waiting for you, thinking that tomorrow will be a day like any other. All these people think of this night as well, one big false alarm, like Orson Well's War of The World. Or maybe it's more like the LA riots except it's in New York. Now Union 57 and all of those experiences are rendered a minor inconvenience. The American people sit glued to the tube, trying to figure out who's at fault. But it's over: as quickly as it started, it's ended."

"What are you getting at?" Benjamin sipped from the bottle.

"Your refineries will continue to run. Terrorist sooner than later will get hold of one again and start this whole thing all over again. That's what bothers me. I wrote briefs on this crap for the past four years and I never could think of something this wild. And now that we all realize the threat, we're gonna do nothing about it."

"Come on, Tom," Bronk nodded his head, "you're a scholar of the game. You know the future threat to the world will come not from armies, but the tiny insurgent guerilla groups. In our day, with our technology and remote bombs, we can keep armies and whole countries at bay, but how do you stop a lone bomber or the solitary trigger man?"

Tom stood silent.

"You can't," continued Benjamin, "anyone could take over a refinery in any major American city and start the whole cycle of events all over again. If they wanted to, they could blow a refinery up. For argument's sake, they could take control of a freighter with chemicals, a nuclear power plant, or hell, just be simple and poison cartons of aspirin at the local drug store. This is simply the world we live in, Tom. It's unbalanced, bizarre, but it's our world."

Tom shook his head, "Maybe that's why Dussant wanted to stop the engine of the world?"

"Don't mock me, Tom," winced the executive, "this planet exists with disproportionate populations in poor, third world, urban areas— poverty stricken masses who reproduce with rampant excess in underdeveloped counties despite the fact that they can't feed their own children. Our food supplies dwindle each year, the ozone's eaten up. But Malthusian prophecies always falls short. We were all supposed to be dead and gone years ago from nuclear war, plague, overpopulation," he wrapped his fingers against the bottle, "but you know what? We're still here. At the core of our global society there is some basic sensibility, a common will to survive."

"What are you saying?" Tom took a deep breath, smelling cigarette smoke and stale liquor in the air, "that we should do nothing about it? Let it all continue as if nothing happened here?"

"Too late to go back. Like it or not, you and I and everyone here in this airport and the world need gasoline to power our trucks, to move food, supplies, people, to pump the blood of the machine we all thrive upon."

"There are options."

"Alternative fuels? If we substituted ethanol and alternative fuels for gas, it wouldn't last the world a single week. Right now, oil is the power that runs the engine of the world. It used to be coal. And one day it'll be something else. The power source is inconsequential. The fact that the engine of the world remains and has always existed: that is the only real truth."

"You'd make a great lecturer at Harvard business school or-"

"I'm trying to talk some sense into an intelligent, brave, and very stubborn kid. The White House has already made you a hero in the eyes of the free world. And despite the details, in my eyes, you are a hero," he pointed out of the bar, whispering in low tones, "but if you want to say your peace to the whole world in exactly the way it happened, CNN's waiting right beyond those security barricades. waiting for you to tell them what really happened. They're dying to hear it. Not because of its socioeconomic value. It's just good old entertainment. Fodder for the TV sensationalists and tabloid magazines. High Drama for the week! We get to take a President down!"

"Would that be so bad?"

"You'll just have another asshole in office. At least this one has a track record—you can predict his moves. You want to break me? Do it. You think the world stops to cry about men like me or Cormon? Our replacements are ensconced in our positions before our blood grows cold. If you want, go ahead and stop the engine of the world. But if I recall, Tom, we've just spent the past three days trying to stop a mad man who tried to achieve to do that very same thing!"

Mack the Knife continued to play through the bar. Tom grabbed the liquor bottle, nodding his head, "It's difficult, Benjamin. I think of Rabb, Remy, and countless names you don't even know. Crimes you wouldn't care to imagine. I'm the keeper of secrets now and the culprits of yesterday are today's heroes. It's just not fair."

"As clichéd as it sounds, the world isn't fair, Tom. You eat what you kill. But today, kiddo, you killed a lot. Name your price. Want to be head of the CIA, FBI, NSA? The world is your oyster today. Want a nice 5 million dollar nest egg? A yacht to cruise the world for the rest of your life? Today you are Vincent Giardino's bargaining chip. He will defend you for as long as he needs you. Hold no illusions though, when you become more of a liability than an asset, he'll hunt you down with all the energy of the United States government. You'll be destroyed, wiped away like the countless bodies that were wiped away in that plant. Your position is tenuous at best. That's why those escorts are waiting outside, watching your every move. Harbor no illusions about that fact!"

"Is this your sales pitch or are you just trying to intimidate me?"

"I'm your friend, Tom," Benjamin leaned close to him. Tom could see the weary lines and black bags underneath his eyes, "I am all you have left in the world besides Candice. You saved my life. You saved my family. For that I shall forever be indebted to you. I acknowledge this whole-heartedly. I would die for you, Tom. I am not the kind of man who is unnecessarily kind or giving. I accepted your invitation here because I feel that strongly about your well-being."

"How much of that 5 million dollar deal you offered me, would you pay?" inquired Tom.

"I would pay all of it. Five million dollars is a cheap price for the lives of my family and myself. I would pay it all right now down to the last penny without a second thought."

"Benjamin," smirked Tom, "I don't want your money. I'm happy you came because I wanted to say goodbye face to face. I never really planned for such a contingent," he sighed, "my plans always had both of us dead or in prison," he smirked.

"Where you going?" asked the billionaire.

Tom thought of telling him, but refrained. Then Tom thought: if he asks me to use his private jet, then he's a traitor. This was the final litmus test. Was he just being paranoid? He'd almost been arrested and possibly killed tonight by the United States government. Tom had grounds to be paranoid.

"Tom," continued Bronk, "take a vacation. Think the offers over. You were correct in one thing: don't tell me where you're going. Hell, I'd offer you my jet, but it would be the worst deal you could ever take. I'm afraid after your stunt with Cormon, they'd shoot you out of the sky."

Tom stared deep into Benjamin's weary eyes, "Thank you, Benjamin."

"For what?" the executive looked confused.

"For everything," his eyes were wet. He stood up, hugging the executive like an old friend. It was a strange hug, but familiar all the same: two tired warriors bidding each other farewell, "I'm afraid I got a plane to catch."

2:39 AM (EST)
Outside Kennedy Airport

Benjamin Bronk took a deep breath.

His body sank into the cold, soft leather seat of the limousine. Slowly, he nursed the Gin and Tonic, taking quiet, slow sips. The limousine exited the ramp of the Delta terminal. Bronk studied JFK Airport with its colorful airline logos and signs. People and cars were piled everywhere—delayed travelers from the pandemonium of the evening. Aircrafts were taking off with every minute—looked like The Berlin Airlift, thought Benjamin. Then for no reason at all, he began to laugh.

He flipped on the tiny television in the limousine. CNN was still running their 24 hour Late Breaking News special on "Crisis in New Jersey". More reporters were regurgitating the same information over and over. Suddenly his own face flashed on the screen. He sighed, shutting his eyes, his mind drifting. Then he thought of his mother and decided to call Mueller on his cell phone:

"Kiddo," Mueller answered, "just about to call and tell ya that your mother's back home safely."

"Good. Amanda and the kids?"

"Due to touch down in Zurich in five hours. Too late to turn the jet around. We did pretty damn good, eh? Got em out by 12:12 AM even with all the crap going on-"

If he hadn't launched his wild mission, thought Benjamin, they'd be dead, "I know," he replied, "Amanda called me from the air. Kids are excited to take a weekend in Switzerland."

"So we got work to do, huh?" sighed Mueller.

Benjamin's mind switched into business mode. He would need to call a news conference first thing in the morning. He held the top secret fax in his breast pocket, the latest government authored lies. Benjamin marveled at the speed in which the politicos could fire out stories. He wondered how many of the historical facts he took for granted, were just impromptu fiction?

As for him, his office already been contacted by CNN, ABC, NBC, FOX, The Star Channel, Time, Newsweek, The New York Times, and USA Today, all asking for morning interviews. It would be a great opportunity to promote the future growth of the company. The press coverage would be priceless especially with the European buy-out coming up in January. Then there was the meeting with the Mayor of New York--he asked for a lunch with Benjamin at The University Club. How could Benjamin refuse?

Not everything was rosy. Benjamin would need to call an emergency shareholders' meeting. He'd need a solid piece in *The Wall Street Journal* to calm any panicked investors who might start a run on the petrochemical sector devaluing his stock and--suddenly, he was struck with the thought:

Look at him.

Just fucking look at him.

His body felt like a thousand pounds of rusted iron. His ribs were still sending sharp aching pains down his spine. He had a gaping wound in his side from a piece of metal. His knees hurt. His elbow was on fire. A massive bruise on his chest burned every time he breathed. He had an infection in the gash on his calf and his ass hurt like hell. He stunk to high heaven and glass was still pouring out of his hair!

Had he so quickly reverted back to his old role— like Giardino and the others? What about all those visions and revelations he had experienced over the past three days? Did it all mean nothing? Was it just back to business as usual? He shuddered at the thought.

"Benjamin, ya there?" asked Mueller.

The thought hit him.

"Yeah. Yeah," his mind raced, "tell me, could you get a jet ready? I'm thinking of taking a long weekend in Zurich with the family."

Silence.

"You think it's a bad idea?" asked Benjamin.

"I was just thinking what a great idea that would be, kiddo," replied Mueller like a proud father.

"You think so?"

"Know so. Only one problem. Ain't got no jets for ya."

"Well, if I recall there's a Swissair Zurich night flight out of JFK. Think you could work me out a first class seat?"

"Think I could do that for the right price. You want me to call you on the cell phone when the press conferences start tomorrow?"

"I was thinking of not bringing the cell phone."

Silence.

"Bad idea?" asked Benjamin.

"Wow, when it rains it pours," replied Mueller, "you've impressed even me, kiddo."

"Screw it," sighed Benjamin, "let the Public relations people deal with it. Hell, Mueller, take your wife anywhere you want—fly in one of the jets tomorrow from Philly. Bill's on me."

"I better go before you start offering me stock options," then he paused, lingering on the line, "remember that question you asked me in the apartment last night?"

"Yes."

"You're gonna be OK, kiddo."

Benjamin laughed.

The line clicked dead.

"Turn the car around," he instructed his driver, "to Swissair."

For the first time in many years Benjamin Bronk looked forward to seeing his wife, Amanda. He would take the kids to Interlochen hiking—no, wait it was winter and there was no way he could hike in his condition. Great, they would get out of Zurich quick— the trains boarded right at the airport. He never liked German Switzerland very much. They'd catch the train to Lucerne for an afternoon and then on to the alps for a little skiing—his family could ski. He'd drink too much Kier and sleep off his wounds. It had been a long time since he had taken a real vacation. He certainly could use a little fun and relaxation.

The image formed in his mind.

He suddenly remembered Felicia: red hair bobbing around her long, thin neck. He remembered the round breasts and pale stomach. She was so graceful, so beautiful, a Princeton grad too-- great in bed. How could he have forgotten about his own frigging mistress all this time? He hadn't even thought about her safety? After all, she was what—twenty eight years old, living alone in New York City. She needed someone to look after her. How could he have forgotten about her during this crisis?

Hah.

Look at him, smirked Benjamin Bronk, as the limousine spun around, heading back towards to the international terminal. He was going to Switzerland for a wonderful weekend which would hopefully restart his entire life and mend his broken marriage and here he was thinking about mistresses. Still, he admitted in a moment of clear sincerity, old habits die hard.

Resolutely, he made a deal with himself— Benjamin was always good with deals. He would try his best to save his marriage and solidify his family. He would give it all of his energy and place it as one of the top goals on his agenda. In the case that it just didn't work, he would continue to take care of Felicia in the apartment in midtown. It sounded like a solid plan, a fair plan, a workable plan. Because Benjamin Bronk will tell you that anyone can change their colors--

but it's very hard to shed your skin.

3:55 AM (EST)
Fort Meade, ML

The room smelled of cleaning fluid.

He studied the Marine Guards which flanked either side of his position. Their cold eyes revealed nothing. He didn't like his escorts but he had to admit that it was quite a show when they all stormed into Fort Meade demanding access to the inner vaults.

He rubbed his weary brow. His fingers had tiny cuts from the sharp ends of the file cabinets he'd searched. The cuts burned with his sweat. Then he heard the clicking of heels against the concrete floor and turned around.

The room was a long hall bordered with massive stainless steel walls of file cabinets. The hallway spanned forever, the lines of perspective converging in the distance. The room had to be a couple of miles long. He rested against the rolling ladder he used to reach the taller shelves. He could see a lone figure nearing, but because of the warped perspective he couldn't tell how close the man was.

He shivered.

The temperature was a chilling 60 degrees Fahrenheit. The air was dry, burning his eyes. From the long elevator ride and the coolness of the room, he knew he was deep within the earth. But then again, The Secret Archives Library of The National Security Agency was constructed to withstand a nuclear war.

He was in the mouth of the beast. It didn't get much more secret than this. Want to know how Elvis died? Who killed Kennedy? Where you could find Jimmy Hoffa? It was all here—time sealed, ready to be opened when such stories were merely the idle babble of forgotten history.

It took a secret Presidential order under The Powers of War act and an armed battalion of Marines to get him in here without a hitch. Other White House staffers were scattered through other subterranean chambers, quietly searching. He glanced down at his wristwatch, he'd been here for almost eight hours.

As for the purpose of this visit, he had no idea why he was here or what he was doing. He was just a Situation Room aid who had been planning to head off on a vacation to Dutch St. Maarten. His plans were interrupted three days before when a ransom note was received on his shift. Since then, things went wacky. He was locked in a room until he was assigned to travel to Fort Meade.

He studied the coordinate label for the file cabinet.

It had taken a great deal of time for the aid to locate this particular file wrapper. The document proceeded the construction of this more modern archive room. The routing computer listed a number of possible locations for the package. In his hand, he held a report of possible alphanumeric positions within this secret library: the locations he'd been forced to search. Only then did he realize that he was standing in exactly the right spot. He opened the drawer.

A clear Plexiglas cover protected the files beneath it, but the files were still coated with a fine dust. He scanned the labels, spotting the file wrapper. He produced the key he'd been given at the archives office. It slipped into the lock. He lifted the hinged Plexiglas cover, grabbing the thick wad of papers carefully wrapped in brown paper liners, strapped with four wire seals with the following label:

<u>TOP SECRET UMBRA ALPHA WAYFARER</u>
NATIONAL SECURITY DIRECTIVE! TOP PRIORITY CLASSIFICATION!
NSD 12444.2, 12444.3, 12444.7, 12444.9, SECRET PLEADINGS (A–Z)
PHOTOS INCLUDED——PLEASE KEEP AWAY FROM SUNLIGHT***
TIME SEALED BY ORDER OF PRESIDENT RICHARD M. NIXON (8/7/74)
<u>AUTHORIZED RELEASE DATE: August 7[Th], 2274</u>

Jesus Christ.

This thing wasn't supposed to be open for nearly 3 centuries! He pulled the file out of the cabinet, anxious to get it to his superiors and-

"Excuse me son," the figure loomed behind him. He was a skinny looking anxious man with curly brown hair--the figure he'd seen walking down the hallway. His long hands shook with tension. These NSA types didn't like White House staffers and their Marine guards treading on their stomping ground, "that's not necessary."

"But," proceeded The White House aide, "my orders are-"

"White House just came through. Whatever caused you to come here, it's over. Your superiors don't require the file. You can put it back."

He returned the batch of files to the cabinet drawer. The nervous man shut the cabinet drawer. The aide was exhausted and his interest in the file already waned. If this crisis was over, then he could probably go home.

He wondered if he could still use those tickets to St. Maarten.

4:09 AM (EST)
In transit from New York to Los Angeles

Tom glanced around the dim aircraft.

Waiting until the last minute, he urgently pressed the government escorts to clear out the first class cabin of the Delta flight bound for Los Angeles. Candice and he set down in their sleeper seats. They held hands and turned on the video monitors. The moment was awkward and strained.

Tom Grant examined his in-flight video screen.

The CNN reporter stared into the camera, peering into millions of viewers' eyes as if she were staring at each of them: face to face, "New details have come to light in our 24 hour coverage of 'Crisis in New Jersey'. White House officials now believe that there is a link between the so-called Bob's Big Boy Mad Man and the bizarre discovery this afternoon of seventy five people found dead in and around their homes in Jersey City and Bayonne, New Jersey.

Government sources claim that these deaths may have been the result of a plot carried out by the so-called Bob's Big Boy mad man and his accomplices--now all believed to have been members of the radical, Midwestern, militia group called The Brothers Of Freedom. Government sources believe that this group experimented with lethal poisons, injecting them into the local water system of the two cities."

The news report cut to an overhead shot of a blazing fire set against the dark, night sky. The CNN reporter continued, "FBI sources corroborate that such poisons may have been cultured in the group's very own make-shift laboratory in Monongahela, Pennsylvania where two days ago, a chemical explosion rocked the town, destroying the lab as well as numerous buildings.

The FBI team dispatched to the area can still not conclusively say, but they believe twenty to thirty terrorists may have been killed in the blast now thought to have been an accident. The FBI now believes that the terrorists may have intended on dumping their copious amounts of poison in the New York City municipal water system."

Tom raised his brow at the next shot. It was strange to see your own face plastered on a television screen—even a four inch wide screen at that. CNN pulled a still shot from his personnel file, "This plan was exposed by undercover FBI agent Tom Grant. The FBI states that Agent Grant infiltrated the group in an investigation culminating day before yesterday at The Bob's Big Boy restaurant in Elizabeth, New Jersey where the group had stopped off to eat dinner just prior to dumping their toxins into the New York City water system.

During that critical dinner, Agent Grant managed to hide the truck with the toxins behind the restaurant and alerted government forces to the group's scheme—a plan which prematurely culminated in a deadly gun battle at the restaurant. Partially surrounded, most of the terrorists managed to escape while one man stayed behind, taking Agent Grant and other innocent patrons hostage, demanding that Secretary of State Vincent Giardino visit the trapped terrorists to act as negotiator. Upon his arrival, the lone gun man took Secretary of State Giardino, Agent Grant, and the others hostage on a car chase, ultimately leading them through upstate New York and central Ohio."

The screen changed to plain clothed men and women exiting a highway tunnel billowing smoke, "In this traffic tunnel just outside of Columbus, Ohio, Agent Grant was able to take control of the van and kill the gun man, ultimately crashing the car into a tunnel wall.

Amazingly, all of the hostages sustained only minor injuries and are currently being hospitalized."

The screen changed to a sweeping, aerial view of The Union 57 refinery, "High level officials at the scene state that some militia members did manage to evade capture, taking control of The Union 57 petrochemical refinery just across the streets from the restaurant. The terrorist gun men allegedly killed all of the employees in the plant. Holed up in the refinery and without their precious toxins, the terrorists then tried to destroy the plant, releasing what they hoped would be lethal gases into the air in and around New York City. A blazing gun battle was initiated at midnight by FBI Agent Dick Osbourne who FBI sources claim, started the attack without government approval. Agent Osbourne also perished in the fire-fight which lasted two and a half hours as the plant was ambushed by government forces.

Within this gun battle, Major Peter Schubert, managed to single-handedly capture of one of the key operational buildings. He is credited by government sources with helping to take control of the plant before he was killed in cross-fire. However, during this skirmish, the terrorists managed to contact various news organizations including CNN.

The terrorist stated that his group was about to release deadly toxins from the refinery which would threaten all lives within a hundred mile radius of the plant. All of the gunmen were subsequently killed or apprehended during the battle, but press reports set off scares and riots throughout New York city and its neighboring boroughs as well as Princeton, Trenton, and Philadelphia. Later that evening, while visiting the refinery in person, President Cormon had this to say:"

The familiar tape of President Cormon's press conference was re-aired. He looked angry, shaking his fist in the air, "This situation that the unbridled freedoms of the media in this country is a time-bomb waiting to be detonated by any would-be terrorist or prank caller. If the media had just listened to government pleas and delayed going public with their story for a few precious minutes, we could have showed everyone that there really was no threat at all. The National Guard would not be patrolling the streets of New York City, Trenton, and Philadelphia this very evening. Certain irresponsible journalists chose to chase a story rather than confirm its validity."

The CNN reporter flashed on the screen again, "In his own press conference, Secretary of State Vincent Giardino, just back from his own role as a hostage in this crisis, is already suggesting hearings on how such an event could be prevented in the future. The Secretary had his own choice remarks:"

The Razorback's face filled the tiny in-flight screen as he wagged a reprimanding finger, "I want the American people to know that my life was on the line tonight. Because when a crazed gunman held a weapon to my head and said he'd pull the trigger if the reporter didn't pull away, do you know what this journalist said? Do it! Do it! And you can quote me on that!"

The shot changed to a Senator standing on the capitol steps, flood lights cast down on his pale, withering face. The CNN reporter continued, "In a strange twist of fate, the Republican Senate Majority Leader Richard Depondit held his own press conference at the Capital this evening, announcing that he and Secretary Giardino will be forming a bipartisan committee to investigate this crisis and the improprieties of the press. Ironically, Senator Depondit also served on the Senate judiciary committee which just tonight, exonerated Secretary Giardino of sexual improprieties in what has come to be known as The Camp David Darling's Crisis."

Senator Depondit shook an angry fist into Tom's in-flight video screen. The wind blew up his thinning hair as he addressed the press, "I want to say that in my eyes, the Secretary of State is truly one of the heroes of this sordid affair."

The CNN reporter flashed back on the screen, "At the source of the proposed investigation is the fact that the captured refinery actually posed little if no threat to the safety of the general public. The Chairman of the Petroleum Refining Association of American at a press conference expressed outrage."

The screen cut to Chairman standing in front of The Union 57 refinery, "Look people, this was a scare. A big scare, but a scare all the same," he smirked, nodding his head, "I will say it again: even if security systems were breached, there is not enough poison gas in a petrochemical refinery to threaten even a city let alone people in a hundred square mile radius. This is preposterous! What we have here are some mad men with insane and unrealistic claims," he pointed around him at the refinery.

Tom recognized the plant, realizing the man was accidentally pointing to the neighboring chemical complex which almost conjoined with Union 57 as well as all the plants in the thirty miles, "you could blow this refinery and all we would have is an oil fire. Some dirt in the air during tomorrow's morning traffic. But," he chuckled, "certainly, nobody's gonna die."

The CNN reporter's face flashed back on the screen, "As for new developments, White House sources claim new revelations will come to light. Press Secretary Sullivan could not be reached for comment-"

Tom turned off the TV, stowing it back in his arm rest.

He sighed, turning to Candice who sat next to him, eyes shut. What was she thinking, he wondered. It was a strange moment, thought Tom, two utterly exhausted, unclean, disheveled individuals who were really stranger to each other. Still, mere fate had forced them together. The government was dying to figure out where they were going. When the aircraft landed in Los Angeles, they would wait around for an hour, forcing their way into the first class cabin of the morning Air New Zealand flight to Auckland, connecting on to Nandi, Fiji.

Tom's mind drifted.

He was too tired to sleep, too exhausted to stay awake, lingering in the half world between consciousness and dreams. Troubled, his thoughts returned to that lucky sonofabitch vomiting in his Virginia apartment 72 hours ago. If he could only go back to that place—when he wasn't contaminated, when Rabb and Remy were alive.

I am like nature, Dussant had told him, *you never know when I come.* Tom felt unclean, unsure of his own soul. The face of Agent Willard turning ever so slowly towards him, haunted his visions. What really terrified him was that he sometimes saw his own bloodied face superimposed over Willard's own. Was he really contaminated like those agents? Ten years from now, would he walk up the stairs to where his children slept, a knife in hand?

Still, an epic tale had finally come to an end. Or so he hoped. But one had to wonder: what exactly was Yves Alexander Dussant? Was he a con man or a messenger of God? Was their death struggle in the tunnels just a dream or had Tom somehow crossed over—crossed over in the way Rabb may have done when he witnessed that beam of light in that basement in Wayfarer? Had Tom really seen the Rabbi in that tunnel?

Or was it just a dream brought on by a concussion or his contamination?

There was no mysticism, thought Tom.

Despite what he had seen, he was still a man of science. Dussant was merely a man with a mutant power which science could not explain. But he was no justification for religious mysticism. As for God and beliefs, Tom saw no will of God here. God hadn't shown his face because God was merely a mental construct of man. God didn't really exist. If Tom actually saw a miracle, not some audiovisual hallucination, but a real miracle --that would have done it, would have made him a true believer on his knees praying. Would have made him believe that Dussant was sent to earth for a reason. But with all that he had seen, he hadn't seen a miracle.

"Are you alright?" asked Candice, slipping a warm hand on his own.

He opened his eyes.

This beautiful woman seemed like a stranger: too beautiful for a man like him. It was funny, when he shut his eyes, the voice was so familiar. . . the voice of the woman who had saved his life and kept him alive for the past 72 hours. It was a logical love: he had constructed a relationship with Candice Cooperman as a voice on the other end of a phone. How strange it was to actually sit with this person. What was he doing here? Rabb was dead! Remy was dead! The--panic took hold of him.

"Tom," her eyes lit up as if she'd just made a momentous decision, "it doesn't mean anything," she nodded her head, tears in her eyes, "I've seen a lot, more than I care to ever imagine. But it's over. They're not here. We have to start living again, breaking out of these shells we've devised for ourselves. I've accepted that fact, just did it in fact a moment ago. There's only one truth."

"What's that?" he took in a deep breath, uncomfortable with his surroundings.

"I'm here," she whispered in his ear.

He smiled. It was a fake smile all the same.

"The guards are gone. We're alone," she sighed, "let's try a different approach," she stared deeply into his eyes, "hello, my name is Candice Cooperman," she rushed forward, kissing him hard. At first it felt strange and then the tenderness of her lips tickling his own, he seemed to fall into her in a way that he had never done before. His arms wrapped tightly around her body. They continued kissing, lost in a soft embrace.

Strangely, his thoughts returned to Dussant: the man who taught him that he was capable of love. He had grown so apart from the world and yet Dussant, the consummate prisoner, taught him to enjoy life, to embrace a freedom Yves Alexander never possessed. Yet at the same time, Tom feared and loathed that creature in the pipes, clawing his face, snarling teeth and red eyes.

Candice finished her kiss, "Much better," she smiled, "leaning over, snuggling in his lap. Suddenly he noticed the flight attendant standing next to them, waiting for their embrace to end, "I just wanted to see if you wanted another drink?" she smiled.

"What wines do you have?" asked Tom.

"A Bordeaux."

"What area of Bordeaux? Pauillac or-" he caught himself.

"I'm sorry sir," she smiled apologetically, "it's just Bordeaux. That's all I know."

"No thanks," he sighed.

What nonsense, thought Tom. Had he actually believed that Dussant could be a messenger of God? God had conveniently failed to show his face in all of this. These were the things of man and man alone. Medical mutations and madness and ultimately solutions forged by real, living men--that a was good way to sum up the past three days. He repeated the thought again: he'd seen no miracles of God to make him a believer.

Only then did he notice the flight attendant still standing over them.

"Yes?" asked Tom.

"It's just that you guys are the only ones up in First Class. Would you like me to keep that window shades open?" she gestured, "we approach LAX from the ocean. With the gasses and stuff from the refineries in Long Beach, it makes for a great sunrise-"

"No thanks," they both moaned in unison-

And their window slid shut.

Fifty Seven

5:58 AM (EST)
10,000 Ft. Over The Atlantic Ocean

Colonel Nathan Sharpe stood alone with his thoughts.

He motioned through the open payload bay, finding his way into the rear hold. The fit, black officer glanced around him at the massive inner cabin of the Lockheed C-130 Hercules. It was a turboprop aircraft carrying heavy machinery. They had trouble fitting the massive amount of equipment back inside the plane without opening the rear paratrooper and cargo door. It always seemed like you picked up more garbage on the way back, thought Sharpe.

All around him, equipment and boxes were piled on top of each other. There were containers of guns, three jeeps, barricades, satellite equipment: everything they had cleared out the New York Headquarters, leaving clean, sparkling floors for the workmen when they returned—and a few shattered windows of course. Almost all of the things were back on the plane-- Sharpe's thoughts returned to dead soldiers, Peter Schubert, Rabb, and General Remy Crandal whose bodies were on a separate aircraft.

Leaning against the back of the troop transport, Sharpe stared through the open cargo door. The clouds had finally broken, moonlight reflecting off the seas of the North Atlantic swelling 14,000 ft. below him, the phosphorescent crests of waves visible even from his distant vantage point. He expected dawn to break at any moment. The aircraft arched over Long Island, heading south along the open ocean back towards Fort Bragg.

Sharpe had just finished watching CNN. Already The White House had announced a press conference scheduled at 08:00 hours. Leaks were already coming through that antagonists in the affair might be Press Secretary Sullivan and Osbourne—both of their whereabouts were still unknown to the general public. They weren't going to find them anytime soon, mused the black Colonel.

As for Colonel Sharpe, he was now the commanding officer of Delta Force--in line for a promotion to Brigadier General, replacing his mentor,

Remy Crandal. In his time, he had disagreed with his commanding officer on many things--that could not be argued: Sharpe and Crandal were two different breeds of men. The Colonel was soft spoken, a loner who didn't enjoy celebrating with his soldiers in the front cabin. Men loved Remy, they respected Sharpe, but both were stubborn and strong willed. The colonel knew that about himself and entertained no allusions. After all, he enjoyed it here in the rear of the plane, alone, lost in his thoughts.

"Sir," the hand tapped him on the shoulder.

Breaking out of his train of thought, the Colonel turned around, facing the officer. It was Ice Man. He didn't look very good, thought Sharpe, his face was pale and damp. But they all looked like shit, didn't they?

"What can I do for you?" asked Sharpe, sensing the officer's awkward look.

"Permission to speak freely sir?" asked the soldier.

God, thought Sharpe, he really does look like he stepped out of some surfer movie, doesn't he? "Permission granted."

Ice's whole body seemed to collapse, "I have a little problem, sir, " in his hand, Sharpe noticed a black duffel bag.

"Is that the problem?"

"Y-yes sir," he stammered.

Ice was nervous, noted the Colonel, the boy's eyes darted about. This looked important. Sharpe woke himself to as much an alert stance as he could muster, "What is it?"

Ice Man glanced from side to side, assuring himself that they were alone. Then he stepped forward, placing the duffel bag at his feet. The wind from the open cargo door, pushed his blonde hair back along his sweaty face. As he continued, he glanced away from the colonel, "Honest, sir, I did my job to the fullest. I never realized that-"

"Whoah! Whoah!" Sharpe put a comforting hand on the boy's trembling shoulders, "slow down. Let's take this thing from the beginning. Shall we?"

"Alright," he sighed, "when I was placed in command of the bomb crew, the first thing I did was to take an inventory of the nuclear shells, right?"

You want me to tell you if you did, thought Sharpe, "Did you?"

"That's what I'm saying. I did. I counted each of the shells. There was only one shell left when I arrived. We fired the other one at the cloud and you don't miscount when you're counting nuclear weapons."

"What are you trying to say?" the Colonel cut to the chase.

"W-well, everything in that room was happening real fast. We armed the missile. Then the over-ride codes came through, but I shut down the targeting computer before I thought the codes could reach the shell. I took it all manually-"

"I remember."

"And Benjamin pressed the firing button. I mean I didn't—I w-wasn't looking directly at him, but I saw the blast of light. It happened right then. And in the refinery, the bodies were all vaporized and we—well, everybody was congratulating me on a job well done. Benjamin took off. I had Sergeant Johnson disassemble the cannon while I helped stabilize our wounded."

"What are you trying to say, Ice?" Sharpe was tired and short on patience.

Ice Man took a deep breath and leaned over, unzipping his duffel bag. Ever so carefully he produced the shining mortar shell cradled in his hands.

Sharpe almost had a heart attack.

"Jesus Christ boy! That's a live nuclear shell!" the Colonel fought to restrain his voice.

"I–I k-know sir," stuttered Ice Man, "that's what I was trying to tell you."

"How did you come to have a neutron bomb?" Sharpe was angry—damn angry!

"Well, like I said, sir," Ice man continued, "when I came back in the bomb room, there it was. And I shit—excuse my language, sir, but how would you feel when there's a neutron bomb left—as if I would miscount! Well, I'm thinking court martial, right? So I formally took the wrong inventory of bombs. There must have been three. Nope. I checked the previous inventory. They had transported only two bombs to New Jersey, fired one--there was only one bombs left. So I asked Johnson where he found the extra shell. He said the mortar cannon was kicked over by the time he examined it. He found the second shell on the floor lying right next to it."

"Wait a minute," Sharpe held up his hands, "are you telling me that-"

"Yes sir," Ice nodded his head, "I'm saying that the shell never fired. Those override codes worked and froze up the whole system."

"So. . ." Sharpe's voice trailed off into silence.

"Even I thought it was real weird. I mean I saw those clouds overhead part. And that light was real tight, like a cylinder, not like a neutron bomb blast. And I found it weird too that our men didn't discover much fried circuitry except for the bombs in that refinery. I mean, if I understood it correctly, Union 57 was in pretty good shape, right?"

Words escaped Sharpe at that moment.

"Now you see my dilemma, sir," added Ice Man, "what am I supposed to do? Say that we mishandled a neutron bomb? I get my ass kicked and everybody who manned that post gets court marshaled? Or do I claim that the blast we witnessed was never caused by our nuclear shell? Then who the hell shot that light into the refinery, God?" scoffed Ice, "they'd lock me in the loony bin."

Sharpe had no reply for him. If the bomb hadn't caused that blast, then what had?

"Colonel, nobody else knows anything about this," continued Ice, misinterpreting Sharpe's confusion as anger, "I didn't say a single thing. I just plopped the shell in the duffel and brought it right to the plane. I was going to give it to you earlier, but I couldn't get you alone."

"It's OK, son. You did the right thing," his voice was a whisper.

"So what do we do?"

Colonel Sharpe had a decision to make. He reached deep inside himself, trying to find the solution. He thought of his training, of what he preached. Then he thought of what Remy Crandal would do. Suddenly, he had a workable solution—a damn good solution!

"Give me that shell."

Ice Man handed it to him.

"We never had this conversation. You hear me, Ice?"

"Yes sir."

"Now get out of here," he barked, "don't worry about it."

The soldier lingered on, "But what are you doing?"

"Saving your ass. Now get out of here. Go have a beer. Forget about it."

Picking up his empty duffel bag, Ice motioned away from his commanding officer, returning to the rear hold where the other soldiers slept and celebrated.

Sharpe now stood alone in the rear cabin.

Quickly and skillfully, he unscrewed the shell into two individual pieces. From his training he knew that the halves of the shell were worthless—it only had value when combined.

The politicians were busy writing their stories, the press busy manipulating it, the people already getting bored with it. Well this story was going to end here, it was going to end now! He'd had enough of it.

With the two individual pieces of metal in his hands, for a brief moment Colonel Sharpe held the most powerful device known to man. But Sharpe was not a romantic man and the notion never crossed his mind-- just as he didn't care about the source of the blast.

Defiantly, he turned around and with a pitchers arm, tossed the front half of the shell out the open cargo door. He took a moment, staring out at the Atlantic ocean, imagining the object falling thousands of feet before sinking to the bottom of the open sea.

Dawn broke in the distance, hints of purple and orange reflecting off the shiny metal disk resting in his hand. It was sad that this mission had nothing to do with God. If it did, such a thing as this shell resting in his hand might have made him a really religious man.

He yawned.

Then ever so slowly, Colonel Nathan Sharpe turned back towards the forward hold. He was the leader now of this ragtag group and despite his instincts, he should be with his men. This was a time of sadness and celebration. He motioned forward, flipping the metal disk in his hand before tucking it into the wide pocket of his Army jumpsuit as he entertained the thought:

It would make a great paperweight.

FROM THE INTERNATIONAL BEST SELLING AUTHOR
DREAMSPACE
ESCAPE C19
SIRIUS
ENTER
BENNETT
JOSHUA
DAVLIN
CENSORED
BY THE
BIDEN
ADMINISTRATION

DREAMSPACE
ESCAPE CITY
WATCH
THE MOVIE SIMULATION
WWW.CENTEREDAMERICA.COM
PG-13

SIRI
ENTER

When free will meets opportunity
you find out who you really are

1990s Hollywood agent trainee, Cullen Gersh, has his life upended after he steals his boss's invitation to the most exclusive Hollywood party. Cullen will lose nearly everything when he's presented with the ability to explore his unknown desires without judgment or repercussion.

Are you
who you think
you are?

CENTERED AMERICA CA CLASSICS

CENTERED AMERICA BOOKS
www.centeredamerica.com

Also available as an ebook

$19.99 US
$26.50 CAN

ISBN 9798988146612

9 798988 146612

90000

HOLLYWOOD
"A pitch-black comedy
about drugs and sexual abuse in Los Angeles"
JONATHAN BING
VARIETY
CENTERED AMERICA CA CLASSICS
The Modern Art of Dating
BENNETT DAVLIN

If your memories aren't your own, then whose are they?

One man is about to find out, as he accidentally ingests a mysterious drug that throws him into a hallucination so vivid that it seems real.

Because it is...

Now Dr. Taylor Briggs will embark on a journey to unlock the mysteries of his own mind—and to find the killer of the innocent victims whose last moments are being played out in his head—in a stunning psychological thriller that explores memory, its crucial role in our consciousness, and its power to deceive...

NOW A MAJOR MOTION PICTURE
Starring

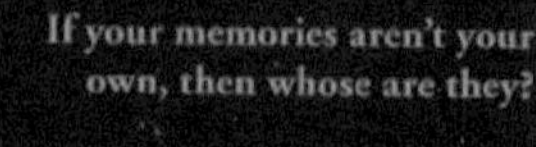

NOVEL
www.penguin.com

$14.00 U.S.
$17.50 CAN

ISBN 13: 978-0-425-20705-5

NOW A MAJOR MOTION PICTURE

STARRING

BILLY ZANE,

ANN-MARGRET,

and

DENNIS HOPPER

NEVER
BEFORE
PUBLISHED

MEMORY

a novel

BENNETT DAVLIN

BILLY
ZANE
DENNIS
HOPPER
ANN
MARGARET
SOMETIMES
MEMORIES
CAN KILL
MEMORY

GOD BIRTHED SCIENCE ON 11/10/1619
SCIENCE WAS USED TO CREATE CONTAGIOUS CANCER*
AND GOD REVEALED IT ALL THROUGH HIS PROPHETS

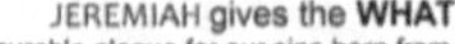

JEREMIAH gives the WHAT

an incurable plague for our sins born from nonbelief

DANIEL gives the WHEN

2020 AD, after the 2,625-year-long Israelite punishment begun in 605 BC when Israel was first conquered, proving their blood sacrifices were no longer rightful

605 BC ◄—— THE 2,625 YEAR PUNISHMENT ——► 2020 AD

and WHERE

The plague originates from the world-ending beast of "Ten Kingdoms" from the Land of 10 Kingdoms, Mainland China's historic name

EZEKIEL gives the WHO

China's King whom God codenamed Gog, launched the plague masked as an act of God, hence his codename so close to God's own

and HOW

Gog invaded with splendidly-clad soldiers dressed as "passengers" on "ascending chariots", airplanes, spreading his lethal, viral cytokine "storm"

JEREMIAH gives the WHY

God placed hooks in Gog, and when His people are powerless God will annhilate Gog and Magog and no one will ever profain His name again

"BE STRONG, DO NOT FEAR
BEHOLD YOUR GOD WILL COME WITH VENGEANCE...
HE WILL COME AND SAVE YOU"

ISAIAH 35:3-4

B. JOSHUA DAVLIN

The Conclusion of Ellen G. White's The Great Controversy
& The Solution to Daniel's Riddle

GOD'S GUIDE TO THE END OF THE WORLD WHEN EVEN YOU CAN BE SAVED

ISBN 9781735873688
90000
9 781735 873688

HOW TO WIN THE WAR

The plan to save the U.S.A

BENNETT JOSHUA DAVLIN

"...I next critized the sex-abuse cover-up scandal, protected for ages by the top elites of their (Catholic) bureaucracy. I disclosed that many of my male homosexual friends, once reaching middle-age, disclosed that they were raped when young by Catholic priests. This wicked conspiracy along with the wrong Sabbath showed the wickedness wrought from the nonsensical Papal infallibility.

I then revealed that my wife and I would never be in a meeting with Catholic Officials except for one, critical fact: **The archangel Saint Michael visited me in the presence of my wife on October 27th, 2017, and altered our lives, bringing us here.**"

- SAINT MICHAEL STOOD UP, PAGE 94

AT THAT TIME (SAINT) MICHAEL
SHALL STAND UP,
THE GREAT PRINCE WHO STANDS WATCH OVER THE SONS OF YOUR PEOPLE; AND THERE SHALL BE A
TIME OF TROUBLE,
SUCH AS NEVER WAS SINCE THERE WAS A NATION,
EVEN TO THAT TIME.
AND AT THAT TIME **YOUR PEOPLE**
SHALL BE DELIVERED,
EVERY ONE WHO IS FOUND WRITTEN IN THE BOOK.

-(DANIEL 12:1)

CENTERED AMERICA BOOKS
www.centeredamerica.com

Also available as an ebook

$24.99 US
$32.65 CAN

SAINT MICHAEL STOOD UP

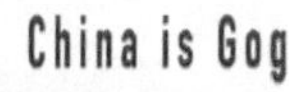

China is Gog

BENNETT JOSHUA DAVLIN

ACKNOWLEDGEMENT

I thank my first mentor, the novelist James A. Michener who kindly took the time to edit my early books when I was only 14, sending me on the path leading to this novel. As a writing sample, *Union 57*'s novel and my adapted screenplay secured amazing reviews in Hollywood, igniting my movie and TV career, and is in this author's humble opinion, is an amazing story.

As always, I'm grateful to my teachers from the *Episcopal School of Acadiana, Tulane University, London's City College, Tulane's A.B. Freeman School of Business*, and *New York Film Academy*. I'm also indebted to *TheGreatCourses.com* which allowed me to continue learning since graduate school.

I thank the late Buckley Norris and the former studio head Dan Melnick for showing me the ropes in L.A. I thank my late, dear friend, the TV creator Glen A. Larson who so loved this work. I thank my entertainment attorneys Robert A. Darwell and Phil Rosenberg. I'm deeply appreciative of *Penguin, Blanvalet Germany, Random House Australia, Sony Books Japan, Centered America Publications*, my Bulgarian Imprint, and other publishers worldwide for translating and printing my novels worldwide. I thank Sony and Tristar Pictures, Warner Bros, and EBE for distributing my films.

And most importantly, I thank my dedicated readers and film fans for making it all possible.

Bennett Joshua Davlin was born in South Central Louisiana and began making films at age five, completing his first novel by ten. He studied at Semester at Sea and London's City College before graduating from Tulane University, later attending Tulane's A.B. Freeman School of Business for his MBA.

In the 1990s, Davlin worked as a combat war correspondent during the Yugoslav conflict. He went on to hold positions in the oilfield industry and in structured and international finance. As a CEO, he successfully turned around the largest manufacturer of high-end decorative goods in America—an achievement that earned him a job offer from Warren Buffett's former turnaround master, which he declined. Due to economic policies under President Clinton, Davlin was later forced to offshore manufacturing production to China. After a period living in Hong Kong and Southern China, he shut down the company, unwilling to contribute further to the rise of Chinese communism that he viewed as a growing threat to America's liberty.

Shifting to Hollywood, Davlin became a studio screenwriter, penning major films such as the Jackie Chan action movie *The Medallion* (distributed by Sony, Columbia TriStar). His novel *Memory* became an international bestseller, published by The Berkley Imprint of Penguin and translated into multiple foreign languages by Sony Books, Blanvalet, and Random House.

He went on to write, direct, and produce the film adaptation of *Memory*, released worldwide by Warner Bros. and EBE. In television, Davlin collaborated with Randy Douthit (co-creator of CNN's *Crossfire* and *Judge Judy*) under a first-look deal with CBS Paramount.

He has guest lectured at NYU, The Tennessee Williams Festival, and other academic venues. Since 2017, he has been a contributing essayist and political commentator at CenteredAmerica.com, focusing on policy, economics, and philosophy. In 2020, he ran as a non-treasonous Democrat for U.S. president. He is a former member of Sigma Phi Epsilon, and a proud member of the Benevolent and Protective Order of Elks.